CONFUSING
THE SEASONS

A Novel

Dan Cavallari

For more information, visit www.danielcavallari.com.

To order copies of this book, please visit www.danielcavallari.com.

Cover design by Filmosity Productions (www.filmosity.com)

Cover photo by Dan Cavallari (www.d2photos.net)

Author bio photo by Joseph M. Arthur (www.josephmarthur.com)

ISBN 978-0615437088

Brown Tie Publishing

To my wife, Rachel.

I

COMINGS AND GOINGS

Einar William Coates. The name his mother gave him. Carved in wood and hanging next to his front door. He pressed his fingers against the letters as he stood in the doorway, a cup of coffee steaming in his other hand and the cold from the morning spearing at his face, and felt each swing and curl of the carving: EINAR. Then, WILLIAM. Then, COATES. The trees rustled in an effort to fight the inevitable: they would lose their leaves with each gust—a stealing thief of moving air, taking bits of those trees with it to the ground or to the lake just past the yard. Einar William Coates looked away from the disk of a long-dead tree with his name carved into it, the one that hung next to his front door, and looked out at the dirt driveway before him and the trees beyond. He saw nothing worth noting.

Willie, as his wife and friends had called him for so many years, no longer felt like a Willie. He felt like an Einar William Coates, a relic, a story in a book, a dead leaf that didn't know it had died and still clung to the tree on which it had grown for so many years. He stood on his front porch and sipped his coffee, too old now for shivering against the cold and yet still alive enough to feel it in his bones. His daughter and two sons had left late yesterday afternoon, and the tracks from their car tires were still noticeable in the dirt of the driveway. Bethany had brought her new husband with her—a hulk of a man in a business suit and a cell phone permanently attached to his right ear, whose name was, stupidly, Askar—and Einar disliked him immediately. What good was all that muscle if all you were lifting was a cell phone and a pen? How the hell could you swing an axe if you were chatting away about stocks on the goddamn phone?

His sons, Robert and Jason, had stayed a bit longer than Bethany and Askar, and they, too, had brought their girlfriend and wife respectively. Jason had spent a good part of yesterday in the axe yard splitting the first of what would be two cords of wood even though Einar told him not to, and at first this obvious challenge of Einar's authority angered him. Then he got tired again, tired thinking about their mother, tired thinking about how he'd burn all that wood alone this winter. He let Jason wield the maul and split almost all of it. Damned if he wasn't a strong boy. Jason's wife, Ginny, whom Einar very much liked, baked two apple pies and made a helluva lunch for all of them yesterday.

Robert had also spent a good portion of his visit on the phone, his cell phone almost permanently attached to his left hand—he was a lefty, despite how hard Einar had tried to make him use his right hand as a kid—but he had good reason. Someone had to arrange the funeral, and Einar just wasn't up for it. He felt like a little baby at times, sitting up on the porch and watching it all happen in the late October mornings, watching people arrive and leave, letting his children cart him into the cars and to the funeral and then to a reception and then back to the house where the house was still just the house and the lake was still just the lake. And when they'd finally left yesterday afternoon, hugs, kisses and handshakes thrown around like so many of those leaves in the dirt on the ground, Einar stood on his porch and watched the cars turn and disappear down the driveway. He was still just Einar William Coates.

As he walked down the steps from the porch, his coffee still in one hand and his name still carved on a piece of wood next to the door, Einar and the morning air mixed and mingled, fought and laughed and tried to reconcile all the years in which he'd forgotten their importance together. How did one find a new companion after spending forty-six years with the same person? Einar William Coates had this breeze, this cold air, and it seemed to fit just right. Sarah Gamble Coates' warmth had been a welcome distraction for forty-six years, but now here was the cold. Here was the air. Here was the morning and its chill.

His legs felt the cold more than any other part of him, and as he made his way down toward the lake, his knees ached in the way they would throughout the winter, a sign of things to come for the next several months. It took some effort to get to the felled log by the bank of the lake, and even as he let his weight rest on the old wood, his knees gave out a creak and a pop that told Einar his walking days were nearing their end. He sipped his coffee and felt the breeze kick up again, watched as a group of leaves swirled in mid-air for a moment, maybe gaining a slight sense of hope that they might escape the ground and find their way to the heights again, then settle slowly back onto the dirt where they would rot. This was how Einar spent the next hour, until his coffee was drained and the cold was too much for him to bear. He retreated back inside and sat at the kitchen table, an empty coffee mug and an unread newspaper in front of him.

That was a Tuesday. Wednesday was much the same, as was Thursday and Friday. But on Saturday, Jason showed up. Einar did not expect to see his son, and the drive from Portland was not a short one, but Einar did not ask questions, either. He was happy to have the company, though Jason looked troubled. Fine, Einar thought, because trouble always followed trouble.

*   *   *

Night had fallen on Saturday. Jason had spent much of the day stacking the wood he had cut the week before, or cleaning the shed out back, or repairing the gutter over the porch. Einar watched his son work, wondered what had brought him here, but said nothing. Jason had lived in Portland now for almost ten years and had gotten himself a damn fine job writing for the Portland Press Herald, a wonderful wife in Ginny, and one comfortable apartment near the water. Any time he made it up this far north was just fine by Einar, and until very recently, just fine by Sarah. But Sarah was gone now, dead and buried, left for the good one above to enjoy. Einar knew that.

"Been meaning to get up there," Einar said to Jason as he finished hammering a nail into a twisted bit of the gutter above the porch. Though night had already fallen, there was enough light from the floodlight above the barn for Jason to see his work.

"Certainly needed some attention," Jason said. He pulled another nail out of his pocket and began hammering.

"Come on down now," Einar said. "Let's have us some dinner."

Jason finished hammering the last nail and sighed, then climbed back down the ladder. He said nothing and followed his father into the house where they made themselves some steaks with beans and rice. They spoke very little, if at all beyond trivialities. When Einar finished his meal, he sat and watched his son eat. Jason's eyes never left his plate.

"Ginny have work?" Einar asked.

"Huh?"

"She didn't come up with you. She have work to do?"

"Oh," Jason said. "She didn't come. She…"

Jason had speared a piece of steak with his fork but had not picked it up off the plate. He stared down at it as if he didn't quite know what he was supposed to do with it. It may as well have been a novel written in German, by the look on his face.

"We're going to be getting a divorce, Pop. At least I think so."

"You think so?"

"Yes." Jason finally raised the fork to his mouth and ate the piece of steak. Einar did not press on.

They cleared the plates off the table and cleaned up. Einar retired to his chair in the living room and Jason sat in the guest bedroom upstairs reading a book until he fell asleep with the light on. Einar climbed the stairs an hour and a half later, turned off the light by Jason's bedside, and went to the living room. He had not slept in his own bedroom since Sarah died. Instead, he would off on the couch or in his chair, opting not to face the empty space that he knew would make him miss Sarah. As he sprawled onto the couch this night, his knees popping and creaking again, Einar felt his new companion—the winter cold—settle up next to him and nestle up close like a lover and doze off to sleep with him.

*   *   *

"Hi Pop."

The phone rang at eight a.m. Einar had already been awake for four hours.

"Robert," Einar said to his eldest son.

"Jason there?"

"Came up yesterday."

"So he told you, then?" Robert said, sounding slightly accusatory

"Told me what?" Einar asked.

"He and Ginny are splitting. Pop, it's not going to be pretty."

"Wouldn't think so," Einar said. Robert sighed on the other end of the phone.

"Listen, I'm going to try and get up there next weekend. Jason will probably still be there. He's taking vacation time. I can't be there until this weekend, though." Robert's voice had a pleading note to it, as if Einar had been trying to guilt-trip him into coming up all along. Einar had no inclination to beg his sons or his daughter to visit him, but he felt as though Robert wanted to hear that from him, hear him plead for his presence.

"Come on up when you can," Einar said.

"One more thing, Pop. Got some news for you. Maggie and I are going to get married. I proposed to her three weeks ago. I didn't get a chance to tell you with all the—with mom passing on and all."

Einar let the last part of Robert's statement pass with the austerity and coldness of the breeze off the lake. "Congratulations, boy."

"Thanks. We were hoping we could have the wedding up there, by the lake."

Einar thought for a moment, then said, "Lots of work to do in the yard there. I can't do much of it, but if you and your brother come up to help—"

"We'll take care of it. As long as it's okay with you."

"Fine by me."

"Good. Thanks. I'll see you next Friday."

Einar hung up the phone and looked out the kitchen window. Jason was standing by the barn, looking up at it as though he were preparing to lift the whole damn thing off the ground. He stood that way for a good minute or two, then finally went inside. Einar got up from the kitchen table and pulled on a coat—one of those Carhartt deals Bethany had bought him down in Freeport two winters ago—and made his way, slowly, across the yard toward the barn. Jason was inside with his head buried in the tractor's engine compartment.

"Only two things end a marriage," Einar said. "Cheatin' with another woman and cheatin' with money. Which one is it?"

Jason righted himself and looked at his father standing in the doorway. Then he grabbed a rag off the seat of the tractor and began wiping his hands over and over again until they were well past clean. "Option A," he said, his eyes cast down at the front wheel of the tractor.

Einar grunted. "Sorry, kid," he said to Jason. He shuffled slowly to the chair to the side of the doorway and sat down with an achy sigh. "I liked Ginny, but yer doin' the right thing by leavin'."

Jason closed his eyes. "I'm not leaving her. She's leaving me." He looked up at his father and saw he didn't understand. "I cheated, dad. Not her."

Einar stared at his son for a moment in the morning sun that shone through the doorway and halfway onto the tractor. Jason suddenly looked old to Einar for the first time ever. He'd always looked like a little boy, always had those happy eyes, always looked fit and spry. But now he looked tired and worn, which made Einar feel ancient and stupid.

Einar grunted again and stood up. He began to walk out of the barn, then stopped. He did not turn to face his son. "Well that sure was stupid of ya," he said, then walked back toward the house. Jason threw the rag back down onto the tractor seat and poked his head into the engine compartment again, trying to un-seize the oil filter, trying to ignore that hot feeling at the back of his neck.

*   *   *

Bethany called on a Tuesday.

"It's fantastic, isn't it, dad?" She half-shrieked through the phone. "They're getting married! Robert just called me to tell me about it. And the wedding…oh, it will be perfect up there at the lake."

Einar listened to his daughter ramble with a smile on his face and his fingers wrapped loosely around the phone.

"They're planning for the spring, late May, I think. Askar said he'd like to come up with Robert a few times this winter to help with the work that needs to be done. It's a long trip from Boston, but it would be so great to spend some time up there."

Einar's smile faded at the sound of his daughter's husband's name. Askar. What the hell kind of a name was that? "Sure he can handle himself with the tools?" Einar said, the sarcasm not readily apparent in his gruff and usually monotone voice.

"He's quite handy, daddy. You should see. He builds these model cars. They're amazing and—well, I'll have him bring one up next time we come visit."

Einar listened to his daughter chat for a few minutes more, his participation in the conversation not at all necessary, and when they hung up and Einar turned away from the phone, he took two steps toward the kitchen and bellowed, "Sarah!"

The silence that echoed back was all Einar needed to realize how much of a fool he was. He wanted to tell Sarah all about his conversation with Bethany and his extreme distaste for Askar, but Sarah was not in the kitchen. She was not in the house. She was in the ground. He looked around the living room and wondered briefly if Jason had heard him, but he'd been outside all morning down by the lake, repairing the dock after he and Henry Johnson from down the way pulled it out of the water for the winter.

Einar put his hands on his hips and let out a slow sigh, then put his coat on and walked out the front door. His boots thumped on the front porch as he looked down the driveway. Years ago—maybe ten of them now—he'd walk down those porch steps every morning at five a.m. to go to the shed and start the tractor, then head down the driveway and across that county road to his potato fields. But ten years had passed, and the fields had been sold for enough money for his retirement, allowing Sarah to do her stained glass crafts and Einar to tend to the house or do some woodworking out in the barn. Ten years had passed. Einar descended the steps slowly and made his way around the side of the house, past the barn and down the slope toward the lake. Jason was there with a cordless drill, repairing one corner of the dock.

Einar waited for the noise of the drill to stop. Jason did not see him standing there, looking out at the lake and the steam rising off it. He was busy checking his work, making sure the screws hadn't poked through the other end of the boards. Einar let the silence last, then finally said, "Your brother's gettin' married."

Startled, Jason pinched his finger between two boards, then pulled his hand out. "Shit," he said. "Yeah, I know. He told me earlier this week. Wants to have the wedding here."

Einar took a step toward the lake. "Lot of work to do 'fore then."

"Yes," Jason said.

"You'll be up?"

"Of course."

Einar did not reply. He took a few more steps forward until his boots almost dangled off the edge of the earth that overhung the lake water. He stood there for a minute or two, quietly staring out at that water. Jason thought how odd it seemed that after so many years, his father looked exactly the same but slower. It was as if time had forgotten him for years and years and only recently remembered to come back and fetch him. Maybe within the last two weeks or so. Since Mom had died. That was when time came back for Einar William Coates.

"I'm going to get started on the barn later today," Jason said. "It'll need a coat of paint in the spring. We should get the eaves repaired before then."

Einar simply nodded. Jason watched his father a moment longer, then returned to his work on the dock, retrieving the screws he'd dropped when his father startled him.

*   *   *

Jason was working on the back side of the barn, high up on a ladder, when Robert showed up on Friday afternoon. Both Robert and Jason were hulking men, both with dark black hair and deep brown eyes, and both tall and straight. But Robert had a slight limp, the result of a car accident on a county road almost a decade ago. He'd been with his girlfriend at the time, coming home from a movie in Fort Kent when he hit a patch of ice and ended up in a ditch on the side of the road outside Nelson Michaud's farm down the way. His girlfriend was irate and injured a little bit of her patience; Robert was scared and had broken his right leg in five places.

Jason saw him pull into the driveway but did not come down from the ladder. He went about fixing the eaves as he'd done for the last two days. Robert limped down the slope of the dooryard and made his way around the side of the barn. He looked up at Jason for a moment, knew he was being ignored, then shook the ladder to get his brother's attention.

"Howdy, brother," Jason said from the top of the ladder.

"Been up here a few days, have ya?"

"Yep."

"Can hear it in your voice," Robert said. "Got that County accent back."

"You say that as if it's a bad thing," Jason said, scraping red, flaky paint away from the eave.

"You want to come down and say hello to your brother?"

"Got work to do up here," Jason said. "Said hello to you last week. We'll say it again when I come down."

Robert laughed with no humor behind it. He stood for a moment longer at the bottom of the ladder, looking up at his younger brother as he scraped away at the red eaves of the barn, then turned and made his way toward the house. When he rounded the corner of the barn, he saw Einar standing on the porch, two cups of coffee in hand.

"Hi, Willie," Robert said to his father. It was strange how Einar didn't register that name as his anymore; it took him a moment to understand what his son was saying.

"Maggie with you?" Einar asked.

"No, she stayed down in Portland this time around. She'll be up next weekend when I come up."

Robert was limping up the steps to the porch now. Einar watched him come, took a step forward and handed him the mug of coffee. Robert took it and looked over at the barn. "He's been here all week?"

"Yep." Einar said.

"He's got to go back to work."

Einar said nothing at first. He took a sip of his coffee, then said, "Tells me he's got vacation time."

Robert chuckled a bit. "Yes, he does. And he's using it all up here. It's not good for him."

Einar considered this for a moment. Yes, Jason was certainly in what his mother would have called the 'mudfunks,' and he'd said maybe a total of ten words since coming up to the farm almost a week ago.

"Man's got to work on a barn sometimes," Einar said, then made his way to the opposite side of the porch to sit in a chair he'd made almost thirty years ago. Its seat was a sawed disk of oak, the back slats of the branches from a birch. Its rigidity made it stiff and uncomfortable to anyone who sat in it, which was just fine by Einar; it freed it up for him, and he thought it more comfortable than any chair he'd put his weight in before.

Robert stood with his weight on his good left leg and looked out at his car sitting in the dirt driveway. A breeze kicked up, loosening the leaves above again and sending one slowly in its descent onto the windshield of Robert's car. It stayed there for a moment, then slid down into the gap between the windshield and the hood. "He cheated on Ginny," Robert said, more to himself than to Einar.

"So he tells me."

Robert turned to Einar. "That doesn't bother you?"

"Sure does," Einar said. "He's bothered plenty, though. Boy don't need my bother, too."

Robert stared at his father with a look that seemed mixed with equal parts awe and revulsion. Einar made no indication that this bothered him, but silently, in his own head, he marked this moment as a sign. Robert was surely bothered by Jason's situation, but there was something else. Einar could see that clear as the sky.

"There's some moose steaks in the icebox. Why don't you go set them out to thaw so we can have them for dinner tonight?" Einar said.

Robert looked at Einar with that same look for a moment longer, then retreated into the house to fetch the steaks. When Einar heard Robert's boots clop through the hard wood of the living room, he stood up and looked out from the corner of the porch again at Jason, just barely visible at the right corner of the barn roof. "Damn fool," Einar said under his breath, then returned to his chair.

*   *   *

They sat at the table in the kitchen in almost complete silence. The dining room was reserved for special occasions. They had used it a few weeks ago for Sarah's funeral, but that was the last time anyone had set foot in that room. Before that, it had probably been the fourth of July. Before that, Easter. Tonight they sat at the kitchen table, the only sounds in the room the clacking of forks and knives, the cleared throats and the slight sounds of chewing. Jason sat to Einar's right, Robert to his left. Robert had all but cleared his plate before he broke the silence.

"Barn's looking good," he said to Jason.

"Lot of work to go."

"You planning on staying up here much longer?"

"Don't know," Jason said as he cut his steak. "I guess I haven't thought that far ahead."

Robert pulled his napkin off his lap and placed it on the table. "Burning up those vacation days pretty quick, aren't ya?"

Jason looked up from his meal and looked briefly at his brother. Einar did not miss the fact that something had been said between his two sons in that glance. Einar was a man of few words and could appreciate a non-verbal conversation, but he damn well didn't like this conversation at all.

Jason went back to cutting his steak.

"You'll help your brother tomorrow," Einar said to Robert.

"I don't need any help, Pop."

"Can't recall askin' if ya needed help."

Robert cleared his throat. "Maybe I should get started on the tractor tomorrow. It needs—"

"I already took care of it," Jason said.

Einar put his fork down on his plate. "Then you'll help your brother with the barn tomorrow," he said, and as if the matter had been closed with those words, the table fell silent again.

*   *   *

The next day, both of Einar's sons were up before he was. Einar dressed himself in work clothes, brown and made for sweat and strain. He had awoken that morning with a strange premonition, or at least a sense that Sarah was watching. The thought made him uncomfortable but would not leave him. His knees hurt less today for one thing, and he intended to take advantage of that welcome vacation. When he made his way down to the kitchen, coffee had already been made and both of his boys were outside in the yard. They had pulled the tractor outside the barn, and Robert was walking with one of the ladders over his shoulder toward the back of the barn. Jason watched his brother as he went, his eyes seemingly following the undulating flow of the ladder caused by Robert's limp. When Robert turned the corner around the barn, Jason went back inside to fetch the other ladder.

Einar watched all this with a contentment that almost brought a smile to his face. He poured himself a cup of coffee, drained it within a few minutes, and went outside as he pulled on his coat. When he reached the barn, both Jason and Robert were high up on the ladders, scraping away at the paint but not speaking to each other. Einar looked up at them only for a moment, then went inside the barn and began clearing off the work bench to the left of the oil-spattered parking spot of his tractor. He pulled all the random scatter off the bench top, pulled all the tool boxes and scraps of wood from underneath, moved all the oil cans and pushed the engine lift outside the barn next to the tractor. He spent the next two hours sweeping, wiping, rearranging, occasionally setting a screw here or a nail there, and essentially enjoying himself for the first time in weeks.

As he rolled the engine lift back into the barn, Jason followed him inside. He began poking around the work bench, looking for some tool or another, moving a can of nails and a jar full of used spark plugs. Einar watched him until he'd moved enough of what Einar had just spent the last two hours arranging before saying, "What are ya lookin' for?"

Jason turned around and looked at Einar as if he hadn't even realized his father had been there at all. "Just need a crowbar or a pike. There's a hornet's nest up there, rotted out and empty. Just out of my reach."

Without moving a single step, Einar reached to his left and picked up the crowbar that had been leaning against the inside wall of the barn. He handed it to Jason, who for some reason looked quite shaken. "You alright, boy?" Einar said to his son.

"I'm fine," Jason replied. He immediately dropped his eyes to the dirt on the floor. "Fine, pop."

"Cold enough them bees should be dead," Einar said, now wiping his hands on a rag that had been hanging from the engine lift.

"Should be," Jason said, walking out of the barn into the sunlight. Einar didn't like his son's manner; Jason had certainly knocked himself down into the cow pies, but now he was rolling in it. Robert was right: Jason was stewing in his mistakes, and Einar knew how much of a trick time could be. But there was something else in his son's gait that told him there was much more beyond what Einar was being told. It wasn't his manner to ask questions about it, so he'd wait. If he knew his son well enough—and he did, by god—Jason would have something to say fairly soon. Maybe not to Einar, but he'd have something to say.

*   *   *

Robert stayed the entire weekend and he and Jason got the eaves scraped on all four sides of the barn. The air had turned warm on Sunday, so they decided to throw a coat of primer all the way around. It was almost sundown on Sunday before they'd finished, and when they came inside for dinner, Robert was so exhausted he took an hour nap before heading back south. Jason sat out on the porch, bundled up now that the sun had gone down and the temperature had dropped, sipping a cup of tea with a nipper of whiskey in it. Einar stood just inside the door.

"Gonna get cold tonight. Think the primer'll set up right?" Einar said to Jason, not looking at him but instead looking out at the dirt driveway.

"Just primer, pop. Most of it's dry already anyway."

"If it gets warm again this week, we can go up there and get a first coat of paint on the eaves," Einar said. "My knees feel good. Could probably put in an hour at a time up on the ladder."

"Sure, pop."

"Frank Jordan could probably come help us. He's been pullin' spuds down the way at his dad's farm."

Jason looked toward the door but couldn't see his father behind the screen. "Frank Jordan's around? I thought he was out in California."

"Was. Came back. Always do, don't they."

Jason thought for a moment. "Yeah, I'll head down that way tomorrow morning and see what Frank's up to. We could get a fresh coat on those eaves with three of us working, no problem. As long as we get a warm day."

"Got a feelin' we'll get one," Einar said. And he did. His knees still felt fresh, and that usually meant warm weather for a spell.

"Yeah, Pop. Me, too."

Einar closed the door and went back into the living room. About a half an hour later, Robert came down the stairs, his duffel bag in one hand and a brief case in the other. "Heading out now, Pop. I'll be up again next weekend, if that's alright."

"Fine by me," Einar said. "Rough potholes on forty-four. Watch out for 'em."

"Got it. Bye."

Einar nodded. Robert walked out the front door and onto the porch with an uneven thump-thump from his boots. He closed the door behind him and Einar could hear him talking to Jason, just for a moment, but he couldn't hear what was said. Then the thump-thump of Robert's boots started down the steps and into the gravel of the driveway. Einar sighed, then picked up a two-day old newspaper and read until he dozed off in the chair.

*   *   *

The next morning, Einar was up before Jason. He cooked scrambled eggs and bacon—one of three meals Einar William Coates to cook—and had it laid on the table by the time Jason came downstairs for his coffee. They sat and ate quickly. It was six a.m. when they finished.

"I'm going to head down the way to see if Frank can lend us a hand today. You need me to get anything while I'm out?"

"Right as rain I am," Einar said.

"Alright. I should be back in an hour or so."

"Dropcloths are up in the loft in the barn. I s'pose I can get those down for us." Einar stood up and took his plate to the sink.

"Your knees okay for that?" Jason said.

"Right as rain," Einar said again. Jason picked up his own plate and set it next to the sink on top of Einar's. He then drained his orange juice, took a sip of coffee, and said, "Alright, I'm off. I'll see you in an hour."

Einar cleaned the dishes, then went out into the barn to pull the dropcloths down from the loft. The day was warming, alright, and by the time he descended the ladder for the second time, Einar pulled off his coat and threw it on the workbench. He'd managed to get two ladders in place, too, by the time Jason came back. Frank Jordan was with him—"not pullin' today," he'd told Einar when he got out of Jason's car—and the three of them began painting by eight o'clock.

It was fine work, Einar thought to himself. The cold had worn off as the day went on, and the wind off the lake was the only sound to be heard as it wove through the trees around the barn and the rest of the yard. That was, of course, until Frank started talking. When that boy got going, he really got going, and he stood perched atop one of the two ladders as Jason lay on his stomach off the roof, brushing back and forth beneath him. Frank would get three strokes in, stop to talk, then three more strokes, then more talking. It was funny to Einar at first, but then it started to grate away at him. He eventually

18

descended his own ladder and went to the house to get away from it for a moment. As he crossed the yard, he could hear Frank up on the ladder: "It's just a matter of time, really. I mean, we're married now, and we both want to go back, so we'll probably head back to California within a month. Maybe two months. Definitely by the spring, though."

He went on, but his voice trailed off the closer to the house Einar got. When he stepped into the kitchen, the phone was ringing.

"Hello," Einar said in his typical monotone voice.

"Hi, dad," Bethany's voice said.

"Mornin' darlin'," he said to his daughter.

"Askar and I are going to be up this weekend. Is there anything you need us to bring?"

No, Einar thought, *but I can think of a few things you can leave at home. Like a bit of luggage and your husband.* "Not a thing. Jason's up here. Frank Jordan from down the way is helpin' with the paintin' on the barn."

"Great," Bethany said. "I have to run, dad. Askar's got a dinner thing going on tonight and I have to get ready. Bye."

She hung up before Einar could say goodbye himself. He hung up the phone and washed his hands in the sink, then went to the closet in the hallway to look for his knit cap—the brown one he'd worn since, hell, since forever. He dug and dug for ten minutes or more, shuffling through boxes and moving old jackets. He got a chair from the kitchen table, stood on it and checked the shelf high up in the closet, moved more boxes, and finally found it, a bit dusty but no worse for the wear. At least, no worse than it had been before. It was ratty, alright, but Einar liked that just fine.

When Einar went back out into the yard, Jason had made his way to the top of the ladder Einar had been using and Frank was still perched atop the other. Neither was painting. Jason was laughing as he watched Frank do what looked to be a dance but could have also been a seizure. "Jackass," Einar grumbled under his breath.

*   *   *

Frank stayed for dinner. Cooked it, in fact. He fired up the grill out back on the patio in the dooryard, even though it had gotten much colder now, and grilled up some moose steaks while Jason made corn on the stove inside. When they all sat down to eat, Frank started in talking immediately.

"Boy, I feel like I've been talking all day," he said.

"Strange," Einar grumbled under his breath again.

"How's life down in Portland, Jason? Big city living, right?" He chuckled.

"It's hardly a *big* city, but it's nice down there. I enjoy it."

"And how about Ginny? Boy, I haven't seen her since—damn, since your wedding probably. She getting along okay?" Frank took a big forkful of meat and shoved it into his mouth. No reply came from Jason, nor Einar, and the silence sat there like a fourth guest at the table.

Frank swallowed. "I say something wrong?"

"No," Jason said. "Ginny and I are…we're taking some time off."

"Oh," Frank replied, pondering Jason's statement for a moment. "I was down in Portland a few months ago and there was this crazy bar Natalie and I went to—you should have dinner with Nat and me, Jason. She's something else. But hey, this bar, they had a fish tank dividing the two rooms and the fish could swim all around you. It was out of this world. You ever been there?"

"Can't say as I have," Jason said, a smile returning to his face. Frank went on talking and cutting his meat. Jason looked to his father briefly, who rolled his eyes back at his son.

After dinner, Jason brought Frank home, then returned to the house to find Einar in a chair in the living room reading a newspaper. When Jason walked through the door, Einar put his paper down. "In behind the workbench by the tractor's a muzzle. We'll fish that out for him tomorrow."

Jason laughed for only the second time since coming to stay with Einar. His father seemed entirely unaware he was being funny, which made it even funnier to Jason. He climbed the stairs, took a shower and fell asleep immediately.

*   *   *

It took another full day of painting to finish the eaves. Frank talked the entire time. With each word, Jason watched another tiny shred of patience rip away from his father and float away into the breeze. When all the painting was done, they had dinner again. Frank talked the entire time. When dinner was over, Einar gave Frank a hundred dollars and wished him well. Frank, of course, turned the money down, and for a moment, Jason thought Einar was going to take the money back just to shut him up, but he apparently had one shred of patience left and finally convinced Frank to take the cash.

*   *   *

Robert came back up to the farm on Friday afternoon. Not long after he pulled into the driveway, Bethany and Askar showed up. Jason had been cleaning out a corner of the basement for more firewood when they all arrived and had no idea they'd come until he heard Robert's uneven footfalls coming down the stairs. When he realized his brother had actually come up to the farm for the second week in a row, Jason shut his eyes momentarily and sighed. He had brought Maggie with him this time, too.

"Hey, brother." Robert said when he reached the bottom of the steps.

"Hi."

"Need any help down here?"

"I got it under control."

Jason busied himself stacking wood on a broken pallet in the far corner of the basement, behind the furnace and bathed in a shadow caused by the only light bulb in the basement—a bare-wire deal that was draped over a pipe and hung in the center of the room. Robert picked up two pieces of wood and brought it over toward Jason's pile. But Jason stopped him before he could stack it.

"I said I got it under control," he said, the irritation rising in his voice. He glared at Robert for a moment, then turned back to the wood pile.

"Are we going to talk about this?" Robert asked.

At first Robert thought Jason hadn't heard him, or was at least ignoring him. But a moment later he was pinned against the stone wall by Jason's two strong forearms.

"No," Jason said. "We are most certainly *not* going to talk about this. Not today, not tomorrow, not this goddamn weekend. You can save yourself the trouble and go home now if it pleases ya."

He released Robert and stormed up the steps to the kitchen. Robert looked at the corner bathed in shadow for a spell, picked up the two pieces of wood Jason had knocked from his hands, stacked them and climbed the stairs, too. He switched off the light bulb that hung from the bare wire as he went.

*　　*　　*

Einar William Coates wasn't always an old man. Didn't always have arthritis. Wasn't always so reticent, so stricken with the idea that words did far more harm than silence. He used to be a young man with dreams, with ideas, with *guts* to make all of them happen. The war had sucked that out of him, had made him cold and ashamed of what he'd seen and what he'd done, not unlike so many other men who'd done exactly what he had done. But he had also made a promise, and then broken it, which made him different from all the others. They didn't have to live with that broken promise on their shoulders all their lives.

He had just begun dating Sarah. They had known each other for no more than three weeks, but they were in love. Very in love. It was at a dance—doesn't it always happen at a dance? So close to the other, eye to eye, pushing and pulling with the slightest movements—down in Falmouth, in that stupid town Einar hated so much and couldn't wait to leave because leaving meant he'd go to war, would go to somewhere other than Maine. But Sarah was in Falmouth that night, in the hall, dancing with Einar, and that was just fine by him.

"Willie," she'd said, her head resting on his shoulder.

"Yes," he had said, quietly, the way he knew Sarah wanted to hear the word.

"You're not going to kill any of those boys, are you?"

"They'll be tryin' to kill me," Einar had replied. Sarah lifted her head off his shoulder and looked him in the eyes. This wasn't some passing, girlish sentiment. Einar knew that just by looking at her. She wasn't concerned really about the men Einar might or might not kill. She was worried about the soul of Einar William Coates. It wouldn't be until much later—decades, in fact—that Einar realized Sarah had not a thing to worry about. When he came back to Maine after his tour of duty, he no longer had a soul. He didn't lose it, per se. He knew exactly where it went.

He spent every moment of his life since then hoping the devil would take good care of it until he made his way down to hell to reclaim it.

But that night in Falmouth, Einar looked at Sarah and said, "If no man tries to kill me, I won't kill no man."

"You promise, Willie?"

"I promise."

Sarah rested her head back on Einar's shoulder and they danced all night long. Almost a year after that dance, Einar William Coates put a bullet in the head of a man who had not tried to kill him, had not so much as uttered a threat in his direction. He'd broken his promise to Sarah, and he'd taken another life to boot.

When he was just a little boy, Einar had picked up a newspaper and began reading the headlines before his father had sat down at the table. Einar read only a few lines about a man who had killed three other men over the matter of money. "What happens to murderers?" Einar had asked his father.

"They die," his father had replied. "They die once for each death they caused."

"But how do you die more than once?" Einar asked.

His father looked very serious and sat down next to his son at the kitchen table. "There are more lives than the ones we live now, son."

Einar put a bullet in a man's head and reckoned he had about a dozen or more lives to die for, but that one would be the one to kill him for good, no matter in this world or the next. This death, the bullet crushed through a man's skull, was laced with a broken promise. If that wasn't a helluva way to seal a man's own coffin, Einar would learn no better method.

When Sarah died, Einar had been by her bedside. Everyone else waited out in the hallway or downstairs in the living room, but Einar sat with his wife's hands in his and watched her eyes close, watched her breathing slow. He watched her go as someone might watch a train leave the platform or the airplane leave the jetway. It was slow, gradual, almost normal, a 'see you later' sort of moment. When her eyes closed and her breathing stopped, Einar sat for fifteen minutes with his wife's dead body and watched her slip away, even after breathing her last breath, still slipping, still floating into whatever world follows this one the way the leaves outside flowed to the ground, swinging, swaying, blowing back and forth, then finally succumbing. Einar pulled the sheet over her face before leaving the room.

Jason and Robert were the only ones in the hallway waiting. Everyone else was downstairs, sitting quietly and waiting…waiting… waiting to make plans, waiting for it all to be official, waiting to grieve and comfort. But Jason and Robert were in the hallway, clinging to a hope they both knew was false, hoping Einar would come out into the hall and tell them she'd made a sudden and amazing recovery, was, in fact, completely okay, ready to do battle with another few decades. Einar saw it painted on their faces plain as the sun off the lake. When Robert read his father's own face, he went downstairs to join the others in the living room. But Jason stayed.

Einar and Jason said nothing. Dry-eyed and serious, they hugged in the middle of the hallway. It was the first time Jason had felt his father's embrace since he was fifteen years old. Jason lost his mother that day, and for Einar, it was the only consolation of that moment that he could be somewhat of a comfort to his son. But in his own mind, he knew there was something else there, too. He'd just watched his wife slip away into a place he'd never get to visit, a heaven he'd never see, because he'd broken a promise and had to be killed so many more times after he died and went away from this life. He would truly never see his wife again. As he stood in the hallway with his arms around his son, Einar couldn't help but feel his mind and heart crush knowing that Jason, too, would never see Einar again once he departed this world. His father would be in a different place altogether, not standing side by side with God and Sarah and whoever else may have passed on in the Coates family throughout the years.

Einar would be wrestling the devil for something he had given away—with the help of the United States Army and the powers that be—so many years ago. How long could that struggle last?

Einar figured the devil had an eternity, and so did he.

*   *   *

Jason went into town—a main street, really. There was no town per se, only a few stores—to pick up a new rake and shovel. Einar's tools had done much throughout the years, and they were certainly worse for the wear. With work to be done and time on his hands, Jason decided to invest in a few new tools—without telling Einar, of course. Frank Jordan had come with him and had been uncharacteristically quiet during the drive, and though Jason noticed, it didn't seem too odd to him. Stoicism grows on trees in northern Maine and rains down on all men their entire lives.

Gibson's Feed was the name of the general store, and as he walked into the place, Jason figured he hadn't set foot in there for a good ten years. It was the kind of place that had the register at the back of the store in front of the booze, cigarettes and candy, because if someone was going to steal from the place, those were the tasty items they would take. Jason made his way through the center aisle toward the counter that held the cash register, and when he'd gotten no more than five feet from it, a semi-familiar voice rang out.

"Jason Coates!"

It took him a moment, but Jason placed the girl quickly enough.

"How are you, Eleanor?"

"By God, it's been years!"

Eleanor Rigby Phillips had been the self-fulfilling prophecy of Jason's high school class. She'd been told all her life she was destined to be alone and miserable because of her name—a gift from her deadbeat dad, an obvious Beatles fanatic and ignoramus regarding subtext—and for years she denied that fate. In fact, she did so to a fault, often portraying herself as a bit too chipper. But over the years, after hearing it over and over again, she began to believe it: she was destined to be alone and miserable. She lived that way now, not because she had to—she was reasonably attractive and quite engaging—but instead because she was expected to. She'd been convinced, just like everyone else had been.

"Sure has," Jason said. "Been down south in Portland."

"Oh, wow," Eleanor said, the fingers of her left hand now twirling through her brown hair. "I always figured you'd find your way south. What do you do down there?"

"I write for the Press Herald," Jason said, now leaning on the glass case dividing him from Eleanor.

"The paper. Wow, that's great. Really great, Jason. God, it's been years." Eleanor's eyes wandered down to the glass case, trying to catch in it a reflection of the many years that had passed since high school, or perhaps simply the days and weeks and months and years since she'd accepted her fate as a hopeless one. Only after a few moments did she snap out of it and smile again. "Well what can I do for you today, young Mr. Coates?"

Jason returned her smile, though hers beamed more brightly than his could in recent memory. He was amazed at how easily her smile rose to her lips despite what he knew to be true about her: she was prone to depression, the severe stuff. She was often unreasonable and angry. Some said she was bipolar. But she was always quick to smile. Amazing.

"I need a few things," Jason said. "Need a rake and a shovel, and probably a new maul."

"Not a problem," Eleanor said as she turned completely around and grabbed a key off a hook behind her. The key was attached to what was once the rear-view mirror of some old car, and it dangled from Eleanor's right hand as she made her way around the glass case. "Out back," she said, motioning for Jason to follow her.

They went through a rickety door that led to a shed in a small, enclosed yard behind the store. Eleanor seemed to float with the breeze across the yard, and Jason noticed her hair catching the air and reaching like arms toward the sky, then falling again. She turned to him when they reached the shed. "You look great," she said to him again. "You really do...but tired."

"I am," Jason said.

Eleanor looked at him a moment longer and her face changed. When she smiled, she smiled completely. And when she didn't smile, she did that just as completely. Jason looked at her as her face changed and thought, if only for a split second, that her brown eyes actually grew darker, as if she'd sensed the weight of his response entirely. He was the first to look away. When he did, Eleanor went into the shed.

"I've been working here a while now," Eleanor said as she rustled through the shed looking for the tools Jason needed. She pulled out a maul first and leaned it against the outside of the shed. "Ten pound okay?"

Jason picked up the maul and said, "This will be fine."

"Was married for a while," Eleanor continued as she dug through the tools. "Betcha didn't know that."

"I didn't," Jason said.

"Was married for two years. The first year was good. The second year wasn't. I left him about six months ago. That's when I moved back here and started working at the store. It's a good life for now. Quiet. I like being alone." Eleanor emerged from the shed carrying a brand new shovel. She handed it to Jason. "You didn't know that, did ya? Didn't know I like being alone. I like it, you know."

"I didn't think--"

"I know you didn't, darlin'."

Eleanor smiled again, then went back into the shed.

"Hey," Jason said as he leaned the shovel against the shed and went inside, "not all of us thought you were that way. I didn't."

Eleanor tugged a metal rake out of one of the racks against the wall. When she did, the handle almost hit Jason in the chest. It was only then that he realized how small the shed really was, and that realization was accompanied by a slight feeling of claustrophobia.

Eleanor was smiling at him again.

"Oh, I know, Jason. I know it. We were kids, anyway." She handed him the rake.

"I mean—"

"Hey," Eleanor interrupted. "I know. Was just kidding with you, Coates. You're one of the good guys, right?"

Eleanor wriggled past him and left the shed. She was already halfway through the yard, the maul in her right hand, when Jason stepped out of the shed. "Good guys," he said to himself. "Not sure about that one, Rigby."

She turned when she heard the name. "Maybe not," she said, her face changed again, somehow darker again. Then she went inside. Jason followed. Frank was leaning on the glass case when Jason and

Eleanor made their way inside. He straightened up when he saw Eleanor. "Hey, Elly," Frank said.

"Mornin', Frank. How're the spuds these days?"

"Okay, I guess."

Eleanor put the maul down in front of the counter, then went around to the other side and positioned herself behind the register. "You helpin' Coates here with some work at Willie's place?"

"Yeah," Frank said. "Got some time before I, you know, head back to California."

Eleanor gave Frank a look that was halfway between a smile and a wink. "Right, Frank."

Frank immediately looked away.

"How's Natalie these days?"

"Oh, she's good. You know. She's—she's good."

"Still in town, is she?"

"Oh, yeah, of course. Still in town. Up at the, uh, up at the farm. With Pop."

Eleanor watched Frank fidget with some light fixtures in the first aisle. He hadn't looked at her since she'd mentioned Natalie's name. Jason watched all this happen and hated Eleanor for it, though he didn't know why. So what if Natalie was up at Frank's Pop's farm. What did that matter to Eleanor? And why was Frank so nervous about it?

Jason made a mental note to ask Frank what was up, then quickly erased it. If Frank had a secret to keep, Jason was not the person to try and uncover it, considering the recent collapse of his own marriage for the sake of...what? Boredom? Anger? Jealousy? What was it?

"Hey Coates!" Eleanor all-but-shouted. "Still with us here?" She snapped her fingers in front of his face.

"Yeah. Sorry. How much?"

"Thirty seven even. Locals-only discount," she said with a slight chuckle.

Jason handed her two twenties and she made change. Jason watched again as Frank fidgeted through the aisles, then returned his attention to Eleanor, who was handing him three brand-new dollar bills.

"You going to be in town for a bit?" She asked.

"Few days, yeah."

"Stop on by again." Eleanor said this with no clear expression on her face. It came off as more of a command than a request.

"I will, Eleanor."

Jason made his way back through the center aisle and Frank followed. Jason put the tools in the trunk of the car and they began driving back toward Einar's place. It was a twenty minute drive that he and Frank spent in mostly silence. Frank still seemed abnormally quiet as he looked out the passenger window, his face so close to the glass that fog formed on it, but Jason let him be. Finally, when they turned onto County Road seventeen, Frank said, "Eleanor's looking happier these days."

Jason didn't reply at first. He thought about the complete smile Eleanor had worn only a few minutes ago, and how it changed so quickly into a straight-faced and bland frown. "I suppose I wouldn't have a basis for comparison," Jason said. "Hadn't seen her in years."

"Right," Frank said. "She and Natalie were spending a lot of time together when she—well, not long ago. Natalie's been spending a lot of time alone. You know. Women need that sort of thing."

Another few minutes of silence followed that, and Jason found it more and more difficult to keep from saying something to Frank. He'd been friends with this guy for years—more years than he cared to count at this point—and he knew when Frank was lying to him. Or worse, when Frank was lying to himself. "Natalie's not around, is she, Frank?"

Frank turned away from the fogged window and looked at Jason with an exaggerated smile. "What? Come on, no, that's silly. She's up at my Pop's place. She's just—"

"She leave you, Frank?"

Frank didn't lose his smile. He stared at Jason, who in turn stared out the windshield at the winding road ahead of them. "Yeah," Frank said finally, turning back to the passenger window. "Yeah, she did."

Jason slowed to a near-stop and took a right turn onto County Road forty-seven, which was not paved. The wheels of the car thumped down off the edge of the pavement and onto the dirt road and whizzed with the sort of whine a dirt road seems to speak with. Jason avoided deep holes full of half-frozen puddles. Pebbles kicked up and bounced off the side panels of the car. Dry dust swirled behind the car, brown ghosts in the rearview mirror exhumed and angered out of their sleep by the spinning rubber tires. "Lots of work to do at Willie's place," Jason said. "Going to need your help."

Frank looked over at Jason again. "Thanks," he said. "Guess we've both got a lot of work to do, don't we?"

Jason made brief eye contact with Frank, then returned his attention to the road. "Yes, I suppose so."

*   *   *

Askar was standing on the porch smoking a cigarette and talking on his cell phone when Jason and Frank pulled up to the house. As he pulled the tools out of the trunk, Jason listened to Askar argue with whomever was on the other end of the line, but he couldn't really understand what the argument was over. Money, of course, but beyond that, it made no sense to Jason. He could see why Willie didn't like Askar, though his own distaste for his sister's husband was not a thing he really dwelled on himself. He was part of the family now, and Jason had no problem with that. He just wished the guy would get off the damn phone for a change.

As Jason and Frank skirted around the porch and headed toward the barn, Bethany came out of the house and stood by Askar. He ignored her and continued his argument. Jason made eye contact with Bethany, and she moved to the railing just above where Jason was standing.

"He gets that way," she said to her brother. "Just needs some time up here, I think, and he'll be fine." She gave Jason the most sincere smile she could muster—a smile Jason had seen countless times throughout their childhood, the smile she wore after disappointment or heartbreak or both—and did not smile back.

"Where's Robert?" Jason asked.

"He and Pop went down to the lake. I think Willie's fishing."

Jason grunted and went to catch up with Frank, who was just stepping into the barn. Bethany watched him go, her hands pressed firmly on the bare wood railing and her ears on the voice of her husband, still arguing about money on his phone behind her. When Jason disappeared into the barn, Bethany turned, gave Askar a kiss on the cheek, and went back inside the house.

*   *   *

It was almost midnight when Jason's cell phone rang. He'd just turned it back on this morning after leaving it in his car for most of the week in an effort to escape whatever life he'd left behind when he came up from Portland. There were several voice mail messages, but Jason listened to none of them. He simply turned the ringer volume to low and placed it on the nightstand. Just before midnight, the slow, soft pulse of the ringer started, and though Jason didn't wake up immediately, he flipped his phone open just in time.

"Hello," he said, his voice groggy.

The reply came slowly: "Hi."

Jason sat up in bed but did not turn the light on. He could feel a nervous heat immediately reach his face, neck and arms. "Ginny," he said quietly.

"I called all week and you never answered."

"I turned my cell phone off. Sorry."

Ginny sighed long and deep, wavering slightly by the end of it. "It's okay. Are you up at your dad's place still?"

"Yes."

"Maggie called me and told me. She says Robert's up there, too."

"Yes," Jason said, the sleep now finally disappearing from his voice. "Robert's up here, too."

There was a long pause between them on the phone in the dark, as if neither really knew how to proceed. Jason knew an apology right then would seem tacky and insincere, so he held back, even though his impulse was to scream it so that she might hear it down in Portland even if they hadn't been on the phone, with sadness and regret in his voice that would rustle the trees. But he held it in his throat, held it for a more appropriate time, held it because it was true and real and deserved to be said in person.

Instead, he said, "How have…you been?"

"My husband disappeared for almost two weeks. How do you think I've been?"

"I wanted to get away. I thought you'd—I thought you'd want to be away from me."

Ginny sighed again. "Part of me does, Jason, but part of me wants you here, right now. I want to scream at you and hit you and hold you and cry into your arms and fucking kill you."

"I know," Jason said.

"When are you coming back?"

"I don't know. Should I come back?" He asked.

"I don't know."

"Okay."

Ginny sniffled, and Jason knew for sure she was in tears. "What are you doing up there anyway?"

"Lots of work to be done up here. The barn. Cutting wood. The tractor. Down basement. Willie wants to get the place looking good for Robert and—well, for the wedding."

Ginny was outright crying now, hard and stuttered between sobs. Jason said nothing. He waited for her to regain control as he pressed his fingers around the bridge of his nose and into his eyes. It took several minutes, but she finally calmed. Ginny was a tough girl; Jason could count on his left hand—okay, maybe on both hands—how many times he'd seen her outright cry, but when she did it, she did it full-on. When she broke, she broke completely. Jason knew this and hated that he'd caused it this time.

"Does Robert know?" Ginny said, finally.

"I don't know. I think he might have some suspicions, but he hasn't said anything. I thought he'd have punched my face through the barn by now if he knew for sure."

Ginny laughed halfheartedly.

"Look," Jason said, "I know it doesn't mean much now, but I'm going to make this right. I'm going to—to fix this."

"Oh, Jason. This isn't something to be fixed."

"But I can fix it, Ginny. I'll tell Robert and work it out with him, and—"

"And what, Jason? Ruin his wedding? And what about me? How

can you fix me? How can you fix us?"

Jason thought about this for a moment. In the darkness of his bedroom, there seemed a million possibilities, but he was no fool. Once the morning sun rose and this all became a reality again, the possibilities whittled down to a few and none of them were really great options. He'd done the damage already, and the only thing he could do now was more damage. The question was, of course, was this damage that needed to be done?

"Ginny, I'll figure this out, I swear to you. I swear to you, okay?"

Ginny cried in response.

"I love you, Ginny."

Ginny cried louder and sobbed hard, then went silent. "Goodnight, Jason. I'm sorry I woke you."

Then she hung up.

Jason didn't sleep again that night until just before sun-up.

*　　*　　*

Einar and Robert were sitting at the kitchen table drinking coffee when Jason came downstairs.

"You look like shit," Robert said to him.

"Good morning to you, too."

"Too cold in the room last night?" Einar said.

"Room was fine."

Jason poured himself a cup of coffee and immediately left the room. Einar never so much as looked at him go, but Robert followed Jason with his eyes the entire time. When he was finally out of the room, Robert looked at Einar. "Dad, this has gone on too long."

Einar nodded.

"What are we going to do about it?" Robert said.

Einar took a sip of coffee. "I 'spect we'll wait a little longer."

Robert looked across the table at his father for a moment longer, then left the kitchen and went through the living room to the front door. Jason was just stepping out onto the porch. Robert followed, then slammed the door behind him. Jason paid no attention. As he walked around the front of the porch and then down the slope of the yard toward the barn, he could hear Robert's uneven footsteps behind him, walking as fast as he could though he couldn't keep up with Jason—a fact Jason silently reveled in at his most angry or devious moments.

"Jason, I want to talk to you."

"So talk."

Jason did not stop walking.

"I want to talk, Jason. No more of this bullshit. Stop so we can talk."

"Got work to do."

Jason took two more steps before he felt Robert's heavy hand slap down on his shoulder. He immediately shrugged it away, but he stopped walking and turned. "I'm not going to talk to you like this. Here. Pissed off."

"I'm not pissed off," Robert said. "I barely know what's wrong with you. But I'm here, you know. I'm here because of you."

"Well let me save you the trouble of babysitting your younger brother. You can leave whenever the hell you want."

"I won't leave until you talk to me. Come on, Jason. I want to help. I know you're in a shitty place now and you screwed up, but we can—"

"Oh," Jason said, his voice getting louder, "thanks for the pep talk, coach. Real helpful, asshole. I know what I did. I know what happened and you don't, so save your bullshit, Robert." Jason started to turn, but he stopped. "And *we* can't fix shit. *We* can scrape the paint off a barn, but *we* can't fix my marriage or my head, or Ginny's head, or—"

"Or what?" Robert said.

"Never mind."

"Tell me."

"I've got work to do."

"Tell me, Jason."

Before Robert could get a grasp on what was happening, Jason had him by the collar. Jason wanted to hold back. He wanted to let it go, wanted to just make it all disappear before he could say what he knew he needed to say. But he could not hold back.

"It was Maggie," He said. "You happy now?"

Robert's massive hand curled into a fist and somehow wrapped around Jason's arms to connect with his jaw. When Jason fell backward, Robert hit him again, and then again. Jason was on the ground now, taking each blow he knew he deserved. Finally, after two more punches, Robert screamed at his brother, "Get up, you fucking asshole! Get up. Get the fuck up!"

Jason did.

Robert punched him in the gut. Then he grabbed Jason's head and punched him in the face. "You son of a bitch," he said, out of breath now.

Robert walked away from his brother who was on his back bleeding in the dirt. Jason didn't move for almost a half hour. He could hear Robert in the barn, on the phone with Maggie, alternately screaming and sobbing. As Jason lay on the ground, listening to his brother's relationship with his fiancé end, he knew he'd done his worst, not because of the rising welts on his face, not because of the blood or the anger…but because Robert was sobbing. Because Jason had broken his brother. First Ginny, then himself, now his brother. What else could he possibly destroy?

Jason got himself up off the ground shortly after Robert stormed out of the barn and got into his car. As Robert sped out of the driveway, kicking dirt in two different directions as he turned, Jason put his hands to his face to feel the damage. It was substantial. Einar was sitting in the rocking chair on the porch. Jason joined him.

"Socked ya good," Einar said.

"Sure did, Willie. Damned if I didn't deserve more."

Einar had brought ice wrapped in a washcloth out onto the porch. He pointed to it as it sat on the railing. "Put that on yer mug," he said, then rocked back and forth in the chair.

Jason did as he was told.

"I messed it all up, Pop."

Einar kept rocking his chair. "Mmhmm."

"What the hell do I do now?" Jason said more to the empty driveway than to Einar.

There was a short moment in which the only noise was the wind through the almost-bare trees, but then Einar said, "Gutters need cleanin'."

Jason chuckled, then said, "I suppose they do." He dropped the ice from his face and started to walk down off the porch.

"Sit down for a spell," Einar said.

Jason turned and looked at his father as he rocked back and forth, arms folded over his brown work coat. He then sat down on the top step of the porch and leaned against the railing, pressing the ice to his face once again.

"I don't really want to talk about this now, Pop."

"Your mother used to love your hockey games."

"What?"

"Down there in Bangor. Used to love the drive down there to watch you play net. Such a boy with not a lick of talent, you were!"

They both laughed.

"She used to sit in the stands next to me, boy. And she'd say, 'he'll be great for his teammates when he's old enough to buy the beer!' She had that way, you know. You'd finish your game and she'd be the first to tell ya how great ya did, not because she believed it, but because she knew ya needed to believe it."

Jason put the ice on the porch and left it there. It was the most he'd heard his father talk all at once in years.

"I was the opposite," Einar said. "Ya know that well enough. I'd tell ya how it was, no matter how it irked ya, an' boy did it irk ya some. That's the balance, Jason. That's how we kept you three level, you and yer brother and sister. We'd tell ya how great ya were, how much you could accomplish, then we'd tell ya what life really is, an' how it would feel to fail and then dust yourself off and keep goin'. I guess ya know that, too."

"Yeah, Pop."

"If yer Ma was here, she'd tell ya you played a helluva game. What-ever that, she'd keep telling ya you had talent and played well, played strong, played with your arms and your legs and your head and your heart. But I'd tell ya different. I'd tell ya you were out of position or you played your angles wrong, or ya weren't keeping your stick on the ice."

"I get ya, Pop."

"Damned if ya do, boy. Because I'll tell ya, your mother ain't here. I am. And I want to tell ya you did the right thing by tellin' him, by takin' your lumps. You're still a goddamned fool, ya are, but ya told him, and now ya get up and dust yourself off. I got a feelin' you got a few more lumps comin' your way. Robert does, too."

Einar paused and looked out at the trees in the driveway. "Ahh, hell. Maybe if your Ma was here, she'd tell ya how badly you done. Maybe we'd switch ourselves, me and her. But it's just me, so I tell ya straight right now. Ya got a lot comin' your way. Keep your stick on the ice and you'll do just fine."

Einar stood up from his rocking chair and put his hands on his hips. It was a slow motion, the kind made perfect by old men throughout the world, though Einar had plenty of vigor and muscles on most men his age.

"Gutters need cleanin'," Einar said, then opened the door to the house and went inside. Jason watched him go, then thumped his head back against the porch railing. He sat that way for ten minutes or more before going inside to clean the cut Robert had opened up above his eye, then went to work cleaning out the gutters.

*　　　*　　　*

Robert came back four hours later. He was drunk and angry. Jason met him in the driveway, but Robert shoved past him and went directly to the barn. Jason didn't bother to follow; instead, he finished cleaning the gutters and went inside to clean up when dinner time rolled around.

*　　　*　　　*

Darkness had fallen by the time Einar decided to go out to the barn. Jason was asleep on the couch in the living room and Robert hadn't come out of the barn since returning home drunk earlier that afternoon. Einar pulled on his brown work coat and gloves and headed out in the direction of the barn; he got about four steps around the corner of the porch when he stopped, turned, and went back inside to fetch his shotgun. He swung the door to the closet open hard and the

41

doorknob banged against the wall behind it. The thump woke Jason, who watched as Einar pulled the shotgun out and loaded it.

"What's going on, Pop?"

Einar said nothing. He took the gun and went back outside with a step more fitting a twenty-year-old man than a man with more than sixty-seven years behind him. Jason immediately got up from the couch, found his boots and laced them as quickly as he could. He had gotten both of them on and was heading toward the door when he heard the first shot.

"Jesus," he said, running outside and into the driveway. When his boots hit the gravel of the driveway, the second shot rang out.

"Don't come back, ya hear me?" Einar screamed in the direction of the lake.

"Pop, what the hell's going on?" Jason was standing next to Einar now, who was reloading the shotgun and preparing for another shot. Jason peered out toward the lake but saw nothing in the darkness. Robert was stumbling out of the barn now, staggering like a drunk, unsurprisingly.

Einar squeezed off another shot. The ringing that followed was immense, the sort of quiet pierced only by the ringing of eardrums that Jason associated with the sound of lightning bouncing off the lake when he was a kid.

"Jesus, Pop, what the hell is going on?"

"Ya goddamn *thief*!" Einar screamed toward the lake again. Then he simply turned and walked back toward the house. Robert was leaning against the barn door, a bottle of whiskey in his right hand. He looked over at Jason and started laughing.

"Thought I'd drink 'em to death if there was trouble, ya know," Robert said, slurring each word in a precise drunken sentence. He turned and disappeared into the barn.

Askar was standing on the porch as Einar approached, a golf club in his right hand and Bethany in the doorway behind him. Einar stopped and looked at the hulking man holding a golf club. "What the hell were ya goin' to do to some gun-wieldin' crazy if he was tryin' to attack my daughter? Huh? Bore him to death?"

Askar stood still, unsmiling and seemingly unfazed.

"Goddamned *golf club*," Einar muttered as he walked around Askar. As he went through the doorway, he looked at Bethany and said, "Damn fool brought a nine-iron to a gunfight."

Jason stood for a moment in the middle of the yard in the dark, peering again at the lake, then at the barn, then at the house. He finally went back inside. Einar was returning the shotgun to the closet.

"What the hell was that, Pop?"

"Goddamn thief. Been coming by here for months now, right around the time your Ma started gettin' worse. Stealin' from the barn, sleepin' out there."

"Who is it?"

"Damned if I know," Einar said. "We'll know for sure when I put a buckshot in his ass."

Einar closed the closet door and put his hands on his hips. Jason was standing in the middle of the living room, hair tousled and adrenaline still pumping. Askar and Bethany were climbing the stairs back up to the bedroom. "Sorry I woke you all," Einar said. Askar and Bethany finally disappeared. Einar looked to Jason. "There's a deck of cards in the kitchen."

Einar left the room and sat down at the kitchen table, not bothering to wait and see if Jason would follow.

He did.

They played cards for an hour without saying a word to each other. By the time the hour had passed, Jason had become sleepy again—

something he wouldn't have thought possible an hour before—and decided to call it a night. Einar stayed at the kitchen table for a half hour more playing solitaire in the soft light of the kitchen. His eyes grew tired, too, but he still had something else to tend to before sleep caught up with him. Einar was a working man, and when there was work to be done, sleep could wait. And wait it would tonight.

He collected the cards and wrapped an elastic band around them. Tossed them in a drawer—the 'junk drawer,' as his kids had called it for so many years growing up—and went to the living room closet to fetch his work coat again. He went outside into the yard, and this time there was no need for a shotgun or any other interruption between him and his son, drunk in the barn.

"Robert," Einar said into the dark.

"Hey, Pop."

Robert's voice came from the back corner of the barn, behind the tractor and Einar's old Ford pick-up. The only light came in the form of a slight glow left over from the kitchen light that swept through the window of the house well behind Einar. It only cast itself about ten feet into the barn. Beyond that, Einar could see nothing.

"Your Pop's old. Where the hell are ya?"

"I'm, uh…shit, I don't know. On the ground."

Einar put his hands on his hips for a moment, then moved around the front of the tractor to the work bench. He shuffled around there for a moment, looking for the flashlight, successfully dropping and shattering a glass container of nails, then found the light behind a can of primer. He clicked it on and wondered briefly when the last time this thing had been clicked on. That flashlight very well may have been older than his youngest child.

It worked, though, and Einar worked his way back around the tractor to the center of the barn, then worked his way back behind the

Ford. Sure enough, Robert was on the ground, empty bottle of whiskey in one hand, his back up against the far wall of the barn.

"You and Jack havin' a night of it?" Einar said, pointing the light at his drunk son.

"You know us, Pop. Always getting into trouble, me and Jack. Can you point that thing somewhere else?"

Einar pointed the light at the ground to his side. Then he looked around for that lantern and found it hanging from a hook on the wall. He pulled some matches out of his pocket and lit it, then clicked off the flashlight. He worked his way back over toward his son and leaned on the back bumper of the Ford.

"I ain't good at talkin'," Einar said.

Robert laughed. "Hadn't noticed."

"Don't be smart," Einar said. "Yer mom was the talker. But I'll hear ya."

"Not much in the mood for talking, Pop. Really. You don't have to fill in for mom, you know. She's gone and that's fine."

Einar said nothing. He looked down at his drunk pile of son, and watched as Robert's eyes opened, then closed, then opened again. His head lolled. His words weren't complete. He'd been drinking a long time today.

"Funny," Einar said. "Three of us Coates men in this house after so many years, and suddenly we're all bachelors."

Robert laughed harder than he should have. Einar cracked a smile only. Robert's voice faded from a laugh to what sounded like a defeated sigh, then he dropped his chin to his chest and let go of the empty bottle. It thumped onto the dirt floor.

"Well, come on then," Einar said, standing up. "I won't have ya sleepin' out here in the barn. Not with that damned thief wanderin' about." He reached his hand down to his son, but Robert did not take it.

"I'm not going inside," Robert said. "Not with *him* in there. Not with Jason."

Einar didn't move. "He's asleep. Can't bother ya if he's asleep."

Robert looked at his father's hand a moment longer, then got to his feet himself. Einar put his hand back in his pocket and watched as Robert stumbled side to side as he made his way out of the barn, his limp now accentuated with the dizziness of alcohol. "You must think I'm—we're shits, Pop. Jason and me both. We're—we're shits. Ha!"

"My sons ain't shits," Einar said, following Robert out into the yard.

"That shit inside, he's a shit."

"He's your brother."

"Not anymore he isn't. He's nothing to me now."

Robert now stood next to the porch, and Einar grabbed him by the arm and threw him against the railing. The sturdy wood of the porch creaked from the force of it. Einar threw his open hand across his son's face hard. Robert winced in surprise. Einar hit him again.

"That's your blood in there, and don't you forget it. I don't care who he diddled to piss ya off. He's your blood. He's a Coates, and so are you."

"Jesus, you slapped me," Robert said.

"Yer lucky I didn't do worse. Ya both deserve worse."

Einar stepped away from his son, who stood stunned against the porch railing. As Einar raised his right boot onto the first step of the porch, he looked toward Robert and said, "If ya want worse, I'll have Askar come down here with his nine iron." This time, Einar laughed and Robert stayed silent.

Robert listened as his father's footfalls reached the door, then the living room, then beyond until they disappeared. He stood unsteady by the porch, wavering through a drunken and dizzying haze, staring at the barn for a moment, then raising his hand to his face. *That asshole fucks my fiancé and* I'm *the one getting a slap?* He thought to himself, forgetting the beating he'd given Jason earlier that day. Robert finally stumbled inside and fell asleep on the couch, his boots still on and a steady stream of drool escaping the corner of his mouth.

*   *   *

When Einar made his way to the bedroom he'd shared with Sarah for more years than he could bear to count, his daughter was sitting on his bed with the light on but her eyes closed. Bethany was sitting Indian-style in the center of the four-poster, her hands folded in her lap and her long, blonde hair falling on either side of her face and onto her shoulders. Einar stood in the doorway, suddenly a guest in his own bedroom, an intrusion on a peaceful moment. But then Bethany opened her eyes, and the feeling that Einar was a piece of misplaced furniture left his mind.

"Sorry, Daddy. It just—it smells like Mom in here."

Einar entered the room and sat down on the rocking chair in the corner. This one was far more comfortable than its cousin out on the front porch, and more presentable, too. Sarah had done a lot of her knitting in this chair, sitting by the window and looking out at the back yard near the lake. Einar used it as a stopping point only to take off his boots. Then he stood up again, put his hands on his hips, and looked at his daughter.

"You miss her a lot, don't you, Daddy?"

"Course I do," Einar said.

"Me too."

Bethany stood up on the bed, bounced once, then stepped down onto the hard wood floor. She gave her father a kiss on the cheek and headed toward the door.

"You and Askar have plans tomorrow?" Einar asked.

Bethany stopped in the doorway and turned. "No, not really," she said. "He's most likely going to spend most of the day on his phone and his laptop. He works too much."

Einar's face softened just a bit. "Laptops and phones get lost sometimes," he said.

Bethany smiled. "Daddy, don't. It's important to him."

Einar crossed his arms across his chest. "Maybe you can tear him away from the phone tomorrow. Jason got through about half of the wood out back that needs to be split. Reckon we could have the whole cord cut and stacked tomorrow, if he'd be willing to help."

"I'll see if he'd do that," Bethany said, then disappeared down the hall. Einar looked at the empty doorway for a moment, then down at the empty bed. A small indentation lingered in the comforter from where Bethany's weight had deformed it, and Einar concentrated for a moment on that space. He half expected Sarah to appear from behind him to smooth out the comforter, pat him on the shoulder and tell him it was time to take off the work clothes and climb into bed, but she did not come. Would not come. Einar closed the door and got changed, then climbed into bed alone. He could hear footsteps in the hallway, softly clopping one way or another, and thought how strange it was to have his kids in the house again without Sarah. This was the second time since she'd died that all the Coates had been in one place, under one roof. Now, one was drunk, one was bloodied and battered, and one was sleeping with a jackass. At one point in his life, all things had been simple; now here he was, with his children, and nothing at all seemed simple.

Einar closed his eyes and listened to the footsteps in the hallway disappear. *Sarah,* he thought, *I'm going to try to be Dad without you. Keep an eye, will ya?*

II

FOOTPRINTS BEHIND...

The drunk Coates slept in the barn until the old man came out to roust him. They blabbered inside the barn for a spell, then came out into the yard. The old man hit the one with the limp, the drunk one, and eventually they both went inside. Quietly, the man waited in the bushes down by the lake for ten more minutes, then crept into the yard and further into the barn. He slept only for a few hours, then left before daybreak.

It happened this way most nights now. The old man would stay outside and watch until he got tired or bored, then go inside and the man would go into the barn to sleep for a few hours. Sometimes the old man would shoot at him, but he had bad eyes, it seemed, and never hit his target. Sometimes the man slept; sometimes he rummaged through the junk in the barn. If it suit him, he'd steal what was there. But only if it would help him. Only if it would get him through another day. He did not take for the sake of taking.

He left this time, just as the sun was about to make its appearance, and he was almost caught. The girl, the old man's daughter, was standing on the porch looking right in the direction of the barn. She must have seen him, or so he thought, but she did not move. She had her arms wrapped around herself—and damn, it was cold, so why not?—and remained still, even though the man was now standing in the opening of the barn door. When he realized she was there, he froze solid, then crept slowly back into the shadows of the barn until she finally went inside. It irked him to wait, because it made him shiver, and he didn't shiver so long as he was moving, and she made him stay still. But eventually she went inside and he left, down toward the lake and into the woods.

Where was he going?

He didn't know.

Did it matter?

No. Not one bit at all.

He'd be back the next night. And the night after. And the night after that.

*   *   *

When Einar woke that morning, Bethany was in the kitchen making breakfast. Askar was sitting at the kitchen table, reading from a stack of papers he'd undoubtedly taken from his briefcase. Einar poured himself a cup of coffee and strode to the front door, put the coffee on the table long enough to get his coat on, and walked out onto the front porch.

As he took his first sip from the steaming mug, he noticed immediately: the barn door, slightly more open than he'd left it last night. That damn thief. Einar went to the barn to see if anything was missing. When he was satisfied that nothing had been stolen, he went back inside and sat at the kitchen table next to Askar. Bethany was scooping eggs onto a dish next to a pile of fatty bacon. Jason entered the kitchen and sat between Askar and Einar just as Bethany was setting the plate of food on the table.

"Need to get the rest of that cord split," Einar said.

"I will, Pop. Going to take care of a few other things first."

"Not you," Einar said.

Askar looked up from his papers.

"Ya want to put all those muscles of yours to work today?" Einar said to Askar.

"Uh," Askar started.

"Maul's down basement. Bulkhead opens easy enough. Just toss it all down. We can stack it later." Einar scooped a spoonful of eggs onto his plate.

"Yeah," Askar said. "Okay. I'll get showered up and do that."

*　　　*　　　*

Robert didn't move from the couch until almost eleven that morning. Askar was in the back yard with the maul, and had done a good deal of the chopping—after Einar showed him how to use the maul correctly, of course—and Jason had busied himself raking the autumn leaves into big piles before digging up that damn stump that had been rotting and taking up half the yard for the last six months. Einar didn't necessarily want the stump gone, but the work was good for Jason. He let him take the chainsaw and shovel to it.

Bethany was still in the kitchen when Robert limped in. She had pulled all the dishes, pots, pans, and miscellaneous junk that had piled up in the cupboards out and began wiping the shelves down with a rag and some Pine-sol. The kitchen smelled strongly of fake pine and dirty mops; Robert's eyes burned when he entered the room.

"Tied on a good one, didn't you?" Bethany said as she knelt on the countertop and reached for the highest shelf.

"Tied it on and double-knotted it," Robert replied.

"There's bacon left in the fridge if you're hungry."

Robert pulled the plate out of the refrigerator and sat down at the kitchen table. He stuck one piece in his mouth before he felt like he might throw up.

"You did a number on Jason." Bethany said, still kneeling on the countertop.

"He deserved that and more," Robert said.

"You two think alike. He said the same thing."

Robert took another bite of bacon. It made him feel worse. "You know what happened."

"Actually, no, I don't. No one seems to be talking to me lately. Not that it's any different from how things usually are. Just quieter, now that mom's gone."

The bacon roiled and rolled in his gut as he wiped his fingers on the edge of the plate. "Jason cheated on Ginny."

Bethany finally turned and sat on the countertop. She plopped the rag down on the counter next to her. "Oh my God," she said. "That's horrible. That's—"

"He cheated on her with Maggie."

Robert's words had the intended effect he'd expected. Bethany's jaw slacked and her eyes got big. "Maggie? Your Maggie?"

"My Maggie," Robert said quietly.

"No," Bethany said. "What are you—what are you going to do?"

Robert took one last piece of bacon and forced it down into his stomach. It seemed to jump and skip and claw at his insides. He stood up. "I'm going to go help him with that stump."

*   *   *

Robert and Jason worked at the stump for most of the afternoon. They didn't say a single word to each other. They barely looked in each other's direction, except when coordinating efforts necessitated such interaction.

*   *   *

When Jason was twelve years old, he and Frank Jordan had a friend named Henry Heinen. Henry was the kind of kid who always seemed to be attached in some way to some sort of adventure. Jason and Frank adored him, followed him wherever he went and more or less did what he said. They'd meet at Gibson's Feed on Saturday mornings and spend the entire day off in the woods, exploring or otherwise making up an adventure to keep themselves occupied until it was time to get on their bikes and ride the long dirt roads back to their houses.

By the time the summer ended that year, Jason and Frank were the only two kids privy to the knowledge that Henry had a disease called amyotrophic lateral sclerosis. Frank had written it down several times so he wouldn't forget it, but they all called it Lou Gehrig's disease—Henry did so proudly, as he was the only Yankees fan in all of Northern Maine, it seemed. Einar would drive Jason to Henry's house in the afternoons, after he'd ridden his bike home from school and finished all his homework, and Frank would already be at Henry's house since he lived closer than Jason did. Henry wasn't in school that year; by the time October rolled around, the most Henry could do was sit up in bed and watch as Jason and Frank bounced around the room, making him laugh and telling him dirty jokes. It was a good time for all three of them, because those afternoons felt like the most effortless times they'd ever spent together. Henry couldn't lead them on adventures anymore, but Jason and Frank could tell him all about their own adventures from school that day. Henry had gotten much quieter, but Jason and Frank talked incessantly, which put a smile on Henry's face.

One Saturday night in November, Jason and Frank passed up their first opportunity to go to a dance—both of them even had dates lined up for the event, or as close to dates at twelve year-olds could get—to go to Henry's house for the night. They sat on Henry's couch watching movies until midnight, then talked and told dirty jokes—Frank had a great one about a priest who goes into a bar with a donkey and a prostitute—until it looked like Henry might pass out from exhaustion. He was a lot paler now, and had lost all mobility in both legs, but he smiled a lot more now, which always made him look energized. Jason helped Henry climb onto the couch, and he lay down while Jason and Frank sat Indian-style on the floor next to him.

Then, seemingly out of nowhere, Henry quietly said, "I'm never going to kiss a girl."

Jason and Frank were so startled by the statement that they didn't even bother to make fun of him—and this was a prime statement for some Grade A ribbing. But they stayed quiet and saw that this was real, that Henry actually had tears in his eyes.

"Sure you will," Frank said. "We all will."

"I'm going to be dead, Frank. Dead. And if I'm not dead, I'll be deformed. A monster. I won't kiss a girl, won't have sex, won't get married."

The silence that followed Henry's words was frightening for all three of them. Henry hadn't said it with any sort of sorrow; it was more like defiance, like anger. Jason thought about it and was suddenly hit with the force of it: yes, Jason would kiss a girl. Would probably be kissing one tonight at the dance, had he gone. Frank would, too. But Henry wouldn't. Would never get the chance. Would never even find himself in the situation to make his move, never have the nervous energy and the sweating palms, never smell a girl up close and feel the softness of her lips, never open his eyes just a crack to see what it was like to look at a girl as she kissed you, never...

Never.

That was the first time Jason had felt any sense of finality in his life.

Three months later, much to the surprise of the doctors, but of no surprise to Jason Coates or Frank Jordan, Henry Heinen was dead.

Robert had just gotten his driver's license, so he drove Jason and Frank to the wake on a Tuesday night. Jason remembered it being a Tuesday because Mr. Simmons had given them both an excuse from doing their homework that night, and Wednesday was supposed to be the big World History quiz. But Jason and Frank wouldn't be there. They'd be at a funeral, watching Henry Heinen go on one last adventure without them.

Robert waited in the car while Jason and Frank went inside the funeral home in Fort Kent. Frank wore a suit with a jacket that was far too large for him, but Jason seemed to fit just right in his suit. As Robert watched him walk into the funeral home, Frank one half-step behind him, Robert couldn't help but think how grown-up his little brother looked. Almost admired him, really. He seemed stoic, calm, as if this were just some perfunctory duty he had to perform, like splitting the wood or raking the yard. He looked like their Pop. He looked like Einar William Coates.

But when they went inside that funeral home, the roles reversed. Jason started crying immediately, and Frank lead him through the front hall and into the room full of chairs that pointed in the direction of the first casket either one of the two boys had ever seen. Jason made no noise as he cried. He simply let the tears fall down his face and hit the floor. He made no attempt to wipe them away, and as a consequence, he could not see through the blur of saline water, so Frank had to take his arm and guide him. They stood in front of the casket together. Jason cried. Frank did not.

For years after that, Jason's only memory of death was the blurred vision of Henry Heinen. He wiped the tears away only once to look at Henry, and then let them take his vision over again. It didn't look like Henry. For some reason, that comforted Jason, made it feel like it wasn't really Henry at all. Was just some stuffed, leathery and fake husk of a human, and Henry had just gone on a trip somewhere. The tears dissipated after that. Unsure of what to do next, Jason and Frank sat in the chairs farthest from the casket and watched as a few folks filed in, viewed the casket, made the sign of the cross, then spoke quietly to Henry's mother and father, both of whom cried several times in the few minutes Jason and Frank sat there.

Watching it all happen, Jason felt suddenly compelled to laugh. It all seemed so silly, really. It wasn't even Henry in the casket.

Frank left Jason's side only once, and that was to say goodbye to Henry's mother. When he came back, Jason was already standing. When they got into the hallway, he stopped, turned to Frank and said, "Hey, don't tell Robert I cried, okay?"

"Okay, Jason," Frank said. "I won't."

They went back out to the car and Robert drove them home.

The funeral was early the next morning, and Robert drove them to that, as well. Einar had given Robert the keys to the pickup truck and told him to dress up nice, too, even though Robert said he didn't want to leave the truck if he didn't have to. But he didn't complain beyond that, and he wore a grey suit with a black tie and a white shirt he borrowed from Einar. When they got to the cemetery, Jason and Frank hopped out of the truck. Robert stayed in the driver's seat and smoked a cigarette, watching the whole ordeal from a safe distance.

Jason cried again.

Frank did not.

When they returned to the truck, Jason's eyes were bloodshot from tears, and so he expected Robert to rib him. But he didn't. They spent the drive in silence.

That night, Jason went to bed with no sleep in his eyes or his heart. He felt no drowsiness, no need for any sort of rest, but also felt no compulsion to get up and do anything. It was an odd feeling—a feeling he would later know to be depression—that made him confused and angry, but tired and helpless at the same time. He'd heard one of his friends say once that he'd been too tired to sleep, and Jason had thought that to be completely stupid. Jason had done all sorts of tiring work, and when he was too tired, he passed out. But now he got it. Now he understood. Now he was too tired to sleep. He was too tired to exist.

It was almost two in the morning when Robert opened the door to Jason's room. "Hey, little brother," Robert said.

"Hi."

Robert closed the door behind him and took two steps into Jason's dark room. Each one of the Coates children had a rocking chair in the corner of their bedroom, just like the one in their parents' room. Each rocking chair had their name on it. Each rocking chair squeaked in a different way. Robert found his way to the rocking chair that had the words JASON ALLEN COATES painted on it, and sat down with the light from the moon painting his face through the window. He said nothing. He just folded his arms and sat down. The squeak,

squeak, squeak of the chair was slight and high-pitched. Back and forth, squeak and squeak. It wasn't the sort of noise that grated on you. Instead, it floated and coasted with a sort of drowsy musical tone that blessed each ear it landed upon with a sweetness and a calm. Robert rocked back and forth for hours, and Jason fell asleep to the sound of it.

*   *   *

The basement was almost full with split wood by the time Askar called it quits for the day. He was pretty useful and strong to boot, so he cut through the pile out back in no time. He and Einar spent a good two hours stacking in the basement after it was all cut, and by the time dinner time rolled around, the basement was packed tight with almost a cord and a half of wood. Askar didn't say much throughout the day, but he also didn't pull out that goddamned cell phone, either. Quiet was alright by Einar, so long as the work was getting done.

He and Bethany were planning on going back down south after dinner. Askar showered and Einar washed himself up, too, but by the time Einar had come back downstairs to sit for dinner, Askar was still up in the bedroom.

"What's he doing up there?" Einar said to Bethany.

"He's probably on his phone," she said as she brought a tray of sliced chicken breast to the table. "He's been up here almost three days and didn't touch the thing all day today. I'm surprised he did as well as he did."

Bethany said this with no humor in her voice, and Einar sensed his daughter's frustration. Felt it, alright, and would do something about it. But now was not the time. Einar sat at the table and waited for his sons and daughter to sit down, and they began to eat. Ten minutes later, Askar sat down at the table. All the Coateses were quiet.

Einar cut a piece of broccoli, chewed it slowly, swallowed, then said, "Askar, let me see that phone of yours. Thinkin' of gettin' one myself."

As Bethany dropped chicken onto his plate, Askar's face revealed his suspicion, but he pulled the phone out nonetheless and handed it to Einar. Einar didn't know this phone from the next one down the line, but it sure did look fancy. Buttons everywhere, and even a little lens for a camera. Askar quietly explained some of the features as Einar turned it over in his hands, flipped it open, flipped it closed. "Only thing is, sometimes it doesn't ring when it's supposed to," Askar said.

Einar looked from the phone to Askar, then back to the phone. "That so?" He said as he pushed his chair back and stood up. "Daddy, no," Bethany said, but it was too late. Einar threw the phone full-force at the wall. Both Jason and Robert let out a small laugh, but quickly quelled themselves. The phone shattered into at least three pieces which settled in different parts of the room.

"I reckon it won't ring at all now." Einar pulled his chair in and sat down again. "Problem solved."

Askar looked stricken. Bethany put her hands on his shoulder briefly, but Askar brushed them away. He stood up and left the room.

"Daddy, that was horrible. Why did you do that?" Bethany said, still standing behind Askar's chair.

"If he'd spent half as much time on you as he does on that damn phone, maybe you'd be a little happier with that marriage of yours." He spit the words out sharply, as though they tasted horrible even to him, and when Bethany heard them, Einar knew they'd been acidic. He looked down at his plate and stabbed at a piece of chicken. "Don't bring him up here again if he's got a phone attached to his ear. I'll break it again, or worse."

With that, Bethany left the room. The three Coates men sat at the dinner table in the middle of the big dining room meant for more people and felt ridiculous for being in there. But they ate their meals in silence the way Coates men did. And when they were through with dinner, they left the room as silently as they'd come and went about their business.

Bethany and Askar left an hour later. They did not say good bye to Einar.

*   *   *

"I'm leaving tomorrow," Jason said to Einar after dinner as they both sat in the living room by the wood stove.

Einar nodded.

"Might be back next week."

"Fine," Einar said.

Jason stood up and went to the wood stove. Einar watched him stand there, bruises purple on his face. "Them bruises going to cause you problems at your job?"

"No, I don't think so. There will be questions, but that's all."

"Ya goin' ta have a talk with yer brother?"

Jason turned and faced Einar. "I don't really think that's my decision. Besides, I think a little bit of time will do us both some good."

Einar nodded again. He stood up and put his hands on his hips—a signature stance for Einar William Coates—and said, "time's a cheat, boy." Then he left the room.

Jason stood by the stove for several more minutes, feeling the warmth of the pot-belly drive into him and wrap around like a thick blanket. It was a feeling he associated with his mother, though for no particular reason, really. It just felt right to think about her while feeling the heat of the stove in the house of his youth, so he did. And for the first time since coming up to the farm to stay with his father, Jason felt just a small sliver of contentment, of peace. Tomorrow that would surely change. Tomorrow his mistakes would find him again, fresh off their vacation, and stick to him with a persistence Jason wasn't sure he could tolerate. But he'd try.

*   *   *

The next morning, Jason lugged his huge duffel bag down the stairs and slung it into the trunk of his car. Robert was doing the same in his own car. They slammed their trunks closed almost in unison and looked at each other. It would have created a laugh between them at any other time, in any other place, but here, in the dirt driveway of Einar William Coates's home in Northern Maine—a little east and north of Fort Kent, if you must know—they didn't laugh. They didn't smile. They didn't speak. They were strangers for the first time in their lives.

"I'll be up next weekend," Jason said. Robert nodded. He was standing with his hands on his hips and his resemblance to Einar was too obvious to miss. "If you...want to talk about this, we can," Jason said. "For what it's worth, I'm—"

"Don't," Robert interrupted.

"Yeah," Jason said, then climbed into the driver's seat and pulled out of the driveway. Robert watched him go, then climbed into his own car. Through the windshield, Robert looked at his father standing on the porch. Einar nodded. Robert wasn't sure what it was supposed to mean. He put the shifter into reverse and pulled out of the driveway.

*   *   *

Jason had no intention of stopping, but when he saw the sign for Gibson's Feed, it only felt natural to pull up to the front and stop in—just to see what was happening, even though he knew damn well the answer was nothing.

Eleanor Rigby Phillips was sitting on a stool behind the cash register, reading a magazine with her lips visibly moving with each word her eyes scanned over. She finished the sentence her eyes followed, then looked up and saw Jason striding up the aisle toward her. She immediately put the magazine down.

"Coates," she said.

"Elly."

"More supplies?"

"Nope." Jason stepped up to the counter and leaned on it, toward her Eleanor. "I want to know about Frank."

"Frank Jordan?"

"Yeah."

"What do you want to know?"

"What happened between him and Natalie?" Jason asked.

Eleanor shrugged. "Split up, I guess. She wanted to stay in California, he wanted to come back here. Simple enough."

"He *wanted* to come back here? Why?"

"They were broke," Eleanor said. "Why else do people come back to this shithole?"

Divorces and deaths, Jason thought. *That's about it.* "So that's it? She wanted to stay and he wanted to go?"

"Can't say, really," Eleanor said. "So far as I know, that's what happened. Frank's been pretty broken up about it. Not doing well at all. He loved that girl." Eleanor sighed as she contemplated that sentiment, as if the entire concept seemed foreign to her.

Jason stood up straight. "How'd you hear about it?"

"How else? This town's small. You linger in this place long enough and you know John Morris's underwear size down the way. Not much to talk about. You know that well enough."

Eleanor watched Jason process this information for a moment. "You headed back south, are ya?"

"Yes," Jason said.

"What are you going to do?"

"What do you mean?"

"What do I mean...I mean Ginny, ya dope. What are you going to do about your wife?"

"How do you know about that?" Jason asked.

"Thirty-six."

"What?"

"John Morris's underwear size."

Jason grunted.

"So, what are you going to do?"

"Ain't none of your damn business," Jason barked.

Eleanor was unfazed. "Wow. You been up here a while," she said. "Losin' that fancy city talk and barkin' like us hicks again."

"Thanks for the info," Jason said as he turned and made his way back toward the door.

"No problem," Eleanor said to Jason's back. She picked up her magazine and started reading again.

"Hey Elly," Jason said, standing by the door with his hand on the knob.

"Coates."

"What would you do?"

Eleanor Rigby Phillips laughed long and hard. "I'd start by keepin' my fly zipped when it counts. Then I'd give her another few days... and beg."

"Beg."

"Yes, Coates. Beg."

Jason stood in the doorway a moment longer, shot Eleanor a smile, then left the store.

When she was sure he'd gone for good, Eleanor threw her magazine down on the counter and sighed. "Ya damn fool, Coates. Beg. It won't do you no good, but beg."

*   *   *

The house hummed with quiet. Einar stood in the center of the kitchen, his hands folded behind his back, and listened to his home speak to him in tones of creaks and dead air. He was the only living thing in the house aside from the mice and spiders and other crawling things inside the walls and in the basement, and it was strange to think it, but it seemed to physically hurt Einar. His legs and back ached; his head throbbed; his eyes felt dry and his mouth chalky. It was an odd sensation to be alone again, and he thought if Jason and Robert and Bethany hadn't been coming up intermittently since Sarah died, he might have gotten used to it by now. But probably not.

With no one to talk to and nothing to do, Einar decided to go to bed early. He made his way through the living room and began to climb the stairs when he stopped and turned around. It was turning into a habit for him, this need to go onto the front porch before going to bed for the night and make sure that goddamned thief wasn't sleeping in the barn again. Einar went to the closet in the hall, pulled on his coat and toted the shotgun out onto the front porch. He stood on the side of the porch farthest east, the side that faced the barn, and squinted into the darkness.

Silence to greet him.

Silence to court him.

Silence to marry him, live with him, die and leave him alone again.

He stared out at the barn for ten minutes, then went back inside and went to sleep. About twenty minutes after that, a man crept slowly through the darkness toward the barn and slept for six hours. Then, in the still-dark morning hours, he crept away having stolen nothing but a few hours' comfort and rest.

*   *   *

The township in Northern Maine that had no real name but more than a few dirt county roads and farms had very little to boast besides the perfunctory residences of farmers who grew spuds and dirt and nothing else. But an oasis for residents nearby and no others *from away* existed in the form of Fernald Lake. So much of the coastline and the lakes inland had been taken over (by force, if you ask the locals) by tourists and rich folks from Massachusetts—known as Mass-holes this far north—and so it came to pass that Fernald Lake became closely guarded throughout the years by residents who lived near its banks. It remained pristine—no cottages, no motor boats, no silly tourists in mini-vans full of noisy kids and hibachi grills to spoil the banks of Fernald. Only two homes bordered the Lake, and it was only incidentally that they were allowed to do so: the Lown residence, on the northern bank of the lake, had been there for longer than anyone could remember and was falling to pieces since the youngest Lown boys moved away in '74. No one had lived there since.

The other residence was that of Einar and Sarah Coates. Or, most recently, Einar William Coates alone. Three miles south as the crow flies from Lown's place, Coates' house, too, had been situated along the banks of Fernald Lake for almost a hundred years, and Coates, in fact, owned most of the property along the southern bank of the Lake. Ten years prior, Coates had allowed the county to build a hiking trail through his property on the condition that no trailhead be built and no advertisement created to publicize it. Therefore, the trail was known only to locals who had been walking the banks for years anyway. Einar William Coates was okay with that.

It was a Thursday morning when Eleanor Rigby Phillips went walking with her dog, a big and old Chocolate Lab named Spurs, down the trail toward the waterfront. It was early and cold—maybe six in the morning, and no more than thirty degrees—and by the time she reached the water, her nose had gone numb. This was not an entirely unpleasant sensation for Eleanor; she quite enjoyed it, in fact. Autumn was her favorite season, and even though it lead into her least favorite season, she took every opportunity to immerse herself in the chill of the mornings and the nip of freeze at her nose. She let Spurs off his leash when she saw water and continued walking west along the banks. She'd been walking for almost ten minutes when she spotted Frank Jordan sitting on a felled log up ahead.

He noticed her immediately. The sound of her boots crunching on the fallen leaves made him stand and turn quickly. When he realized who was walking toward him, Frank rubbed his eyes with his gloved hands and yelled a bit too loudly, "Hi, Elly."

"Hi Frank. What are you doing out here so early?"

"Oh, uh, just, you know, enjoying the water." He swept his right hand out in a grand gesture of presentation that almost made Eleanor laugh. "How about you?"

"Just out walking Spurs."

"Oh. Right."

Eleanor was standing next to Frank now, which seemed to make him slightly uncomfortable. She sat on the log he'd been sitting on only moments earlier. Frank did not follow suit.

"Sit," she said, patting the section of the log next to her.

"Oh, that's okay. I'll stand."

"Suit yourself," she said. "How are things, Frank?"

"Good," he said with a fake smile. "Real good. Been helping my Pop with a lot of projects, and I've even been over at the Coates's place a lot, helping them out with some things."

"I hear they're getting it ready for Robert's wedding in the spring," Eleanor said. Spurs sprinted up to her—he was quick for an old man—and dropped a drool-covered stick at her feet. Eleanor picked it up and threw it down the path.

"Oh, right, Robert's wedding," Frank said. "I don't, uh, don't think that's happening anymore."

Eleanor didn't inquire further; she simply made a mental note the way so many folks up that way did. Peoples' business was peoples' business, and Eleanor wasn't one to spread or perpetuate rumors. If they happened to come her way occasionally, she'd hear them out, but she wouldn't perpetuate them.

"—and finishing up the barn."

"I'm sorry, what?" Eleanor said.

"I said I was up at the Coates's place a bunch this past week fixing the tractor and finishing up the barn. It's been nice being back here. Natalie likes it, too. She says—"

"Frank," Eleanor interrupted.

He didn't seem to understand at first, but as Eleanor's eyes met his, he remembered she already knew. "Oh, right."

"You don't have to pretend, Frank. Natalie's gone back to California, and most folks know. It's nothing to be ashamed of. I mean, I don't know anything about you two beyond what you've said or what I've heard, but you don't have to be ashamed with me, at least."

"I'm not ashamed," he said. "I'm just…"

"Just what?"

"Never mind."

Eleanor laughed. "Wow. For a second there, I thought I was going to convince a *man* from up here in *Maine* to talk about how he feels. But men don't have feelings, do they, bucko?"

"I'm just…"

"Go on, Frank."

"Shit, Elly, I'm so sad."

Frank sat down next to her on the log. Eleanor hesitated, but eventually threw her arm around him. They sat this way for several minutes, and though she didn't look at him, Eleanor knew he was trying to compose himself, keep from letting tears loose. She waited for him to speak…and eventually, he did.

"She left because of me," he said. "Not because of California or Maine, or anything like that. It was because of me. Maybe I'm boring, or not enough for her. I just don't know. And she won't answer my calls. I can't even talk to her."

Eleanor rested her head on Frank's shoulder.

"I just miss her, Elly. And I don't know what to do."

For a moment, Eleanor thought she might know what to say. She usually did. Whether it all made sense or not, that was irrelevant. She usually had something to say that would at least make whoever was listening think for a moment, but now she had nothing. Why? She couldn't say. Frank was no different than any other man from Northern Maine she'd ever met. He was stoic when it counted, even though Frank tended to be chattier than most, but he always remained closed off when it came to anything beyond the realm of crops, tractors, hockey, or cutting wood. Now this. Now, with little provocation (though it *was* provoked; Eleanor had to keep that in mind) he was broken down, opened up wide. She didn't know what to say to that. When she was married, Eleanor couldn't do that to her own husband. But Frank seemed ready and willing—though reluctant—to fall apart. It scared Eleanor, to tell the truth.

"I don't know either, Frank."

They sat in silence for almost a half hour before Frank stood up suddenly. "I was supposed to go up to the Coates's place. Damn, I forgot!" He took two steps toward the trail, then stopped. "You want to come with me? I just have to check in on Willie. Jason asked me to do it while he was gone. Just to see, ya know?"

"Sure," Eleanor said. "I'll come along." She whistled and Spurs came bounding up to her. With the big old Chocolate Lab leading the way, Frank and Elly hiked up the trail back toward the dirt road above.

*   *   *

As a young man, Einar watched his father lose his arm in an accident at the paper mill in Millinocket. The Coates lived there for only three years, and it was a miserable time for Einar and his parents. Both Einar and his father worked in the paper mill, but since they worked in different areas of the plant, it was only by a fluke that Einar witnessed his father's accident. He'd been called to the loading dock on the east side of the mill to help load the train that had just pulled in an hour earlier, since the crew on that side of the mill had been short-staffed after the flu broke out earlier that month. When Einar received the order to go to the loading dock, he was on the west side of the mill, in the packaging room. As he made his way through the mill, he passed his father's work station and had no intention of stopping—until he heard the emergency alarm and screaming voices. His father's voice. Clear as day.

His father lost his right arm that day, and from that moment on, Einar was sure he believed in God if only because of his newfound fear of fate. Only two months after his father's accident, Einar was sent to war. It was during that time he learned that he believed in God, and was also deathly afraid of Him. Years later, when his oldest son, Robert, was in a car accident that could have and should have claimed his life, Einar was sure of one more thing: God was looking out for him. This made him more terrified of the big man upstairs, and he knew exactly why.

Sarah had once told him she knew she'd marry Einar because of something her father had told her when she was just a little girl. "Sometimes you need to let go of the things you love for the things you need," he had told her and her younger sister, Constance, over and over again as they'd grown up. It had become a staple expression in her mind, but at the same time she tried so many times to reconcile herself with a life that didn't exist with that constraint, that necessity of giving up what one loved for what one needed to exist. When she met Einar, she had found what she needed—and what she loved. He had been her saving grace, and she wasn't afraid to tell him so. It became difficult after the war for Einar to hear Sarah say such things about him, but after time, even he began to believe it, mostly because he felt the same about Sarah.

And so, Einar feared God.

Einar William Coates knew the debt he owed. He knew it was no coincidence he led the life he did, nor was it a coincidence that he found himself blessed with a wonderful family, wife, and sense of place. For a suspicious man like Einar, it was too good of a situation to have no strings attached to it. Now that Sarah was gone and his family seemed to be faltering under the weight of a thousand crosses, Einar saw his debt soon to be collected. He was standing on the front porch again, looking out at the barn and the lake beyond, wondering if he was up to the task of taking what was being presented to him and changing it all for the better—a real philosophical bender for a man who restricted emotional thought severely and allowed himself to talk even less—when he heard tires crunching on the gravel of the driveway behind him.

He turned to see who was coming up the driveway but saw no one at first. It was almost a quarter of a mile from the county road to the house, on a twisting and rutted driveway that weaved and bobbed until it finally steadily descended toward the even clearing in front of the house; Einar had no problem allowing the driveway to be run over with weeds, rocks and the occasional puddle of mud, and if you were listening close enough, you would hear the tires of any car crunching on that gravel down by the road well before seeing the vehicle pull into view. So he waited.

He was unsurprised to see Frank Jordan's pickup truck bounce around the final corner and into the even clearing before the house. His companion was somewhat of a surprise, but not an unpleasant one. Eleanor was a fine girl in Einar's book. Smart as a whip and sometimes a bit of a smartass, but fine nonetheless. She'd been working at Gibson's Feed for a while now, but Einar remembered she'd been married only a few years ago and moved away—he couldn't recall where, exactly, but he knew it was south. Maybe Boston. She'd come back minus a husband and a smile, but at least one of those elements seemed to be seeping slowly back into her personality. Einar stood on the porch with his hands on his hips and waited for Frank to turn off the truck. Both he and Eleanor got out at the same time.

"Mornin', Mister Coates," Frank said, a little louder than was necessary.

"Frank," Einar said, nodding. "How've ya been, Eleanor?"

Eleanor seemed momentarily surprised that Einar had spoken to her, but a bright and beautiful smile quickly swept across her face. "Finer than a Sunday morning," she said as she followed Frank up the steps to the porch. "And you?"

"Just fine, just fine. What can I do for ya two young folks today?"

"Just stopping by to see if you needed anything," Frank said.

Einar grunted. "Jason tell you to stop by?"

Frank nodded nervously. Eleanor smiled again, this time looking at Frank as she did so.

"Well, since you're here, maybe you could help me lug some wood up from the basement. Got the woodstove in the kitchen and the fireplace in the livin' room."

"Sure thing, Mister Coates," Frank said as though he had spoken through the eager voice of a sixteen-year-old boy. And really, Eleanor thought, that's what Frank Jordan really was: a teenager who had simply grown up without realizing he'd done so. It wasn't so much that Frank was immature; that wasn't it at all. But he was…innocent, Eleanor thought, for lack of a better word. It seemed as though Frank belonged nowhere but exactly where he was, in the woods and fields of Northern Maine, his good heart loving too much at all the wrong times. As Frank followed Einar inside and Eleanor tracked them both, she couldn't keep herself from feeling a slight pang of anger toward Natalie for hurting Frank, and a slight amount of embarrassment just the same. Poor Frank…he just had no idea.

When Einar and Frank disappeared into the basement, Eleanor was left standing alone in the living room. It was a sparse space, dark but welcoming with its wood tones, fireplace and framed photos scattered across tables, shelves and the mantle. Eleanor went from one to another, peering quickly at each one: Robert as a high school senior. Jason, presumably graduating college. Bethany with long, beautiful hair and a flowing white gown on her wedding day. Einar and Sarah standing side by side on their own wedding day, Einar in his army uniform and Sarah in a lovely white dress that bathed the floor beneath her with its fantastically long train. And then, on a shelf behind glass in the corner of the room, a three-sectioned frame that drew Eleanor's attention.

The first section, on the far left of the frame, showed Jason playing hockey in high school. He was skating fast, it seemed, wearing the green and gold jersey of Fort Kent High School. The second frame showed him raising his gloved hands and his stick in victory after scoring a goal. And the third depicted Jason standing between the stands and the locker room, smiling proudly. It wasn't this beaming smile or this boy in his hockey uniform that so captivated Eleanor; instead, it was a young brunette girl sitting in the stands behind Jason, only half-looking in his direction as whoever held the camera snapped his picture. The young girl had a soft face that wore a slight, demure smile. Her hands were folded in her lap, her forest-green coat wrapped around her as though protecting her from the bitterest cold ever to blow through that ice rink. She sat alone in those stands, though she hadn't been alone the entire game. She had sat with her friends until the final seconds of the game on the other side of the stands, but when the time ran out, she quickly but casually shifted her position toward the path between the stands that led to the locker rooms so that she might catch the eye of Jason Coates, whom she'd had a crush on since freshman year. That young girl in that picture. That soft face. It used to be Eleanor Rigby Phillips.

It came as a surprise to Eleanor that she remembered that day so vividly, could picture herself there, could still feel the cold coming off the ice and the hard, metal stands beneath her. Could still feel her crush on Jason. Looking into that photo felt like looking into a yesterday you weren't supposed to see anymore, opening up that section of the brain marked, "ready for disposal" and poking around just enough to make yourself wonder if this really was a memory in need of being thrown away. Eleanor thought not. She stared at the photo a moment longer, then turned away just as Frank and Einar were climbing the stairs, each carrying armfuls of wood. Einar turned toward the kitchen; Frank came to the living room and stacked the wood in a neat pile to the right of the fireplace.

"Did you play hockey in high school, Frank?"

"Sure did," he said as he straightened himself up and brushed off the dirt from his arms. "I was the Varsity goalie for two years," he said, a proud smile painted vividly on his face. "Good year senior year… we went to the state championship game. Jason scored twice, and I played pretty decent, but we lost four to two."

Eleanor nodded. She had no recollection whatsoever of Frank being on the team that year. She'd gone to plenty of the games—presumably to show school spirit, but really to watch Jason Coates—and knew several of the boys on the team, but for whatever reason, she just couldn't remember Frank Jordan playing on that team. It disheartened her for a moment, but she let it pass. She smiled at Frank and he began walking back toward the door to the basement.

"I remember you always watching the games," he said as he descended the first step. Then he laughed. "You were always tripping up Mikey Valance. He had such a crush on you and he knew you were in the stands." Frank's voice faded as he descended the stairs, but he just continued talking. Eleanor stood in the living room, listening to his fading story. "He used to fall all over himself," Frank continued. "I remember once he crashed right into me in the net because he was looking up at you instead of at the puck." Frank let out a laugh and continued talking, but Eleanor couldn't make out what he was saying.

She'd been Elly back then. Elly Phillips. Until senior year, when Mikey Valance started calling her by her full name—Eleanor Rigby Phillips—and everyone latched on to the idea that she was going to end up just like the character in the song. If Mikey Valance had a crush on her, he had a hell of a way of showing it. She'd been miserable that senior year: Jason Coates was dating Rochelle Parks and ignoring Eleanor at every corner; she was beginning to believe her destiny was written in a Beatles song, and every member of the senior class took every opportunity to remind her of that; then there was the "Big Accident" of senior year, which folks still talked about, when Helen Michaud and Keller Johnson hit a patch of ice on the way to school in Keller's old Plymouth and drove clear off the CR12 bridge. They both died that morning. Helen had been Eleanor's best friend, the only person in school who didn't hound her incessantly about her name. And then she was dead.

Senior year had been awful for sure, but then, just before prom, Jason Coates broke up with Rochelle Park and asked Elly to the prom. She was beside herself. It was perfect, and it turned out being a magnificent night—even though Coates never made a move on her, and Lord knew she wouldn't have minded a bit if he had. That memory brought a wide grin to her face as she stood in Einar's living room, but it quickly dissipated.

Why couldn't she remember Frank Jordan playing hockey?

The more she thought about it, the more she realized she only had a vague handful of memories of Frank from high school in general. It wasn't as though he and Eleanor had been great friends back then—they barely spoke, really, but they had always been cordial—and really, it was nothing to get upset over, but for some reason, Eleanor's heart continued to sink as she searched her memory for any vision of Frank wearing the Fort Kent hockey jersey and his goalie equipment.

She just couldn't seem to do it.

Frank appeared suddenly in the living room, another armful of wood ready for the stack by the fireplace. He was still talking, though Eleanor hadn't been listening at all, and Einar, too, had gone down the stairs and come back up with an armful of wood without Eleanor noticing. She'd been that lost in thought. How odd, she thought to herself, that she should allow herself to disappear into her own mind so suddenly and over something so strange, so seemingly trivial. She shook herself out of it and listened to the tail-end of Frank's story before Einar interrupted him.

"You two want some coffee while you're here?" Einar said from the doorway to the kitchen.

"Tea for me, if you have it," Eleanor said.

"Coffee sounds great, Willie," Frank said.

Einar smiled and disappeared into the kitchen. Eleanor couldn't remember ever seeing Willie Coates smile before this day. Frank and Eleanor followed Einar into the kitchen and sipped their warm drinks before returning to Frank's truck and pulling out of the long driveway. Einar watched them go from the porch, and long after they'd left, Einar stood there, looking out at the driveway and the trees that had now lost most of their leaves, and still saw nothing worth noting.

* * *

Midnight.

Einar slept intermittently. Then woke. Walked downstairs. Heard a noise. Knew it was the thief. Grabbed his gun. Fired off the porch. Saw the damn fool run down toward the lake. Einar fired again, shouting after the thief. No one would hear the shots. No one was close enough to the Coates house to hear them. Einar had no idea if he'd hit the thief. He figured not. He stood on the porch for almost twenty minutes before going inside. He was in bed and asleep again when the thief returned, slept the full night in the barn and left just after sun-up.

*   *   *

Mainers recognize the seasons with all their senses. Aside from the obvious bite of the autumn and winter chills, those tougher New England souls taste their seasons; smell them; hear them; touch them and see them. As Einar sat in the living room of his home in Northern Maine, not far from Fort Kent, he knew it was cold, knew winter was on its way and the first snowfall wouldn't be far off—before Thanksgiving, for sure. He knew this by listening. His silent house gave way to other noises: the crackle of the burning logs in the fireplace, the groans and pops of the house settling into its joints, arthritically cracking from the blasting of heat from within and cold from without. The windows knocking from the gusts of wind outside, interspersed with the crunch and scatter of the dead leaves across the ground and each other outside. These were the signs that the snow was coming, but without them, Einar would still simply know. That's just how Einar was.

With Thanksgiving only a week away, Einar had been preparing for a trip south to Robert's house in Portland, but considering recent events, Einar knew well that Thanksgiving would not be taking place there this year. Might not take place at all—sure, that was a possibility, but not a strong one. No, Einar expected a phone call, most likely from Bethany, within the next day or two, announcing grand plans to have Thanksgiving at Einar's home 'up north.'

Bethany called around three in the afternoon that day. For the first time in as many weeks, the home of Einar William and Sarah Coates would be filled with the voices of their children.

And it was those voices intermingling that had Einar just a tad nervous.

What was happening between Jason and Robert would be a volatile and ever-present kink in the gathering of the Coates this Thanksgiving, but Einar took solace in the fact that eventually, the two Coates boys would talk. Or fight. So many times growing up, problems between them had been resolved with both words and fists, and as long as they didn't get carried away with either, Einar was just fine with it. It had only come close to going too far once before, after Robert's accident, but that, too, had eventually fizzled and the Coates brothers lived their lives.

But Bethany.

Oh, Bethany.

She would not speak. Not without Sarah here. Einar knew very little about communicating with his daughter and even less about recognizing when the problem was serious. He had a sneaking suspicion now, however, and he intended to at least try to help. Though he felt not at all as though he'd helped matters much with anyone in his family in recent weeks…Einar just wasn't good at it. But Sarah was gone, and he wasn't, and so by default, he had a responsibility to try to fix up his family as if it were just a tractor engine or a barn to be repaired before the winter. And winter was coming, after all.

He wouldn't have called it an unwelcome distraction, his kids being at the house and in a bit of turmoil, because the truth was, he missed Sarah. Missed her more than he thought he'd be capable of. No one asked him how he was doing and that was just fine by him. He'd just as well deal with it himself over a glass of scotch and a conversation with the wind outside his windows.

But he felt entombed already.

The house. That must have been it. The house wasn't just a home anymore; it held stores and stores of memories and voices and little reminders of lives that no longer existed, that no longer tied together or crossed paths to make other paths. It was, at its basest form, a filing cabinet marked "closed cases." Einar remembered the day his mother passed away. He had just gotten back from the war and was staying with a friend in Millinocket. That morning, he drove up to Fort Kent where his parents were living then. It was a newer house, small, not far from downtown, and it had never felt like home to Einar. He had his own place in the world, and his parents had left long ago the place Einar considered his childhood home. They'd lived in Millinocket for a spell, and that, too, felt nothing like what Einar could call home. When he drove up to Fort Kent that day and walked into the house his father now inhabited alone, not only did the place not feel like home, but it had no signs of his mother anywhere. Sure, there were photos and the like, but where were the tell-tale signs? The stains on the countertop from her cooking? The dish rag hung over the back of the kitchen chair? Her bathrobe hanging from the back of the bathroom door? That place was not his mother's, and his mother did not belong to that place.

Sarah was everywhere in Einar's house. He was thankful, at least, for that.

The chip in the banister where Sarah had dropped her sewing basket.

The still-lingering smell of her cooking around the stove.

The faded spot on the floor just inside the back door where Sarah had left her boots in the winter and her gardening shoes in the summer.

These things and so many more.

The worn-out hollow on the other side of Einar's bed where the weight of his wife had rested for decades.

These small signs.

Robert's old bedroom, which Sarah had repainted by herself and converted into a half-office and half-indoor-garden.

The small reminders.

Were they gifts or curses?

Any other man may have thought the latter, but Einar had seen his father's house after the death of Einar's mother. He saw how his father walked around the place and with the one hand he had left, felt the walls and the banisters and the tables and the windows for any signs of his wife and found none. Einar knew this was no curse. It was a presence. Sarah may have left this world, but she never left her husband.

The phone rang. It was Bethany. Thanksgiving would be next Tuesday at the home of Einar William and Sarah Coates.

*   *   *

In Portland, Robert Coates had found a home in a pub. It was familiar territory for him, a flashback, really. He'd gone through this once before after his accident, not looking for answers in a glass of whiskey but knowing if there was one there, he'd find it. Back then, the alcohol thinned his blood, making him susceptible to an infection in the still-unhealed wounds he'd collected in the accident. He'd only been out of the hospital for three days when he hit the bottle hard, and in his mind, that had been three days too many. But now his drinking was simply a matter of boredom, an antsy need to do something with himself. He hadn't spoken to Maggie in almost a week, the last conversation being more of a one-sided shouting spectacle, and every time he thought of Jason he had a concurrent thought of guns and strangulation, but really, that was all just filler. He was bored. He was tired. And though he knew he was splitting apart at the seams, he couldn't quite tell where those splits were. Maybe he'd drink so much whiskey it would pour out of those cracks in him. At least then he'd know where they were. At least then, he could pretend as though he had intentions of mending them.

He hadn't noticed the name of the pub when he entered it. He didn't care. It was a loud, raucous sort of place when he entered, but as the hours ticked off, it became more and more subdued. It was a Wednesday, after all, and the happy-hour suits had ordered their wings and drank their pints and returned home to the suburbs to their wives and kids and dogs, and Robert, the one true altruist of the place since he was still there to keep the stools and the shine off the bar-top from the lights above company, stuck around to see what would happen. Not that he expected anything. He'd been there for almost four hours and hadn't breathed a single word to anyone beside the bartender, and those conversations never went beyond orders and money exchanges. For a drunk, Robert was surprisingly subdued. His eyes grew heavy and the reflection of the light off the top of the bar became a silent companion, the only character listening to the long and rambling discourse taking place in his mind. He'd forgotten his surroundings and was alternating in his head between reviewing the events that lead up to this moment, imagining killing his younger brother, and imagining reducing his former fiancé to tears, then worse, then forgiving her, then getting revenge on her, then simply recalling her face. It was an exercise in sweet torture.

In his mind, the perfect situation to play out would include Jason walking unsuspectingly into the bar. Robert would see him immediately, though Jason would walk up to the bar with no idea that his older brother was anywhere near him. Jason would order a drink. The bartender would put the glass down on the bar, and Robert would grab it before Jason could. He would throw it across the room. It would shatter against the wall. Jason would try to say something, but Robert would grab him and throw him. Jason would crash through a table and hit the floor. Robert would pick him up and punch him in the face over and over again until there was nothing but blood and pulp. He would stop, say something really horrible, something that Jason would hear and know he'd ruined everything—Robert wasn't sure what, but he knew it would be fantastic—and then he'd keep punching. Maybe throw in a knee to the gut. And then Jason would fall limp to the ground, Robert vindicated and his brother punished. All the while, Maggie would be standing by the door, watching this go down, watching because she'd been searching for Robert everywhere and someone had tipped her off that he'd be here, and she'd see him beating his brother, see how much he'd loved her, and she, too, would feel how horrible this all was. Feel what Robert felt.

That's how it would go.

And, as if by some cruel trick of time or irony, Jason did, in fact, walk into the bar. And Robert did, of course, notice him before Jason noticed Robert. But Jason had known his brother would be there. Had been in the bar twice, in fact, since Robert arrived four hours prior. Jason did walk up to the bar but did not order a drink. Instead, he asked the bartender to call a cab. Robert stood up and stumbled over toward Jason. His hobbled leg betrayed him and he briefly tumbled toward the bar, but he righted himself and continued on toward his brother. Jason was not watching his brother walk toward him. He was digging through his wallet, making sure he had enough cash for the cab when it arrived. When Robert threw his first punch, Jason still was not looking. It didn't matter; Robert was a good four feet away when he threw his punch and missed Jason by a longshot. He fell to the ground in a heap. Jason closed his wallet and put it in his back pocket, then looked down at his brother on the ground.

"Missed by a hair," he said, then bent down to help Robert to his feet. When it seemed Robert was standing solidly in front of him, Jason let him go and said, "Hi, brother."

"Hi," Robert said, then took another swing, missed and fell down.

"I take it you're still upset," Jason said, helping Robert to his feet again.

Robert grunted.

Jason nodded toward the bartender and then helped Robert put on his coat. They walked outside and waited on the sidewalk for the cab.

At first, the two brothers were silent. They looked in opposite directions, Robert alternating his glances between the streetlights that lined the streets and the sheen of the rainwater on the pavement by the curb. Jason looked up the street toward the center of town, the town green just barely visible to the far left. Jason had no real intention of talking to Robert tonight. A friend from work had told him he'd seen his brother at the pub and he wasn't in good shape, so Jason swung by to take a look. He took a late lunch around four. Robert was there, alright. Then he stopped in after work, around six. Robert was still there. Then at eight. It was nine-thirty now.

His only intention in coming to see Robert was to make sure he got home. So he drove over to the bar once more, ordered him a cab (they lived on opposite sides of town and Jason couldn't bear the thought of a silent drive across town with Robert drunk) and that would be it. He didn't think Robert would say much, either. But then he spoke.

"You ruined me twice," Robert said, still alternating his glances between the south side of the street and the slush by the curb.

Jason closed his eyes for a moment, then reopened them. "I know."

"You know," Robert said. "You know. You know. You know. So what if you know?" He toed a pile of the slush and almost fell off the curb. Jason reached for him, but Robert slapped his hand away. "Hey, why'd you do it, anyway?" Robert asked the question as if he'd just asked Jason where he'd left the mayonnaise or if he remembered to turn off the living room light.

"We'll talk when you're sober," Jason said.

"Don't be condescending to me, tough guy. We'll talk now." Robert teetered. Jason wondered when his next plunge toward the ground might come. "Tell me why you did it. Tell me why you fucked my fiancé. Tell me why I limp, Jason. Tell me why my body doesn't work anymore."

"Oh, for God's sake, Robert, that was years ago. Let's focus on one thing at a time, here."

"No," Robert shouted, "because they're the same thing. Yesterday and today. Tell me!" Robert rushed toward Jason and missed. He hit a streetlamp and leaned on it, then said quietly, "Tell me, Jason. Why did you take her from me?"

"I didn't take her," Jason said.

"Don't...lie."

"I'm not lying. She came to me."

"Stop lying!"

"I'm not lying, Robert. She came to me because she was scared of you."

"Oh, fuck off."

"She was scared of you. Terrified. You were drinking so much you had no idea you were hurting her."

Robert tried to stand up straight. "I never—*never*—hit her. Never hurt her that way. I wouldn't."

"Like I said, big brother, you were so drunk you had no idea."

"Oh, oh, okay, so—ohh! Well then! So Maggie and I had a spat. She comes to you and your solution was to bend her over?"

"Jesus Christ," Jason said, turning away from Robert. "I'm not going to talk about this while you're drunk."

"Tell me, Jason. Why did you do it?"

"She didn't want to marry you." Jason shouted this, and it silenced Robert. Made him deflate. "Maybe if you'd talked to her, you'd know that. What happened with Maggie was a mistake. It ruined my marriage and your relationship. I can't even begin to tell you how sorry I am for that. But I will not—" Jason stepped toward Robert and poked his forefinger into his chest, "—keep apologizing for what happened years ago. I won't apologize for your accident."

"*My* accident?" Robert said, laughing.

Jason threw his arms out to his side. "Yes, Robert, *your* accident. You were part of it, too. Now focus, because I want you to hear this loud and clear. I fucked up here. My marriage is over. I screwed over my big brother. I made a mistake. Maggie made a mistake. We fucked up big, and I'll have nothing now." Jason stepped toward Robert again and almost whispered. "But you can fix it with Maggie. So step up to the plate and fix it."

The cab pulled up just then, and both men watched it as its tires plunged into the slush and mess by the curb. It stopped with squealing brakes and a splash. "Get in," Jason said. "Maybe when you can stand up straight, we'll talk about the rest."

Jason opened the front door of the cab, handed the driver enough money to get Robert where he needed to go, then closed the door again. He opened the back door, glanced back at Robert, then walked on down the street. Robert watched him go. He watched so long the cabby beeped his horn. It startled Robert into action and he climbed into the back of the cab.

Maggie was sitting on Jason's front stoop when he got home.

He lived on a frontage road not far from downtown, and he lived on the second floor of a three-family place. Despite the appearance of the outside, the apartment itself was quite nice, and Jason loved it. He could walk or ride a bike to work if he wanted to, though he opted to drive most days, especially in the winter, and the view from his window was of the river and the blinking lights of the buildings on the other side. It was comfortable. Unfortunately, since Ginny left, the apartment had taken on the air of a bachelor pad, complete with a card table posing as a kitchen table and a ratty couch that had been left on a curb three blocks away.

And there was Maggie.

She did not stand when Jason approached the stoop. "Hi," he said stupidly.

"Hello, Jason."

"I found Robert. He was…pretty drunk."

"Not surprising."

A long silence followed, and though Jason was facing Maggie and looking at her, she was far away and seemingly concentrating on some far-off place across the river. Jason bounced his car keys in his hand and started to climb the stairs to the door. When his hand reached the doorknob, Maggie said, "Have you talked to Ginny?"

"No," Jason said immediately.

"Are you going to?"

Jason's head drooped. His hand was still on the doorknob. "What would I say?"

"I honestly don't know," Maggie said. She finally turned but did not stand. "Robert do that to you?"

At first, Jason had no idea what Maggie was talking about, then he remembered being worked over by his brother up at Einar's place. The swelling in his lip had just recently gone down, and his right eye still had a good shiner on it. "Yeah, he sure did."

"Sounds like him."

"I deserved it."

"He deserves the same."

Jason turned. Maggie was no longer facing him. "Let's not forget something here. We screwed him. Not the other way around, okay?"

Maggie stood up suddenly and laughed. "Are you kidding me, Jason? I mean, honestly. You know what he was like."

"Yes, I do. And I also know you never said a word to him. Instead, you went behind his back and…"

"And what, Jason? And what? I went behind his back and fucked his brother? Is that what you were going to say?"

"Look," Jason said. "You and Robert have a chance. You were going to get married, for chrissakes! That has to mean something to you."

Maggie laughed again. "Yeah, it means something. It means you're not paying attention."

"It's not my responsibility to pay attention to you. That was Robert's job."

"And he didn't do it," Maggie said.

"Why did you come here tonight?"

"Because I thought you'd understand. I thought I could talk to you. And I thought you could use someone to talk to, yourself."

"And that person was supposed to be you?"

"Geez, Jason, I don't know. You threw away a marriage once for me. Doesn't *that* mean something?"

Jason stared at Maggie through the orange glow of the street lamp above. She'd never looked so ugly to him. "What makes you think I threw it away for *you?*"

Maggie's mouth opened as if she were about to say something, but no sound came out. Jason turned and disappeared through the doorway.

*　　*　　*

"Jesus, we're going up there again?"

Bethany and Askar had just finished eating dinner and Bethany was clearing the dishes when she told Askar Thanksgiving would be at Einar's house. "Yes, we're going up there again," Bethany said.

"Your dad hates me."

"He doesn't hate you. He just doesn't like you."

"That's the same as hating me."

"No it's not. If he hated you, he would have shot you by now."

"That's comforting."

"Look," Bethany said, two plates still planted in each of her hands, "it's either that, or we hang around here and do nothing. Say nothing." Then, added as a whispered post-script, "Like every other day."

"Come on, that's not true at all."

"Oh, no? It's not true?"

"Bethany, I'm doing my best, here."

"It's just dinner, Askar. We'll be up there overnight. It's not that big a deal."

Askar took off his reading glasses and put them down on the dinner table. "I have work to do here. I can't be spending every weekend up in the middle of nowhere. I have a life, you know."

Bethany slammed a plate down on the countertop and turned to face Askar. "Yes," she said. "You have a life. And I used to be a part of it."

With that, Bethany left the room. Askar put his glasses back on and finished reading the newspaper.

*   *   *

Eleanor knew a boy back in high school who epitomized the very concept of the term, 'dumb hick.' Surprisingly enough, there weren't many of them around—most of the folks around Northern Maine certainly had a backcountry way about them, but the derogatory idea of a hick was fewer and farther between than one might have thought. Nevertheless, there were a few, and Angus McCausland was one of them. He drove a rustbucket of a truck with tires that stood higher than the roof of normal cars, and it belched exhaust in a steaming cloud every time he pushed the gas pedal, leaving a trail of stink and noise behind him at all times. Eleanor thought this appropriate since Angus did the same thing as he roamed the hallways during school.

Converse to the existence of dipshits like Angus were an equally strange and lazy breed of humans: the Hippies. They had infiltrated some sects of Northern Maine during the summer months and simply never left. Their children in turn became hippies and went to school with Eleanor. She felt nothing toward this group—she found them to be lazy and inoffensive, if not rank and boring, but otherwise nondescript. But the Hicks and the Hippies hated each other with a passion, and it was not uncommon to find Angus and a few of his friends beating on a random Hippie behind the baseball diamond or by the auto shop. None of this mattered a bit to Eleanor until the last two months of her senior year.

Angus's truck became a mainstay of the parking lot at the high school. It was either parked there or driving through it toward the auto shop to get its intake tweaked or glasspack muffler re-welded.

On a Tuesday in late April, the big rustbucket was parked in the lot in a spot normally reserved for teachers. This surprised no one. What was surprising, however, was the sticker that adorned its bumper that afternoon when school let out. The bright orange rectangle stuck slightly askew on the driver side of the bumper, and in bold white letters, it proclaimed: IF THIS COUNTRY IS FREE, THEN WHY IS EVERYTHING FOR SALE?

This, of course, was not the doing of Angus McCausland. It couldn't have been, for two reasons: first, this sort of thought dwelled well beyond the mental capacity of a dolt like Angus, and second, this sticker was situated only a few feet below a decal of a confederate flag. Angus had no such Hippie ideas in his mostly-vacant mind, and his staunch patriotism was eclipsed only by his monumental egoism. A small crowd gathered on the opposite side of the parking lot, waiting for Angus to come out of the school and discover the sticker. He would inevitably take a moment to read it carefully—Angus was barely literate—and this would cause a few chuckles. But as soon as that part of the show ended, the crowd would disperse; no one would want to bear the brunt of Angus's anger.

The 250 pound hulk of a boy trudged out of the school at 3:15. He had been hung up in the hallway by a peeved Mr. Reeve, who took a few minutes to lecture Angus on the finer points of manners and the damage of marijuana smoke. If it had been possible for Angus to roll his eyes continually for ten minutes, he would have. As it was, he simply stood there and turned off his mind, a simple and effective method for tuning out teachers throughout the day. As he plodded his way through the parking lot, Mikey Jessiman following his coattails as he always did, Angus took a moment to throw his arm around Sarah Gorman, who quickly shoved the massive arm away with a look of disgust indicating she had just touched sewage or an animal carcass. Angus laughed a stupid laugh and walked on.

Then he saw the sticker.

As expected, he took a good long moment to read it. And, as expected, the crowd that had gathered—comprised mostly of Hippies—laughed heartily, then dispersed. Angus immediately launched into a tirade. "I am going to kick the ass of every one of you fucking *Hippies*," he bellowed at the running crowd. "Every fucking one of you!"

The next day, a new sticker covered the Hippie orange sticker. This one read, "HOW AM I DRIVING? CALL 1-800-EAT-SHIT." Very satisfied with himself, Angus walked with a smile into the school. That afternoon, the sticker had changed again. This one read, "ONE PEOPLE, ONE LOVE, ONE WORLD." This one so angered Angus after school that he punched the quarter panel of his truck and put a good-sized dent in it. The next day, the dent was gone and a new sticker proclaimed, "MY OTHER RIDE IS YOUR MOM."

This sticker swap went on for almost a month and a half. Then, on a mid-June day during finals, all of it stopped. Not suddenly, but violently. The weather had been mild all through late May and early June, but this day had been a scorcher. The school, which had no air conditioning and poor ventilation, had all the students glistening with sweat and stink throughout the day, and thankfully, Eleanor thought, the day would be a short one. Her exam that day ended just after noon, and when the bell rang, students were too lethargic and sticky to do much more than drag their feet toward the door. But school was over for the day, and there were only two more days until graduation, so when she reached the hallway, Eleanor's step quickened just slightly. As she navigated her way through the crowd toward the parking lot, it happened.

Eleanor's interactions with Angus throughout her four years of high school had been limited to one encounter. Sometime during junior year, Eleanor had been standing by her locker, gathering her books for the next class and taking a quick peek in her mirror to make sure her hair was behaving itself. She had worn a skirt for the first time that year—a green number that showed off her long legs that she felt were the nicest parts of her to look at—and she felt especially pretty that day. This was, of course, a strange and foreign feeling for Eleanor, but it did not make her enjoy it any less, especially after she had caught Jason Coates taking a peek at her legs during third period. As she stood by her locker, however, Angus managed to change that enthusiasm with one simple, ignorant and greedy motion. As he and Mikey Jessiman cruised down the crowded hallway past Eleanor, Angus dipped his upper body just enough to catch his finger on the hem of Eleanor's skirt and pulled it up so everyone in the hallway could see what hid beneath. Everyone laughed. Eleanor was mortified. That had been the only time Angus McCausland had had any sort of influence on her life.

Until she stepped through the doors and into the parking lot that afternoon after her final exam.

A massive fist grabbed her shirt and picked her up, quite literally, two feet off the ground. Angus had her gripped firmly with his left hand, and another boy, Thomas Moon Griffith dangled from his right. If there had been a sliding scale of Hippie-dom, Thomas would be the benchmark by which all others would be measured. It was by pure coincidence that Eleanor happened to be walking next to him as she left the school, and had she been thinking a little more clearly and a little less panicked at that moment, she might have realized she was dangling from Angus's fist simply because of association: Angus saw her walking with a Hippie, and therefore, she, too, was a Hippie.

Angus tossed them both to the pavement. When Eleanor looked up, she realized she was lying directly behind Angus's bumper. He had pulled the truck right up to the front entrance to the school. Eleanor read the bumper sticker: "IMAGINE PEACE." She had tears in her eyes now, but she could read the sticker clear as day. Angus grabbed both Thomas and Eleanor by their hair and pulled back hard. "You think this shit is funny?" He screamed. Mikey Jessiman laughed as he sat on the tailgate of the truck. A crowd was gathering now, but in typical high school fashion, no one did anything to stop him.

Eleanor's palms and knees were bleeding from the fall to the pavement. She tried to say something—to this day, she wasn't sure exactly what—but Angus was pulling back hard on her hair and she couldn't breathe in enough to so much as cry, let alone speak. "You think this is *funny*?" Angus yelled again, then pulled Eleanor's head back so hard she literally sprawled backward. Angus had turned his full attention to Thomas Moon Griffith, who was laughing despite his impending beating. This only infuriated Angus more.

At that moment, Jason Coates grabbed Eleanor and pulled her backward and onto a patch of grass adjacent to the main entrance of the school. When Mikey Jessiman saw Jason coming, he immediately disappeared. What happened next both terrified and fascinated Eleanor. Angus still had Thomas firmly gripped by his long hair, but he had now taken to slamming Thomas's head into the bumper, directly against the bumper sticker. The first thump sounded so horrible that a girl directly behind Eleanor screamed. The second thump sent a stream of blood spurting left of Thomas's face. He was no longer laughing. The third thump sent another spurt. The fourth, fifth and sixth thumps were equally horrible but almost noiseless, terrifying in their existence but numb in their performance. "Funny now, you *fucker*?" Angus was screaming over and over again. "Funny now, you shithead Hippie?"

He thumped Thomas's head once more before Jason Coates grabbed

Angus by the right shoulder, turned him, drove a fist into his forehead and dropped him to the ground.

Thomas's body lay limp by the bumper of the truck, and Angus's body lay just as limp adjacent to his. Jason immediately knelt down and turned Thomas over to view his face. There wasn't much left. He was very much dead. Jason fell backward and sat on the pavement. "Oh, God," he said. No one else said a word. When Mr. Reeve came rushing out of the school, he saw Jason Coates sobbing between the unconscious body of Angus McCausland and the dead one of Thomas Moon Griffith.

"Call the police," he shouted, and that was when the same girl who had screamed the first time screamed again. The crowd went into a panic.

Jason had spent the afternoon in jail until enough students had testified about what had happened. Angus McCausland eventually went to trial, and then straight to prison where he would stay for the rest of his life. He was tried as an adult—and he was an adult, as he had stayed back twice already, making him the oldest student at the high school as a twenty-year old senior. Thomas Moon Griffith was buried in Fort Kent Memorial Cemetery three weeks after he was killed. It seemed like all of the students in the school showed up to the funeral—even the Hicks.

Except for Eleanor Rigby Phillips.

Eleanor stayed home and locked herself in her bedroom. No one came to see her, and her mother never even so much as knocked on her door to see if she was okay. Not once. This marked the beginning of a slide into depression that would plague her all through college and for years after, the dark shadow of realization that descended upon her and made her certain the jokes were true: the cursed name her deadbeat father had given her would, in fact, play out to be true.

She would be alone. She would be insignificant. She would be just another face in the crowd. Yes, this was the beginning. As she sat curled on her bed that day, Eleanor wondered when the ending would come, if it came at all.

*   *   *

As Einar slowly paced his way down the driveway back toward his home, he took a strange, disjointed solace knowing that his own darkness could, like his shadow, dwell behind him, constantly chasing but never catching. He didn't wholeheartedly believe this, but knowing it was an option was enough for the moment.

He had spent part of the morning walking along the county road, gazing out at the fields he had spent so many years of his life tending to. This morning was a bitterly cold one, the wind scraping through the air and slicing across Einar's face the same way Jason's scraper had ripped against the flaked and tattered paint of the barn a few weeks prior. The sun hid behind the clouds and out of sight, casting only a dull and empty pallor across its needy and implacable child, the earth. Einar could smell it in the air: another snowfall loomed near, and this one would leave more than a dusting when all was said and done.

It was getting on toward dark when Einar looked out the kitchen window and spotted that damn thief again, heading toward the barn at a slow hobbled pace. Einar immediately headed for the living room closet to fetch his shotgun. He checked to make sure it was loaded—and it always was, but checking was a good habit nonetheless—and headed outside. He did not bother to put on his coat, and the cold breeze immediately frosted his fingers and arms. But Einar went on anyway, toward the barn, ready to put an end to these nightly visits.

He stood in the opening of the barn door and cocked the gun. "Come on out now," he said to whoever might have been in the darkness of the barn. "Come on out and save yourself a hole in your chest."

Einar listened for a moment but heard only the slight sound of stuttered breathing in the far corner of the barn, just below the ladder to the hay loft. "Now," Einar said, then waited. He held the gun in place as the sound of car tires crunching on the driveway gravel reached his ears. "Shit," he muttered. "Come on now. Ain't a need to make this hard," Einar said to the darkness again, and this time he heard the rustled movements of a man trying to stand up. Einar took four steps back so he now stood in the yard just outside the barn door. A car door slammed. Einar looked left briefly, then returned his attention to the barn.

Someone was running toward him from the driveway.

"Willie!" A man's voice called. "Willie, no, don't shoot!"

"Frank?" Einar yelled back. "That you?"

"Yes, Willie, don't shoot."

"This here trespasser's been stealing from my barn for too long," Einar said, loud enough for both Frank and the night visitor to hear. "Get on out of there, ya hear me?"

More rustling.

Frank was now standing next to Einar, panting and trying to catch his breath from the short run. Einar supposed it had more to do with adrenaline than with real strain, but why? "Just don't shoot him, okay, Willie?"

"Now why the hell not?"

The thief appeared in the doorway of the barn. A short man. Old. A long beard hung down to the middle of his concave chest, and his clothes hung off him as if they had been placed on him to dry in the wind.

"Because it's my dad," Frank said. "Please don't shoot him."

Einar lowered his gun.

"I'm ready, Doctor Billings," Frank's dad shouted. "I'm ready. Tell my wife I love her."

"Th' hell's he babblin' about?" Einar asked Frank under his breath. Frank simply sighed in return.

"Come on, dad. Let's get on home."

"Doctor Billings? That you?"

"No, dad. It's Frank. It's your son...never mind. Yes, it's Doctor Billings. Come on home now. You need your rest."

"I'll rest here," he shouted. "Here, in the mud. In the trenches. Good enough for the grunts, good enough for me." With that, he turned and disappeared into the barn.

"I'll go fetch some flashlights," Einar said. He turned and walked off toward the house. Frank followed.

"Suppose I owe you an explanation," Frank said.

"Don't owe me nothin'."

"He's gone senile. Also has Alzheimer's. A good one-two punch."

Einar stopped on the porch and looked at Frank. "Gerald? Alzheimer's?"

"Yessir."

Einar ran this over in his mind for a moment, then went inside. "Known your dad a good long time," Einar said. "Only a few years older than me."

"Yessir," Frank said again.

Einar pulled two flashlights out of a drawer in the kitchen—the 'junk drawer'—and handed one to Frank. "Why didn't ya say anythin'?"

Frank looked down at the floor. "Sorry, Willie. Should have said something."

Einar considered this for a moment, then walked toward the front door again. "No sorry, boy. No need for one. Let's get your pop on home."

They walked out onto the porch together and went around the side of the house through the dooryard. Einar stopped here. "He's got some of my tools," he said, almost ashamed to bring it up.

"I know. I have them all in a box. Been meaning to bring them back, but..."

Einar grunted. They went to the barn.

"Doctor Billings?" Gerald Jordan shouted from inside. "That you?"

"Yes," Frank said. "It's me. Let's get on home."

III

TO GIVE THANKS...

The date was December seventeenth. Eight years ago. Jason remembered that much for sure. The rest was a blur of details, flashing lights, and semi-drunken conversations with friends and family. But it was definitely December seventeenth, and it was late—after midnight, for sure—when the accident happened.

Jason was in the midst of his senior year of high school, the events pertaining to Angus McCausland still months away, midterms staring him in the face. Robert was, for all intents and purposes, a college drop-out and quite unemployed. This was the third time Robert had stalled his college education, each delay lasting a year or more. Though when asked, anyone close to him called it a 'break' and reassured everyone that he would be enrolled again for the spring term. That would have been true, had Robert not had the accident, but as it turned out, it was a good year before he'd see the inside of a college classroom again.

Robert had been dating a girl named Renè for about a year by the time December of that year rolled around. Sarah Coates did not like Renè because she had tattoos—two of them, in fact: one visible all the time, and the other visible only to 'special' friends; Jason and his friends knew this kind of tattoo as a 'Tramp Stamp'—and she smoked cigarettes. Robert liked her exactly for all those reasons. They had spent the majority of their evening in Fort Kent, first having dinner at a cheap diner, then buying a handle of whiskey and partying at Del Cormley's place down by the mill. The house stunk like shit and cabbage all the time, a common smell in towns that housed paper mills, but Robert wondered if the stench came from someplace inside the apartment rather than from the hulking mill across the street. Either possibility seemed likely.

When they left Del's, both Robert and Renè were sufficiently drunk. They drove across town to the movie theater in hopes of letting the buzz wear off before heading back out on the road to get Renè home and Robert back to Willie and Sarah's place, where he was crashing for the weekend instead of driving back down to Old Town to his apartment near the university. The movie ended up being a slasher flick, and a piss-poor one at that, but it didn't matter to Robert and Renè, who had spent the entire time fooling around to an almost absurd degree. When the movie ended, they went to the parking lot and continued where they had left off in the theater before heading back out of town toward Renè's place. But they had one more stop to make.

When they passed the mill again, heading in the direction of Del's place and that shitty bar beyond—the Hog Hut, it had been called—Robert decided to cap off the evening with some fine dining courtesy of the Irving gas station down the road. This would also give him the opportunity to take a squirt in the men's room—something he'd been putting off for a few hours now. He pulled into the parking lot and saw two things he didn't like: one, his younger brother Jason hobbling around the parking lot, obviously drunk; and two, the pick-up truck Jason was headed for, obviously intent on driving it home. Robert pulled up behind the truck Jason had borrowed from their father and put the car in park. Jason saw this happen but had no idea who had just blocked him in the parking lot. He was that drunk.

"Hey little brother," Robert said as he stepped out of the car. Renè stayed in the passenger seat, checking her makeup in the mirror and making it clear she had absolutely no interest in what was happening outside.

"Hey," Jason said, loudly and far too jovially. Frank Jordan was sitting on the curb with a few of the other varsity hockey players, laughing at Jason through their own inebriation. "What are you doin' here?" Jason said with slurred words as he threw an arm around Robert. "I mean, what—what are you *doing* here?"

Robert couldn't help but laugh a little. "I know you weren't thinking of driving Pop's truck home drunk, now were you?"

"Me? No. No, of course not. Well, maybe. I mean, yeah, I was just going to—you know—*drive* home. *Drive* it." Jason laughed for no reason.

"And you shitheads were going to let him," Robert yelled toward Frank and the other hockey players. They all stopped laughing. "Come on," Robert said. "Hop in the back seat. I'll get you home."

"No, I—okay." Jason climbed in the backseat and started laughing again for no real reason at all.

Robert walked over to the truck, grabbed the keys from the ignition, then made his way around the front of the truck to Frank Jordan. "You ride here with Jason?"

"Yes," Frank said.

"You sober?"

"Yeah," he said, honestly. Robert tossed Frank the keys to the truck. "Make sure that gets back to my Pop's driveway before morning."

"Sure thing, Robert," Frank said.

With that, Robert climbed back into the car and pulled out of the gas station parking lot. He got maybe two miles down the road before he couldn't stand it anymore: he had to pee. He pulled off the side of the road just outside of Nelson Michaud's farm—Robert knew this was Nelson's property because Einar and Nelson often loaned workers to each other, and it would be fair to say Robert had been traded to Nelson's farm more than once—and turned to Renè. "Just need one second," he said, planting a kiss on her lips.

"Jesus," Jason said sarcastically from the back seat. Robert turned to him. "You sit tight," he said. "In other words, don't move your ass from that seat."

Jason laughed. Robert got out to pee. He immediately hit a patch of ice that he saw reached clear across the road, picked himself up, and trundled down the embankment. He was halfway through his business when he heard Renè shout something. Before he had a second to so much as turn around, the car was peeling away from the side of the road, full-throttle.

Robert zipped his pants and ran up the embankment in time to see the car zoom down the road, skid to a stop, slam into reverse and streak back toward him. "Oh, shit," he said, waiting to see where the car would go so he would know in which direction to jump out of its way. Luckily, the car streaked right past him in reverse. Robert saw Jason's screaming, smiling face in the driver's seat, drunk as a skunk and having the time of his life. Renè was screaming in the passenger seat.

"Jason!" Robert screamed as the car hit a patch of ice, went slightly askew, then stopped. Jason slammed the car into first gear and gunned the engine. The rear wheels of the car spun dramatically on the ice before catching and propelling the car forward right at Robert. Jason drove the car a good fifty yards before hitting another patch of ice, sending the car sideways and eventually up onto its side. It skidded toward Robert, who tumbled down the embankment and came to rest at the bottom. When he looked up, he saw the roof of the car staring at him. The car had come to rest exactly where Robert had been standing, propped up on its side, hanging halfway off the side of the road and down the embankment, wheels still spinning.

Robert scrambled back up the embankment and climbed on top of the car so all his weight rested on the passenger side door. Renè hung sideways inside, screaming and crying. Jason looked stunned as he hung sideways, bleeding from his face and neck. Robert opened the door and propped it open with his right leg as he pulled Renè out of the car and placed her safely on the pavement. Then he looked down at Jason. "Come on," he said, reaching his arm inside the car. When Jason stood up, he stumbled a bit, causing the car to shimmy back and forth.

"Easy," he shouted. "Car's not stable."

"Okay," Jason said, more to himself than to Robert. He reached upward toward Robert's hand, then stumbled backward again. "Whoa," he blurted. "Sorry, Robert. Sorry about this."

"Just grab my hand," Robert said. Jason did. Robert pulled him up, but Jason was far too unsteady. He kicked and flailed, and his grip loosened from Robert's. Jason tumbled back into the car and fell in a heap against the roof of the car. That was when the car lurched.

Robert had enough time to yell, "Fuck!" before jumping off the side of the car and down the ditch. He hit the frozen ground and tumbled, shattering his right leg as he went. The car tumbled down the embankment behind him, and he rolled out of the way just in time to keep from being crushed by its weight. The trunk of the car, however, rolled over his right leg as it rolled down the embankment, crushing it again. He screamed a bloody and horrible shriek as the pain shot all the way through him. When the car settled, Jason climbed out of the car.

"Fuck, oh fuck!" Jason screamed, pressing his palms against his forehead.

"Robert," Renè screamed from the road, more as a question posed in a 'when the hell are we going to go home' tone than a question of genuine concern. Robert screamed again.

"I'm going to get help," Jason said. "Just…I'll go get help."

"Go!" Robert screamed.

Twenty minutes later, Jason returned in the passenger seat of a pick-up truck. The truck belonged to Nelson Michaud, who was now clambering down the embankment, unsteady with arthritis in his legs and frozen ground beneath him. When he reached Robert, he said, "Don't worry, son. We got an ambulance on the way."

Robert said nothing.

"What happened, boy?" Nelson asked.

"I was—" Jason started to say, but Robert cut him off.

"Hit a patch of ice," Robert said through clenched teeth. "Didn't see it. Sent me sideways."

Nelson looked from Robert to Jason, then from Jason to Renè. Jason had made no movement whatsoever, but Renè nodded. "Yes," she said, her arms crossed and her face serious.

"Why don't you get in the truck," Nelson said to Renè. "Warmer in there."

She nodded again, then did as she was told. Nelson looked at Jason again, and even though he was still drunk, he could see Nelson saw right through the lie that had just been told. He could also see it didn't matter; Nelson would say nothing.

The ambulance and police arrived quicker than any of them had expected them to. They were there within five minutes of Nelson's arrival. Einar and Sarah met Jason at the hospital—Nelson gave Jason a ride there—and Jason told his tale. He'd been at the gas station with Frank, then decided to head home. He had gotten down the road and saw Robert's car in the ditch. He ran to Nelson's place—his driveway was only a few hundred yards up the road—to get help. He had sent Frank back to the gas station with the truck to call the police, but the official call came from Nelson's. Jason explained this, saying he must have gotten to Nelson's before Frank got back to the gas station. No one had bothered to check and see if Frank really had called the cops at all (he hadn't); no one questioned the stink of booze on Jason's breath; no one pressed Renè for her take on what had happened; what mattered was that everyone was alive. That was simply good enough.

"Why'd you lie?" Jason asked Robert almost a year later. They hadn't spoken about that night before then.

"Because you would have been in a lot of trouble you didn't need," Robert said. "You've got too much going for you." He paused, looking down at his leg that had been shattered a year earlier. "Just don't fuck up like that again. You've broken me enough."

Robert had intended that comment to be funny, but they both knew it wasn't. Jason had every intention to keep that promise—never fuck up like that again, especially at Robert's expense—but life changes us all, and years later, he would break Robert yet again. This time, he wouldn't need the weight of a car to crush his brother.

*   *   *

Thanksgiving.

Five A.M.

Einar woke with an ache in his knees and no other real emotion to speak of. To him, this day would reflect in on itself, the way all other days had looked like since Sarah had died. An exercise in remembering. An exercise in disappointment. An exercise in guilt. Promises made. Promises kept. Others broken. Einar stepped into the bathroom and took out his shaving cream and wondered if, somewhere down the line, the pain of not having Sarah with him would leave. He wondered if he'd miss it when it was gone, the way he missed Sarah now. Was this the consolation? The pain? Was this what was to fill the gap? Einar patted the shaving cream on his face and watched as the streaks of the stuff disappeared beneath his razor, taking the age of the night with it.

Robert arrived first. He was standing on the porch when Einar made his way back up from the lake. His hands were shoved into the pockets of his coat and he looked neat and tidy for the holiday. "Hey, Pop," he said as Einar climbed the steps to the porch.

"Mornin'," Einar said.

"Surprised Bethany's not here yet. Figured she'd be elbow deep in stuffing and turkey guts by now."

"Suspect she'll be here any time now," Einar said, now standing next to his son.

"Askar coming up, too?"

Einar nodded. "Suppose he is."

Robert laughed.

"What's funny?" Einar said.

"Give him a chance, Pop. He isn't that bad."

Einar grunted. Robert laughed again. "Come on," Robert said. "I could use another cup of coffee."

They turned and went inside. As Robert pulled the door closed,

Bethany and Askar pulled into the driveway.

"Bethany's here," Robert yelled to Einar, who was already in the kitchen. "I'm going to give them a hand."

Robert limped down the steps and into the driveway just as Askar was putting the Jeep Cherokee into park. Bethany popped—literally popped—out of the car and hugged Robert with a smile and a 'happy Thanksgiving.' Askar stayed in the car, cell phone glued to his ear and his mouth moving a mile a minute. Bethany watched Robert take that scene in for a moment, then said, "Come on. Lots to carry inside."

She didn't wait for his reply. She went to the trunk and began loading Robert up with random foodstuffs.

Inside, Bethany immediately began cooking. She was chatting away at this and that, and her hands moved quickly over the turkey, the stuffing, the pots and the pans. Robert and Einar both watched this spectacle for almost five minutes before Robert said, "Beth."

"What?" She said, not stopping her movements at all.

"You're going to be here a while. Why don't you take off your coat?"

She finally stopped moving, looked down and saw that she still had her down coat securely fastened around her, then laughed. "Oh," she squeaked. "Thought it was hot in here." She laughed again, loud and artificial, as she pulled off the coat and slung it over one of the chairs at the kitchen table. She immediately returned to cooking. Einar shot Robert a look and Robert nodded in return, then walked back through the living room and out the front door. Askar was just now getting off his phone and climbing out of the car. "Morning, Robert," he said with a wave as he slammed the door closed. "Happy Thanksgiving and all that."

"To you, too."

"Beautiful morning for it," he said, climbing the steps and settling into place next to Robert, who was looking, arms crossed, out at the morning that really wasn't that beautiful at all.

"What's going on with Bethany?" Robert asked. "She seems pretty wound up."

"Oh, I don't know," Askar said with a hint of exasperation in his voice. "She's been bouncing off the walls all morning. The drive up here was almost painful."

Robert nodded with a fake smile curling his lips. He suddenly felt just like his father. This was a good time to keep his mouth shut.

"Well," Askar said, sensing the demise of the conversation, "I suppose I'll head in and see what I can do to help."

Robert nodded again. He was now watching Jason's car pull into the driveway. Askar disappeared inside the house. Robert tightened his already-folded arms. Here was Jason. Here was his brother. Here was the reason for all of the anger in his life.

Robert dug his fingers into his side hard. "Just for today," he mumbled under his breath. "Shut up just for today."

*   *   *

"Doctor Billings coming today?"

Frank sat at the kitchen table with his father opposite him as they both ate breakfast Thanksgiving morning.

"No, Pop. Not today." Not any day, really, Frank thought. Doctor Billings had been dead for over twenty years and Frank wondered if he'd ever actually met the man. He had no recollection of such. Frank finished his eggs and brought his plate to the sink. When he turned to fetch his father's plate, Gerald was wearing his eggs on his head and was about to place his toast in about the same place.

"Dammit, dad," Frank said. Gerald, unfazed, placed the toast in a neat stack on top of the eggs that now covered his bald spot. Frank watched all this with no humor at all, his hands on his hips and his head hanging. This was the pose in which he stood when the doorbell rang. "Shit," Frank muttered. "Stay here, Pop. I have to go get the door."

"Should be Doctor Billings. Show him in," Gerald said, giving the toast on his head a final pat.

Frank shook his head and went to get the door.

It was Eleanor.

"Happy Thanksgiving," Eleanor said with a big grin on her face. She threw her arms around Frank, which both surprised and pleased him. Eleanor picked up a paper bag that she had set down on the porch, then walked around Frank and into the living room with the intent of going to the kitchen. "Got some cooking to do," she said.

Frank closed the door.

"Uh, Eleanor," Frank stammered.

She stopped by the door to the kitchen. "Yes?"

"I have to tell you something if you're going to stay."

A confused look overtook her face. Frank tried to find the words to tell her about his father's condition and the overwhelmingly horrible life that had piled upon him over the last several months, but as he grappled with himself, he suddenly found he had no need to catch those words after all.

"My Pop," he said, pointing directly behind Eleanor. She turned, and there stood Gerald Jordan in the doorway, two over-easy eggs perched on his head and dripping into his eyes, one remaining slice of toast complementing them absurdly. He wore no pants, only boxer shorts and a sweater. "He's not doing so well," Frank said, hoping she wouldn't laugh. That sound might break him completely.

Instead, Eleanor looked to Frank with a face that said, no, this isn't funny at all, and yes, I'm glad I came.

"You Doctor Billings's nurse?" Gerald said. Eleanor turned back to him, speechless, then crossed the room back toward Frank. She gave him a kiss on the cheek. "Come on, let's get everything settled," She said.

*   *   *

It had been Robert who had convinced Jason so many years ago to give up playing goalie—which he loved, but he was terrible at it—and take up playing forward. Halfway through his sophomore season, Jason relinquished his claim on the net to Frank Jordan, who was a far superior netminder, and took up left wing somewhat hesitantly. At first he was klutzy and had no confidence in player skates, but Robert worked with him tirelessly. Jason would practice with the school team in the mornings and then again after school, and when he got home, Robert would be there. "Finish your homework," he said, and Jason knew what this meant. Robert would be waiting on the lake's ice out behind the house. If the sun went down, he'd pull his car down there and turn the high beams on. Einar didn't like when he did that, but Robert knew there were more important matters at hand.

Eventually, Robert turned Jason into a stellar forward. He made it onto the all-state team that year, and the next year, and the year after that. He wasn't just decent as a forward; he was phenomenal. Every opponent knew his name, and the University of Maine was recruiting him to play on their team. This excited Jason to no end—UMaine had won the national championship two seasons prior, and in Maine, the college team *was* Maine's pro team. Through all this, Robert sat back and smiled. He'd had no real talent as a hockey player himself, but he could teach it, and by God, he did a fine job with Jason, if he didn't say so himself.

Then that business with Angus McCausland happened, and Robert could do nothing but watch as Jason threw it away.

He remembered sitting back and watching as Jason broke up with his girlfriend—a really sweet girl who was good for him in every way—and drink the remainder of his senior year away. It had really all started with the accident, and for a while afterward, as Robert healed and Jason wallowed in his own guilt, things had gotten better. But then Jason hit the bottle again. Then Angus McCausland. A ladder downward, so to speak. Jason took Eleanor to the prom, and that was the end of Jason and his girlfriend—not that Jason seemed to mind—and that following summer turned into a retrieval practice: Robert retrieving Jason from a bar, or from the granite pits, or from a party. He was always hopelessly drunk. It occurred to Robert that summer that it really hadn't been him that had been crippled in the accident. It was Jason.

Sitting at the dinner table that afternoon for a Thanksgiving meal expertly prepared by Bethany seemed almost torturous to both brothers. And they certainly weren't the only ones to notice. Jason did make the UMaine team and played three strong years there, and with that atmosphere came a certain strange ego that Jason had never had before. Bethany had been the one to bring him down from it—she was a strong girl then that had become fawning and somewhat servile only recently—and it would be her that would bring him down again.

But not just him. In a single stroke, she would take down all four men sitting at the table that Thanksgiving. No one saw it coming. Not even Bethany.

*   *   *

Maggie had been sitting in her apartment on Thanksgiving afternoon. She had nowhere to go, really; her parents both lived in Oregon, and she had not made the commitment of flying there for this holiday, though she would for Christmas, and since the mess with Robert and Jason, she decided a day alone in the apartment would do just fine. So, at three in the afternoon, Maggie sat on her couch in her apartment in Portland, Maine and watched a movie.

Someone knocked on the door at 3:17. She opened it to find the least likely candidate for a visit to her apartment.

"Ginny," Maggie said, stunned.

"May I come in?"

"Yes. Yes, of course."

Maggie stepped out of the way and Ginny walked in. They went to the kitchen and sat at the table there. "Can I get you something? Coffee?"

"Coffee would be nice," Ginny said as she sat with her hands folded across her lap. Maggie busied herself getting some coffee ready, nervously dropping spoons and clunking mugs onto the counter top. It would not have been accurate to say Maggie and Ginny had ever been friends—hadn't even met, in fact, until they both started dating the Coates men at UMaine—but they were friendly for sure. Being integrated into a family always went smoother when you weren't doing it alone, and they were doing it together with the Coates's. Sure, they *would* have become friends. But that was before...well, that was before. Now was different.

Maggie got the pot of coffee going, then sat at the small table in the narrow kitchen. Ginny sat sideways, facing the counter instead of Maggie, and that was fine by Maggie. Neither woman wanted to look the other in the eyes. "Should only be a few minutes," Maggie said, her eyes glued to the coffee maker as if it would stop working if she looked away.

"Okay," Ginny said. This was followed by a prolonged and strange silence in which both women indulged in the running monologues taking place in their respective heads. What to say next…well, that was the question, wasn't it? Ginny wanted to be angry but couldn't. Maggie wanted to be apologetic but knew how it would come across—the term, 'too little too late,' came to mind—and so they sat in silence. Watching the coffee brew. Watching hands fold, then unfold, then fold again. By the time the coffee pot was half full, fifteen minutes had passed but no words had done so between them. Maggie got up to pour the coffee.

"Have you talked to him?" Ginny asked.

Maggie almost dropped the pot of coffee. "Which one?" She asked.

"Either one."

"I haven't seen or heard from Robert." Maggie's voice faltered when she said his name. "But I did talk to Jason. Once. Briefly." She looked to Ginny for only the second time since her arrival, and immediately looked away. "It was nothing. He—he was angry. I suppose I was, too."

Ginny wore a look on her face that Maggie could not read, so she turned instead and poured two cups of coffee. "You take milk or sugar?"

"Black is fine for now," Ginny said softly.

Maggie handed her the steaming mug and sat down again.

"I want to be angry at you," Ginny said. "I want to scream at you, want to say nasty things and then storm out of here."

"What's stopping you?"

Ginny took a slow sip from her mug. "I don't know."

Silence again.

"That's not true," Ginny finally said. "It's guilt, really. I mean, this didn't happen because of you. It happened because of me and Jason. I just can't figure—just can't figure out what went wrong."

"Ginny," Maggie started, then stopped. Tears were welling up in her eyes, and she thought it best to keep quiet if she didn't want to start bawling outright.

"But the thing is, Maggie, I *am* angry with you. With you, with Jason, with me. I hate it all. Hate *us* all." She paused. Maggie held in a sob and Ginny noticed it; there was no sound to it, and Ginny hadn't been looking, but as if it had given off light, Ginny saw it. She sighed. "Jason. He had a smell, you know. A scent of…December. I used to tell him that. It was a cold smell, but somehow wonderful, sweet. I didn't realize his scent wasn't the only thing cold about him."

"Robert, too," Maggie whispered. Ginny heard this but ignored it.

Ginny stood up. "I don't forgive you for this," she said. "The fact is, I don't forgive any of us. But I wanted to see you and say that. Maybe I wanted to come here and see if I could forigive, but I can't. I just can't."

Maggie was crying now. She wanted to say she was sorry, and she was, but Ginny had spelled it out quite clearly: there was no forgiveness to be given or had. So she just cried as Ginny walked out of the kitchen and left the apartment. Maggie sat at the kitchen table until both mugs of coffee had lost their steam and gone cold, then stood up on legs that felt no steadier than those of a newborn. By the time she made it to her couch, a fatigue stronger than she'd ever felt swept over her and she slept through the rest of the day until the sun went down. Thanksgiving had been a bitter holiday for her this year, and Maggie succumbed to it. With her hands folded tightly between her thighs and her head sinking into a pillow wet with tears, Maggie let the day go…and the next, and the next.

*   *   *

While the Coates family sat down to Thanksgiving dinner, Eleanor Rigby Phillips stood in front of the stove in the Jordan household. Frank sat at the table behind her, watching her stir pots, reach for ingredients left waiting on the counter, and pull her hair back into a pony tail.

At the same time, Maggie lay on her couch, intermittently crying in between bouts of drowsiness and sleep.

Ginny, in that very same moment, walked slowly through the Old Port in Portland, Maine, her arms wrapped around herself and a breeze taunting and pulling at her until tears finally leaked down her face.

For each of them, in their own minds in their own homes, changes were taking place without their consent.

Askar left the dinner table to take a call. Bethany held her composure only for a moment, then hurried off up the stairs to the bedroom.

Ginny stopped and leaned against a wooden railing, staring out at the water and feeling one more gust of wind take a tear and drag it across her cheeks and into her hair.

Maggie dozed off again, then woke, then cried, then slept.

Frank stood up from the kitchen table and crossed the room to stand by Eleanor, who faced him only momentarily to smile, then return to her cooking.

Gerald Jordan sat in the living room, waiting for a doctor twenty years deceased to come and give him a check-up, and wet his pants.

And then there were the Coates men left. Robert, Jason, and Einar. At the table. They ate their meals and searched their minds for some calming words to break the silence and make the quiet stop provoking them. But no words came to any of them. They sat and ate and let the world march on around them.

When she was a little girl, Bethany had formed an odd kinship with the family cat. Einar hated the thing. It made him sneeze and it often clawed at him, but his daughter loved the furry little nuisance, so it stayed. Bethany had named it Delia and let it sleep in her bed every night. When Bethany would sit at the kitchen table to do her homework, Delia would curl up into a ball on top of Bethany's feet or find its way to Bethany's shoulders to perch itself and preside over the studying. The two of them existed peacefully as no other creatures possibly could.

It was a Tuesday when Delia died. Bethany was twelve years old. Sarah had found the cat underneath the porch steps, lying on its side and dead as a ghost could be. Bethany came home from school to find Sarah waiting for her on the porch, and she immediately knew her mother had bad news to give her. The tears came without provocation; Sarah had not said a word yet. "Delia?" Bethany had said, and Sarah had nodded with a solemn and calm expression on her face. Bethany hugged her mother and cried for nearly ten minutes.

"I don't want her to die, Mama," Bethany said between choked sobs.

"We'll all die someday, darling. It's part of life."

"I don't want any of us to die. Ever. We're not dying, Mama. Never."

"Everything in the world is dying," Sarah had said softly. "If it ain't dying, it's already dead. But there's something beautiful about it, Bethany. You need to see that. Someday you will see that."

On Thanksgiving day, as her father and two brothers sat at the dinner table eating the meal she had spent the last several hours preparing, Bethany stood by the bedroom window looking down at the driveway. Her husband paced back and forth, talking with distinct animation to his cell phone to someone he felt must have been more important than his wife, than Bethany. She watched him walk left, then right, then left again, the whole time his hands waving and his arms gesturing, and she finally saw what Sarah had tried to tell her so many years ago. Everything was dying, and there was beauty to be seen in it. Yes, certainly so. Beauty to be seen in death.

But looking down at Askar, Bethany could see no beauty in what she now knew was to happen to her marriage. Just like coming home to find Delia had died, Bethany felt as though she'd come to the house in northern Maine this Thanksgiving to find her marriage lying on its side underneath the porch steps. And just like her disbelief then, when Sarah had told her Bethany would find the beauty in Delia's death, Bethany hoped Sarah would be right again and someday she'd see the beauty in this. Someday she would see the purpose and the far-reaching good to come of this.

But that day was not today.

Bethany did not waste too much time mourning. She was sitting at the dinner table again before Askar hung up his phone and returned to the scornful glances of the men sitting around the dinner table. She did not look at him. She would never look at him again, if all went her way.

*   *   *

"Can I help with anything?" Frank asked Eleanor.

"Umm, you can chop those vegetables. That would be helpful."

Frank obliged and began chopping the vegetables that sat on the cutting board next to the sink. First the broccoli. Then the onions. Then the green peppers. He cut methodically. Eleanor saw this and smiled.

Gerald let loose a howl from the living room, then followed it up with a gassy and vibrating fart. Frank stopped chopping, mortified. In that dead moment after the fart, the silence asserted itself and Frank turned red. Then, faintly, both Frank and Eleanor heard the quiet chuckle from Gerald in the other room. Eleanor looked to Frank, who was still staring down at the vegetables, and they both began to laugh.

"I'm sorry, I shouldn't laugh," Eleanor said.

"Didn't stop *him*," Frank said, nodding toward the door to the living room. They both laughed again. Frank resumed chopping the vegetables.

"How long has he…" Eleanor started.

Frank's face turned visibly red. "Started last year. Got real bad about six months ago. Got worse when Natalie and I moved back. When she…when Nat left, it seemed like it got a hundred times worse. Suppose it's because I was alone with him."

"Have you thought about putting him in a home?" Eleanor asked.

"Thought about it, yeah. But I can't."

Eleanor placed a lid on top of the pot of boiling potatoes, then turned once more to Frank. "Is he the reason you and Natalie moved back to Maine?"

Frank nodded.

"And is he the reason Natalie left you?"

All of the vegetables were cut now, but Frank still poked at them with a knife and occasionally cut them into finer bits, some as thin as paper and inedible now. "No," he said. "No, she didn't leave because of Pop."

Eleanor thought for a moment. "There's a good home in Fort Kent, you know. They could take care of him and—"

"I can't do that, Elly."

"I know it's hard, Frank, but they could take care of him better than you can."

Frank put the knife down on the cutting board. "That may be so," he said as he wiped off his hands on a dish rag, "but they aren't me. And he needs me." He threw the dish rag down onto the counter and paced to the window above the kitchen table. He stared out at the dooryard outside, his hands on his hips and his back now to Eleanor. "You remember Henry Heinen?"

Eleanor thought for a moment. "No, I don't."

"He was my best friend. Henry and Jason Coates, anyway. Henry died when we were just kids. Coates and I spent every day with him while he was dying, and I tell ya, Elly, I believe it in my heart and in my head that the only reason that kid lasted as long as he did was because Coates and I were there for him. If we weren't there, he wouldn't have any reason to live. You know how easy it would be to die if you had no reason to live? Toward the end, he would get snippy with us and tell us to leave. We wouldn't, but he would always tell us to go. We didn't understand it then, but you know what, Elly? I get it now. He wanted us to go because we were all that was keeping him alive. If we weren't there, he could have died, and he would have been okay with that because what was there to live for? He spent most of his time in bed, in pain. He spent the rest of the time scared out of his mind. But we stayed, Elly, and he died with whatever he had left of a smile on his face. Henry was my best friend." Frank turned to Eleanor and crossed his arms at his chest. "That's my dad. I owe him this much. I owe it to him to hang around until he's gone, because even if it's only me, Elly, he has something to live for. Even if it's only me."

Eleanor opened her mouth to say something, but then closed it again. She looked across the room at Frank, who would no longer look back at her, whether out of embarrassment or fear or whatever else had plagued the man's mind since his wife left him. The pot of potatoes on the stove boiled over, sending a loud hissing noise into the air. Without looking, Eleanor turned down the heat and crossed the room to Frank, the hissing and spitting sounds still skipping through the air. She went to him and uncrossed his arms. She pulled them around her. And she kissed him. Then she pressed her head into his chest and they held each other that way as the hissing and spitting sound slowly dissipated and the room went silent. In the other room, Gerald mumbled and laughed to himself. Eleanor and Frank stood

in the kitchen, holding each other and listening to the lost voice of
the man in the other room who, at one time, had been Frank's father,
the most important man in his life. And that was how Thanksgiving
stayed for them. Within the silence mixed with the vacant ramblings
of a man Frank used to know, he and Eleanor stayed close to each
other.

*   *   *

Einar watched as his family reassembled at the dinner table. Robert
and Jason had never left, but really, neither had been entirely there
to begin with. The silence between them may as well have been a
lead weight placed in the center of the table next to the squash and
potatoes. Bethany sat down again and placed her napkin on her lap,
and no more than a minute later, Askar returned to the table as well.
No one said a word; it seemed everyone was waiting for someone else
to make the day right, make it better. Einar cleared his throat. Jason
shifted in his seat. Askar reached across for the basket of bread. And
then Bethany picked her fork up and put it back down again.

"I won't have this," she said in a near whisper.

"What?" Jason said, his voice gravelly from the prolonged silence.

"I won't have *this*," she repeated. "This quiet…it's ridiculous. God,
it's so ridiculous! You," she said, looking over at Robert. "Say something to your brother if it eats at you so much. And you," she said,
pointing to Jason. "Apologize. Beg. Buy him a goddamn car, I don't
care what you have to do to fix whatever's going on between you two,
just do it." Then she looked at Askar. "And you."

Askar looked to his wife, then dropped his gaze again. Bethany
stared at him with an intensity Einar recognized instantly. It was
Sarah in that stare. "You," Bethany repeated. "You lose that phone or

you lose me."

With that, Bethany picked up her fork and began eating again. For a moment, the men at the table did not follow suit; they simply exchanged glances, each one wrought with its own version of guilt and embarrassment, its own sheepish grin for having been called out so easily and perfectly. Then they returned to their meals, too, and with their thoughts on everything and anything beyond the wonderful meal that lay spread before them, the men at the table cleared their throats. Chewed. Clicked forks on plates. Wiped their mouths. And waited.

Had Einar not asked for a second helping of mashed potatoes, the silence surely would have sustained itself. But he did, and that seemed to have broken some invisible rule, the rule that stated no man should speak until spoken to because all men present were guilty of something. All men here now had no rights but the right to defer to Bethany, and they respected that rule. But not Einar.

"I got off scot-free there, didn't I?" He said, half under his breath. Bethany shot him a glance that could have cut through stone. "Yes, scot-free," he said again, scooping mashed potatoes into his dish.

"I—" Bethany started.

"Thing is," Einar interrupted, "we're all guilty of something. And we're all here. In front of us, here's this table. And ya know, it's empty, really. So, like Bethany says. Let's get it all out on the table."

Einar finished scooping the mashed potatoes onto his plate and returned the bowl to the center of the table. Then he folded his hands in front of him and looked directly into the eyes of his daughter. She nodded.

Again, the silence at the table became something physical, heavy, dull and throbbing. They all noticed it. They all observed the rules. They all waited again.

But then they couldn't wait any more.

"You don't love me anymore," Bethany said quietly, her head down and her hands folded. She did not address this statement to anyone, but Askar knew whose ear she sought to reach.

"You ruined my life…twice." Robert said.

"You beat your fiancé," Jason replied.

"You boys let each other down, which means you let *me* down," Einar said, and as if this statement had carried the most weight of all, each person at the table closed their eyes and winced just a little bit. "And neither of you two dolts has bothered to take care of those girls you supposedly love so much. Yer Ma raised ya better than that."

Jason and Robert caught each other's eyes and held them. "Now we got that out," Einar said, picking his fork back up. "Let's eat before it gets cold."

Einar began to pick at the turkey in front of him. He had downed three bites before anyone else at the table had dared to so much as lay a finger on their fork. But eventually Jason did. Then Robert. And Askar. But Bethany did not. Instead, she looked over at Einar and watched him eat.

"You're not mom," she said.

Einar looked over at Bethany and saw a face that was half his wife and half the frightened workings of a girl lost in the woods. Before he could think of what to say to that, Bethany picked up her fork and began eating.

*   *   *

Ginny stood by the water and watched. Nothing in particular really held her attention, but she looked out at the water and allowed her mind to latch on to the idea of ripples in the water, tiny waves, particles of dirt below floating in the mass of liquid. This calmed her, and the tears disappeared shortly after they started. Not that they had been intense to begin with, but she felt better knowing she could control herself. She had spoken to Maggie, and that had been difficult, but she still had to talk to Jason, and that would be much harder.

She didn't think about it much anymore, but not long before she met Jason, she had been briefly married to a man named Sergeant. He had been raised with that name: Sergeant Willow Jackson. When they had met, his name had been a source of amusement for both of them, a cute but silly way to interact until those nervous jitters of dating disappeared and they became official 'boyfriend-girlfriend' material, then on to 'engaged couple,' and, of course, on to 'husband-wife.' How strange it was, she thought, that a man who had grown up with such a ridiculous but masculine name acted nothing of the sort. He had been kind and understanding while they dated, even to the point of near feminism. While Ginny didn't trust these sentiments at first, she grew to trust him and took him for his word. Sergeant, for his ridiculous name and hellishly harsh father, seemed a kind and gentle man.

That changed. It always does, doesn't it?

They had been married for two months when he beat her for the first time. Before that, he hadn't so much as said an unkind word to her. Then, one day, out of the blue, he stormed into their bedroom in a tiny apartment near Freeport while Ginny had been reading, and without making any sound of warning or aggression, proceeded to pummel her. She had been so taken by surprise that she didn't have time to react. She took her beating, then lay there afterward in shock. When he came back ten minutes later, she felt she had no option but to let Sergeant strip her clothes off and have sex with her. She didn't want it, and she knew she could fight it, but for whatever reason her mind had conjured in that moment, she simply did not.

She went to work at the Herald the next day with bruises on her arms and legs which were covered by her sweater and pants, respectively. She had a welt behind her left cheek, but if one had glanced only quickly, they would never have seen it at all. And no one did—except for Jason Coates. He saw it for sure, but he said nothing. At that time, Ginny and Jason had been no more than acquaintances, their conversations limited to a polite 'hello' in passing in the hallway or an 'excuse me' around the coffee machine. But he had noticed; she knew that. Had seen him spot the swelling and look away quickly, seemingly embarrassed. This had worried Ginny, but again, Jason had said nothing, so she went on living.

Sergeant seemed to have enjoyed the taste he had gotten that night, and the beatings continued steadily over the course of the next four months. The last beating put Ginny in the hospital with a broken forearm, which she explained at work was the result of a fall while playing racquetball. Jason noticed all the swellings, all the marks, all the make-up cover-ups, all the lies and all the times Ginny would look away when explaining her injuries to friends or peers at work.

But Jason never asked, and she never told.

Sergeant wasn't much of a drinker, but he had a friend in town from down in Boston who was staying in the Old Port area of Portland. He and Ginny met him at a bar called Horatio's, a semi-classy place that was both clean and comforting and dark and frightening at the same time. They had sat for most of the night in a booth by the door, laughing and having a generally good time. When Ginny excused herself to go to the bathroom, the trouble started.

Her right arm knocked over a martini glass, which, in turn, knocked over Sergeant's beer, the contents of which spilled on the lap of his friend from Boston—Thomas, his name had been. Ginny's breath immediately caught in her throat, and her eyes darted to find Sergeant's. He was laughing, as was Thomas, but Ginny could see it plain as day:

there was no humor at all in those eyes. Sergeant was angry. Sergeant was beyond that: he was irate. But he went on laughing, and Thomas went on saying, "No worries, dear. Needed a good washing anyway."

Ginny faked a smile and fetched a bar rag from the bartender, then went to the bathroom, where she spent five or so minutes trying to calm herself down so she wouldn't cry. She had never been a meek girl or one prone to tears, but since marrying Sergeant, she found herself doing much the same thing she was doing now just about every night. She had gotten very talented at holding back her tears, and tonight was no exception. When she returned to the table, Thomas and Sergeant both had their coats on and were ready to leave. Ginny followed suit.

When they walked outside into the coolness of the spring night, Thomas and Sergeant shared a few more laughs as they accompanied Thomas to his rental car down the street. After the usual arm-punching and bantering, Thomas got in his car and Sergeant and Ginny walked back up the sidewalk toward their own car. When they reached the front of Horatio's and Thomas was safely out of sight, Sergeant lashed his right hand out and connected with Ginny's left cheek. Then he did it a second time. Then a third. It was the first time he had hit her in public.

She regained her composure and faced her husband, who was already yelling at her, though hushed. She saw his lips moving and heard his voice, but her mind could not wrap itself around the words. She only felt fear. When he raised his hand to hit her again, however, something strange happened.

Sergeant hit the pavement.

At first, Ginny had no idea what had happened, but slow comprehension dawned on her as she tried to decide whether what she was seeing was actually happening, or if it was really just wishful thinking. Jason Coates had given Sergeant a right hook that had sent him crashing to the pavement, stunned and bleeding. He hadn't even seen Jason, let alone his fist flying at Sergeant's face. Nor had Ginny. She and Sergeant had been so intensely focused on each other that Jason must have walked right up to them—though Jason later told Ginny he had seen Sergeant hit her from inside the bar; he stormed out of the bar making quite a bit of noise by his account, but neither she nor Sergeant noticed.

Before Sergeant could regain his composure, Jason grabbed him by the scruff of his neck and pulled him to his feet. He slammed Sergeant against the faded brick wall to his left, bashing his head into the wall twice.

"Feel good?" Jason said.

"Who the fuck are—"

Jason threw another punch, this one into Sergeant's gut. He doubled over, but Jason pulled him back up and slammed him into the wall again. By this time, Frank Jordan was standing behind Jason. "Come on, Coates, that's enough," he said, though he knew Jason wouldn't stop until he'd finished all he had to say.

He leaned in close to Sergeant, and almost in a whisper, said, "Touch her again and I'll find you. You want to hit girls, fine. But just know that for every lump you give her, I will give you a hundred."

With that, Jason threw Sergeant to the pavement once more. Ginny looked briefly at Jason, who was walking back into the bar, then went to Sergeant to tend to him. He slapped her way. As soon as he did, he turned his head to make sure Jason hadn't seen the slap. He hadn't; Sergeant got to his feet and began walking toward the car. Ginny followed.

"Don't," he said. "Don't fucking follow me, you bitch," he screamed. Ginny stopped in her tracks and watched as Sergeant walked on toward the car, occasionally touching his hand to his face to assess his lumps. Ginny waited until he disappeared, then went back into Horatio's.

Jason was standing by the corner of the bar, a Bud Lite in his left hand and his right hand resting tentatively on the wood of the shiny bar top. He was chatting with Frank Jordan, but when he saw Ginny come in, he turned to see her come toward him. His face bore no revealing expression, and Ginny saw no pride in his face. No shame, either. He simply stood there, watching her come toward him. When she finally stood before him, she had a hard time deciding what she should do, so she did both things that readily occurred to her.

She slapped Jason across the face.

Then she kissed him.

Then she slapped him again.

"Thanks," Jason said.

"For the slap or the kiss?" She asked.

"Both, I suppose."

For an odd and tentative moment, Ginny and Jason just stared at each other. Frank Jordan took a sip of his beer, smiled, then looked away.

"You gonna be okay to go home?" Jason asked.

"Not going home," Ginny said. Jason nodded. Again, another odd moment in which they merely stared at each other. Then Ginny sat down at the bar and ordered a drink. "Think I earned this one," she said as the bartender placed a martini in front of her. Jason nodded again.

They didn't speak again after that. Jason and Frank found a table and sat down. Ginny stayed at the bar. She stared into the mirror behind all the tall bottles of liquor and imagined what it might feel like to stand up and scream, not a meek scream but a terrifying and brutal one. What would it feel like, she thought, to just stand up and rage? What would it feel like to make every person in the bar fear her, want to run from her, want to cower in her presence? She watched her hand pick up the martini glass in the mirror, watched her hand raise the glass to her lips, take a sip, replace it on the bar top.

Then she decided she never wanted to find out what that might feel like.

Never.

Nor did she ever want to feel afraid again.

She threw down a five dollar bill and three singles and stood up to leave. Jason and Frank watched. Frank jabbed Jason with his elbow. Ginny saw none of this, but a moment later, Jason was walking next to her as she made her way to the door.

"Hey," he said. She did not stop walking. "Uh, look, if you need—"

"I don't need anything." They were both outside on the sidewalk again, standing exactly where Jason had dropped Sergeant.

"I know, but, uh, I'm just saying if you *do* need anything—"

"Look," Ginny said, now facing Jason. "I appreciate what you did, but I don't need anything. Not from him, not from you, not from anyone. *Get it?*" She then turned to walk away.

"Okay, yeah, but—"

Ginny wheeled around on Jason and raised her hand as if to slap him. He raised his arm to block the shot and his face contorted in expectation. "I'm not going to—" Ginny started, but then she stopped. His face. His arms. Was he—could he be afraid? *No*, Ginny thought immediately. *He's not afraid of you. Not you. He beat the shit out of Sergeant. Why would he be afraid of you?*

But really, he looked that way, didn't he? She dropped her hand and Jason slowly followed suit. "I'm sorry," she said. "Really. I should go."

Ginny began rushing off down the sidewalk.

128

"Where are you going to go?" Jason shouted after her.

Ginny stopped and turned once more. "I don't know. I have a friend not far from here."

"Let me give you a ride then."

"No, it's okay."

"Then let me walk with you."

"Really, it's fine."

"Ginny, please."

"I don't need help, Jason. I'm okay."

"But I'm not."

This so struck Ginny that she didn't really know how to reply. It wasn't so much that she believed what he had just said, but something in how he had said it made her believe that, yes, he needed to walk her to wherever she was going. He needed to know. He needed to be safe in his knowledge that he had, in some way, solved a problem. She started to say something, then stopped, started again, then stopped again. She wrapped her arms around herself and looked off down at the water. "Okay," she said. "Okay, fine."

Jason smiled. Ginny thought for the first time—though it certainly wouldn't be the last—that she loved that smile. "Let me grab my coat," he said, then ran inside the bar, told Frank he was going—Frank only laughed—and a moment later, stood by Ginny's side again.

They walked on mostly in silence.

Ginny walked ahead of Jason only by a step. Nothing of importance passed between them as they wove their way through the city toward wherever it was that Ginny was leading them, and Jason did not ask. When they reached the doorstep of Ginny's friend, Theresa, Ginny turned to Jason. "Thanks for the walk," she said, then climbed the stairs to the front door. She stopped, turned, and looked down at Jason. He stood on the sidewalk with his hands in his pockets, his eyes looking up at her.

"Well," he said, "I'm sure I'll see you soon," he said, then walked down the road without another word.

*   *   *

As Ginny stared out at the Portland waterfront, still reeling a bit from her meeting with Maggie, she decided it was time to talk to Jason. It was time to decide—and it was she that needed to do the deciding. She walked back to her car and drove home with the intention of calling Jason.

*   *   *

Frank and Eleanor sat down to dinner around the same time Bethany was returning to the dinner table at the home of Einar William Coates. Frank's dad had fallen asleep in his chair in the living room—blessedly devoid of pants and drooling more than slightly—and they did not bother to wake him. In fact, Frank gladly let the old man snooze. Eleanor had made quite a dinner, and the two of them sat at the kitchen table with little fanfare and even less in the way of accoutrements. This disappointed neither of them; they smiled at each other as they sat down, nervously, as though on a first date...which was, suddenly, what it felt like to both of them.

Gerald's snores in the other room droned on in a musical drumbeat, punctuated occasionally by the rattling windows reacting to the slight wind outside. It all felt wonderful to Frank, who periodically glanced out the window as the sun dove down beneath the horizon over the course of ten minutes or so. Eleanor made small talk and they both took comfort in that, if only a temporary one. Frank asked for more squash. Eleanor re-filled her glass of wine, then Frank's. They ate, they

130

talked, they laughed.

Then Frank got nervous.

Gerald's snores had stopped.

"I should check on him," he said, his face suddenly worrisome.

"I'm sure he's fine," Eleanor said, more to herself, as Frank stood up. He left the room and Eleanor wiped her mouth with her napkin, then waited with her hands folded. *Fine,* she thought, *just fine. Woke up, probably reading or watching the T.V. or just staring off into space...*

But Frank came back into the kitchen and Eleanor knew immediately that nothing was fine. Nothing was just fine at all.

"He's gone, isn't he?" Eleanor asked. Frank looked at her with shame on his face and said nothing. "Come on, then," Eleanor said as she stood up and went to the breezeway to fetch her jacket. "Let's find him."

She grabbed Frank's jacket, too, handed it to him and headed for the door. "You think he went—"

She stopped short. Frank hadn't moved yet. "Frank?"

"I'm not going to get him."

"What? Frank, you have to."

"I can't."

"Yes, you can. Come on, it's freezing out there. We should—"

"I'm not going, Elly."

"Why not?"

"Why should I?"

Eleanor leaned against the counter by the door. "Wait a minute, buddy, weren't you the one who was telling me not one hour ago about how you were the only thing he had, the only person left, the only reason to live? What happened to all that?"

Before Frank could answer, Gerald banged on the window above the sink.

He yelled from the back yard, "The tomatoes are menstruating, Frank! Get the car started and tell your mother to put on some water to boil!" With that, he ran off toward the side yard.

Eleanor watched this with the disbelieving face of someone who has seen a ghost but is still in severe denial over that fact. Then she turned to Frank. His face had not changed from its blank expression from a moment ago. "He's not wearing pants, you know," Frank said.

"We need to get him inside," Eleanor said.

"No."

"Why not?"

"Every time he disappears," Frank said, pulling out the chair to the kitchen table and settling in, "I chase him. The man can't remember his own name, but he could find his way through those woods faster than any hunter, any deer. He know exactly where he was going in any direction, even up. Hell, he could reach the moon's doorstep faster than an astronaut and be back here before nightfall. But I chase him every time anyway. And I stay up all night doing it most times. But ya know something?"

Frank took a gulp of wine from his glass and sat it back down gently. "He runs because I chase. He leaves because he knows I'll follow." He smiled, and though he didn't tell Eleanor, he heard, just then, the faint sound he'd been hoping to hear. "Go take a peek in the living room," he said with a slight smile on his face.

Eleanor did. Gerald Jordan was back sitting in his chair in the living room again, nodding off and mumbling as he went closer toward sleep. Eleanor closed the door again and sat down across from Frank.

"He's gone," Frank said, "but that doesn't mean I have to chase him anymore."

*   *   *

Einar stepped out into the breezy yard in the dark with his flashlight in his left hand and his eyes barely open from the wind. He needed a hammer—nothing needed fixing aside from his attitude, it seemed, but he felt as though the presence of a hammer inside the house might help calm him, might lead him to some sort of way to reason this all out. He pulled out his tool box, the same tin piece of junk he'd had since he came back from the war so many years ago, and dug through the tools in search of his hammer. It didn't take him long to figure out it wasn't in there, and suddenly the fact that the head needed to be reset on the handle and he couldn't do it because he couldn't find it made him irate, made him want to throw the damn box across the barn.

He closed the lid of the tool box and stowed it away beneath the bench and searched around again for the hammer. It was not on the bench; was not beneath it; was not behind it or in front of it, not near the tractor or on the ground near the barn door. "Dammit, Frank," Einar said out loud, then thought, *yer pop stole m'damned tools and I need 'em back!* He immediately regretted the thought but let it remain, let it become justifiable in his mind. Sure, others had their troubles, but these troubles were Einar's and he wanted to own them for the moment.

"Need a hand?" A voice said from the barn door. Einar turned slowly—it seemed he reacted slower and slower since Sarah died—and saw Askar standing there, his face ashen in the darkness that was broken only by Einar's flashlight.

"No," Einar said, re-commencing his search.

Askar stood by the barn door a moment longer before he turned to go back to the house. But then he turned again and entered the barn, stood next to Einar. Turned him. "I want to fix this," Askar said.

Einar faced him and looked him in the eyes. "Do ya now."

"Yes."

"Gimme your phone."

"No," Askar said, his accent—something Einar could not place as any one nationality, but he knew damn sure it wasn't French-Canadian—now thicker. "Last time I did that you smashed the damn thing."

"And I intend to do it again," Einar said. He looked away, down at the bench, then over at the windowsill. " 'Cept I can't find m'damned hammer."

"How do I fix this?" Askar said.

"Told ya already. Give me your damn phone, let me smash it, and be on your way."

"I fail to see how that will—"

Einar grabbed a plumber's wrench from the shelf just below the workbench and slammed it on the leg of the bench. "Well then open your eyes, boy. Ya can't listen to your wife with a phone glued to yer ear, now can ya? Ya can't tell her what she needs to know if yer yappin' to some fool down south." Einar slammed the pipe wrench down on the bench hard. The sound made Askar flinch and take a step back. "Yer problem ain't got nothin' to do with m'daughter," Einar said in an accent most would have recognized at Northern Mainer, but Askar did not recognize at all and could barely understand. "S'got to do wit' you, ya damned fool. Now give me yer damned phone!" Einar slammed the wrench down once more.

Askar pulled his phone out of his pocket and threw it down on the bench. Einar smashed it with the wrench without looking. It shattered into four separate pieces. Askar could hear the acid from the battery sizzling on the ground, mixing with whatever had soaked itself into the dirt floor. "Now ya wanna fix it? Stop talkin' to an old man in his bahn and go tahlk to yer damned wife."

As if that closed the conversation, Einar threw the wrench onto the bench and continued searching for the hammer. Askar turned to leave, and just as he crossed through the doorway, he heard Einar mumble in a small voice: "Talk to yer wife. Ya dummy. Like t'were a goddamnt mystery."

Askar walked slowly through the dark across the yard. Like a mystery. Sure. Einar was right. The old fart that hated Askar's guts was right, and he knew it, and yet the old man still told Askar how to fix it all. So what if it had been right in front of his face? To be honest, Askar liked to hate the old man, liked to think Einar was just being an ass smashing his phone the first time, but this time it made sense. It made sense because it wasn't about him, wasn't about the business down south, wasn't about making phone calls or landing contracts. It was about his wife, and he had loved Bethany at one point in his life. Why not now? What had he done differently? Why had he changed? He knew. He really did. Bethany was, in fact, everything he wanted, was just what he had needed when he had needed it. And maybe, as ridiculous as it sounded now, that was what irked him about her. He resented her for it. Felt as though she'd figured him out, had deconstructed him so perfectly that there was nothing left of him that was secret, unique, different. Had he lost his identity because of Bethany? He wasn't so sure, but Einar was right. He needed to ask her, didn't he?

*   *   *

Einar could not find his hammer. Instead, he returned to the house with a hatchet and two screwdrivers. For what, he could not have told you, but when he tossed them down on the kitchen table and took off his coat, he knew he had made the right decision in tool choice—in lieu of the hammer, of course. He hung his coat next to Robert's on the rack in the breezeway and turned to find Jason standing by the stove, arms crossed, apparently waiting for Einar.

"I want to fix this," Jason said.

"Ah Jesus," Einar said in a sincere voice of exasperation that Jason recognized all too well. "You been around yer sister's man too much." Einar sat down at the kitchen table and examined the hatchet, took the flathead screwdriver and scraped a fleck of rust off the hatchet's head, then put them both down. Einar sighed. "I ain't yer mother. Bethany said so at dinner tonight. What can I tell ya? If she calls ya, answer yer phone. If she don't call ya, go find her and do what men have to do sometimes."

"See, I've been trying to figure that one out. What do men have to do sometimes, Pop?"

Einar looked at his son and with a sincerity he could not have feigned had he tried, Einar said, "Beg."

Jason opened his mouth to speak, but then closed it again.

"Ah, damn, boy, I ain't got the right answer fer ya. Yer mom, she'd have othingg' right smaht to tell ya, but I got othing'. You wanna know how to pull spuds? Sharpen an axe? I got that covered. But makin' a marriage work…yer mom made ours work. So long as I showed up, she'd tell me what to do and where to be, and boy, I liked it that way."

Einar sat back in the chair and Jason couldn't help but notice the old man looked terribly uncomfortable. He winced with every movement nowadays, as if he'd aged years in just a few weeks. "What about Robert?" Jason asked.

"What did you two do when you were kids? Go out back, give each other a whoopin' or two, have a beer and shut up."

Jason laughed a little, but it was a patronizing laugh. Einar knew that well enough. He sighed again. "Jason, I don't know where I was when you two grew up, but one day, you two were adults. Not kids no more. Used to be that you'd go out on the lake and thump each other with hockey sticks when you had a spat. Ten minutes later you'd be laughin' and shoutin in the barn. Now? Now you're a man, and if there's one thing I know, boy, it's that one man can't tell another how to use his brain…or his heart. Robert's a problem, sure. So's Ginny. They're your problems. But you, ya dummy, you're your biggest damn problem. So fix that one first. Stop mopin'. You've worked on yer barn and got it all out a'ya. Now fix yerself, fix yer brothah, and find your wife and hope she wants to be fixed. Cuz if she don't, well Jason, I'm out of barns fer you to fix."

Jason stood with his arms crossed a moment longer, then crossed the room and stood by Einar. He placed a hand on his father's shoulder and said, "That's the most I've heard you talk all at once in…well, ever." He patted him once more, then left the kitchen. Einar sat at the table, the screwdriver still in his right hand, watching as Jason walked through the doorway to the living room. Yes, Jason was certainly right. Einar was not a man of words, and that had been quite a little speech he'd just given…but it felt good, it did. Felt right. Just then, the floorboards beneath the table creaked for no reason at all and the windows rattled with the wind. Einar looked up at the dumb framed drawing of a woman standing by a stove that hung above the kitchen table and thought of Sarah. *I ain't yer mother,* he'd said, but looking up at that picture and thinking of what he'd just said to his son, he wondered if that was sincerely true.

*   *   *

No one saw it Angus's way.

Not even the other shitheads at Thomaston State Prison, not even the new prisoners when Thomaston shut down and moved to Warren.

No one got it. No one bothered to listen, and in a place like Warren, prisoners had a lot of opportunities—none of which were the option to grow up. Maturity simply wasn't a trait many of the folks at the prison held on to very tightly, and Angus McCausland was certainly no different. He had not grown up. And he had not moved on. Probably never would.

But he didn't really want to move on. He wanted to get the hell out of jail, find every fucker, every Hippie, every single piece of Maine shit that stood there that day and got him caught. Hell, he just wanted to rough the kid up a little, not kill him…even if he *did* think the fucking Hippie deserved to die. But he wasn't going to kill him. No, no way.

He did, though, and Angus blamed that on everyone but himself. If that Hippie hadn't put the sticker on his truck, well then there wouldn't have been any problem at all, would there? No. Angus knew that. He *knew* that. But no one saw it his way. No one could grasp that concept with their shit-for-brains heads, and no one would hear him out. The judge put him in jail, life in prison, enjoy the meal, don't bend over and shut the fuck up. And though he'd already been in for a few years, it still felt temporary to him, as if fate simply wouldn't dare leave him in the shithole prison for more than a few years. He behaved himself—only found himself in solitary once—and kept quiet. He'd seen movies as a kid, and that was how they always got out early. They were good. They were quiet. And then they got out.

Angus wanted out.

High on his list of things to do:

Find Jason Coates.

Oh, yes, he remembered that name. Remembered it well. Angus could have skipped town. Could have gone to Canada. Could have just gotten in his truck and left the fucking country behind, damn the

Hippies and screw his father, fuck Maine and all that. Canada. Yeah, he could have made it okay. But Coates. That shithead knocked him out—one punch, he'd heard, but he couldn't believe that—and so he ended up in the joint watching his asshole at shower time and sleeping with one eye open. Sure, okay, Angus could make it work for now. But not forever. Fate wouldn't let that happen.

And it didn't.

On Thanksgiving day, almost nine years after he went in for murder, Angus McCausland saw fate walking past him on the street. And Angus stopped him, told ol' fate he owed Angus a handshake. Fate did just that; as the bus bounced and bucked down a rutted dirt road, thirty-two prisoners aboard—including the illustrious Angus McCausland—Fate shook Angus's hand and shook it firm, with meaning and intent. They were headed up the Stud Mill Road northeast of Old Town on paper mill property, a regular excursion that would take them to the middle of nowhere and ten to twelve hours of hard, manual labor clearing slash, when the bus blew a tire and flipped.

Angus didn't know it, but five of the nine guards were killed almost immediately when the bus slammed on its side and slid down into a ditch. The head bitch, Officer Utley, flew backward through the windshield of the bus. Angus saw that clear as day from his seat near the middle of the bus. Out of the four remaining guards, one was unconscious, another had lost his left arm and was screaming rather constantly, and the other two were busy pulling their buddies from the wreck.

Angus had two cuts. One on his left hand and one on his left shin. That was all. He knew none of the other prisoners on this particular excursion and felt no strong desire to heave their bodies from the wreck. Some were dead, some were not. But his chains had broken—yes, Fate shook his hand and shook it well—and so he climbed through the nearest window and simply walked away, into the woods and down the road. Nearly an hour had passed before anyone realized he was gone, and another two and a half hours before anything could be done about it. By that time, Angus had already hitched a ride on the back of a logging truck back to Old Town, then north to Passadumkeag, where he stole a jacket from a general store to hide at least most of the bright orange jump suit he wore. The storekeeper, realizing a prisoner had just strolled into his *fine* establishment, was the first to trip the alarms on Angus McCausland.

It took him the better part of the night, but Angus hitched his way up Interstate 95 to Medway, where he ditched his jumpsuit altogether after stealing a pair of pants and a t-shirt at an all-night truck stop. He slept in the bathroom there, and when morning broke, he hitched a ride up north with a long haul trucker named Perry, then walked for almost three hours on route 11 before hitching all the way up to Fort Kent. It took him most of the day, but he was finally back home. Fort Kent.

Angus remembered the town as though he'd tromped through it only the day before. Not much had changed—there was a Walgreen's and a new Shop N' Save, but otherwise everything looked exactly as he'd left it—and he navigated his way to CR44, out toward his Pop's place. He'd gotten word two years ago that his old man had died, but he wanted to see the place anyway for two reasons: one, spitting on that shit shack would be a satisfying pleasure, and two, it was only a three mile walk through the woods from his Pop's old place to the home of the Coates. Angus figured Jason didn't live there anymore, but he also figured his Ma or Pop might have a good idea where Angus's old high school buddy Jason might be.

As the afternoon sun fought the wind to warm him, Angus began walking north on CR44 toward his Pop's place, toward home.

Toward Jason Coates.

IV

UP 'TIL NOW
— or —
DECEMBER

Hello?

Hi.

…Hi.

How are you?

I'm okay. Good. I'm up at my Pop's.

Yeah, I figured.

How are you?

Not bad.

Good. Good. That's good, Gin.

…

I really want to…talk about this. Can we?

I don't know, Jason. I don't know. It's just…a lot right now, you know?

Yeah. I know. But I want to try and make this right. I have to try, you know? I have to at least…I have to at least try. Is it bad to try?

No. Not bad to try.

141

Good. Can I...can I see you soon?

...

Ginny?

I want to see you, Jason. I do. But I don't—

Look, we can try, and if it gets uncomfortable—

It will *be uncomfortable, Jason. If you don't know that—*

I know it will, but the sooner we try the sooner it might be less strange. I mean, we've got a lot to talk about, right?

Yes.

So. Can we?

Yes. I think so.

Good.

But Jason.

Yeah?

I can't promise anything.

I know.

No, I mean it. I mean I can't. Promise. Anything.

...

Jason?

Yeah, I got it.

Goodnight.

Yeah, goodnight.

*　　*　　*

Jason remembered the first time he made the drive down to Portland. The first time in the driver's seat, that is. Robert sat shotgun. It wasn't long after Robert had been released from the hospital and he still had that big dumb cast on his leg. Robert couldn't drive with his leg molded into position with plaster of Paris and whatever else they put in that damn thing—it felt like iron to Robert—so Jason, who was still seventeen at the time and was three weeks away from his eighteenth birthday and seven weeks away from his encounter with Angus McCausland, sat in the driver's seat on the long ride down to Portland.

Jason did not hold this day in his memory as something momentous or special because of the drive itself. What happened after the drive was, in fact, the more important memory that kept kicking at him every so often throughout his life since. Maybe he wasn't entirely sure why, but that's how it went. He'd sit at his desk at the Press Herald and remember running through South Portland. He would be up at Einar's chopping wood and see the police lights and smell the stench of the dumpsters behind the gas station. Those memories, obtrusive and unwelcome, always seemed to peck at him at all the right times.

As he and Robert loaded their respective cars for the journey back south, occasionally eyeing each other with a mix of malice, anger, and yearning for reconciliation, Jason knew this was his moment to talk to his brother...but all he could think about was that night in South Portland, his night alone, his single slip-up that sent him on an adventure of sorts that he wished more or less every day he had never taken.

*   *   *

"Next left."

"Here?"

"No. Second driveway."

Robert pointed to the second driveway and said, "Just beyond the gas station sign there."

Jason turned the wheel and pulled into the parking lot of a shitbox motel named The Docks. They were nowhere near the waterfront, but that, Jason supposed, was exactly what cheap motels counted on: the illusion of and yearning for better places. He parked close to the office, ran inside to get a room, and came back out five minutes later with a key. He pulled the car over toward room seventeen and slotted Sarah Coates' Buick into the parking spot closest to the door. Getting Robert out of the passenger seat then proved to be a task—the cast didn't allow much in the way of wiggle room—but after a brief struggle they got him extracted from the car and safely on crutches.

When Jason opened the door to the room, he was hit with something he had only really expected in his imagination: a stench. Subtle, but there.

"Oh, jeez," he said, waving his hand in front of his nose. "What the hell's that smell?"

Robert hopped on his crutches past his little brother and into the room. "The smell of destitution, brother," Robert said. Destitution. Robert had been in school up until the accident and took every opportunity—though subtly—to remind Jason of that fact. The word destitution was one such method: big word equaled big disappointment. Robert had ways of keeping Jason in tune with the fact that a life had been ruined that night and it was by Jason's hands. They didn't need to talk about it for that fact to remain ultimately clear.

Jason followed Robert into the room. "Smells like a hooker died in here."

Robert plopped down on the bed. "Probably did. Recently. And violently."

"That's gross."

"Grab the bags out of the trunk."

Jason did as he was told.

They had come to South Portland for Willie and Sarah. An old friend of theirs was flying into Portland the following day—Jason couldn't for the life of him remember their names, though he had apparently met them once several years ago—and Jason and Robert had come down to pick them up. Since their flight in was an early one, Jason and Robert came down the day before to stay the night and get to the airport early. They had driven around parts of Portland for almost an hour and a half, looking for a cheap hotel or motel, but the ones that weren't too expensive for them were full this particular weekend because the Portland Sea Dogs had made the playoffs (finally) the same weekend as the Harley rally down by the Old Port. The city was packed. So they headed to South Portland, the cheaper, not-so-pristine area where tourists rarely ventured. South Portland was an okay place, but it had its blemishes. Jason and Robert were sleeping in one of them tonight.

Jason dropped their bags on the floor in front of the tiny table that held the television. They lay on their beds for the next three hours, watching T.V. and waiting for the pizza delivery guy to drop off their dinner. By the time he finally did arrive and Jason and Robert polished off the pizza, night had fallen and Robert had dozed off. Jason hung around for another half hour before he got bored enough to wander outside toward the gas station next door.

He went inside and bought himself a six-pack. Jason looked twenty-five easily, so he never really had much trouble buying booze at seventeen, unless he was buying up near home, where just about everyone either knew who he was or knew Willie and Sarah. But here, he looked twenty-five and could act the same when the mood suited him, so he bought himself a six-pack of Milwaukee's Best and left the store. A group of five guys—all of them maybe in their late teens or early twenties, and all fairly big men—stood in a huddle by the payphone that hung on the wall by the corner of the gas station. Jason glanced at them briefly, then began walking down the street to find a nice stoop on which to rest and imbibe. His foot had barely left the cracked pavement of the parking lot when a voice shouted out from behind him.

"Hey, man."

Jason turned, expecting to see one of the guys from the huddle, but instead a grizzled, dirty and old man stood not three feet to the left of the huddle. "You got a dollar so I can…get a, uh…sandwich?"

Jason smiled. He tore one of his beers from the six-pack and looked back at the man. "Nah," Jason said, then tossed the beer toward the homeless wreck of a man.

But the beer never reached the man's hands. The can left Jason's hand and he immediately knew he had thrown off-course. The can spiraled toward the huddle of guys who were standing by the pay-phone and hit one of them squarely in the back. They all wheeled around as a single unit, it seemed, and Jason's breath caught in his throat. "Shit," he mumbled.

"What the *fuck*," one of them yelled. It wasn't even the one that the can had hit. They were all walking toward him now. "You got a fuck-ing *problem*?"

"No, man," Jason stammered, "I'm sorry about that. I didn't mean to—"

"Yeah, you didn't mean to, but you did."

The entire group of them were now huddled around Jason. "Look, take the beer. I didn't mean to hit you guys, so here's the rest of the beer."

The only one of them who had spoken so far looked at the beer. As Jason watched the man's hand reach out and take the five remaining beers, he took the opportunity to examine the man's face: he had a goatee, dark skin and even darker eyes, and a shiny, bald head. He was probably in his mid-twenties, if Jason had to guess, but to Jason, anyone above the teenage years were, in his mind, in their mid-twenties.

The bald man began to laugh. The group laughed with him. "Look around, boy," the man said. "How many of us do you see?"

Jason did as he was told. Eight. Eight guys. Eight very large, very angry guys, most of them smoking and wearing black. Half of them looked Puerto Rican and the other half looked…pissed.

"This is five beers. What we gonna do with five beers?"

"I'll go buy some more."

"Damn right you will, boy. Now get the fuck in there and buy us some beer."

Jason did just that. When he came back out with two more six packs, he only had seventy-five cents left in his pocket. Jason was not a small kid—hockey had built his muscles in a hurry—but even he, in his cocky, youthful and stupid attitude, knew he could not take these guys on without getting worked over. He looked at the beer and sighed. He would drink none of these tonight, he thought.

The huddle of guys stood outside the door. He handed the six packs over and began to walk off again, this time back toward the motel.

"Where you think you're goin'?"The bald guy said.

"What?"

He took a step toward Jason. "I said, where. Do. You. Think. You're. Going."

Jason opened his mouth to say something, but nothing came out. The group laughed. "Get over here, kid," the bald guy said. Jason did as instructed. When he reached the group again, they began to walk—again, it seemed, as a whole unit—down in the direction Jason had initially started to walk after buying the first six pack. "Come on," the bald man said.

"Look, I'm sorry, and I bought you guys beer. We're straight now. I just want to go."

"We ain't straight, kid," the bald man said.

"Well what would set us straight?" Jason said, now getting nervous to the point of being shaky.

The bald man cracked open a beer and handed it to Jason. "Drink a beer with us. That might set us straight."

Jason took the beer, almost unbelievingly, and drank from it. The group laughed again as the bald man handed out beers. They all cracked one open as they walked down the street, and Jason, though he didn't intend to, felt a bit more at ease now. He was drinking a beer with them. That couldn't be so bad, right?

The group walked south for a mile or more, drinking their beers and keeping an eye out for cops. Jason listened to the banter and occasionally laughed, but he kept quiet for the most part. When they reached the southern terminus of the street on which they had been walking, Jason could see the bright lights of yet another gas station/mini-mart. The bald guy stopped walking. The rest of the group followed suit.

"I'm hungry," he said, and two of the guys laughed. They began walking again toward the gas station and they entered the store, again it seemed, as one solid entity. This time, Jason was a part of that entity. As soon as they passed through the doors, four of the guys went left, two went up the center aisle, and Jason and the bald man went right. As soon as they dipped into one of the aisles, the bald man grabbed Jason tightly by the back of his coat. "Stay close," he said, then shoved a handful of candy bars into Jason's left pocket. They turned a corner and the bald guy shoved a bag of chips down the front of Jason's coat. The motion of his arm was so fluid and quick that Jason never even saw it clearly. In fact, each time the bald guy swiped something and shoved it in one of Jason's pockets, it seemed as though nothing unusual were happening at all.

Jason snuck a peek at the man behind the counter. He was leaning on his elbows, a magazine splayed out on the countertop in front of him, alternately glancing at whatever rag he was reading and scanning the store for anything suspicious. But the bald guy and his friends were smart. One of them stood close by the counter, apparently contemplating what flavor of beef jerky he wanted to pull from the bins to the cashier's right, and another approached the cashier directly. "You got a key to that bathroom over there?"

The cashier gave him a suspicious look, then ducked his head beneath the counter to fish out the key. When he did so, Jason watched as every member of the group, at various locations throughout the store, swiped something off the shelves and shoved it in a pocket without so much as a whisper of sound. It was like a perfectly executed break into the offensive zone on a power play, Jason's hockey-obsessed mind thought. It seemed choreographed, scripted, a dance that had been rehearsed over and over for months and months.

"Never mind," the guy said, "I don't have to pee anymore."

He walked through the electronic sliding glass doors, leaving the key on the counter. The guy contemplating the beef jerky slabs followed closely behind. Five seconds later, two more of them left the store. Then another. Then another. After all of them had left, Jason and the bald guy made their way toward the door...but the cashier noticed. He saw. The wrapper of a Mr. Goodbar poked just far enough out of Jason's right sleeve by his wrist, a tiny yellow flag waving hello to the cashier.

"Hey!" He yelled.

The bald guy wasted no time. He bolted, and Jason, always a quick learner, followed. When they reached the parking lot outside, the entire group saw them running and joined in. They took a right, then a left, then went through an alleyway and took another right at the next intersection. They ran into a park and stopped by a swing set. They all laughed. Jason laughed, too.

They spent the next twenty minutes or so digging through all that they had stolen, picking out what they wanted and tossing the rest aside. They ate. They finished up the beers that one of the guys had the wherewithal to grab off the curb by the mini-mart before running off down the street. Jason felt good. He did.

But then the blue and red lights flashed and they had to run again. They ran fast. They did not stop. Jason had no idea at all where they were going or where they had been. A slight pang of panic reached him when he realized he no longer knew how to get back to the motel. The cops followed. There were cops on foot. There were cops in cars. It seemed there was a cop at every intersection they came to, a shouting voice down every alley, a reason to keep running after every step. Now Jason grew more and more nervous. Now he grew scared. What if the cops caught them? He would go to jail. Willie would kill him. *Robert* would kill him, would take that stupid cast right off his leg and beat Jason to death with it.

Suddenly jail didn't sound so bad.

They ran down a street that, surprisingly enough, turned into dirt. The slope of it made it difficult to keep a good footing as they ran, and Jason slipped twice on the loose gravel. He lost track of how much time had passed, but he figured it had gone on past midnight by now. The air was certainly chilly enough now to warrant that assumption, and it felt like he'd been running with these guys for just short of a century. They all made their way as a group down the dirt road until it flattened out into a large parking area of sorts. Jason recognized it immediately: it looked just like the public works garage up in Bangor, but this one was bigger and had more sheds. The massive garage door to one of the sheds stood wide open, its dark mouth staring at the guys in a semi-inviting and semi-mettlesome manner. They began to run toward it.

"Find yourself a good spot to hide or you'll be hiding in jail tonight," the bald guy said as he ran past Jason. It was the last time Jason ever saw him. At least four of the guys were running toward the garage door when suddenly the lights inside the garage flickered on. They all stopped, reversed direction and scrambled to find another refuge. Jason simply froze in the middle of the dirt yard, staring at the open garage, then turning and staring at the dirt road he had just run down. Sweat stood out on his forehead, cool and damp and dripping quickly down into his eyes. The blue and red lights of the cop cars shone up at the top of the hill and progressed quickly toward him. As they began to drop down the hill, Jason ran to his left and huddled between a massive plow blade that was being held up on concrete blocks and a salt mound that was covered by a blue tarp. He crouched in behind the plow blade and pulled himself up underneath the blue tarp.

Then he closed his eyes and waited.

Silence.

For a horrendously long time, silence.

He was vaguely aware of the cop cars retreating back up the hill after what must have been a half hour or so, but he didn't dare crawl out from underneath the tarp. He considered it, but then he remembered the cops on foot. Yes, they would be down here, too. He stayed put, and it was a lucky thing he did. A few minutes after he first considered crawling out from underneath the tarp, he heard a voice shouting. Then another voice. Then the slam of something metal hitting something else metal. A cop car returned. One of the guys from the group was getting arrested. Then two of them. Then a third. An hour passed. The cops did not find any more of the men. Jason stayed put.

The night had turned chilly and Jason's sweat made his clothes cling tightly to his body. After a while of hiding and nervously waiting, he began to shiver. Then he got drowsy. Then he fell asleep. He slept until his shivering woke him up. He opened his eyes and listened: silence yet again. How long had he slept? Minutes? Hours? It didn't matter; he could not stay under the tarp any longer, cops or not. He was freezing. He crept out slowly and hunkered behind the plow blade again. This time, he saw no lights, sensed no movement. The light to the garage was off and the door shut tightly. It had to be early morning by now. Jason stood up and began walking up the dirt road, back in the direction from which he had come earlier.

His Pop had once told him that the worst thing one could do in the woods of Maine was get lost. And if you were going to get lost, you at least needed to know how to survive. Jason had no problems being lost in the woods, and he knew he could survive there, but this wasn't the woods. And he certainly was good and lost. As he kicked his way up the dirt road, he zipped up his coat as far as it would go and flipped the collar up high. Then he shoved his hands in his pockets and fought the urge to panic. "Shit," he said under his breath. He could feel the tears wanting to find his eyes, could sense his muscles wanting to react to the adrenaline that was surely still creeping through his body. He fought it. He fought it all the way up the dirt road until it turned to pavement, then fought it some more as he wandered through a random neighborhood. Then another random neighborhood. And another. And another.

An hour or so passed before Jason finally spotted a payphone. He dialed the operator and asked her to patch him through to the Docks Motel in South Portland. She did so, and he deposited his last quarter into the phone.

"Docks Motel," a man's voice said on the other end of the line.

"Hello, can you please ring Room Seventeen? It's under the name Coates."

"Just a second."

Click. Then click again. Then ring. Ring. Ring. Ring.

"Hello." Robert's groggy voice.

"Robert, I'm...shit, I'm lost."

"Jason? Where the hell..."

"Look, I'm at a payphone. It's outside some building...shit, hang on." Jason let the phone dangle from its cord as he went to check the nearest street sign. Then he returned and said, "Ellsworth and Lagrange streets. That's where I am."

"Where the hell is that?"

"If I knew that, do you think I'd be calling you at midnight?"

"It's four in the morning."

"Jesus. Can you come get me? I'm freezing."

"Jason, I can't drive. How the hell am I going to drive?"

"I don't know. I don't know!" Jason nearly shouted. He slammed the receiver against the side of the phone kiosk. When he pressed it to his ear again, he heard the operator's message: *To continue this call, please deposit twenty-five cents now.* "Shit! Robert, you have to come get me. You have to—"

Your call has been disconnected. Please hang up and try your call again.

Jason returned the receiver to the cradle.

He walked up the street without the slightest hint as to whether he was walking in the right direction or not. A half hour passed. He began to panic. And shiver. His teeth chattered. He rubbed his arms on his chest. A cop car passed by but the cop did not so much as cast a curious glance at Jason. He walked on.

Then he saw headlights.

Robert.

Sarah Coates' car pulled up to the sidewalk. Robert sat in the driver's seat.

"Get me out of the driver's seat," he said, then added, "and get in the damn car." Robert was sitting half in the driver's seat and half on the center console, his massive, white cast propped up and over the console and into the passenger's side of the car. Jason made his way to the driver's side door and helped Robert get out. "How did you even get *in* the car?" Jason asked.

"Don't ask. Just get me out."

He did.

"How did you find me?"

"Asked the guy at the front desk. What the hell are you doing out this late? In South fucking Portland of all places? What the hell is wrong with you?"

The question hung in the air between them as Jason followed Robert's directions back to the motel. What was wrong with him? How did he continually find himself in these ridiculous situations? And why did he always manage to make them worse?

And how was it, inevitably, that he would involve Robert in it? Robert, who always seemed to have a solution, or a way out, or the directions home?

"I don't know," Jason said finally. "I have no idea what's wrong with me."

Robert looked at Jason's face as the street lights washed over it and disappeared. He punched Jason in the arm. "Shake it off, little brother. Tell me what the hell happened to you tonight, then forget about it."

He did. And then he forgot about it.

Because Robert said so.

And Robert was right.

He always was.

*　　　*　　　*

December First.

Einar William Coates woke early and began walking up his dirt driveway toward the county road. He didn't know it yet, but he was walking to Sarah's grave that day.

Jason left his apartment in Portland around six-thirty to meet Ginny at the coffee shop down the block. She was not there when he arrived, so he ordered a coffee and sat at the corner table. She walked in ten minutes later and sat down without a word. Jason had not taken a single sip of his coffee and would not do so throughout their meeting.

Bethany had not slept at home the night before, so this morning she left her cousin's place and took a cab downtown. She wasn't sure where one went to file divorce papers, but she felt confident she would find out.

Robert had not slept at all last night. He stayed up late with an old and dear friend, his buddy Johnny Walker, instead. Jason had been right about one thing: the booze made him forget who he was sometimes. Before the night was over and the morning sun hit his eyes for the first time, Robert had driven his fist through a wall and thrown an entire stereo across the room, shattering it into a flotsam of pieces on the carpet.

And Askar, sans-cell phone, had no way of contacting anyone. All the important numbers he had stored in his phone were gone and he had never bothered to memorize any of them. Not even Bethany's. And suddenly, that seemed the only important phone call he could make. He spent most of the morning looking for her in lieu of going to work.

All of this on the morning of December First.

155

*　　*　　*

Maggie had not been to work in three days. Robert knew this because he had been watching her every morning. Well, not exactly watching *her*, per se, because she had not yet come out of her apartment. But he was aware of where she was and was not throughout her day. He had not been to work himself during those three days, and he had stayed consistently drunk since returning from Einar's the day after Thanksgiving. Each passing day felt like an exercise in purging, but really, he hadn't purged at all. He dwelled. He wallowed. This was Jason's doing, not Maggie's, and although he had not talked to either of them about what had happened—at least not beyond the cursory facts of the matter—he was certain the blame was to rest squarely on the shoulders of his younger brother. Maggie? No. Maggie needed to be watched. Maggie needed *protecting*.

What Robert did not realize was that Maggie did, in fact, need protecting…from him.

He stood across the street from her apartment for almost an hour, drinking a bottle from a paper bag and pacing his stuttered, broken limp of a walk. He left at noon. Went home. Showered. Fell asleep naked on his bed, the bottle of Johnny Walker tipped over and spilling over his sheets and mattress as he slept.

The next four days would be a carbon copy of this one for Robert.

*　　*　　*

Maggie watched from her kitchen window, the curtains drawn closed except for a tiny slit through which she peered, and counted his paces. Ten. Fifteen. Thirty. Seventy-five. Robert. Robert. Robert.

She loved him and she feared him, depending on the day and

whether his right hand held on fast to one of his buddies, his bottles. She watched him pace, but she kept her eyes on the brown paper bag in his right hand that undoubtedly held a bottle of whiskey. He was a sucker for the whiskey. She looked at his thick hands and remembered, vaguely, the times when that hand stroked through her blonde hair in a loving motion, a gentle one, a sincere one. She remembered times when that hand wrote her letters on post-it notes: Miss You. Love You. You And Me Tonight. Stuck on her refrigerator or on the clock radio, the glass of water on her nightstand or on the mirror in the bathroom.

Then she remembered that hand swinging at her. Connecting with her cheek. Curled into a fist and plunging into her gut. Never hard enough to *really* hurt but plenty hard to get the message across. That hand. It never acted without the bottle, but really, how often were the two separated?

One hundred and twelve paces. Maggie pulled the curtains tight and walked away. The last sliver of light that had slipped through the crack in the curtains disappeared and Maggie was glad to see it go.

*   *   *

There's a difference between a November cold and a December one. The cold in November seems more moist, comfortably chilled but not biting. The biting cold doesn't arrive until December, that dry, cracking bitch of a cold that strikes and strikes and abates only long enough to let you forget that it might strike again. On this first day of December, though he stood nearly a hundred miles from any ocean, Einar recognized the dry cold for what it was. He walked on down CR44 without gloves or a scarf nonetheless, the ground underneath his feet crunching and crackling in response to the moisture that had seeped its way into the dirt and frozen there.

His intention that morning had not been to go to Sarah's grave. In fact, after the funeral, he did not intend to go visit the grave at all. Why would he? Sarah was no more in that hole in the ground than she was in the Empire State Building or the Upper Peninsula of Michigan. Einar knew exactly where Sarah was. The house. The walls. The creaks and the cracks. The smells and the sounds. The textures and the tastes. His wife was at home.

And yet as he walked down CR44, he knew exactly where he was going. He could not have said why, but his certainty only grew with each booted step, each crack and crunch of the frozen ground beneath him. His knee ached miserably. His back did the same, and the walk certainly wasn't a short one. But he had all day, and he intended to use it. The wind had been more active this year than it had in autumns past, and with his hands tucked in his pockets and his eyes cast down, another gust pressed unpleasantly against his face. It pushed him backward as if to warn him to go back, forget the whole thing, nothing good waited for him down this road. But Einar kept on. Einar always did.

It took him nearly an hour to walk to the cemetery and another twenty minutes to find Sarah's headstone. Against Einar's desires, her headstone was small, unassuming, hard to spot amongst the much larger, imposing ones that surrounded it. Sarah had wanted it this way. "Didn't make a fuss in life, don't want to make one in death," she had said to Einar just over a week before her death. Einar had not broached the subject, had no real desire to do so, but Sarah wanted to know everything was worked out for her. So it could be easy. So Einar would not have to take care of it. So no one would dwell. She didn't make a fuss.

When Bethany was in grade school—Einar couldn't quite remember what grade she had been in, but she was around nine or ten years old at the time—her art teacher took the class on a field trip to Bangor. They all loaded up onto a bus and drove the nearly three hours south to visit the Children's' Museum and Mount Hope Cemetery. The cemetery was famous throughout Maine and even throughout New England because it was supposedly one of the oldest garden cemeteries in the country, and Hannibal Hamlin was buried there. Sarah's hackles had risen at the thought of her young daughter wandering around an old cemetery—what if she gets scared or if a gravestone falls on her? Those stones are rickety, Sarah had said—but they signed the permission slip nonetheless and off Bethany went.

When she returned that evening, Sarah picked her up at the school. It was around six in the evening by then and Bethany sat in the back seat, quickly firing off all the details of the day and pulling random slips of paper or leaves or other souvenirs out of her backpack. Sarah occasionally glanced in the rearview mirror to see what her daughter was holding up to her, but after a while, Bethany's words meshed into one long sentence and Sarah lost track. She just smiled and said, "Very nice, dear."

It wasn't until later that night, after Sarah had tucked Bethany in and watched her fall asleep, that she noticed the thin sheet of tracing paper on Bethany's tiny desk. Sarah picked it up and walked into the light of the hallway, then gasped and put her hand to her mouth. She stared at it a moment longer, then made her way downstairs to the living room where Einar was sitting and reading a newspaper.

"Look at this," Sarah said to Einar. He put his newspaper down on the table next to him and held the paper Sarah handed him. Einar knew what it was immediately, and he knew what Sarah *thought* it was immediately, too. "Grave rubbin'," Einar said as though he had just clarified a muddled word in a newspaper.

"I know what it is," Sarah said. "It was in Bethany's things. From her field trip. Can you believe that?"

Einar examined the paper once more. Scrawled in blue crayon at the bottom right of the paper was Bethany's name, big, sloppy letters. The rubbing itself had been taken from a stone of a man named Jeshua Billings Drinkwater. Born 1822, Died 1890. Loving Father. "Just an art project," Einar said. "The boys did 'em when they were her age."

"Our boys?"

"Ayuh."

"I never saw them."

"Robert never cared much for his," Einar said. "Jason brought me his in the barn after school when he did his. Long time ago now. Had me hang it next to the window. Don't know what happened to it from there."

Sarah looked stunned. "You never told me?"

"Just a grave rubbin'," Einar said, handing it back to her. "Don't mean nothin'."

"Nothing?" Sarah said, exasperated. "This is *someone*, Willie. This is a ghost in our house."

"Then it'll be a ghost in good company," Einar had said. He intended this to be a joke, but Sarah was obviously not amused. She returned the rubbing to Bethany's room and they never talked about it again.

As Einar looked down at Sarah's headstone, he thought of that conversation and realized how wrong he had been. He didn't really believe that Sarah's soul lingered in this place, this empty, grassy knoll, but then he thought of some young kid coming along with a crayon and some tracing paper, hunkering down on top of Sarah's grave, holding that piece of paper up to the stone and rubbing the crayon on its side against the words: Sarah Gamble Coates. Taking the years she lived, the year she died. Copying who she was, why she was. Taking it home and thinking of her as a novelty, as art. As a *lesson*. It seemed suddenly and horribly wrong to Einar.

He knelt down slowly, his knees popping and grinding as he descended, and pressed his right hand against the cold of the smooth stone. Fallen leaves had gathered around the base of the stone, but Einar did not bother to brush them away; they covered the fresh dirt that still swelled from its new placement and his knees drove into the earth beneath him that swelled similarly, not yet settled from Sarah's interment not long ago. The glassy smoothness of the face of her headstone reflected the clouds above with such a fierce sheen that Einar felt compelled to hunch just a little further to catch his own reflection in it. He did not. That would be too horrible, too real.

Instead, he ran the index finger of his right hand over the carved letters: SARAH. GAMBLE. COATES. Over and over again. He went on for so long tracing his fingers over the letters that someone passing by might think he had carved the letters themselves with his bare finger. Over and over again. SARAH. GAMBLE. COATES. The feel of the stone did not so much bother him as did the sheen of it, the reflective surface and its smoothness in direct opposition to its surroundings. Einar hated the stone then, wanted it replaced immediately, wanted to knock it down right then and there with his booted foot and replace it with something misshapen, rough, dull.

He stood up finally, his knees again popping and grinding in protest, and stood back a few feet from the stone. He pressed his right hand to his face, just underneath his nose, and rubbed it side to side. He could smell the stinging scent of the rock on his fingers, could imagine particles of it dancing and jumping on his fingertips. Then he dropped his hand again, ending the moment that had come closest to being an outward sign of emotion Einar had had since Sarah's death. Einar finally pried his eyes away from the stone and looked to his right, up the slight, grassy incline toward the mausoleum and the cemetery entrance beyond.

That was when he noticed another man, maybe a hundred yards to his right, standing at another headstone, his hands folded in front of him and his head dropped. He stood alone, unmoving, and though Einar could not see the man's face, he imagined the man's eyes were closed tightly and his features sagged only slightly. Einar watched the man lament silently, stoically, for five minutes or more before the man looked up and turned his head in Einar's direction. Einar could not have said whether he and the man had truly made eye contact from such a great distance, but he could have believed it so. The man looked at Einar for only a brief moment, then walked away toward the cemetery gates, his hands shoved solidly in his coat pockets.

Einar waited another few minutes, then followed suit.

The walk back home took much longer than the walk to the cemetery had. Einar felt distracted, maybe even a little angry, but he could not pinpoint why. The wind beat him the way it had done on his walk in the other direction, but this time he did not notice as much; it seemed now to be a triviality, a minor inconvenience that paled in comparison to the larger issues at hand, which were…what, exactly?

When Einar finally climbed the steps to his front porch, the sky had clouded over and threatened either rain or a dusting of snow. His booted feet thumped on the worn steps, pounding a dull, hollow thud into Einar's ears that, contrary to what should have been the case, comforted him. Told him he was home. Told him he was not alone in his house, because his house was Sarah, or so he had convinced himself. He reached the front door and began to pull it open, but then stopped.

He placed his left hand on the wooden placard that hung next to the front door, the raw disk of a felled and sawed tree, the wood with his name carved into it with sweeping curves and distinctly artful letters. Einar ran his fingers over the letters of his name as he had done to Sarah's on the gravestone: EINAR. Then, WILLIAM. Then, COATES. He did this twice, then dropped his hand to his side. Einar swung the door open and looked inside his house and finally, finally, saw something worth noting.

*   *   *

Frank sat in the driver's seat of his Pop's pick-up truck as he made his way back home with Gerald Jordan sitting shotgun—sans-pants, as usual. They had just visited the doctor, and though Gerald continually addressed the man as the long-dead Doctor Billings, this younger and very tolerant Doctor Paquette told Frank that aside from the Alzheimer's and senility, Gerald Jordan was in good health. This assessment seemed slightly ironic to Frank, but he said nothing.

As they made their way north on CR44, crossing that very distinct line between the end of the pavement and the beginning of the ruts of frozen mud and dirt, Frank spotted someone walking up ahead on the side of the road. It appeared to be a man, but the figure was still too far off in the distance for Frank to be sure. The sun was starting to dip behind the horizon and the ghost-moon had already risen, but Frank was sure his eyes weren't playing tricks on him: the man had turned, saw the truck coming, and ran into the woods. This was verified when Gerald piped up and said, "Must've heard our sirens and seen the flashing lights. Weeeooohh weeeooohh!"

They drove past the spot where Frank estimated the man had dived into the woods but he saw no trace of him. No sooner had Frank and Gerald passed that spot than Frank had forgotten all about the man, his thoughts returning to the spot in his mind he so often returned to as of late—the spot occupied by two women that seemed to dominate his every emotion recently: Natalie and Eleanor. Because of this sudden inundation of thought, because of his preoccupation with these seemingly polar-opposite women, Frank did not notice that same man standing by the road only a few yards past where Frank had last seen him. Frank did not notice his face, did not recognize the glare in the man's stupid and mostly empty gaze, did not realize he had just passed Angus McCausland, former schoolmate and current escaped prisoner. He simply did not notice.

*   *   *

Angus made his way north on CR44, the biting wind nipping at him occasionally and the dead leaves, remnants of autumn, rushing past his feet like a traffic jam finally freed of obstruction. After diving into the brush and bushes to avoid being seen by the pick-up truck, Angus did not see another vehicle pass him. He walked all the way to his former home, now just an abandoned shack mired in brambles and overgrown weeds, and kicked his way down what used to be the driveway all the way up to the front steps. The wood of the house had turned a deathly gray, the kind of uninviting material that would bite fingers with a sliver or two the second you got within a close enough distance of it. All the windows had been shattered, and though Angus himself would have been the one to do the deed in his younger days, he now felt bitter resentment at whatever stupid kids had taken rocks and carelessly thrown them through the windows.

He pressed his right hand against the front door, which hung askew on only one hinge. It crashed to the floor when he pushed on it. His footsteps creaked and thudded on the rotted floorboards as he stood in what used to be the living room—or, as a more apt description, the room in which Angus's father sat and drank, alone, in his stink and cigarette smoke. The room still stunk, as if his father's cigarettes had bled into the walls for so long that the stench had found permanent residence there. Except now, the stench mixed with another sour smell, the smell of rotten wood and decay. Angus grunted and walked into the kitchen.

It was here he first saw his father beat his mother. It was also here that he saw his mother for the last time. The kitchen table—no more than a glorified card table that was at one time flanked by folding steel chairs—surprisingly still sat in the corner of the kitchen, a hole rotted through the middle and the legs bent at odd angles. The chairs were gone. Angus looked at the table for a moment, remembering his bitch of a mother standing by it, serving up some sad excuse for dinner and then sitting quietly by her husband's side. Angus remembered this and hated the memory, hated the taste of it, the smell of it. The goddamned smell of this place! Had it always been this bad?

He thought of the day his mother died and felt a quick and slight pang of remorse, of sadness. She had died from 'complications resulting from a kidney rupture,' a rupture Angus's father had caused with a swift punch to his wife's side. It was almost two years before he went to jail for it, but by that time Angus was already in jail himself. And this was what became of their home. Not surprising, Angus thought. He picked up the kitchen table and threw it at the cabinets above the stove.

The back yard played host to weeds so high Angus could not see over them. But a path had been worn from the back door to the bulk head through the brown grass and weeds that seemed to hover over the house itself. He followed the path and pulled the bulkhead open. A familiar smell of moisture and dirt reached his nostrils and made him smile. The first time he had gotten drunk took place among the asbestos and rat shit in this basement. The first time he got high, too. One time he and Bennett Kingfield had snorted coke down there, but that stuff gave Angus such a headache he never did it again. Kingfield died of it shortly after Angus went to prison. Too much of a good thing, Angus supposed.

The steps, a cracked concrete overwhelmed with spider webs and filth, had always felt stunted and short to Angus growing up, and even now he took them two at a time until he reached the earthen floor of the basement. Bums had been here, he knew that much. Beer bottles everywhere—not his dad's brand—and scraps of cardboard, ashes from a fire, the smell of soot and creosote, the smell of other rot and decay that only the human body could produce. Angus saw all these signs and more, but he ignored them in favor of what he had been looking for in the first place: a sleeping bag, dirty and bunched up on itself in the corner. He went to it and picked it up. It held its shape, a crusty, dirty and frozen V. Angus sighed.

He carried the sleeping bag back upstairs and into the house, smoothed it out straight, then started a fire in the middle of the living room using stale old wood and a fold of matches he had stolen from the general store in Where-The-Fuck-Ever, Maine. He put the sleeping bag as close to the fire as he could get it without burning it and watched it thaw. For the next several hours, that was what Angus McCausland did: sat by the fire in the middle of his living room, staring into the flames and wondering what he would do next, after his sleeping bag thawed and he got himself a good sleep. Never one for plans, Angus decided to let things happen as they might. He stayed at his house that night, slept by the fire, warmed himself and, with what little intellect he had swimming in his brain, wondered what tomorrow would bring him. Fate was, after all, on his side.

*   *   *

Jason looked at his wife through eyes strained, eyes fighting the urge to give up everything, eyes ready to try and make it all better with just a look, eyes that knew they would fail at that endeavor. Ginny wrapped her hands around the warm cup of coffee in front of her, and she, like Jason, had not taken a sip from it. For a long time, neither of them spoke a word. They would glance at each other, then let their eyes float away to something over in the corner, or outside on the street, or down at their coffee. In those silent moments, Jason felt something like hope. Ginny, in those same moments, felt an acute despair knowing she could still be in love with this man who had cheated on her, this man who had taken their marriage and dragged it through fire and mud. She felt despair because she wanted to forgive him and probably could. But she could never trust him.

"How's your dad doing these days?" Ginny finally asked.

"Willie's good," Jason said, glad the silence had ended and fighting a smile because of it. "Talkative these days…at least by his standards."

Ginny's eyes met Jason's briefly and she saw the hope in them. This should have been good, should have made her smile, but it made her angry instead. Irate, even. The audacity to have that kind of hope after what he did…well, that may have been just too much for her. "So what do you have to say?" She said, her voice unmistakably terse.

Jason was thrown. This had caught him off guard and he cleared his throat as he shifted in his seat. "I have so much to say," he said, "that I really don't know where to start."

"Why did you do it? Start there."

Silence. Then, "I've been thinking about that one for a long time. The why. The reason. And to be honest, I don't know what the bottom line is. I don't know what compelled me to do what I did on the base level, the everyday common sense level. But what I can tell you is something you will most likely not believe. And I can understand that. But you deserve the truth, so here it is."

Jason cleared his throat. Ginny sat silently, her eyes fixed on the table between them. She could not bring herself to look at him as he spoke of what was so obviously ruining everything for them.

"My brother. I did it because of him. This is going to sound strange, but here goes. First off, he drinks because of me. Did you know that? My brother is an alcoholic because of me. He spent his life paying for my screw-ups, doing the legwork for making *my* life good, taking the tough knocks for *me.* And so for a long time I let the guilt swamp me, take me under. I figured, hell, I'm the shithead here, so I owe him. I owe big brother. Gotta let him have the glory once in a while, right? He had Maggie, and Maggie was great for him, but I knew. I knew what he did to her the way I knew what Sergeant was doing to you. But I let it go on because Robert needed her. He needed her, Gin, and I couldn't bear the thought of taking something else away from him."

Ginny snickered. Jason leaned in close.

"Look," he said. "I know this sounds like some bullshit so far, but please just hear me out. I ran into Maggie in the Old Port one night while some of the guys on the team and I were drinking after a game. She was sitting alone at the bar and I went to her to say hello. She had a welt, Ginny, a welt the size of a goddamn baseball on her arm. And I knew. That was the first time I talked to her about it. That was the first time I heard her say she had to do something about it, something to make him realize he was hurting her, something to make him realize she could go away at any moment. She didn't have to love him, she said, and I agreed. I didn't know then, Ginny. I swear to you it was honest to God concern and nothing else. But then it changed about a month later."

Ginny looked up and locked her eyes on Jason's. He immediately knew his words had just crushed his wife, knew that by his simple statement he had admitted that he had held another woman in his arms, had taken another woman to bed, and it had gone beyond just a *mistake*. There was something, maybe not love, but something. And that, that simple sentiment, had just crushed Ginny.

"You need to understand. Please. She had called me one night after Robert had gotten drunk and thrashed her. She called me because she didn't know what to do, thought he might kill her. So I went over there. Robert was passed out on the couch. I took her to a motel and told her to stay there, told her not to go to her apartment or to Robert's, told her to just lay low. I paid for the room. The only reason I did it, Ginny, was because I wanted to approach Robert about it. I wanted to be in control of the situation so that maybe I could fix things for once. I've always been good at screwing up, but I'd never had the opportunity to make things right. This was my chance.

"So I went to see Robert the next morning. We had a pretty huge blowout in the hallway of his apartment building. I stormed out. Then I went to the motel to tell Maggie what had happened. She broke down and I watched, but Gin, I felt the same way watching her as I did when I watched you go through it and it killed me. It killed me because of what was happening, but it killed me more because it was Robert, and in that moment I hated him more than anyone. I wanted to hurt him. I *wanted* to ruin his life this time, and I did. But for whatever reason, that part of my brain that would have told me I was going to ruin my life, too, was going to ruin your life, shut off the way it has so many times in the past. I blew it. I had the chance to fix things and I dug deeper, made them worse.

"It just happened, Ginny. I have no other excuse besides that, and I know it's a weak one at that. But if you could know how sorry I am, how badly I want to take it all back, well, I don't know. Maybe you'd at least be able to look at me again someday. I won't ask for your forgiveness. But I will tell you that given the opportunity, I'd like to try and earn it."

Ginny sat with her head slightly hanging, tears streaking down her face despite her best efforts to keep them from doing so. She did not say anything for several minutes and Jason did not try to provoke her. They just sat with the table and two cold coffees between them, the minutes ticking off the clock like so many meaningless papers in a breeze.

"I want to forgive you," she whispered, "but I don't know that I can. I want to hate you, but I don't know that I can do that, either." She looked up at Jason's face, which was now bracing for a crushing heartbreak. "Most of all, I wish I hadn't been so stupid as to trust you." She paused again. Jason looked stricken. "I don't know what to do from here, Jason. All I know is that if there's any chance of forgiveness, any chance of reconciling with each other, this is only step one out of a ninety step process. You've got some work to do."

Ginny stood up and slung her purse over her shoulder. Jason made a motion to stand as well, but Ginny put her hand out—which Jason noticed was without its wedding ring—and told him to stay sitting. "Make it right, Jason. We'll go from there."

With that, she walked out of the coffee shop. Jason sat for a long time by himself at the table, his hands still wrapped around the coffee cup, feeling for a warmth that was no longer there. Ginny's still-full cup stood motionless only a foot away from his own, but it seemed far enough away that he could never touch it, never lay his fingers on it to feel for himself that it, too, had gone cold and lost its primary function. Almost a half hour passed before Jason stood up. He picked up his coffee cup to throw it away and started to reach for Ginny's cup as well, but then he stopped. He could not touch it. Instead, he left it on the table and walked out of the shop into the cold morning air beyond.

*   *   *

Eleanor had been sitting behind the counter at Gibson's Feed for almost two hours before she couldn't take it anymore. Not a single person had come into the store all day and she had been staring at the same damn display of shovels for two solid hours now without moving so much as an inch. Even Spurs, lying on his side on the floor, seemed ready to gnaw off his own paw just for entertainment. Eleanor stood up and walked around the entire store once, up every aisle and back down, Spurs plodding along quietly behind her, before she decided to lock the store and take a walk down the street.

It was almost noon on December second. The wind had turned bitterly cold and the sky's overcast face peered down at her as she walked up the street with Spurs by her side. She reached the corner of CR44 and stopped, looking up the street at the gas station maybe seven hundred yards north. There was a pickup truck parked at the pumps and no other human life to be seen…at least, not at first glance. Then she saw something that seemed so strange, so incongruous and so chilling that she almost felt a need to run back to the store and lock herself in there.

A man stood outside the gas station. But he wasn't just standing casually the way a man waiting for his truck to gas up might stand. This man, instead, was leaning against the side of the gas station, his head cocked to his right, as if waiting to pounce whoever might be unfortunate enough to walk past. Something about the man's stature seemed familiar to her. She couldn't quite make out all the features of his face, but she felt that familiarity as sure as she felt the water in the shower every morning. She knew this man.

Eleanor walked closer toward the gas station until she could just about make out the man's face…and that was when she stopped dead, pivoted on her heels and ran back to the shop. She ran faster than she had done since she had been a little girl and when she got back to Gibson's Feed and Spurs was safely through the door, too, she slammed the door shut and locked it. Bolted it. Went to the back door and checked that one.

She had just seen Angus McCausland.

*   *   *

Any Mainer will tell you there's only three seasons north of New Hampshire: bug season, mud season, and snow season. While snow season takes up a good chunk of Maine's time throughout the year, bug season certainly claims its fair share in the warmer months. Mud season, however, comes once a year right after the snow thaws and hangs around as long as it wants. If it overlaps into bug season, well, that's just bug season's problem, now isn't it?

This past year, mud season never really ended. It kept right on going through bug season—and to be honest, bug season just loves it when mud season sticks around—and continued on through until just before snow season. Mud season ended on December first this year, the day of the first real hard freeze. The mud does funny things during the freeze. Sometimes it carves itself out into deep, frozen ruts. Other times, mostly in the thick of the woods, it freezes in layers of moss and thick muck, creating a false-ground that crashes and crumbles the second a foot falls upon it.

It was this latter kind of mud, the stuff Jason and Robert—as young boys—had called *glass ground*, that made the remaining hours of December first extremely difficult for Einar William Coates. Jason and Robert had called this frozen mud glass ground because when your foot plunged through it, it crackled and shattered like a horizontal pane of glass, and you never really knew what might be hanging out beneath. On December first, just before the sun began its slow descent below the horizon, Einar's foot shattered the glass ground.

He had spent the majority of the remaining daylight after his hike to Sarah's grave inside on the couch, napping after what had turned into an exhausting walk. When he woke finally, the light that shone through the windows in the living room had already become faint at best, but Einar had been struck with a sudden and strange idea as he shook off his grogginess.

Maybe Gerald Jordan left some of his tools on the path by the lake.

Sure, he'd seen Gerald heading down that way before he'd known the intruder camping out in the barn *was* Gerald, and yet he'd never thought to go check what he might have dropped along the way. Surely he didn't take everything he pilfered back up the road to his place. Maybe some of Einar's tools—hopefully his hammer—had been neglected there, tossed in haste or simply dropped by accident. Einar decided his hunch was worth checking out.

He pulled on his boots and his thick jacket and headed around the side of the house past the barn. He plodded along slowly, not in any real hurry to get anywhere, when he felt the first crunch of the glass ground beneath him. His foot crashed through the frozen mud and sunk into the ground an inch. Einar tripped but only stumbled. He kept on walking toward the lake without so much as a second thought about it.

When he reached the edge of the lake, which was already beginning to freeze around the edges, he skirted the left side of the dock that

Jason had pulled out of the water almost a month earlier. There, in the brush and trees, lay the beaten but almost overgrown path that wove its way most of the way around the lake. Einar hiked on, his booted feet plodding on what felt like very solid, very sturdy ground. And it was…in most spots. The county had gotten a late season rain not four days prior and the runoff from the showers usually washed the trail out in various spots. These sections were not difficult to spot—they often looked mucky and left a trail of underbrush detritus wherever they flowed—and Einar spotted most of them. He did not, however, make any attempt to avoid them.

He hiked about thirty yards down the trail when he came upon one of these washed out spots. The water had flowed, the mud thickened, and then the two elements froze in place like a miniature frost heave of fine crystals. Einar's right foot hit the glass ground and plunged through. His leg sunk almost a foot into the false ground, which had apparently washed out beneath the glass ground as well, but Einar's momentum had already taken him this far and it intended to go further. His body lunged forward but his foot stayed lodged in place, locking his leg at the knee and eventually snapping it about midway up his shin.

The sound Einar made was not a scream. It was not a horrified grimace. It came out as something like a question. "Whaaa," is what he said, and it sounded neither pained nor surprised. It felt more perfunctory than anything else, an escape of air that just happened to have grabbed on slightly to his vocal cords. When the reality of what had just happened settled into his mind, the pain rushing toward every receptor in his body that it could find, Einar issued a miserable, "Ohhh." It did not last long and it was not loud, but for Einar William Coates, it was quite enough.

He quickly sprawled on his left side and sent his hands in the direction of his damaged shin, but he did not touch it. He knew better. He had broken bones before and knew what one felt like. He didn't need the touch of his hands to confirm it, so instead he pulled his hands back and rested his weight on his palms. He sat that way for five minutes or more, pondering the situation and watching the sun sink beneath the tree line and down below the horizon. As soon as the sun disappeared entirely, the cold attacked him, tapped him on the shoulder as if to say, hey, don't forget about me. I'm still here. I'm still all around you. Einar noticed, thank you very much.

He gave out a sigh and laid back straight, reaching out to his left to feel for any loose branches thick enough to splint his leg with. There were none. He reached to his right and found one long branch, good enough to split in half and use as a solid splint. The only problem was getting leverage enough to break the branch. Every movement sent throbbing pain to his leg, every swing in his weight sent a crashing crescendo of lightning and needles straight to his shin. It took him the better part of ten minutes to finally break the branch in half, which had done two things, one bad and one good: it had made him sweat, which was bad—the wind and cold would certainly make his sweat more than just a discomfort—but it had also gotten his blood boiling enough to warm him up for the time being, which was good. He simply needed to take advantage of that warmth immediately and get himself back to the house.

Einar took off his coat and piled it on the ground next to him. Then he took off his shirt. The wind immediately enveloped him, slapping his skin and freezing the sweat that stood out on his back and chest. He worked quickly, tearing his shirt into strips—or close to strips, at least—and tied the sticks to his leg. It hurt like a sonofabitch to do it, but it was better than having the lower part of his leg flopping all over the place. He snugged the splint tight, grimacing with each movement, then put his coat back on. He managed to get himself to his feet but realized quickly enough that supporting himself on saplings and the occasional birch or pine was not going to get him back to the house. How would he get through the yard?

"Get to that when…" he said to himself, and finished the statement in his head: *when I get to the yard.*

And so, slowly, Einar made his way back toward the dock by the lake and rested there, contemplating how to make his way across the dark yard in the cold and wind. After a short while of sitting, thinking, and aggravating himself, Einar decided there was no shame in crawling. So he did. It took him almost an hour to get from the lake to the house, but he did it, by God, and it hurt like mad. But he made it. Always did. Always survived. For what purpose, he could not be sure, but he always survived.

Einar crawled up the steps to the porch and into the house, across the living room and onto the couch by the phone. When he finally made it to the sitting position, he first called Jason. Then he called Robert, who did not answer. Then he called an ambulance. December first had proven to be a killer, and the early morning hours of December second proved to be just as tough as the doctor re-set Einar's bone. No, there would be no sleep for him this night. December had come in hard and fast to make certain of that.

*   *   *

Dusk had fallen over the water and Portland's skyline looked like a painting from some overzealous artist too eager to sell his work to a tourist. Maggie looked at it from her window and knew the scene to be beautiful, but she simply could not convince herself that the image was that in a pure sense. It seemed a false front to her, a façade hiding the real events of the past day. She was sitting at her kitchen table watching the sun fall farther and farther, painting the sky its insultingly beautiful colors, when someone knocked on her door.

She knew immediately, without having to strain herself to think, who it would be standing on the other side.

Robert had walked past her apartment at least a dozen times today—at least, a dozen times that she had noticed—and he had been drunk every time.

A knock again. Then a muffled voice: "Maggie?"

Maggie stood and went to the door but did not undo the deadbolt she had set in place early that morning after seeing Robert outside the first time. She peered through the peephole and saw him, disheveled and still obviously drunk, leaning against the door with one arm. His head hung low as if the weight of it were too heavy for the rest of his body to manage.

"Go away," she said. "Come back when you're sober."

"No," Robert bellowed, "I need to talk to you now. I can't wait, Maggie. I need to see you."

"I—I—I. Fuck you, Robert. It's always about you, isn't it? Get the hell out of here before I call the cops."

Silence. Maggie pulled her eye away from the peephole and leaned her back against the door. Then a shock hit her back hard. Robert had punched the door. "Let me see you!" He screamed.

"I'm calling the police," Maggie said, crossing the room to get her phone. She immediately returned to the door and looked through the peephole again. This time, Robert was standing up straight, his head still hung low.

"I'm sorry," he said quietly. "I'll leave. Can I come back when I'm… more…uh…together?"

"When you're sober."

"Yeah."

"Yes, Robert. When you're sober."

"Okay."

"Robert."

"What?"

"You can't keep sitting outside my apartment."

"I was just waiting for you. I needed to talk to you."

"It scares me."

Silence.

"Robert?"

"Why does it scare you?"

"You scare me."

"I scare you?"

"Yes."

Maggie watched as this information sank into Robert's brain. He looked down at the floor, then up at the door, then back at the hardwood shining back up at him from the floor. He opened his mouth to speak but said nothing. He simply walked away.

Maggie turned and pressed her back against the door again, her face contorted into one that indicated tears were on the way, but none ever came. Just the fear. Just the hurt. Just every other horrific and gut wrenching emotion that came with tears both before and after they had fallen. But no tears came. She would not cry for him. Not while he was drunk. She had done that plenty of times before. Not this time.

The next day, Maggie left her apartment and went to work, where her boss put her on probation for missing three days of work without bothering to call. And for some reason, that made Maggie feel alright.

Frank had to put his father to bed.

To Gerald Jordan, this faux-reversal of roles did not seem strange at all—after all, as a child, Frank had never really been put to bed by his father; his mother had always done the honors—but to Frank, this went beyond humiliation. His father could not brush his own teeth without shoving the toothbrush down the drain of the sink or getting toothpaste all over his chest. He had to make sure his father wiped himself after using the toilet. He had to make sure his father had put his shirt on right side in. He had to see if Gerald had showered with the curtain closed so the water didn't go all over the floor. These, the little things, the daily struggles that made his father look like an infant rather than the hulking, strong and stoic man Frank had known as a child were the moments that made Frank want to give up and put Gerald in a home.

But the closest home was in Bangor, and Frank just could not do that to his father. And to himself. He hated this life, living with his father in Maine while his wife lived in California and pursued a divorce. He hated knowing his father would never revert back to that strong man he'd once known, the man who had taught him to play goalie, the man who had taught him to drive all the tractors and rebuild the carburetor in the truck. The man whom Frank had once loved so much and admired. He was just a child now. A drooling, foolish and forgetful child.

Frank pulled the covers up over his father's chest. "I'm not a goddamn infant," Gerald bellowed and coughed, then rolled onto his side, clutching the blanket the way child scared of the dark might do.

"Okay, Pop," Frank said as he turned off the light by Gerald's bedside. The light from the hallway shone in a streak across the floor and up onto the foot of Gerald's bed. "Goodnight. I'll see you in the morning."

"Call Doctor Billings first thing," Gerald mumbled almost under his breath. Frank closed his eyes, bearing the weight of the statement as if the words had individually scorched his skin or cut him open all over.

"Okay, Pop. I will."

He crossed the dark room and headed to the hallway, closing the door behind him.

"Frank," Gerald said from his bed. Frank stopped in the doorway.

"Yeah."

"I know it's hard," Gerald half-mumbled. "I know it's hard."

Frank sighed.

"Goodnight, Pop."

He started to close the door, but just before he clicked it closed, he heard his father speak one more time. His voice came to Frank's ears as the slight voice of a little boy, mumbled, strained from impending sleep, honest.

"Love you, boy."

Frank pulled the door closed all the way and closed his eyes, his hand still clenched tightly around the doorknob. The hallway light suddenly seemed too bright, shining through his closed eyes with that red transparency showing on his eyeballs. The light burned. The light showed everything. Frank closed his eyes tighter. The light faded but did not disappear. It knew everything.

*   *   *

The next morning, the morning of December second, Frank drove Gerald's truck—leaving Gerald alone, against his better judgment—

180

down to Gibson's Feed. His motives were, of course, twofold: he needed a new snow shovel, since the one in the basement was the same shovel Frank had used to clear the steps of the house as a kid, and of course, the other reason, the one he had not yet admitted to himself, was to see Eleanor.

Every smile Frank let cross his lips as he thought about Eleanor also killed him a little. That smile, he thought, should be for Natalie. So in a sense, his own happiness hurt him, as if it, too, knew its existence was a betrayal. Frank tried his damnedest to control it, this irrational and somewhat silly misery, but in the end, the memory of Natalie always won. He hadn't seen or heard from her in months now, and so memory was all she had become. Frank knew this now, admitted it to himself at the worst times, in the darkest times of sleep that would not come, at the most shining moments with the most wonderful people. Natalie's memory dominated him, as if it were stronger than the actual reality of her.

And it was, really.

Frank pulled into the dirt lot in front of Gibson's and closed his eyes in anticipation of the backfire the truck was sure to shoot off at any moment. It did, he winced, and got out of the truck. As soon as he opened the door, the wind whipped up hard and pushed the door against its hinges, creating a creaking sound that was both familiar and horrible to Frank. He slammed it shut with a little more effort than was probably needed and climbed the three wooden steps to the door of Gibson's.

The door was shut tight.

Locked.

Silence inside.

"Elly?" Frank shouted.

No response.

"Elly, it's Frank. You in there?"

No response again.

Frank left the porch and made his way around back to the fence that surrounded the small lumber yard. He peeked through the slats to find the back door closed and locked as well. Gibson's was dark and closed up tight.

Eleanor lived in a house southeast on CR44. It was the only house on that side of the road between the town and the next town over, Fort Kent. Her mother had left the house to Elly in her will, and Eleanor, to Frank's knowledge, lived there alone and had done so ever since returning to town. He had never been in Eleanor's house, had only been by the driveway in his truck and by the house itself as a kid tramping through the woods, but he figured now might be as good a time as any to drop on by. It seemed odd that Eleanor wasn't at the store, and if she was sick, Frank figured he'd go cheer her up.

So he drove on down CR44 until, fifteen minutes later, he reached the left-hand turn of her driveway. It was a rutted, potholed, dirt affair—much like every other driveway up these parts—that wound around trees and crabgrass patches for about three hundred yards. It emptied into a small dirt lot in front of the dooryard of a beautiful house, deep brown wooden slats and windows perfectly painted a subtle and pleasant white. Eleanor's tiny hunk of a car sat parked in front of the house, exactly where Frank assumed it would be. He pulled Gerald's truck up next to it and waited again for the backfire, but this time it did not come. Frank was grateful for that.

He hopped out of the truck, and the wind kicked up again when he did. This time it wasn't so strong and didn't buck the door on the hinges, but it was uncomfortable enough that Frank hoped Eleanor would answer the door quickly after he knocked.

She did just that.

Eleanor looked stricken, as if she had been slapped.

"Come in, Frank," she said, pulling at his right arm.

"How are you, Elly? You sick today?"

"No, not sick," Eleanor said as she bolted the door, an action that occurred so rarely in these parts as to seem absurd to Frank.

"Why you lockin' the door?"

Eleanor peeked out the front window through the closed curtains. She had a blanket wrapped around her shoulders that draped down past her legs to the floor.

"Elly, what's up?"

She turned. Frank saw a face on her that looked close to panic.

"I saw something yesterday...some*one*."

"Who?"

Eleanor opened her mouth to say the name but found she could not. *Angus McCausland,* she thought. *Yes, I know, he should be in jail, but I saw him and I'm scared to death. Scared of what? Maybe he remembers me. Maybe he doesn't. Does it matter? He's still crazy. He's still dangerous. And I'm still scared of him.*

"Come sit down," she said instead, guiding Frank to the kitchen. They sat at the table on opposite sides.

"You weren't at work today, so I—"

"I saw Angus McCausland."

Frank sat stunned for a moment as if he, too, had just been slapped. To be honest, it had taken Frank a moment to recall what that name meant—Angus...Angus...yes, that's right, high school. Killed that kid. Frank hadn't seen it happen, but he had been there. Yes, oh, how could he have forgotten? Eleanor was...

"Elly, he's in prison. Prison far south. You couldn't have seen—"

"I saw him, Frank. Saw him plain as the sun shines."

Eleanor rocked back and forth, just slightly, on the couch. The blanket that still hung from her shoulders shuddered slightly, Frank could see, either from a slight draft in the room or from Eleanor's shivers.

"Where did you see him?"

"Gas station on 44. I saw him, Frank. Please believe me."

Frank twiddled his thumbs, then shifted nervously in his seat. Angus McCausland? There was no way. He was in prison. He would have had to break out of prison—unlikely in and of itself, if Frank remembered Angus's mental capacity correctly—and then find his way all the way back up to the northernmost tip of the state. It was near impossible.

"Okay, Elly. We should call the police and let them know, then."

"Already did."

"You did?"

"Yes. They said…"

"Said what?"

"Well, they said it might be possible. They said a bus carrying a prison work crew down near Old Town flipped. Some of the guards were killed and they can't find all the inmates. Angus could have been one, Frank, and he's up here, he's in our town. He's around here."

Eleanor looked close to panic. Frank had never seen her cry but imagined she was close to it now, and though it made him feel guilty to admit it to himself, part of him wanted to see her cry. He wanted to see the tears and be there to throw his arm around her. It made a certain sense, he supposed, but god, she was a friend. Why would he wish that on a friend?

Not a friend, Frank thought. *Not anymore. Something else now.*

Then, as if an incongruous caveat had lurched its way slowly into his mind, he thought, simply, *Natalie.*

But Eleanor did not cry. She smiled instead. "I know it sounds nuts, Frank, but I saw him. I haven't thought about him in years," she lied, "but there he was, and I recognized him right away. He hadn't changed much, to be honest. More facial hair and less of it on top of his head, but otherwise, he still had that face. Angry, you know?"

Frank nodded.

"What did the police say when you called?"

"Got the sheriff's office. Said they'd be on the lookout. They sent someone out to McCausland's house, which is abandoned, by the way. I've been past it myself."

For a moment, Eleanor just stared off into space. Frank watched her mind leave the room, rove around and come back all at once, but said nothing. Finally, Eleanor looked at Frank as if seeing him for the first time that day. "Come on in the kitchen. I'll make some coffee."

Without waiting for a response, Eleanor got up and went to the kitchen. Frank followed, slowly, trying to wrap his mind and heart around whatever change had occurred in Eleanor since he last saw her. Something was not quite right about her, and it went well beyond fear or even paranoia. Something had shaken Eleanor to the core, and Frank just could not believe simply seeing Angus McCausland would do that.

Frank sat down at the kitchen table and watched as Eleanor shuffled around the kitchen. "You're awfully quiet today," Eleanor said.

"Suppose I am."

She turned and faced Frank. He hadn't seen her do it, but she had left the blanket that had been draped over her shoulders on the couch in the living room. She wore a thick wool sweater that looked both extremely comfortable and itchy as hell. "Look, it's no big deal, really. I think I just over-reacted, that's all."

Frank nodded. Eleanor shot him a smile, then continued getting the coffee ready. She began to fill the glass coffee pot, humming a tune and changing her mood almost completely from only moments before. Frank sat silently for a minute or more before realizing what had struck him as odd. *It's not that odd, though,* he thought as he looked down at Spurs's water bowl on the floor, his leash hanging from a peg just above it on the wall. *Probably outside in the dooryard or—*

"Where's Spurs, Elly?"

The coffee pot smashing in the sink startled Frank far less than the look on Eleanor's face when she turned toward him.

*   *   *

Jason came home from work to find Robert passed out on his couch. The spare key Jason kept behind a crack in the molding around his front door sat on the end table next to the lamp. He made no effort to be quiet as he came in, and he figured it didn't matter, anyway; Robert would not wake up if a marching band had followed Jason through the door.

For the next fifteen minutes, Jason ignored the drunken pile of a man on his couch. His lunch hour only gave him so much time, and he did not intend to spend his time listening to his drunk brother ramble on about how Jason ruined his life. Jason already knew that, didn't need reminding. He made himself a sandwich and poured a glass of orange juice to go with it. Then he sat on the chair adjacent to the couch and watched Robert sleep, intermittently biting into the sandwich or drinking the orange juice.

When he had finished his sandwich and drank most of the orange juice down, Jason got up and went back to the kitchen. He drained what remained of the orange juice, put the glass in the sink, and headed for the door.

Robert was standing in front of it.

"Mornin' sunshine," Jason said.

Robert grunted.

"I gotta get back to work. Sleep if you want. Lock up if you leave."

Jason made a move for the door, but it was apparent Robert had no intention of moving.

"I want to talk," Robert said.

"Jesus. I have to get back to work."

"You fucked my fiancé. Give me five minutes, you asshole."

"No, Robert. Not five minutes, not two minutes. Not now. You don't get to choose. You want to talk tonight over beers, fine, but it don't seem like you need any more of those. You want to talk later, great. Let the healing begin, big guy."

Jason made a move for the door, but Robert shoved him back. He fell backward over the end table and onto the couch.

"We'll talk now," Robert bellowed. Jason looked up at him from the couch, his shirt now untucked and his hair tousled. He wanted to rage at his brother, swing endless fists and kick him in his kidneys. But instead, he began to laugh.

"What's funny?"

"You."

"Oh, I'm funny?"

"Yeah."

"Tell me, little brother. Why am I funny?"

Jason stopped laughing almost abruptly. "Because you want to talk, Robert, and all that really needs to be said just happened. Just now. You push. You get drunk and you push. You want to solve the great big mystery as to why Maggie's scared of you?" Jason stood up. "Well there it is. There it is, big brother. She's been tossed just like you tossed me. She's been tossed one too many times. I'll get up, Robert. I grew up with you. I can take you. But Maggie..."

Jason tucked in his shirt, then approached his brother. "Hope I solved the mystery for you." Jason pushed Robert gently away from the door. "Lock up when you leave."

With that, Jason left his apartment. He walked down the hallway. He descended the stairs, hit the sidewalk, clenched his face against the cold. Walked three blocks back to work. Wrote all day. Made phone calls. Attended two brief meetings. After work, he shuffled back the same way he had come. He wanted to call Ginny, wanted to try again. He thought about what he might say as he walked home, the breeze biting even more fiercely now that the sun had disappeared. Einar had called him from the hospital and told him he had broken his leg, so Jason intended to go up to Einar's this coming weekend. He wondered if Ginny might go with him, might give him a chance. As he opened the front door to his building, Jason thought about what he might say. He thought about what Ginny might say in response as his hard-soled shoes clicked on the wooden stairs. When he reached the second floor, he pulled out his keys with his right hand. He wanted to call her right then and there, but he would wait until he was inside, out of his work clothes, until he was sitting on the couch, maybe listening to soft music, just relaxing in general. The mood would be better if he was relaxed. He knew that. He put his key into the lock and turned it, pushed the door open. Flipped the light switch. The lights came on bright and sudden.

And in that one moment, that shred of time between the lights being out and the lights turning on, that bitch of a split second, Jason's mood changed. His heart sunk and his mind exploded. He knew he would be going up to see Einar this weekend, but not because of his Pop's broken leg. He knew he would see Ginny again, but there would be no smiles on either of their faces. He would not have time to take off his work clothes and relax on the couch. Because on that couch where he had only seconds before planned to be sitting, talking on the phone to his wife, lay the crumpled and bloody body of his brother, Robert.

*   *   *

Einar made two phone calls when he finally reached the hospital. The first call was to Frank Jordan. He had taken an ambulance to the hospital—and it had taken a good two hours for that little trip to Fort Kent from Einar's place in the woods—and he needed someone to pick him up and bring him home. The second call was to Jason. He told him what had happened—glass ground, fractured tibia and fibula, long time on crutches—and, though he thought it would do no good at all, recommended he tell his brother and sister. Jason called Bethany, who, as expected, lost her mind and told Jason she would be leaving for Einar's as soon as possible. Robert had been too drunk to comprehend any such information, so Jason avoided him altogether until he had found his older brother sleeping on the couch during his lunch break.

And that was all Einar knew of his children's current states of being. Frank showed up at the hospital an hour or so after he had called, and when Einar saw Frank walk into the hospital lobby, he immediately saw a stricken face that probably had little or nothing to do with Einar's broken leg.

"Frank," Einar said with a slight nod of his head. "Thanks for comin'."

"Sure thing, Willie."

Frank helped Einar to his feet and eventually led him out to the parking lot and into Gerald Jordan's pickup truck. They were well down the street and on their way toward CR44 by the time Einar realized that the truck was quiet—which was, in the presence of Frank Jordan, a rare occurrence.

"Usually talkin' up a storm, you are, Frank. Quiet today."

"Yeah," Frank said, a slight shake in his voice. "Uh…helluva day today, Willie."

"Sure, sure," Einar said, nodding.

"It ain't gonna get much better," Frank said, his voice shaking even

189

worse now. Einar looked over at him, this man he had known since Frank was knee-high, and saw in that face that stared straight out the windshield a sign of something ominous, like the way Einar's knees ached before a storm. He saw it coming, alright.

"You gonna set me up for a story, or just come out with it?"

Frank looked over at Einar briefly, then pulled the truck over on to the frozen dirt by the side of the road.

"Willie, something bad has happened."

Einar examined Frank's face once more. "By the looks of it, it ain't my leg you're talkin' about."

"It's Robert, Willie. He…"

"What happened to my boy?"

"He's dead, Willie."

"What the hell you talkin' about?"

"He killed himself…in Jason's living room. Just happened a little while ago. I'm sorry, Willie."

Frank could not look at Einar anymore. He put the truck in first gear and pulled back onto the road. Einar's eyes, however, did not leave the side of Frank's face for nearly a minute. His boy was dead? Not Robert. No, that couldn't be right. Einar decided he would call his boy when he got home to set things straight. Frank had gotten his facts wrong, that was all. Just got them wrong and—

"My boy killed himself?" Einar said finally.

Frank did not reply.

Einar said nothing for the rest of the ride back to his home. When they got there, Frank helped Einar up the steps and into the living room. "Jason should be up tonight," Frank said. "Do you need any-thing?"

Einar looked at Frank and what Frank saw staring at him fright-ened him. This was the first time Frank had seen any sort of hurt cross

Einar's face, any sort of panic. Growing up, he had known Einar to be the kind of man that could shrug off the fires of hell, if the need arose. He had watched Einar look on as Jason left the ice arena in a stretcher after being knocked unconscious against the boards back in high school. Sure, Einar had been worried, but his face painted a picture of complete calm. When Robert had been crushed by that car years and years ago on CR44, Einar had gone to the hospital and stood by Sarah's side with a face that suggested he was barely conscious at all, no worry whatsoever crossing his mind. When his own wife had died, Einar had folded his hands in front of him, bowed his head, sat through the services, and gone home with that same look on his face.

What Frank saw now was terrible.

This was not Einar William Coates. This was someone else.

Einar shook his head, then stared off at the wood stove. Frank took this to mean the man wanted to be alone. "I'll stop by later, Willie. If you need anything, you just call."

Einar nodded.

Frank left the house and drove back to his own place. When he arrived, his Pop was sitting on the front porch, sans-pants as usual, holding a pot from the kitchen in one hand and the cordless phone in the other. He was fast asleep.

As he sat in the truck, parked in front of his Pop's house and watching the man he had grown up fearing snooze like a baby on the porch, Frank began to understand something he could not and probably would never be able to articulate. As with most moments in life, understanding and articulation did not coincide on this day and this did not bother Frank in the least. What did bother him, however, was the ease in which humans tricked themselves into believing a detrimental action could save a life—or prolong one, at least. Frank sat in his dad's truck, a grown man without a wife or a job or a sense of belonging, watching his Pop sleep in what would have been an embarrassing scene had anyone else been in the truck with Frank, and he decided the time had come to make a change or two. Step one sat sleeping on the porch.

Frank's boots clopping up the steps to the porch woke Gerald Jordan. He had always been a light sleeper, and any time Frank saw signs of the man his father used to be, he could not help but be astounded how little the man had actually changed. This made Frank regret the decision he had just made, but only slightly. This was the right thing to do.

"Hi, Pop," Frank said as Gerald shuffled to a more upright sitting position. Gerald did not reply. He merely grunted.

"I need the phone, okay? I need to make some important phone calls."

"Coates boy's dead, ain't he?"

"How'd you know that, Pop?"

"Heard ya on the phone. It's been ringin' since ya left."

Frank felt a sudden embarrassment wash over him. Had his Pop answered the phone? What did he say? "Did you answer?"

"Course I answered. The hell else ya do when th' phone's ringin'? Go for a swim?"

Wouldn't be out of the question these days, Pop, Frank thought. "Who called?"

"Coates boy. The younger one. Forget his name. Was lookin' for you. Also Doc Billings. Says I should come in for a checkup."

Jason Coates and a dead man had called. All part of a normal day, Frank supposed. "Can I have the phone, Pop? I need to call Jason Coates back."

"Doc Billings, too. Make the appointment for me," Gerald said with his usual fervor. Then, almost like a child, he added, "I'm so tired these days. So tired now…"

He trailed off and his gaze fixed on some far off place where Doc Billings still made house calls and pants were optional accoutrements in society. Frank took the phone from his father's hands and walked inside the house. He sat at the kitchen table for a long while, staring at the phone in his hand and the phone book open on the table in front of him, wondering if he could really go through with this. But after time, he decided it was no longer a matter of what he could or could not do; it had become, a long time ago, a matter of what *needed* to be done. And as had been the case since Natalie left, Frank had no one to rely on but himself.

He ran his finger down the page until he found the number to Bergen Convalescent home in Fort Kent. He began to dial the number, then stopped, hung up, and re-dialed, this time a different number.

Eleanor picked up.

"Hi, Elly," Frank said.

"Hey there, Frank. Thought you went done got yourself lost in the woods. Haven't heard from ya today."

"It's been quite a day. How are you doing?"

A long pause interrupted what had been a nicely flowing conversation, albeit a short one. Then Elly sighed. "Doin' okay, Frank. I just wish Spurs would come home. I'm so worried about him. But otherwise, I'm okay."

"I could really use you here," Frank said, almost embarrassed.

"Okay," Eleanor said. "I can come over now if you like. Everything okay?"

Frank did not answer. He did not know how to answer, to be honest. No, everything was not okay. In fact, everything was downright horrible. A shitshow, as he and Coates used to say back in high school. A real down-home shitshow cooked up in a pot and served on a stick.

"I could really use…really need you now, Elly."

"Okay Frank. I'll be there in ten."

She hung up before Frank did. He sat silently at the kitchen table for a long time, listening to the occasional grunt or clang of a pot out on the front porch, where, despite the cold, Gerald Jordan sat with an old work coat and no pants. Eleanor would see him when she arrived and Frank would not try to stop that from occurring. She needed to see it, because what waited beyond Gerald Jordan, inside the house, sitting at the kitchen table, would make the man sitting on the porch just a passing instance of a strange refraction of light on an otherwise normal day.

*   *   *

Night arrived on the evening of December second with the discordant note of rain in the air. While Angus believed it could go either way—rain or snow, depending on the whims of the sky above—he dreaded both prospects as he lay on the kitchen floor of what used to be his home, tucked in a sleeping bag and leaning against the wall. He had not felt so cold in years, and even if he had ever felt this cold before, this frigid air compounded his misery in combination with an odd sensation he never thought he'd have: he missed prison.

Angus had not eaten much in three days. Whatever he managed to steal from the gas station in town had been a pittance to begin with and was just about gone now. He had never been much for stealing; he had never really honed his talents as a thief throughout the years, choosing instead to bully his friends into doing the deed for him. Now, as his stomach grumbled and his body racked with shivers, Angus wished he had practiced more as a kid. Maybe he could have grabbed a few more packages of beef jerky before the old fart behind the counter at the gas station noticed him and called the police. The man knew, after all, Angus was up to something. Probably even recognized him from all the newspaper photos from years ago after he killed—

Angus sat up suddenly.

He heard a familiar sound.

Rats, he thought, but then he thought better. The footsteps were too heavy to be that of rats. Maybe a 'coon. But no, the steps are...too spread out, too slow. Something bigger with longer legs. Angus crept out of his sleeping bag and crawled on his hands and knees through the dark. He could just barely see the walls and floor, the random scattered messes left by who the hell knew over the years, in whatever pittance of light shone from the sky outside and through the holes in the ceiling. It wasn't much, but it was enough; he could see his guest visitor sniffing around the opposite side of the living room: a medium-sized dog, probably wandered in from town—those dumb mutts wandered for hours if they smelled a cat or an asshole to sniff. When Angus turned his body to face the room, the dog's head reeled around and spotted Angus. Its first reaction was obviously to run, but it did not. Angus cooed to it.

"Come'ere, pup," he whispered. "Got some food for ya." Though the dog probably could not see it, Angus held out his hand as if to indicate he held food. The dog took a few tentative steps toward Angus, then stopped. Angus called to it again. It took quite a while, but the dog finally approached close enough to realize Angus had nothing in his hands and was probably dangerous, but by that time Angus had already seized his opportunity. He pounced on the dog, quickly snapped its neck, and sat back breathing hard. *Matches,* he thought. *I took matches from the gas station—right in front of that old fuck, too. I can start a* "Fire," he said out loud. And he did.

Almost a half hour later, the stench of burning dog hair filled the house, but Angus did not notice. As he twirled the dog's collar around his index fingers, the tags that read SPURS tinkling like bells as they spun, Angus only felt the anticipation of an impending meal, stench be damned.

V

CONFUSING THE SEASONS

The first real snowfall of the season happened on December fifteenth—the day of Robert's funeral, which had been delayed twice, once because two of Robert's cousins were out of the country and were having trouble getting back into the U.S., and once because the Cumberland County medical examiner delayed Robert's autopsy. So the funeral happened on the fifteenth, in the midst of the first snowstorm of the season, one that would dump nearly a foot and a half of snow when all was said and done.

Everyone trudged through the accumulating inches with their scarves raised and cinched tightly against the wind and driving flakes. They packed into the church and the warmth of it enveloped them. After the services, it took nearly forty minutes for everyone to get their cars dug out and ready to make the trek to the cemetery where Robert was to be buried in the same plot as his mother. Jason was a pall bearer, as was Frank Jordan. Two of Robert's friends—drinking buddies, actually—from down in Portland took care of that duty as well, and Einar, his weight leaning on crutches after he refused to be carted around in a wheelchair, watched all this with a stern face that suggested he was not there at all.

For Jason, the days following Robert's death played out something like a television show playing in the background of a crowded room. He understood what was happening but could not stick to the plot-line, could not really grasp the characters' names, could not keep track of everything that had lead up to this point. It was all background events. What stood out in the foreground for him was the process: the funeral arrangements, the meetings and planning, the dinner and receptions, the mundane events that would fill rooms with chatter and hearts with heaviness. The rest remained background, only subtle noise, lights and movement that flickered off walls at night time.

The day he had found Robert on his couch had been a strangely hopeful one for Jason. He had intentions of making everything right, working through it all and resolving it, and when he found Robert asleep on his couch at lunch, it almost delighted Jason. This was a mountain he could, indeed, conquer. He felt assured of that. But when he came home from work and found Robert dead, that changed so quickly and so drastically that Jason's mind and body never even no-ticed the difference. He felt as though misery had always been an overwhelming presence in him.

This feeling had followed him everywhere he went up until the funeral and the familiar list of things to do associated with such a day: buy the casket. Arrange the wake. Call the church. Attend the ceremony. Clean the house. Invite friends and family. Obituary in the paper. He couldn't help but think his mother's funeral had been practice for this more somber, more awkward event. But Jason floated through all of this with his mind and heart switched off, his consciousness operating only halfway, the bare essentials left firing just enough to get him through it all without being really cognizant of what was transpiring. This changed after the funeral.

As friends and family left Robert's casket underneath the canvas tent that covered the hole that would swallow him forever, only Einar and Jason remained. They stood in silence for several minutes before Jason put his hand on his father's shoulder and said, "Give a wave when you're ready. I'll help you down the hill." Einar made no acknowledgement that he had heard Jason's offer, and Jason did not wait for one. He plodded through the snow down the hill toward his car.

Maggie was standing by his driver's side door, the snow pelting her face as she wrapped her arms around herself. Jason approached her tentatively with his hands shoved in his pockets. As he stood before her, Maggie's face changed; she had been somewhat weepy throughout the funeral ceremony, but now her features changed to something harder, something lost. Jason did not speak; he only listened.

"Because of all this," she said, "I thought I didn't love him. But I did, you know. I did love him. He abused the shit out of me, Jason, but I loved him."

Jason nodded but never took his eyes away from Maggie's.

"It was a mistake to do what I did. What you did."

He nodded again.

Maggie looked to her left and watched the snowflakes snap past her face. "I never want to see another Coates man again."

She never looked back to Jason. Maggie walked away in the same direction as the snow flying sideways and got into her car. She drove off and Jason watched the tail lights flicker through the heavy white precipitation until he could no longer see the car at all. When he finally turned around, Einar was looking down at him from the top of the hill, leaning on his crutches. Jason could just barely make out his father's face through the blinding snow, his black outline in the fierce white. Seeing his father standing there was what made Jason's mind and heart turn back on and crumble immediately. Einar raised a hand to Jason and Jason did the same back. He then trudged back up the hill to help Einar down. By the time he reached Einar, Jason had tears streaking down his face. Whether Einar simply did not see them or if he chose to ignore them Jason did not know, but by the time they reached the car and Jason had helped Einar in, the tears disappeared and never returned. They drove off through the snow toward home.

*   *   *

Angus watched from the gates of the cemetery as Jason Coates walked with his Pop. He watched as the snow fell, as the people cried, as the pall bearers carried the casket. He watched through eyes that blurred from the wind as his arms and chest shuddered from the cold. And he hated. He hated more than even he comprehended.

Tonight would be just fine to kill Jason Coates.

As Jason and his Pop drove off through the cemetery gates in the snow, Angus trudged along the road with his thumb cocked up and out to hitch a ride, but no cars were coming other than those leaving the funeral. He walked for forty minutes before someone picked him up and dropped him off back at his house, the shack in which he had grown up, and he started a fire as quickly as he could in the fading light of day. The snow fell through the roof and piled up in corners of the room that shook from the wind and creaked as if they, too, shivered. But all Angus could think of was summer.

He remembered his first summer in prison. The sticky heat. The brutal, intense ovens that were the cells, the ill-tempered guards made even more cranky by the near-hundred-degree temperatures. He hated that summer in a different way than he'd ever hated anything before, as if it had been baked and intensified, solidified and cracked like a desert landscape. The heat became a companion, a cellmate that Angus both embraced and despised, but more than anything else, that heat brought him to a new place in his mind, one he had only experienced in one other place in his life. That new place had a sign above its doorway, written in bright neon and blinking with bugs flying around it. That sign read FEAR, and until prison, Angus had known that place to house only one person: his father. But now, now that place was packed full, to the brim, his father relegated to the storeroom at the back, and the showroom displayed brand new shining examples of what was out there in this world to *really* fear…and Angus now knew most of those things existed in prison.

Eventually he became one of those shining displays. He feared himself more than anything or anyone else, and that, in and of itself, was a miracle. Angus had never been one to examine his own existence, but in prison, what else was there to do? The deeper he got into his own mind, the more he took all those aspects of himself that he feared and hated and turned them around, made them face the wall and take on the shape of something else: blame. He could blame anyone and did. As years passed, Angus found that one person could shoulder the bulk of that blame simply because that one person had stopped Angus, kept him from finishing the job, kept him from *getting away with it*. Jason Coates. Yes, Coates. Surely this was all his fault.

That first summer crawled by and felt acidic to Angus. By the end of it, he wondered if he could survive another day of that heat and hoped like hell the fall came sooner than later to cool that damn shithole off. But the summer hung on, and whether he was sitting in his cell or out swinging an axe on a work crew, the heat clung to him. He named that heat Coates. He named that cell Jason. He named that moment in his life Hell.

But Angus didn't just want to kill Jason Coates. He wanted to make him suffer. Torture him, embarrass him, make him feel the pain before he got off the hook and died. As Angus thought about it, a smile inadvertently swept across his face in a twisted version of a grin only a man left for the toil of jail life could muster. Yes, twisting Jason Coates until he broke in half, gouging his eyes out with his fingers and cracking open his chest with a hammer—that would solve it all. Maybe Angus could sleep then. Maybe he could feel okay again.

Maybe.

*　　　*　　　*

Einar was there when Tommy Barnes lifted two full kegs over his head. Most folks wouldn't believe that if they heard it but Einar saw it with his own eyes in seventy-nine, eighty-two and again in eighty-six. Tommy liked to do it to impress folks, and he only did it on the rarest of occasions because when it came down to it, Tommy was not a showy fella. But he had a talent and he liked to use it, even if it was only sparingly.

Tommy died in ninety-one.

Then there was Sheryl Frost. She and Sarah Coates had been great friends for nearly two decades until Sheryl and her husband, Gene, moved three towns away. They may as well have moved to a different planet. The last time Einar could remember seeing either Sheryl or Gene was sometime in the mid eighties down at Gibson's Feed. The definitive last time he saw Gene was in a photo in the obituaries. He died in ninety-seven. Sheryl went seven months later in early ninety-eight.

All of these folks were in their seventies or eighties. Done with life. Closer to Einar's age than to Robert's. As Einar sat at the kitchen table, watching the snow streak past the window at a brutal angle that indicated—along with the whistling and creaking of the house—intense winds, he did something he had never done, not once, in his life before.

He questioned God.

Years and years ago in a town with an unpronounceable name in a country Einar would just as soon raze to the ground as *liberate*, he made a promise to himself and to whatever God happened to have an ear turned to him at that moment. The promise, in his mind, was simple: Einar would not kill another man in his life. He asked for nothing in return but the love of his then-fiancé and whatever family they might be lucky enough to produce someday. After Robert's funeral, Einar went over it all in his head: had he had a hand in killing his son? Had Jason? Or had no one really, other than Robert himself?

Einar came up with no good answer.

But through all of this, there was God. Maybe this was a karmic payment. Maybe those years in the war were finally catching up with Einar all at once—first he had to bury Sarah, now Robert. Who next? All he had left was Jason, and could he even look at the boy right now? Not since the funeral.

In the end, though, Einar knew he would have to foot the blame for all this. Since Sarah died, his life had become an exercise of going through the motions, of placating those who felt it necessary to placate and comfort him. He did not want comfort. He wanted to be alone in his pain, alone in his mourning. And now he had that wish fulfilled, only with the added solemnity of knowing he was mourning for two now. Where had the humor in his life gone? He'd never really been one to laugh all that much, but Einar knew funny and welcomed it when it came. Humor seemed to be the only one not hanging around his house after the funeral, the only one not making the effort to console and placate Einar. And so Einar, on so many occasions, stood by the edge of the lake and looked for its hiding place, wished for its return, but did not wish too hard. There was still too much pain to wallow in. And hadn't it been Einar himself who had told Jason to stop wallowing in his self-pity? Why hadn't Einar heeded his own words?

With his crutches laying on the floor next to him and his broken leg propped up on a chair, Einar listened to the wind slapping against the house, carrying with it tiny flakes of snow that seemed malicious both to the eye and to the ear, and for the first time he could remember, for the first time since he wore short pants and fished in the river on the edge of his Pop's property as an eight year old boy, Einar let a tear sneak down out of his eye and down his cheek. He felt no relief in letting another one go, but he did it anyway. He did it in silence, let the hum of the refrigerator and the cursing of the wind narrate the moment. When both tears had fallen, Einar closed his eyes and shut off that kind of self-indulgent mourning for good.

*   *   *

Elly had her left leg wrapped around Frank's as they lay on the couch together listening to the storm outside. Night had fallen only a half hour ago and neither had bothered to turn on a light or stir from their position. Her head rested nestled on Frank's shoulder. Her left arm stretched over his chest so her hand could cup itself around the right side of his rib cage. And though Frank lay completely still, almost fully rigid, he was not uncomfortable, was not nervous.

When a friend dies, all other problems disappear like a fog as the sun rises. Frank knew this from experience as a boy, when Henry Heinen finally died. Knew the feeling the way he knew the lines to a song he'd known in college—bits and pieces came back slowly, but not all at once, so that you had to hum the pieces you couldn't remember until it all finally clicked into place. Frank pressed his hand over Elly's forearm and knew immediately he was humming the parts he could not remember.

When he had heard about Robert's death, Frank was surprised to feel anger well up inside him. Jason had called him and told him what had happened, and the next day he was up at Einar's place. Frank went over there immediately and had a shouting match with Jason. He was not sure why that anger had come out at Jason—or rather, he *was* sure and did not want to admit it—but the words that came out of his mouth that day frightened him as much as they had shook Jason. After all, Robert's death wasn't *really* Jason's fault, but Frank wanted it to be his fault that day. Just for that one day.

Two days passed after the funeral before Frank laughed. Elly had been cooking dinner in his kitchen as Gerald sang an unintelligible song in the living room, blessedly devoid of pants as usual. Frank was in the hallway taking laundry out of the dryer, a relatively new task for him. He had taken to it quite well, actually enjoyed it even, but he kept running into the same problem.

"Damn," he said as he pulled a shirt out that had two socks and a pair of boxer shorts stuck to it.

"What's the matter?" Elly said from the kitchen.

Frank took the shirt and showed Elly. "I put these shirts on and I feel like they're attacking me. The static just sticks right to my body." Frank tore one of the socks off the shirt.

"Did you put a dryer sheet in with the load?" Elly asked.

Frank's face went blank.

Elly laughed.

"Frank, you have to put a dryer sheet in." She went to the closet and pulled out the box. "See? They keep the static down."

"Really? I thought those just made the clothes smell good."

Elly laughed again. "No. See?" She rubbed the dryer sheet on the shirt Frank still held and the static started to dissipate.

The laughter snuck up on Frank, and it hit him all at once. He and Elly stood in the hallway and let the laughter overtake them for as long as it would last. When their voices finally subsided, they could hear Gerald laughing in the living room, most likely at some unrelated and irrelevant something that only he understood.

Now, lying on the couch with Elly, laughter felt far away again.

"I don't want to do it," Frank said.

"You have to and you know it," said Elly, almost in a whisper.

"I know."

Then they lay there again, quiet. Gerald slept soundly upstairs in the bedroom he had slept in every night for the better part of forty years, sleeping without the knowledge that Frank had packed Gerald's bags and planned to take him to the convalescent home in Fort Kent tomorrow.

"I don't want to do it," he said again, and this time Elly did not reply.

*   *   *

"Funny how all the Coates men befriend Jack Daniels and all his cohorts in the worst of times," Jason said as he sat on the floor of his apartment in boxer shorts and a t-shirt. Ginny stood over him, her arms wrapped around herself and her purse hanging from her right shoulder. Jason could not tell if she was angry or sad or frightened—in fact, couldn't really see her at all—and so he just laughed and watched the room spin.

"You're disgusting," Ginny said. "Why didn't you call Frank? Let him baby-sit you?"

"I'll tell you where Frank is," Jason yelled. "Frank is…not…here." He punctuated the notion with a wave of a finger and a spill of whiskey down his shirt. "Frank, Frank, Frank. Probably up north where he always is. You know, *pining* away for his lost love." Jason laughed again. "*Pining.*"

"You wouldn't know anything about that, would you?" said Ginny.

Jason looked up at her as if he had just been kicked in the ribs, then immediately dropped his face again. "Ya know, fuck off. I'm—"

He stopped there and looked up at Ginny again, waiting to see if she would leave. She did not. Instead, Ginny stood over Jason with the same stolid look she had worn since walking in the door ten minutes before.

When she had arrived at Jason's apartment, she wasn't sure she wanted to see him at all. It felt right, though, she couldn't deny that, so she went, and when she walked down the hallway and saw his door wide open, a flutter of panic washed through her. Where it had come from and what it had meant was beyond her, but it left as quickly as it came when she saw Jason on the floor.

"I hear you got fired," Ginny said to him from the doorway, and that was how the exchange began. It continued nearly incoherently for the next ten minutes right up until this moment, this awkward and tense moment in which Jason watched and waited to see if Ginny would walk away. But she didn't.

She never did.

"Get up," she said to Jason. It took almost a full minute, but he did. Ginny pushed him through his apartment to the bathroom as Jason mumbled and swore, Jack Daniels always at hand. She flipped on the bathroom light and wasted no time in pushing Jason into the bath tub.

"What the *Fuck!*"

As Jason lay in a heap in the far corner of the shower, whiskey spilt all over him, Ginny turned on the cold water and let it hit Jason full force. He struggled for a moment, tried to get out of the shower, fell back in, and cursed again: "*What the goddamn fuck!*"

"If you're not going to get it together, I'm going to get it together for you," Ginny said without a trace of anger in her voice at all. She put her purse down on the counter, then pulled off her coat. She grabbed the shampoo off its ridge on the side of the shower and squirted it at Jason. "Take your clothes off," she said, an overwhelming calm fixed in her voice.

"Ginny, what the—"

"Just take off your clothes, Jason. Don't argue with me."

"I can't even stand up."

"Then don't stand. Just take your shirt off."

Ginny threw a bar of soap at him. It landed on his chest. He pushed it off and peeled his shirt off. Ginny grabbed the now-empty bottle of Jack Daniels and put it aside, next to her purse.

"Get up."

"I'm trying."

"Try harder."

Jason shot her a look that told Ginny two things: one, he was getting frustrated. Two, he was sobering up quick.

He finally stood.

"Can you at least turn the warm water on?"

"Do it your damn self."

Ginny sat on the toilet and watched the astonishment sweep over Jason's face. Jason turned on the hot water.

"Take off your boxers. You look ridiculous in the shower with shorts on."

"You gonna stand there and watch?"

"Is that a problem?"

Jason exhaled short and hard, then pulled his pants off. In between glances at his wife, Jason began to do normal shower motions: soaping up. Rinsing off. Shampoo. Then he stopped. "This is really odd."

"What's odd?"

"You're watching me shower."

Ginny stood up and without a word, took off her clothes and stepped in the shower.

*　　　*　　　*

In the spring of 1999, the University of Maine Men's Ice Hockey team won the national championship, beating the University of New Hampshire in double overtime by a score of three to two. Jason Coates had started the season with that team. He did not end it.

Instead, his season ended in mid-February after he jumped off the roof of the entryway to Androscoggin Hall. He was, of course, drunk at the time, and he missed the snow pile he had aimed for by a good four feet. The result was a lot of embarrassment and a broken left femur.

It healed quickly—miraculously quickly, the doctors at Eastern Maine Medical Center had said—but Coach Walsh wouldn't let Jason skate with the team. Wouldn't let him in Alfond Arena, in fact. Walsh wanted Jason Coates nowhere near hockey until he sobered up. It was tough love, but Jason did not recognize it as such. Instead, he quit the team altogether and dropped out of school in late March of that year.

"Get your act together," Walsh had said. He'd followed that statement up with an offer to help Jason do just that, but Jason had stopped listening by

that point. Get your act together. If there had been a soundtrack to Jason's life, that would be the chorus of the very first song. He didn't do it, though, and he missed out on a national championship.

And much more than that.

Luckily, Jason had a sense of humor. Of course, only he could see the humor in the situation, and certainly Robert saw none of it. When Robert came down to Orono, his limp more pronounced now that his leg had healed wrong after a surgery the previous year, he wasn't laughing at all. He was irate, in fact. But, that lasted only a week. Robert moved in with Jason instead—Jason's roommates had kicked him out after too many drunken stumbles, fights, and rages—and forced him to stop drinking. That part wasn't easy. Jason Coates, it can be said, was crafty in his ways of procuring alcohol, but luckily for him, Robert Coates was just as crafty at disposing of all of it. One of those crafty methods Robert employed, Jason would not find out until later, was to sink down a fair amount of the booze himself. But he never showed it if he was drunk—or at least Jason was too drunk himself to realize it.

Only Einar knew that Robert, too, had a drinking problem, but he kept it quiet. He figured his boy was strong enough to get over that mountain, and besides, he couldn't be that bad off if he was doing so much good for Jason. And in the end, he was good for Jason. By the first day of summer, Jason was completely sober and ready to re-apply for the fall semester. He had no idea Robert had been keeping in touch with Coach Walsh, updating him on Jason's progress or lack thereof.

In June, Robert began training Jason. Cardio, weights, bike, you name it. Robert had Jason doing it. Robert didn't know if Coach Walsh would give Jason another shot, but if he did, Robert wanted Jason to be the best-conditioned athlete out there. If he was going to try, he was going to try hard. If he was going to fail, he would fail knowing he took his A-game to the arena.

By the fall, Jason's drinking problem became no more than a bad memory, a nightmare he had awoken from in early summer. But for Robert, that nightmare was just beginning. The boys at the Bear Brew Pub knew that winter that if Jason Coates walked through the door, they could count on two things for sure: a helluva bar tab and a helluva bar fight. When Robert Coates started coming in mid-summer, the boys behind the bar again knew two things: a helluva bar tab and a brooding, frighteningly somber drunk that seemed to disquiet the other customers. Neither of the Coates brothers were welcome at the Bear Brew for all that long.

But as it turned out, Jason Coates did get back on the UMaine hockey team, and when Jason went back to school, Robert decided he would do the same. The 2000 season would be Jason's last as a player and as a student, but Robert had at least two more years to go beyond the current school year if he wanted a degree. This thought weighed on him heavily; solving Jason's problems had been easy, but what about his own? In December of that year, Robert finished the semester and did not enroll for the spring term. Instead, he moved out of the apartment in Orono and went back up to live with his parents, and as any good Mainer will tell you, there ain't much for a young man to do in Northern Maine but drink and screw. Robert did plenty of both.

By the spring, Jason was vying for another shot at the national championship—a bid that eventually failed during the national quarterfinal versus Boston College—and Robert was drinking more heavily than Jason ever had. His limp seemed more pronounced now, too, and though Sarah Coates fretted about it and Einar did the same in his own cut-off and stoic manner, Robert continued on.

Until one day in early May, the day of Jason's graduation.

Robert had driven down to Orono with Einar in the passenger seat, Sarah in the back seat, and Jack Daniels sitting shotgun in his bloodstream. He wasn't drunk per se, but he wasn't exactly sober, either. Nevertheless, he made it down to Orono with his parents in tow and parked near the steam plant along the Stillwater River, where they met up with Bethany—who was living in a sorority house not far from the steam plant. They walked up past the Alfond Arena to the football stadium and climbed high up onto the bleachers, a chilly wind biting through the crowd and a buzz of excitement following it. The ceremony went on for a long time, longer than Robert could bear to sit still, and so he excused himself and made his way back down the bleachers and behind the stands toward the doors of the arena. He lit a cigarette—a very new hobby for him, one that would not last more than a few months, in fact—and pulled a flask out of his jacket pocket. He took a long, deep drink of whiskey from it and was about to shove it back inside his coat pocket when a voice startled him from behind.

"Got a little to spare?"

He turned to see a young and gorgeous blonde with a soft face and a mischievous grin looking at him with arms folded and hair floating and bobbing with the breeze.

"Suppose I do," Robert said.

He handed the flask to her and she took two big gulps without flinching, then handed it back to him. "I'm Maggie," she said, to which he, of course, replied, "I'm Robert."

Maggie was studying chemical engineering, a subject that Robert found to be both intriguing and boring at the same time. Regardless, the two started dating immediately and moved into a small apartment on Hamlin Street in Orono only a few months later in the late summer. Maggie encouraged Robert to go back to school and Robert encouraged Maggie to refine her taste for liquor in great quantities. She did, at least for a while, and things went along smoothly.

It was the first week of school when Robert hit her for the first time.

They had been drinking all night—not an unusual occurrence, especially during the first week of classes—and Maggie had made a joke about Rob-

ert's limp at a party. This, too, was not uncommon, as Maggie had, if noth-
ing else, taught Robert to laugh a little at what had happened to him. But
that night felt different, felt acidic and stingy, and as soon as the words
passed through her lips, she knew she'd made a mistake. Robert said noth-
ing to her the entire walk home, but when the door to their apartment
clicked closed behind them, something inside of him switched on—or off,
Maggie couldn't tell anymore—and Robert unleashed a forehand slap that
sent her flying into the side of the refrigerator.

And that was all. He walked to the bedroom and fell asleep immediately.

The next morning, Robert seemed to remember nothing at all about the
end of their evening, and Maggie said nothing about it. Her face swelled
slightly, enough to be painful but not enough to be noticed unless someone
was really looking. She wrote the incident off as just that: an isolated inci-
dent. And that's what it remained for several months.

But then it happened again.

Then months passed.

Then again.

Then almost a year.

Then again.

Waiting for it to happen was almost worse than the actual slaps or punch-
es or beatings, but even worse than the waiting, worse than the beatings
themselves, was the next day, the after, the moment when she would wake
up next to Robert and he would say nothing, as if it hadn't happened at all,
and Maggie would wonder if he really remembered at all, convinced her-
self he must remember but was ignoring it, then turning that logic around
and thinking, well, maybe he doesn't know, his drinking's out of control, the
booze makes him forget, makes him angry, makes him—

And that was the burden Maggie made her own.

She graduated in 2003 with a degree in Chemical Engineering. Robert
graduated a year later and they moved to Portland. Two years later, in

2006, Robert proposed to her and she said yes.

By December of 2007, Robert was dead.

Through it all, Maggie wondered if he would change. She thought he must change, he loved her, after all, and she loved him. He would stop drinking if she asked him to, and she would ask. If it got to a point where it was unbearable—oh, but wasn't it always unbearable?—she would ask him to stop. And she did. What she got for it was a sprained wrist and a bruised abdomen. So she tried something else.

She first ran into Jason by accident. She saw him occasionally down near Congress Street, running around on some assignment or another for the Herald, but rarely did they stop and say hello to each other. But one rainy day in May, she stopped him. Grabbed his arm. Pulled him into a covered bus stop bench and told him everything.

"When it happens, or when you think it might happen," he told Maggie, "you come to my place. I will help."

I will help.

Yes, she thought, he'll help and everything will be fine.

But that changed one night in early July, when helping became betraying. Maggie knew Jason was married, knew Ginny, in fact, from Umaine. They had never been friends, really, but they had always been cordial. She liked Ginny, in fact, in a very passive way. Their apartment down by the Old Port was spacious and comfortable, completely unlike the apartment Maggie shared with Robert only seven blocks away. Ginny had gone to Massachusetts to visit her family for a week when Maggie came over, her lip bleeding and tears streaking down her face, and she knew, didn't she? She knew that night would be the night, because Jason had been protecting her, and if she let him protect her, maybe Robert would notice, maybe—

She regretted that night immediately, hated herself for it, went home that night and actually hoped Robert would beat her again.

But he did not.

He never did again.
And that made things so much worse.

*   *   *

     Just before Angus left the shack that used to be his home, he looked around long and hard. Night had fallen and he had quite a walk ahead of him, the cold bit at him from every angle, but despite it all, he felt good. He left the shack, spit on the ground and began walking up CR44 toward the home of the Coates's, not really knowing if Jason would be there but somehow *knowing*. Yes, he'd be there alright. Angus felt that in every inch of him.

*   *   *

12:30 a.m.

Gerald Jordan woke and knew a trip to the bathroom was necessary. Despite his failing mind, this thought came to him clearly and quickly. Without turning on the light, he slipped out from beneath his covers and made his way slowly down the hall in his bare feet, stopping only once to peek into the guest bedroom where his son was fast asleep with his new lady friend. Gerald did not remember her name but she seemed nice enough. He had no recollection whatsoever of talking to her once a week for the last four years down at Gibson's Feed. No matter. He continued on down the hall and snapped the bathroom door shut behind him, stood over the toilet in the dark for a moment, then decided sitting might be a better option.

    As he did his business there in the dark, Gerald closed his eyes and thought about the past, weaving together his life with those stories and memories that did not belong to him. A part of him knew his mind was betraying him, knew his sanity had slipped away sometime over the course of the last year, but the rest of his mind ignored that sentiment and allowed the deterioration to continue unabated, almost gleefully, into what would become a big, empty black hole. Every day he remembered less and made up more. Why didn't he wear pants anymore? He could not remember, but he suspected Doctor Billings recommended it. He couldn't be sure, though.

As Gerald sat on the toilet in the dark, the slow creaks of the house sounding off in the wind, he closed his eyes and fell asleep silently, feeling somewhat relieved and more than a little confused. But that would do until morning, he thought as he drifted off, and when contentment came, who was he to argue?

*   *   *

Einar, too, had woken that morning in December just around midnight, but it was not his bowels that roused him. He had spent a restless few hours in bed, tossing and turning until finally the ache in his leg and the nagging thoughts in his mind poked and prodded him out of bed. He made his way around the house on his crutches before his sore palms told him it was time to sit, so he went back upstairs to the bedroom and sat in the rocking chair by the window in which Sarah had spent so many hours sitting and knitting. It felt good to sit in the chair; it, like many inanimate objects in the house, felt to Einar as though it held just a bit of his dead wife. But where and how could he feel Robert?

Einar stared down at the yard, looking away only once into the darkness of the bedroom to stretch out the muscle in his neck that had stiffened just a bit from the angle he held it at. Then, sometime around twelve thirty, Einar saw something.

No, someone.

"Ah, Gerald," he said to himself, his voice sounding unnatural in the stillness of the dark room. Einar had seen this sight before: a shadowy figure skulking across the yard and dipping into the barn. This time the figure appeared silhouetted against the snow that had accumulated on the ground, and Einar had no doubt in his mind: Gerald had made another escape from his home and decided to spend the night in Einar's barn filching tools.

Einar sighed and picked up the phone. It was late but he figured Frank would want to know about it, so he dialed the number.

"Frank. Einar Coates here."

Frank tried to shake the sleep from his voice. "Hello, Willie. Is everything okay?"

"Oh, fine, fine," Einar said. "Yer Pop just found his way into m'barn 'gain. Cold out tonight, thought you'd wanter know."

"Damn," Frank said somewhat under his breath. "I'm sorry, Willie. I'll be over in just a few minutes."

"I'll put some coffee on," Einar said.

"You don't have to do that. You've been bothered enough."

"Was awake anyway. Could use another voice and you'll want somethin' warm ter keep ya 'wake on th'drive back home."

"Thanks, Willie. I'll be there soon."

Einar picked up his crutches and slowly made his way downstairs to the kitchen. He had always liked the house at this time of night, dark and still, the only sounds coming from the creaks and groans of the settling floorboards and foundation. As he made his way down the stairs into the living room, Einar kept the lights off to bask in that familiar memory a bit longer, just until Frank arrived, just a few minutes more. It felt good to be there, in that old house, just by himself. As he passed through the living room past the front door, Einar checked to make sure the front door was unlocked—not that it ever *was* locked, but wasn't it strange when those kind of compulsions hit us?—and then went to the kitchen to make coffee. Only then did he turn on a light, the low and soft one just above the stove that threw just enough light to make visible the stove itself and the counter tops surrounding it.

As the water boiled, Einar sat at the kitchen table, his leg throbbing, wondering what it must have been like to be Gerald, slowly oblivious to the world. Einar's first thought on the matter was, like that of so many others, of tragedy. The man had essentially lost his mind. But as Einar looked around his kitchen and tried to shake off the memory of his wife and the recent death of his son, he wondered how bad it *really* could have been for Gerald to lose his mind. Could Einar do it? Would he want to? Sometimes he thought he would, he could, but then the rational side of him, the side of him that got up at four thirty every morning for thirty years to tend to the potato fields, told him no, his mind was too important, his cognizance all he had left. Those two sides of him fought each other daily now as his body began to fail and his spirit weakened. Einar wondered if he was destined to become a lonely old man.

By the time the water had come to a boil, Einar heard his front door open and then close. He decided then, as he heard Frank's footsteps clop across his living room floor, that his mind was fine where it was. Whether Gerald Jordan's deterioration was a blessing in disguise or the curse it overtly appeared to be was beyond Einar, but as far as he could tell, his own mind was just fine the way it was.

"In the kitchen, Frank," Einar hollered. He had been struggling to get himself out of his chair when he yelled to Frank, but now, as he stood leaning on his crutches, Einar stopped and listened…listened because beyond the hiss of the now-boiling water on the stove, there were no sounds in his house at all.

The footsteps in the living room that he thought had been Frank's had ceased entirely.

*   *   *

Frank crawled out of bed and Eleanor stirred. "What's wrong?" She said.

"Willie Coates just called. Says Pop's in his barn again. I'm going to go take care of it.

"Frank," Eleanor said softly. Frank sat back down on the bed and leaned over her. Eleanor reached up and cupped her hands behind his neck, pulling him down toward her softly. She kissed him, and though she had done so before, Frank's body still tensed up at the touch of her lips on his. "Be careful," she said, letting go of his neck and turning back onto her side. Frank ran his hand down over her curled arm and then got up.

He dressed himself and made his way quietly down the hallway. He stopped at his father's bedroom and pushed the door open, flipped the light on. The covers had been tossed aside and the bed was empty. "Dammit, Pop," Frank said, flipping the light back off and heading down the stairs.

By twelve forty-five, Frank was driving through the settled snow toward Willie Coates's house.

*   *   *

It had taken quite a while for Angus to make it all the way up to the Coates place, and when he got there, he was shivering so hard he thought he might break his own spine. He had no gloves, his boots

219

were low cut and let the snow sneak in around his ankles, his neck felt as though it had frozen solid, and he hadn't been able to feel his nose for the last two hours. But he was here, and that was a step in the right direction.

Angus approached the house and decided to warm himself in the barn before trying his hand at whatever waited for him inside the house. He'd be no good if he was shivering so hard he couldn't keep himself standing up straight, so he went to the barn and spent some time huddled underneath the hay. The barn itself was warmer than the outside, but not by much; once he settled underneath the hay, he warmed up surprisingly quickly and felt his will regenerate. It didn't take him long to feel heat course through him; his blood felt like coffee, his eyes like stew. Angus got out of the hay and rifled through the barn for a few minutes, searching for something long, heavy, blunt, deadly. He found what he was looking for in the corner of the barn in front of the tractor.

Einar's axe.

He handled it with a reverence he had never shown anything in his entire life, not even his life itself. This axe would be the equalizer. He felt it as his calloused hands ran up and down the wooden handle and over the blunt end of the metal head. The sharp end, the wonderfully sharp end, seemed to gleam at him even in the darkness of the night that swallowed him in the barn. The axe.

The axe.

Angus crept out into the yard and around to the front of the house. He climbed the steps to the porch. Curled his hand around the doorknob, knowing no one locked their doors in Northern Maine, knowing it would turn easily, and it did. He pushed the door open, startled himself when the door hinges squeaked loudly—something else he should have expected but something that had slipped his adrenaline-riddled mind—then calmed himself down as he stepped into the dark living room of the Coates house.

*   *   *

When he thought about it, Einar couldn't believe so much could happen in one instance. He had always felt individual moments were designed to play host to individual events, maybe two at most, but when the door to the kitchen swung open, too much happened all at once for it to have really happened *all at once.*

As soon as the words had passed his lips, Einar knew he had not called out to Frank in the living room. He had called Frank's name to someone else, and that someone else had been spooked at the sound of Einar's voice. Einar leaned one of his crutches against the counter top and picked up the pot of boiling water with his free right hand. Then he slowly approached the door between the kitchen and the living room.

It swung open before he took more than two steps toward it.

It swung open with such ferocity that it hit the wall behind it and ripped off its hinges. Einar took a blind swing with the pot of boiling water, which made contact with whoever was storming into the kitchen, but Einar had no idea where he had made contact. He immediately fell to the floor, a product of his own force and imbalance on his good right leg, and a scream filled the room. It was not Einar's.

Einar looked up to see a massive man he did not recognize reaching for his face with his free hand, the hand that wasn't holding Einar's very own axe. The coffee pot had landed on the left side of the man's face and had left a burnt streak of flesh across it. The man quickly recovered, however, and he brought the blunt end of Einar's axe down hard and swift. It re-shattered Einar's left leg and Einar howled.

In that same moment, Frank walked through the front door.

Then came the man's scream, followed immediately by Einar's. Frank ran through the living room, saw the kitchen door off its hinges, and felt adrenaline shoot through his body. The moment he entered the kitchen, however, he was on the floor, bloody and unconscious. The butt of the axe handle had made solid contact with Frank's forehead. Blood screamed into the air in three different directions and Einar thought Frank was dead.

In case he wasn't, the man sent a fist into Frank's face, then one into his gut, then another into his face. All this happened in what seemed, to Einar, to be the same moment.

When the man turned to face Einar again, the man's face lit up into a grin. That was when Einar recognized him: Angus McCausland. He had seen plenty of that face years ago during court proceedings. These were memories Einar would just as soon forget, but here they were, staring him in the face with a sharp and maniacal grin.

Angus looked toward the door next to the stove. "That the basement?" He said, his grin not fading even a little bit, as if this were pure ecstasy for him. Einar did not reply. Angus sent the axe through the door—which was entirely unnecessary considering it was unlocked and half open anyway—and swung it aside. The steps that led to the basement were only barely visible in the slight slivers of light cast off by the bulb above the stove. Angus grabbed Frank underneath his armpits and sent him tumbling down the stairs. Einar heard Frank's body hit the dirt floor of the basement with a dead thud he had heard over and over again back in the war, and it sent a shiver through him.

Angus slammed the basement door closed. It ricocheted back open and Angus slammed it again. Then he let out a growl and grabbed the kitchen table, swung it across the kitchen and propped it against the door.

Then he turned his grin once again to Einar.

"Knock knock," he grunted at Einar. "Jason home?"

Angus sent the axe down toward Einar again, this time with the sharp end. Einar rolled to his side and the axe lodged into the kitchen floor. Angus laughed. "Just want to play with him," Angus said.

"He ain't here," Einar said, far too calmly for how he really felt.

Angus dislodged the axe and leaned his forearms on it. "Well I guess we'll just have to wait for him."

"He ain't comin' here any time soon."

"Everyone comes home sometime," Angus said.

"Ya damned fool, Jason ha'n't lived here in years."

For the first time since he stormed into the kitchen, Angus's grin disappeared. He lifted the axe again and tapped the underside of Einar's chin with the heavy head of it. "What you mean? Where's he live then?"

"He's a grown man," Einar barked. "Lives where he wants to live."

"*Where does he fucking live?*" Angus screamed.

"Portland," Einar said, once again too calmly for how he felt. Now it was Einar's turn to smile.

Angus's face contorted and pinched, making it look as if he was holding his breath to spite his parents. He stomped his feet on the kitchen floor, making the pots in the cupboards rattle and clang against each other. "Shit," he spat. "Shit, shit, shit!" Angus sent the axe into the wall where the kitchen table had been, then kicked the handle and pulled the axe out of the wall. He then knelt down next to Einar and once again pressed the head of the axe underneath his chin.

"Where in Portland?"

Einar laughed an old man's laugh. It immediately irritated Angus. He pressed the axe head harder into Einar's chin.

"Where in Portland?"

"Boy, even if I told ya, cops'd be all ovah ya by the time ya got down the forty-four."

"You ain't gonna call the cops," Angus said, "because I'll kill you first."

"Then you'll kill me without knowin' where m'boy lives."

"You think I'm kidding, old man?"

"Don't make no nevahmind t'me."

Angus stared at Einar for a long while, trying to work through what he might be able to do next. The old man was right: if he left now, the cops would find him quick. He supposed he could get into the woods quick enough, but if he really wanted to go to Portland, the cops would be on the lookout down there. And if he killed the old man—well, he was going to kill the old man anyway, but he wanted more info from him, wanted to know how to get to Jason, wanted—

Angus had a thought.

"Get up," he said to Einar.

"Can't get up, ya damnt fool, I—"

"Just get the fuck up!" Angus screamed.

Einar worked his way up with the aid of the countertop and felt a thousand electrical circuits erupt into flames inside his left leg. As he gritted his teeth, bearing the pain of his shattered leg, Angus crossed the kitchen and picked up the cordless phone off its cradle hanging from the wall. He handed it to Einar.

"Call him. Call him and tell him you…you fell down the stairs and broke your leg again. Tell him it hurts bad and he needs to come up."

"I won't," Einar said.

"You damn well *will*," Angus shouted, swinging the axe and burying the head in the door of the refrigerator.

The last time Einar William Coates feared for his life was during the war. Squatting in the bush, soaked from the rain, bullets seemed to come out of the air like flies and bite you just as frequently. He had been lucky for the most part, only getting grazed by a bullet once, and it had shaken him badly. For weeks after, he felt as though his life would be taken from him at any given arbitrary moment, stopped in mid-sentence maybe, or in mid-piss or in mid-sleep. He feared. And when he got back from the war, he stopped fearing.

Until now, in the company of Angus McCausland. There was something about the way Angus grinned despite the bubbling burn across his face from Einar's coffee pot, something in his obsession to find Jason. Einar figured Frank could have been dead already, and he also figured he was next, but he did not want Jason to enter into this. He'd lost one boy. He'd be goddamned if he lost the other.

When Bethany had been just a little girl, no more than five or six, she developed a fear of the barn and would not go in there for any reason, especially at night. When Robert and Jason found out about her fear, they of course compounded it by playing tricks on her. Soon enough, they had tormented her so much that she then feared the basement, the dock down by the lake, and the underside of the front porch as much as she feared the barn. So Einar sat her down one day, bobbing her up and down on his thigh until she giggled hard, and he said to her, "If them brothers of yers bother ya, you tell me and I'll put a hurt to em."

Bethany shook her head. "No, daddy, they'll scare me even more after that if they know I told on them."

"Okay," Einar said, looking out at his yard. He didn't know what to tell her at first, but then, staring at the tractor down by the barn, it came to him. "How about this. If you're ever scared, or if somethin's wrong, or if them brothahs of yers put a fear in ya, you come to me and you say, 'Daddy, tractor's got a flat,' and I'll know what you mean."

"Like a code word?" Bethany said, a smile beaming across her face.

"Exactly," Einar said, and for years after that, that phrase acted as a secret communiqué between them. Einar figured Bethany hadn't said it to him in ten years or more, and as he leaned on the counter, the phone in his hand, he hoped with every inch of his battered and broken body that she remembered.

"Fine," he said to Angus as he started to dial the number. A few moments passed and Angus looked as eager as a dog with a ball in its mouth.

Bethany picked up on the other end of the phone. "Hello," she said, sleep deep in her voice.

"Jason, it's Pop," he said.

"Daddy, this is Bethany, not Jason. Are you okay?"

"Had an accident, Jason. Need ya to come up. Fell down the stairs and re-broke m'leg. Can ya come?"

"This isn't Jason, Daddy, but I'll come up. Did you hit your head? Can you call Frank Jordan to come get you?"

"Nah," Einar said, looking over at Angus, who was grinning again. "Truck's not runnin', and, uh, tractor's got a flat."

There was a long pause on the phone, then Bethany asked again, "Daddy, did you hit your head?"

"No, goddammit," Einar barked. "Tractor's got a *flat*." He looked over at Angus to see if he sensed anything, but Angus's face kept its dumb look as it had moments before.

Bethany whispered now. "Tractor's got a flat? Is someone there, Daddy?"

"Yes."

"Should I call the cops?"

"Yes."

"Okay, I will. And Askar and I will come up now, fast as we can."

"You call your br—your sister, too, before you come up."

226

Angus took a step toward Einar.

"Daddy," Bethany whispered, "you want me to call Jason?"

"Yes," he said. "Now get goin'!"

Einar hung up the phone.

*   *   *

Jason quickly transitioned from drunk to hung over. He suspected that had something to do with Ginny's presence; had she not shown up that night, he would have drank all the way through until morning and been drunk when the sun came up. As it happened, however, Ginny had come to the apartment and made sure the hangover hit him during the night and not midway through tomorrow morning.

For weeks now, Jason's apartment resembled very closely the tiny hole of a place in which he and Robert had lived during college. The furniture consisted of whatever was cheap at Goodwill and milk crates that were always free if you hung out long enough in the alley behind the coffee shop on the corner. He had a coffee table that Ginny was sure he'd found on the side of the road and a television he was probably borrowing from a friend. That was it, for the most part, aside from a card-table that acted as a kitchen table and a coffee maker that smelled and looked older than Jason and Ginny combined.

When she had shown up, Jason had been surprised but not unpleasantly so. She had dropped in a few times over the course of the last few weeks, especially since Robert died, and Jason had been drunk on the majority of these visits. Each time she had come and stayed less than ten minutes, and Jason remained perplexed as to why she paid such visits if only to discuss trivialities. But then tonight, Ginny had shown up and proved herself to be a motivated woman. When she climbed into the shower with Jason, she bathed. And that was all.

Jason stood behind her, dumbfounded and more than a little aroused, and when she turned to him and said, "not a chance," he couldn't help but laugh almost uncontrollably.

So they both bathed and by the time they got out of the shower, Jason felt his senses returning. He was still drunk for sure—you don't shower off half of a fifth of Jack Daniels—but he could see why Ginny had come. And stayed. And he loved her for it.

Jason dressed himself in sweatpants and a hoodie sweatshirt, and Ginny pulled a similar outfit out of Jason's pile of clothes and wrapped herself in it. Jason loved the way his too-large UMaine sweatpants fell down over Ginny's hips, the way she rolled up the sleeves of his Bruins sweatshirt, the way she tossed her wet hair back and into a tight ponytail. Ginny was not oblivious to his drunken observations, but she ignored them entirely. She had to. She was here for a reason.

Jason sat on the couch in the living room and Ginny dumped two cans of soup into a pot to boil. Ten minutes later, they sat together on the couch, in silence, around midnight, sipping soup and nothing more. Ginny sat with her feet tucked underneath her. Jason sat with legs splayed out until Ginny told him to sit up straight. When he did, the room began to spin but he did not complain.

After they finished the soup, Ginny went to the sink and washed the pot and the bowls they had each eaten out of. She left the remaining pile of dirty dishes sitting in the sink where she had found them, but carefully placed the pot and two bowls in the dry rack next to the sink. It was empty except for those items, as if the dry rack's presence had been an afterthought for Jason, a perfunctory object necessary to complete any dwelling fit for living. Having apartment equaled having dry rack. Ginny thought she would never understand men.

Jason's bedroom consisted of four bare walls, a closet with clothes vomiting from it, and a mattress lying on the ground in the corner beneath the window. Ginny was certain Jason hadn't washed the sheets since moving in. She lay down next to him anyway, and there she slept for the rest of the night as Jason fought off drunken sleep and listened to his wife breathe. It felt good to be next to her, but he couldn't help but feel out of place, as though he had guilted himself out of any pleasure associated with interacting with Ginny. And hadn't he? Certainly he did, and so around two-thirty, when his drunkenness wore off and his hangover set in, he nudged Ginny awake. With her head resting in the hollow of Jason's shoulder, she ran her right hand up his chest and down his arm, as though she had expected him to wake her exactly at that moment, as if she had calculated the exact time.

"Why did you stay?" Jason said.

"Because I love you and you don't."

"I *do* love you, I really do."

"I know that, you dope. I mean *you* don't love *you*."

Jason let that sink in for a moment. Was it true?

"Jason, just know that—this doesn't mean anything, me being here. I don't want you to think—"

"I know," Jason said, and he intended to say more, but his cell phone started ringing.

Ginny lifted her head first. "It's late," she said, almost inquisitively.

"Yeah," Jason said as he reached for his phone, which was lying on the floor next to the bed. He looked at the display screen. "It's Bethany." He flipped open the phone. "Hey," he said. Ginny listened to the muffled sound of Bethany's voice coming through the phone, but she could not make out what she was saying. But she could read Jason's immediate worry right away. Something was wrong. Something had happened—something bad, of course, because misfortune only follows misfortune.

"Slow down," Jason said. "What did he say?"

Muffled voice again.

"Did you call the police already?"

Muffled voice, and what Ginny could have sworn was crying.

"Bethany, are you sure? Are you absolutely *sure*?"

Muffled voice, and Ginny could hear aggravation in Bethany's voice now. She still couldn't make out words, but she recognized the urgency.

"Okay. Okay, I'm getting up. I'll leave right now."

Jason hung up the phone. Ginny was already sitting up in bed, ready to get up, ready to go wherever they needed to go…but then she stopped herself. She needed to keep that distance. Whatever was happening had nothing to do with her, at least at this stage in the game. She had to keep her distance.

"What's going on?" She said as Jason reached around her for the light switch of the reading lamp on the floor beside the bed.

"Bethany said my Pop called her. She says something's wrong."

"What's wrong?"

"She doesn't know. She…she said something about a code word. I have no idea what the hell she's talking about, but she called the police and she wants me to go up there."

"Are you going?"

"I guess I have to," Jason said as he climbed out of bed.

"You should try calling him first," Ginny said as she, too, climbed out of bed.

"Yeah, I should." And so he did. No one answered. He tried again. No answer. He tried again. Still no answer.

As Jason hung up the phone for the third time, Ginny recognized real apprehension cross his face for the first time. He changed into a pair of jeans and pulled some boots on. "I'm sorry," he said to Ginny, not sure whether or not he should try to hug her, or kiss her, or just leave. "You can stay the rest of the night," he offered as Ginny stood in the doorway of the bedroom, still in her bare feet, still in Jason's sweatpants and sweatshirt.

Ginny watched as Jason turned to go, knowing she should just go home and forget about it, but also knowing she wouldn't. "Wait," she said, then went to the bathroom and undressed. Five minutes later, she emerged in the dress she had worn when she came to Jason's apartment earlier that night. "I'm coming, too," she said, and so they left together, bound for The County, bound for Einar's place.

*   *   *

Eleanor could not sleep after Frank left, so she got up and made herself a cup of tea. Sitting in the darkness of the kitchen, the snow outside looked electric, bright and white contrasted against the red of the sky. The sight had made Eleanor uneasy ever since she was a little girl, the thought of looking out into the yard and seeing clearly the trees and the ground when she should see nothing but thick black dark, the stuff of night, the setting of sleep. The landscape always seemed menacing to Eleanor when it had a fresh coat of snow on it, and tonight as she sipped her tea and looked out the window at the woods beyond the yard, it felt no different.

Frank had been gone for almost an hour and a half now. It wasn't too much of a stretch to think that Gerald was giving him an extra difficult time over at the Coates place. Maybe he was running around the yard. Maybe he wouldn't come down from the hay loft in the barn. Maybe they were all sitting in Einar's kitchen drinking coffee and talking about nothing in particular.

But the thought of Frank being gone so long, much like the snow outside the window, seemed menacing to her.

She sat in the kitchen and waited. As she leaned against the counter, she began to think if there was something else she should be worried about—namely, the fact that she was getting very attached to Frank Jordan. Their interaction, while seemingly good for both of them, felt like dangerous territory to her, as if Natalie might return at any moment and sweep Frank away from her, leaving her alone yet again, leaving her to live up to her name yet again, the stupid, cursed name her father had given her. It felt silly to do it, but she worried about it every time she got close to Frank. They hadn't gotten *too* close just yet—sex had been something they both stumbled around often but both were too afraid to actually initiate it—and Eleanor kept it that way. She figured Frank did, too, but she wished like hell they didn't have to keep each other at arm's length, as if the other might be gone for good at any moment.

But it made her smile, if only for a moment, thinking about how the nervousness of it all made her feel so young, like high school all over again. After she had gotten divorced, she often sat behind the counter at Gibson's Feed and thought about what it might be like to go back to high school and do it all over again with the maturity she possessed now, the knowledge of the world she had accrued since then. What difference it would have made! Maybe she would have been confident. Maybe she would have been more popular or made better decisions.

But the fact of the matter was, you could never go back. She knew that better than anyone, and she figured if being with Frank Jordan gave her a sense that she could renew whatever feeling in her had been lost when she got divorced, then she would do it, danger and nervousness be damned.

At two in the morning, Eleanor could not stand it anymore. She picked up the phone and called the Coates house.

"Answer it," Angus said, his voice raspy from almost an hour of complete silence. Einar hesitated, then did as he was told.

"Hello," he said.

Eleanor's pleasant but worried voice responded. "Hello, Einar, this is Eleanor Phillips. Has Frank been there yet?"

"Ayuh, he has," Einar said.

"Oh, good. And has he left for home with Gerald?"

Einar thought for a moment. According to the clock on the wall, it was coming on two o'clock and the police had not come. That meant one of two things: either Bethany hadn't called them, or the police in Fort Kent figured any disturbance way out CR44 at two in the morning could wait until morning, especially with the roads as slick as they were. Einar figured on the latter. He knew well enough folks up this way saw more than their fair share of domestic abuse cases, and the police had learned, for better or worse, that most could wait until morning.

Some couldn't.

This one couldn't. And this one went beyond just plain ol' domestic abuse.

Should he tell Eleanor to come? She might be able to help—and then again, she might just get herself killed.

"Ayuh," Einar said. "Left just a little bit ago with Gerald."

Eleanor sighed. "Okay, thanks, Einar. I was just…just worried with the roads the way they are."

"He'll be just fine," Einar said. "Goodnight, Eleanor."

"Goodnight, Einar."

When Einar put the phone down, Angus smiled. "Smart move," he said, the axe head resting in the palm of his right hand.

"The hell you want wi' my boy anyway?" Einar said, his voice stronger than maybe it should have been. Angus, who had been plopped heavily and splayed in the only chair in the kitchen that hadn't been smashed or overturned, stood up and hovered over Einar, who sat on the floor with his back pressed against the counter and his shattered leg bleeding and pulsing beneath him.

"Guess you'll see when he gets here. You'll have front row seats when I smash his goddamn face in."

"Why th' hell ya want to go and do a thing like that?" Einar asked the question with sincerity laced in his voice, but he really had no interest in the answer at all. In fact, Einar figured he had Angus McCausland pretty well figured out. Einar had known Angus's father, a shit of a man named Linus. Linus smoked like a chimney and had only a few teeth left by the time he settled into his deathbed. He drank more than any man Einar had ever seen, and Einar had seen his fair share of drunks. Any time Einar had the distinct privilege of interacting with Linus, he could be assured he would see a man wearing no shirt smoking a cigarette, even in the dead of winter, as if the snow, too, made him sweat.

Looking at Angus made Einar certain the beer never strayed far from the six pack, and Angus's anger was no surprise at all to him. So far as Einar could figure, Angus had been in jail since high school when the whole fiasco with Jason and that boy who got killed happened in late spring of that year. That would be enough to piss anyone off, but a slow mind like Angus's would latch on to one thing and one thing only: anger. Simple, stupid anger. And who would he focus that anger on? Why, the last boy from his school that he would ever see, the boy who testified against him at the trial, Jason Coates. No, Einar had no question in his mind what Angus wanted to do to Jason. But he had no intention of letting Angus get his way.

Angus made like he was going to throw the axe in Einar's direction but then stopped and laughed. Einar did not flinch. He stared up at Angus instead, his eyes unmoving, and though Angus would not admit it to himself or show it to Einar, it unsettled Angus to his core.

*   *   *

As Eleanor finished off her cup of tea and made her way back up to the bedroom, she decided worrying in the comfort of the bed sheets was just as well as worrying in the cold of the kitchen. She knew she wouldn't sleep either way until Frank returned, so she decided to warm her numb toes in the bed rather than shuffle them underneath her body in a chair in the kitchen.

She climbed the creaky stairs to the second floor of the house, the creaks now becoming familiar to her, how funny that was, and when she reached the landing, she shuffled toward the bedroom. When she reached the dark doorway, she stopped.

"No," she said softly, negating to herself that she had heard what she had just heard. She listened closely, and a few seconds later, the sound came again.

Snoring.

Eleanor stepped lightly back down the hallway, listening for more of the snoring, and when it came again, she knew it was coming from the bathroom. "No," she said again, just as softly as the first time. She curled her hand around the doorknob to the bathroom, turned it, pushed it open and saw exactly what she thought she would see, exactly what she hoped she would not see: Gerald Jordan, pants down, sitting on the toilet, fast asleep in his own stink.

Panic set in immediately, but she tried her best to calm it. She wanted to run downstairs, but instead she walked. When she looked out the window onto the driveway and did not see the truck parked there, she wanted to scream but didn't.

And when she climbed into her own truck, shivering from the cold and kicking the snow off her boots before she closed the door, she wanted to drive a hundred miles an hour all the way to Einar Coates's house. But she didn't. She drove slowly and prudently until, almost a half hour later, she pulled into the driveway of the Coates house.

*   *   *

It had barely snowed at all in Portland. The storm, as it was, hadn't done much more than temporarily wet the pavement of the streets. But as Jason and Ginny drove north through Bangor at around one-thirty in the morning, the snow had accumulated to a stout and steady one inch. With still another two and a half hours of driving to go, Jason knew exactly what Fort Kent and CR44 beyond would look like: an un-plowed mess of at least three or four inches of snow. Sure, the major roads in Fort Kent would probably be clear and a little icy, but CR44 would be a tough drive, especially when the pavement turned to dirt. Jason knew this but said nothing to Ginny, who had driven the first hour and relinquished the driver's seat to Jason near Hermon.

Bethany had called Jason's cell phone about a half hour earlier. Askar would not leave Boston for yet another supposedly pointless trip to Northern Maine in the middle of the night, and he and Bethany had spent the last two hours fighting about it. When she called Jason, she sounded completely broken and told him she couldn't make the drive by herself. "It's fine," he told her. "I'll take care of it. Ginny's here and *we'll* take care of it."

Jason could hear the surprise in Bethany's voice when she said okay, but she did not make a big issue out of it. Instead, she hung up the phone and faced whatever was going on down in Boston between her and her husband.

*   *   *

Frank was not dead.
He felt like death, but he wasn't dead.

*   *   *

Years ago, when he had first met the woman who was to be his wife, Frank sat down at a dirty table in a dirty diner in Southern California and waited. He waited for an answer from this beautiful woman he had been terrified to even approach only a week earlier. He waited for an answer to a question he could not believe he had asked.

"How is it that you are completely unafraid to believe in God?"

The question had come as a surprise to both of them, had come somewhat out of the blue, for neither of them were religious in the sense that they went to church or read the bible. But Frank had lost some sort of direction, some balance that he, as a young man, attributed to a loss of faith or an estrangement with God, if God actually existed at all. It was a crisis he kept to himself; he did not mention it even to his best of friends, nor to his family. Instead, he worried about it only in dark rooms intended for sleep, in quiet places like waiting rooms or libraries (on the off chance he visited one), or in the most public of places where it was necessary to ensconce oneself within oneself in order to protect from stray eye contact or involuntary touching. Only then did he wonder.

But then he met Natalie. Actually, he had met her months before in, of all places, a waiting room. They were applying for the same job,

237

the same go-nowhere job that everyone was dying to get in L.A., and had Natalie not been the one to speak to him, Frank would not have ventured to give her a second look—even though all he wanted to do was stare at this beautiful woman. As it happened, Natalie was not so content to be coy. She piped up immediately.

"You shouldn't be so nervous," she said to Frank. "They're going to tell us all no, and then call one of us later on and say yes. That's how it works around here."

Frank nodded and smiled politely, but nothing more.

"You're new in town. I can see it written all over you." Natalie had been sitting two seats away from Frank, but now she scooted over into the seat next to his. "You know how I know?"

"No," Frank said quietly. He immediately thought he sounded dumb and shy. Natalie immediately thought Frank's response was distant and stoic, yet endearing.

"I know because you listened when I started talking to you."

Frank allowed himself to smile honestly this time, and Natalie smiled with him. Moments later, Natalie's name was called for the interview, and he must have missed her in the transition because when he came back out from his own interview, Natalie was gone.

Three weeks passed before he saw her again.

As she had promised, they told him No immediately and then called him four days later to tell him yes. He was the new manager of The Sports Heaven sporting goods store in East L.A. He had no idea why he was even in California to begin with, other than to not be in Maine anymore, but this seemed like a good start. At least he could pay his rent now.

He had been on the job for four days when he saw Natalie again. She was waiting for the bus at the stop around the corner from The Sports Heaven, and when Frank realized that he would be standing no more than two feet away from her in only a moment's time, his heart did a somersault that ended ungracefully in a belly flop. And so he did stand next to her, but he could not speak. And she did not notice him. She read her paperback book and got on the bus. Frank sat two seats behind her. She did not notice him. He got off at his stop and she did not notice him.

Frank poured himself a whiskey and Coke that night that was three parts whiskey and no parts Coke.

Three days later, she was at the bus stop again, just as Frank had so desperately hoped. This time, he vowed to talk to her. She was reading the same paperback and Frank stood right next to her this time. He did not nudge her or poke her or try to gain her attention. He simply began speaking.

"It was four days," he said out loud, seemingly to no one in particular. "Four days until they told me yes."

Natalie was the only one standing at the bus stop to look up at him. Frank smiled. "That's how I know you're not from around here," Frank said coolly, though he was shaking all over and sweating a little. "You're the only one who actually listened to me."

For a moment, Natalie did not respond, and it was a moment in which Frank felt like a complete fool. But she finally smiled and said, "Frank, right?"

As if that validation, that simple recognition of his name, were enough to split the clouds and reel the sun right into his pocket, Frank's unease disappeared entirely.

They went out on their first date the next night.

A week later, they sat in a dirty diner across from each other, picking at apple pie neither of them really wanted to eat, and Frank asked his question about God.

"How is it that you are completely unafraid to believe in God?"

Natalie put down her fork. She had told Frank what it was like to grow up the way she had, with her father being a pastor and her mother working full time at the church. She told of her rebellion against religion, the drugs, the drinking, the sex she had with boys she didn't even like just to upset her parents, the way she would leave marijuana in plain view on her dresser in high school so she would get caught because getting caught was the only way to rebel. She told about the last time she had seen her father, when she told him that God was just a story people told to scare others into being submissive, how she made her father believe she really felt that way. And Frank listened to every word as if it were gospel.

But then she had said something surprising.

"But I do believe in God. I just don't know what he wants from me."

She said it with a nonchalance that shook Frank out of his daze caused by his crush on Natalie. He could not understand it and said so immediately.

He started slowly. "I grew up in Maine," he said, and Natalie smiled. Frank didn't know why she smiled, but he loved it anyway.

"I've never been there," Natalie said.

"Neither has God," Frank replied. "My Pop, he doesn't believe in God. Lots of folks up where I'm from don't, but I guess just as many do. Me, well, I guess I stopped believing in that when I was a kid and one of my best friends died. Henry was his name. I had hope after that, you know, just enough to get me by, but then in high school something else happened. This boy, Angus McCausland, he—well, it doesn't matter what he did, but that was when I knew God didn't exist. At least not in Northern Maine. At least not for me."

Frank stared down at his uneaten pie. Natalie looked at him from across the table and wondered something she had wondered periodically throughout her life: how did she talk someone into believing in a God that sincerely and honestly did not exist to that someone? She supposed she couldn't, because for some, God did not exist at all. That, she had figured a long time ago, was the wonder of being a human. Our minds create reality. Each mind is different. Each reality, therefore, is different. Some folks just can't conjure God in their minds. Natalie knew this.

"Maybe that's true," she said. "In fact, it *is* true, Frank. If God doesn't exist, if you say He doesn't, then he doesn't. But you know how I know He exists?"

Frank looked up. "No."

Natalie leaned across the table and kissed him on the lips. "You're here, and if it's God or just plain energy or some fluke of nature, you being here is a good thing. That's why I believe in God and that's why I don't give a rat's ass if people bash me for it."

They both grinned childish grins for a moment, and just as quickly as the topic had come up, it vanished entirely.

Four years later, Frank was on the brink of being divorced from the woman he loved fiercely from the moment he met her. He had never believed in God, not even after that night at the diner with Natalie, but he entertained the notion at least after that. But now, tonight, pummeled and beaten and sprawled on the ground with at least two broken bones, probably more, and his face exploding in a pain he had never in his life felt before, Frank figured there might be a God out there somewhere. He still believed God had never been to Northern Maine, and he was not here tonight, but maybe he was out there. How else could this much misfortune befall one place all at once? Only if God was not looking, that's how.

Frank managed to prop himself up on one arm, then immediately fell back down sprawled. His arm was broken. That much seemed certain. He tried his left arm this time, and it supported his weight. That was a good start. He let out an involuntary groan as he prepared to try and stand up, not knowing what limbs might give out or shriek in pain, not knowing exactly where he was or how he got there, and not knowing why he felt as though he needed to get up in the first place, or why he felt a certain sense of urgency and dread mixed together in his mind and heart.

Frank took two deep breaths and tried to stand in the pitch black of Einar William Coates's basement.

*   *   *

Angus was digging through the refrigerator when Einar heard a familiar sound. Owning the same home for as long as he had allowed him to become almost eerily familiar with it, the way a husband and wife know the nuances of each other without really thinking about it after time. Creaks and pops, tricks of opening certain windows or un-jamming certain doors, knowing where the bathtub leaks; these slight variances from smooth existence were what made his house lovable, or so Einar believed, and one of those variances had just—well, varied.

Whenever the heat kicked on, Einar knew the furnace would groan, a fierce sound that always forced an image of a sick elephant into his mind. Sarah always told him he needed to pick a new image for that one, since she knew damn well Einar had never seen an elephant, let alone a sick one. He also knew that when the snow piled up on the southeast corner of the roof, the water dripped right on the window-sill of what used to be Bethany's room, causing a tapping sound that sounded like a helicopter built to miniature scale.

He also knew that when someone walked up the front steps onto the porch and the temperature was just right, the first board lying across the porch itself was liable to pop up hard and give off a report like a gunshot that echoed off the trees in the yard. He heard such a gunshot as he sat sprawled on the kitchen floor, watching Angus McCausland dig through the refrigerator in search of some sustenance.

This sound worried Einar for two reasons: first, whoever was climbing the front steps right now was in a heap of trouble because they had no idea what they were walking into, and second, whoever was walking up the steps was not a member of his family. Bethany would know to come to the back door after the phone call he had made, and even if she didn't, she would know to step over that board. Jason would, too. They had learned the nuance of the front porch over the years just as Einar had. Sarah, however, had never really taken it to mind and managed to step on that board each and every time she climbed the steps, startling herself out of her shoes as the gunshot-like pop echoed through the yard.

But Sarah was dead and that left only strangers as a possibility for their guest.

Angus closed the refrigerator door immediately and glared at Einar as if to say, without words, *what the hell was that?*

"Don't getcher killin' shoes on just yet," Einar said, hoping to hell he sounded calm. "Was just the water pipe downstairs in th'basement. Jumps in cold weather and knocks against th'floorboards sometimes."

Angus looked at Einar a moment longer with a look that suggested he didn't believe a word that was coming out of the old man's mouth. Einar recognized the look and tried even harder to keep himself from panicking. "Check fer yerself if ya want. Downstairs in th'basement near the only window down there."

"Maybe I'll just take a look around," Angus said, then smiled. He tooled out of the room with bounding steps through the living room and toward the front door. He swung it open with no caution whatsoever and stepped out into the cold, onto the porch to see what he could see.

What he saw bothered him.

A pick-up truck sat parked in front of the house.

Angus plodded down the steps and into the snow-covered driveway toward the driver's side of the truck and glanced in. No one inside, nothing much to look at. He turned his attention toward the house and scanned, in the darkness, the perimeter of the porch and then toward the barn. Nothing. Angus ran back inside the house.

"Your boy drive a pick up truck?" Angus said to Einar.

"Drives some damn foreign car," Einar replied, not bothering to lie this time. His contempt for Jason's car mirrored almost equally his contempt for Angus, who now stood glowering over Einar.

"I think you're lying, old man."

"Think all ya want."

Without another word or any other indication that he might do what he was about to do, Angus lifted the axe above his head and brought the blunt end of it down on Einar's left ankle. Einar howled, his face turning red and his hands shooting as far down his leg as he could reach, which wasn't far enough to appease the pain. Then he blacked out.

Angus returned to the living room, turned the light on, then off. He returned to the kitchen and stared out the back window until his eyes went blurry.

VI

HOME AGAIN

When Eleanor arrived at Einar's house, she made an effort to pull into the driveway silently, turning off her headlights as soon as she got within range of the house. She didn't know what was going on, but if it was nothing, she had decided she didn't want to disturb anyone. But when she got close enough to the house and saw Frank's truck parked out front, she knew something had happened. Why else would Einar have lied to her on the phone?

She parked in front of the house, almost perpendicular to Frank's truck, and hopped out. When she climbed the stairs to the porch, she remembered to step over the tricky board that made the gunshot sound Frank had told her about last time they visited Einar—he had said it almost in passing, as if it floated up to his mind ethereally, an unsuspecting memory intruding only for a moment—and was about to knock on the door when she thought better of it. No, she'd try the back door instead. She would be able to look in the window back there.

Eleanor turned to head back down the porch steps but failed to miss the tricky board this time. The gunshot-sound erupted and echoed off the tree, and with adrenaline shooting through her body, Eleanor ran down the remaining steps and around the porch toward the back of the house.

*   *   *

Frank, too, heard the gunshot. He had been in the middle of trying to hoist his battered body to its feet when the sound pierced through the basement. Frank immediately fell back down to the dirt floor and held in a groan. Then he listened to the eerie silence that followed the loud bang to see what might happen next. What he expected was some sort of scream of pain. What actually sounded though the air was a series of bounding footsteps above him bouncing through the house toward the front door.

To the best of his knowledge, Frank figured he had a broken nose, maybe the part of his skull around his left eye (he would later know this bone to be his orbital bone), and definitely his right arm. His right leg, well, that was a chaos of pain everywhere below the belt. He didn't think he had any breaks, but something was definitely dislocated. Every movement made a symphony strike up throughout every inch of his leg and putting weight on it seemed impossible. Nonetheless, he tried to sit up once again, wondering what had happened to him and where, exactly, he was now. He remembered going to Einar's house to pick up his Pop, but beyond that, he had no recollection of what happened once he got to Einar's.

Frank figured he must be at Einar's place—by the sounds of the footsteps above him, he was in the basement, which would make sense since he was lying in dirt. But why? And why all the injuries? *Come on, Frank,* he thought. *Think. What happened to you?* But he honestly had no recollection, which was not surprising, given the amount of time—or lack thereof—that had passed between his arrival and Angus's attack.

He could not see a thing except for a single sliver of faded light coming from a dusty window behind him. It was the only window in the basement and it gave off next to no light at all, but it was enough to discern a staircase not far from Frank's feet. He sat up, turned himself, and began to drag himself toward the stairs. When his fingers grabbed on to the bottom step, he heard something that made every muscle of his clench up, every gland produce a gleam of sweat: a massive thud, followed immediately by a piercing scream.

Einar's scream.

Frank thought twice about trying to climb those stairs, but did not actually stop. He got his hip up on the first step, then managed the second step, then stopped to rest. He stopped for a good long time to control the immense pain and his heavy breathing, because he figured whoever was up there was not real friendly, and he figured too if that person heard him, he'd be the next to be screaming like Einar. So he went slow, very slow. Almost a half hour passed before he reached the top step. There he stopped and waited, listening to what was happening in the kitchen beyond, listening for an idea of who might be on the other end, but all he heard was silence.

*   *   *

Jason and Ginny pulled onto CR44 in the early morning darkness, and it was every bit as snowy and slick as he had expected. He remembered once, as a child, his mother had to take him to the hospital in Fort Kent early in the morning as he battled pneumonia. His Pop had been away—Jason couldn't remember where, exactly, and Willie rarely went anywhere without his family in those days, but he was not there, Jason remembered that clearly enough—and so Sarah Coates loaded Jason into the '83 Buick she kept around for grocery runs and pulled out onto the snowy CR44 toward Fort Kent.

He had been scared then and he was certainly nervous now, but neither time was he scared because of the snow itself. No, then it had been fear of the entire course of events—mom didn't get panicky and head out into a snowstorm if junior just had himself a little bit of a cold or a fever—and the slick roads hadn't made his unease any better then. Now, it was the panic-held-in-check of what he and Ginny might find once they got out to his Pop's place. It felt to Jason that this road, when covered in slick winter snow, signified nothing but the worst of events, especially at night, in the dark, immediately following a fresh snowfall.

Sarah had gotten him to the hospital that night safely, only sliding in a corner once and coming out of it gracefully as though she had meant all along to do it that way, and Jason intended to do much the same. Despite her nervousness, Ginny had dozed off in the passenger seat and Jason had no intention of waking her until they were near the driveway, ready to pull in and find out what the hell was going on in Northern Maine this snowy night.

When that moment finally came, Jason pulled the car over—the car Willie referred to only as *that foreign car*—and waited before waking Ginny. That moment, as it turned out, was a moment of waiting for many folks, including Bethany, who sat anxiously by her phone in her home outside of Boston, waiting for word from Jason; and for Frank, who sat in agony on the top step of the basement stairs in Einar's house; for Eleanor, who had retreated to the barn to think about what to do next after watching that man—she *thought* it might be Angus, but then she thought that was just her mind playing tricks on her—smash Einar's ankles with the blunt end of an axe; and for Einar himself who, in is unconscious mind, still waited for the moment when it might be time for him to make good on his promise to God, the one he had made when he married Sarah and started his family. Yes, he had certainly been waiting the longest out of all of them.

And would God be here to watch him make good on that promise? Einar certainly thought so the moment Angus entered the house. And in his unconscious mind, he knew so.

*   *   *

Jesus it's cold in here, Eleanor thought over and over again as she wrapped her arms around herself. She stood just inside the barn door, occasionally peeking out across the yard at the house, wondering what she should do next. In her haste to leave Frank's place, she left her cell phone sitting on the night stand; as her shivering grew more and more intense, all she could picture in her mind was the image of that damned cell phone sitting next to Frank's bed.

After seeing that man smash Einar's ankle the way he did, Eleanor fought the urge to vomit right then and there standing on the back stoop by the door. Instead, when she heard Einar's piercing scream, she ran across the yard to the barn, and that was where she stood now, almost a full half hour later, trying to get her shivering—borne partly from the cold and mostly from fear—to stop and her mind to slow down a bit and formulate a plan. She had heard the man inside stomp out to the front porch already (*It just couldn't be Angus,* she thought),

249

so she knew he had realized by now someone was here. She also figured Frank was somewhere inside the house, too, and God only knew what the man had done to him. So what now?

Eleanor peeked out of the barn doors once more and saw a light come on in the living room, then shut off again. But in that span of three seconds that the light had been on, she caught another glimpse of the man who had smashed Einar's ankle to bits. His face appeared to her cold and stupid, not the face of a strategic genius at all. Instead, it seemed the face of a boy, an angry boy who didn't know how to control his—

"Angus," she said out loud to herself, recognizing that boyish, stupid anger all at once. Yes, she had seen that face before when it was younger and had shorter hair atop it. Eleanor's mind exploded as she digested this information. *Oh my god it is Angus it's fucking Angus what do I do he hurt Einar he hurt Frank fuck it's Angus it's Angus Angus fucking McCausland! Have to get to the road, have to find someone—*

"Who the mighty hell are you going to find on the road at this hour in the freezing cold, Eleanor?" She said quietly to herself. *Gotta get to the truck then, sweetheart. You want to do some good for those men inside, then get the hell out of here and quick.*

"Okay, then," she said as she peeked again out of the barn door at the house. So far as she could tell, the only light on in the house was coming from the kitchen, but could she really be sure Angus wasn't sitting in the dark of the living room, waiting for her to make a move? She didn't think Angus was much of a planner, but she didn't think he was *completely* vacant, either. *Gotta take that risk, honey,* she told herself in her mother's voice, oddly enough.

Eleanor did not hesitate. She slinked out of the barn and went around to the back side of it, then slipped into the woods. Several minutes later, she approached her truck from the back side, hoping like hell no one saw her.

No one did.

She hopped in, started the truck and jammed it into reverse as quickly as she possibly could.

*   *   *

Angus heard the truck start and ran through the kitchen, into the living room and out the front door. He got there just in time to see the tail lights of Eleanor's truck bouncing their way back up toward the road. Angus stormed off after them, and when he got within twenty feet of the truck's rear bumper, he launched the axe into the air. It struck the rear gate of the truck with its handle, which smashed into two pieces. Then the truck disappeared on up the driveway toward the road.

Angus screamed but did not bother to use any coherent words. Instead, he ran back to the house, bounded through the living room and into the kitchen. He stood over Einar, who was still unconscious. Angus screamed. "Where the hell is he?" Einar did not stir. "I said where the hell is he!" Angus brought his booted right foot down hard on Einar's smashed left ankle. That was when—

*   *   *

Einar woke to astounding pain and the sound of his own voice screaming again. He had blacked out screaming, too, he knew that, but had he ever stopped in between? That he didn't know, but at the moment, he couldn't have cared any less. The pain of it sent all the blood in his body rushing to the surface of his skin, pushing to get out and explode, pushing to escape. Finally Angus let up and Einar's scream dissipated.

"I said, where the hell is he?"

Einar struggled to catch his breath. "I don't know," he said.

"*Bull*shit!" Angus boomed. "He was here. He was here in that god-damn truck and now he left. Now the police will come. Now I gotta—now I have to—"

Angus's face went blank. He obviously had no idea what, exactly, he had to do now. Then thought returned to his face and he did something so instinctively it was frightening to see it happen. Of course, just about every sane man in Northern Maine kept a shotgun in his house, and Angus of all people certainly knew that. But how did he know where to look? Einar chalked it up to a bit of luck and good ol' Maine man instinct, but boy, didn't it startle him to watch Angus walk over to the closet and open it as if he had done so a thousand times in his life, pull out that shotgun as if it had called out to him. He grabbed the gun, checked the chamber for a cartridge, checked the closet for the ammunition box that was most definitely in there somewhere (he found it just inside the left jamb), then slammed the door closed. He returned to Einar.

"Get up."

"Th'hell makes ya think I can do that?"

Angus pointed the gun down at Einar.

"Get up."

Einar got up. Every inch of him screamed as he did it, but he got up. Angus positioned himself behind Einar as he struggled to get his crutches into position, then pressed the muzzle deep into Einar's back. "Walk," he said, and Einar walked. When they reached the back door, Angus poked Einar's back again. "Wait," he said, then turned back toward the kitchen. He looked toward the refrigerator, then toward the cellar door.

For the second time in as many minutes, Einar watched Angus do something so instinctively it was too eerie to be believable. Angus lumbered across the kitchen, threw the kitchen table out of the way, and swung open the door to the cellar.

Frank sat perched on the top step.

"What are you doin' awake?" Angus said, and before Frank could utter a single word, Angus sent the sole of his boot crashing into Frank's face. Einar watched as blood spurted in several different directions and disjointedly thought, *geez, Frank, one more blow like that and your face will be all out of blood completely.*

Frank tumbled backward down the stairs and settled once again into the dirt of the floor. Einar listened to that final, sickening thud of Frank's body hitting the ground and shuddered, but he didn't have much time to dwell on it. Before he knew it, Angus was standing behind him again, poking him with the barrel of the gun and goading him outside across the snowy yard toward the barn.

*   *   *

"Jesus," Jason said, startled. "Whose damn truck was *that?*"

He and Ginny were still sitting on the side of the road in the car, the lights off and the engine cooling. He had awoken her but hadn't even had the chance to tell her where they were before Eleanor's truck came barreling up the driveway and motoring down CR44. She was heading north, away from town, and Jason recognized the truck just in time to have the wherewithal to turn the car on and flash the high beams.

Eleanor slammed on the brakes and skidded to a stop. Then her truck just idled there, in the middle of the road, no more than seventy-five yards up the road.

"Who is it, Jason?" Ginny asked.

"I think it's Elly—Elly Phillips. From the feed store. She and Frank have been—"

Jason did not finish his thought. Both he and Ginny watched as Eleanor's truck came barreling toward them in reverse. For a moment, Jason thought maybe he'd made a mistake, maybe it wasn't Eleanor at all but instead the trouble that he had come up here to discover, but the truck came to a stop next to Jason's car and there was Elly, her face ashen and worried.

Jason put the car in park and got out. Eleanor motioned for him to open the door. When he did, she did not say anything at first, but then the words came quickly, all at once. "Sorry, the window doesn't open. Listen, you're not going to believe this, but Angus McCausland is inside Willie's house and it looks like he's hurt—Willie, not Angus—and I think Frank is in there, too, but I don't know what to do and I forgot my phone at Frank's, so I didn't call the police or anything but—"

"Whoa," Jason said. "Hold on there, Angus McCausland? Elly, you've got to be kidding me."

Eleanor's face turned stern and sour. "I am *not* kidding you. Angus is in there, now what do you intend to do about it?"

Jason's mind flashed back to the last time he could recall being asked that question in that same manner. Shortly before he and Ginny had gotten engaged, they had gotten into something of a fight. It hadn't been all that ugly, really, and Jason couldn't for the life of him remember what it was even about. But the two of them had been standing in the middle of the sidewalk in the Old Port in Portland when Ginny had stormed off. Jason followed, then stopped. He knew she would come back. Knew it. Hated himself for knowing it, but knew it nonetheless. And she did. But she didn't do what he expected her to do. He had expected a heartfelt sorry or something of the like, maybe a make-up hug and a walk back to one of their apartments for some make-up sex. But that wasn't what happened.

Instead, Ginny stood before him, slightly drunk but not incoherent, just as Jason was, and she said to him calmly, sharply, "I love you. Now what do you intend to do about it?"

To be honest, he hadn't any intentions at all until she had challenged him to it. He said nothing in response to her curt question, only stood there until she took his hand and walked with him back to his apartment where they did, in fact, have make-up sex. The next day, though, Jason suddenly knew what he intended to do. Had intentions all day long, in fact, and that night, he proposed to her.

Now, standing in the snow in between his own car and Eleanor's truck, he had no idea what he intended to do and did not have until tomorrow to think about it. So he said the first thing that popped in his head. "We'll call the police again."

Eleanor rolled her eyes, but Jason dialed 911 anyway. When the dispatcher picked up, Jason fought the urge to scream at her for not taking action earlier when Bethany called. Instead, he calmly told her the situation, told her the address, told her they needed police there immediately. The dispatcher seemed stunned. "We sent two cars out there earlier tonight," she said. "No one home. No cars in the driveway, no lights on anywhere in the house, nothing."

"You didn't go inside to check it out?" Jason asked.

"Doors were locked," the dispatcher replied.

"The doors are *never* locked."

"They were locked for us, sir. We'll gladly send another officer out there now, but it will be a while on account of the snow."

"This is an emergency, okay? Get a few officers here now!"

"Sir, we'll be there soon. In the meantime, please stay calm and keep a safe distance from—"

Jason hung up the phone. "Jesus," he said.

"We have to do something now," Eleanor said. "He'll—he'll kill him, Jason."

"Why would Angus McCausland be at my Pop's house? It makes no sense. What the hell would he want with—"

Jason stopped and closed his eyes. Ginny got out of the car and stood next to him. "Dipshit," he said to himself. "Of course he's looking for me. I'm going."

Eleanor immediately got out of her truck. "He'll kill you, ya damn fool. Are you crazy? You'll be in just as much trouble as Willie and Frank."

Jason ignored her. He turned and jumped into the car and slammed his door closed. Ginny banged her fist on the window. "You wait," she said, acid in her voice, and Jason froze. He rolled down his window and looked up at her. "What are you going to do, go be a damn hero? Wake the hell up, Jason. If this guy is really in there, and Willie's already hurt, and Frank's already hurt, what the hell you think he's going to do to you? You think you're going to go in there unarmed and *talk* him out of bludgeoning you, or worse, killing you? You know Willie's got a shotgun in that closet. You think Angus hasn't found it?"

For a moment, Ginny thought she had reached Jason. He sat in the idling car, steam leaving his mouth with every breath, looking down at the bottom of her jacket with a blank, childish expression on his face. But then he looked her in the eyes, and before he said a word, she knew immediately she had done nothing at all. "I'm going to go find out," he said calmly. "It's my fault, Gin. I'm going to fix it. Go with Elly. Wait here for the police."

"For what, Jason? For you to go be a hero? For you to go get killed?"

"I don't know!" Jason screamed. "I don't know, okay? But my dad's in there."

"Don't do this," Ginny said, reaching through the window. She placed her hands on either side of Jason's face. "Don't do this, okay? I know you want to make up for Robert, but please don't do it like this."

Jason placed his hands over Ginny's, held them for a moment, then pulled them away from his face. "I'm sorry," he said as he rolled up his window, "but I have to go."

Ginny watched as Jason pulled away, then climbed into Eleanor's truck. The next time she saw Jason, she wasn't sure if he was dead or alive, nor was she sure which would have been better.

*   *   *

"You smell like—like December."

Jason had heard that before, but never like this. Never from her. And coming from Ginny, it felt right, felt okay. Growing up, that had been different.

"Ya smell like a December season," Sarah Coates would say to Jason whenever he came home late from hockey practice. The December season she referred to was, of course, the hockey season, and the scent she spoke of was not a pleasant one. Hockey equipment stunk like musty socks and sweat all the time, and wherever he left his bag full of skates, shin guards, helmet and the like took on the same musty and damp smell. So Sarah had made him leave the bag in the barn where it stunk all the time anyway. But Jason soon realized the sweat-logged equipment would freeze if he left it out there, so he started to store it in his bedroom. Every time Sarah Coates walked past that room, she would pop her head and say, "Smells like a December season in here, Jason." She would then go to the bathroom, fetch the can of Lysol spray and douse the room in it. After that, it smelled like musty hockey equipment and fake flowers.

But that night, as Ginny lay on top of Jason on the floor of the living room, the words meant something else. Her hair tickled his face as she rested her cheek against his, and with her breath shooting pleasantly into his right ear, she breathed the words as though she meant it as the highest compliment anyone might ever conjure, and Jason took it that way.

"You smell like—like December."

He hadn't asked for an explanation as to what she meant by that, didn't really need one. Though she was a small woman and did not weigh much at all, her weight pressed gently into him and he knew exactly what she meant. December. Not the frigid part of it, but the warmth. The inside, the moments looking out the window and knowing there were so many things to fear but none of them resided in here, in the warmth, on the floor together. Not with him. Not with her.

They had fallen to the floor almost an hour ago in a fit of laughter, stupid laughter relegated only to those in love and ignorantly comfortable with each other, and they had just frozen there the way those in love will often do. Neither had spoken a word before Ginny's, and neither spoke anymore after. They instead allowed the scent of December to complete the night, to allow the silliness to turn into what was to become a memory, the answer to the question of "how did you fall in love" or "how did you know" or "were you ever scared." They knew the answers to those questions now, knew them as clearly as Ginny had stated them with a simple breath of air in Jason's right ear as they lay on the living room floor of a crappy apartment in Portland, Maine.

*　　　*　　　*

Askar sat at his workbench in the basement, picking away at a scale model of a Chevy Bel-Air when he heard two thuds above him. He looked up momentarily, but then went back to work. Then he heard the front door open and close again a few minutes later. This time, he got up and climbed the stairs.

Askar made his way through the kitchen and down the hall. He then found himself standing at the foot of the stairs that led upstairs to the bedrooms. "Beth?" He called out to his wife. "Bethany?"

No response came back to him.

"Beth, you up there?"

Again, nothing.

Askar opened the front door and saw Bethany's car was gone. And so it passed that Askar never witnessed the moment his wife left him in the middle of the night on a cold night just outside Boston.

*   *   *

Frank could not believe he was conscious.

He did not want to be—the pain that shot through his face had turned into something hot, unbearable, electric—but he had his eyes open and saw red. The blood had coated his eyeballs. His head ached as though it had hit every step with force on the way down—and most likely had come close to exactly that—and when he had finally settled on the ground after being kicked back down the stairs, he *had* passed out, thankfully. But now he was wide awake, scared, and unsure of how much time had passed. He had no desire to climb those steps again, and the bulkhead—which was in, oh, some dark direction or another from where he lay—seemed like an impossible destination, so he let his head rest on the cold ground.

The dirt that coated the basement floor kicked up into the air at the slightest provocation, and Frank assumed he was coated in it by now. He could not see anything to prove that notion, but he figured it was obvious enough. He also had no idea what parts of him were

259

broken, bleeding, or otherwise bruised. All he knew was every inch of him hurt, and that was not going to change any time soon. Was this what Henry felt like? The hopelessness? Frank's left eye throbbed. He lifted his hand to touch it, and it seemed the socket screamed out before his fingers even got within an inch of it. Frank stifled a scream and dropped his hand back down to his side. When he did, a lightning bolt of pain shot through his fingers, through his hand and up his forearm. This time, he did scream. It was a short expulsion and he stifled it quickly, expecting the door to open and whoever it was that had kicked him back down the stairs to come barreling down to finish him off.

But nothing happened. No one stirred above him. No other sound but the echo of his own voice reached his ears.

How long have I been down here?

Frank was fairly certain he could not have mustered the strength to get to the stairs at this point anyway, so he simply stayed put and tried to assess his injuries, tried to piece together a timeline of what had happened and why.

Start from the beginning. You left the house to go to Willie's to fetch Pop...

*   *   *

As a younger man, Einar had spent the better part of his working life standing in the barn, fixing this machinery or that, sharpening this axe blade or cleaning that carburetor. He could climb to the hay loft as easily as though he were simply walking across the kitchen, could pick up a tractor tire, could throw hay bails. He had been a strong man, a worker, maybe even a bit of a grunt. But he had always done well for himself.

Now he could barely keep his eyes open.

Part of it, logically enough, had to do with the severe injuries Angus had been so generous as to bestow upon him, but part of it was something else, too: the knowledge of a conclusion. Einar didn't remember much from his days of schooling, but he had always loved English class with Ms. Bennington. Freshman year of high school, he was fairly sure that was. Einar loved stories, loved the books. His own writing was weak and convoluted, but he could read and lose himself in the story any time he had a free moment. Ms. Bennington had taught them about the process of a book: the introduction, the plot, the complication, the climax, the resolution, and a word Einar loved to say when he was a kid: the denouement.

Here he was, peaking at the climax. Angus would most likely kill him. And then the denouement. And as much as Einar hated to admit it, he feared that word now, what it implied, what it might mean in reality. He and Angus were in the barn now after an arduous journey across the yard. Einar's leg felt like a thousand pieces of smashed glass, and it had taken him several minutes to catch his breath about halfway across the yard. But now Angus sat on the tractor, a shotgun pointed directly at Einar, who lay in a pile of hay, probably in the same place Gerald Jordan had slept on warmer nights. Einar wore no coat and was shivering uncontrollably, and Angus seemed to be taking a lot of pleasure in that fact. Nonetheless, he pointed that shotgun at Einar as though he might jump up at any moment, dance a jig and bolt for the door. It made Einar tired just thinking about moving.

Something had changed in Angus since they transferred to the barn, however. He became visibly nervous, which in turn made Einar nervous as hell. This guy seemed about ready to let fly a few rounds just to get the killing bug out of him and Einar figured he would be target number one. Einar had no idea if anyone was coming for him. A big part of him hoped no one was; as much as he had grown to resent Jason over the course of the last few weeks—and he had done so; he finally admitted it to himself earlier that night—he didn't want to see another one of his children die for no good reason at all.

So as he sat and watched Angus watch him, he thought about Jason. Thought about Robert. About Bethany. And of course, about Sarah. What was there to pick apart? Well, for starters, Einar had known for years and years that Robert and Jason fed off each other, bled each other, lifted each other up and kept each other down. Hadn't he seen the signs of that same impending denouement for them after Maggie left Robert? And what had he done about it? Not a damn thing. He coddled Jason and thought fixing the relationship between his two boys had some odd philosophical relationship to fixing the eaves of a goddamn barn. Now one of his boys was in the ground and the other was heading there, if not by the gun of Angus McCausland, then by his own alcoholism and knack for self-destruction. He would have been dead by now, Einar knew that well enough, but Robert had been there years ago to fix it. Always Robert. Never Einar.

Angus was pacing now. He had climbed down from the seat of the tractor and was walking back and forth, the shotgun slung over his shoulder like a baseball bat, pacing and occasionally kicking dirt or spitting.

"Sit down," Einar said. "Lots of waitin' still to come."

"Shut up, old man," Angus said, not bothering to look at Einar. The only light in the barn came from a lamp that Angus had lit when they first entered. Einar had told him where it was, and Angus fired it up quick with some matches he pulled from his coat pocket, but after he fired the lamp up, he turned it down as low as it would go. The result was a ghastly sort of haze of light that made the inside of the barn look like a scene from an old movie, a combination of brown and orange that wasn't quite brown or orange.

Angus continued to pace and Einar followed him with his eyes. Several minutes of silence passed before Angus said, for the fifteenth or so time this hour, "Where the hell is he?"

Einar sighed. "Sit down and relax. It's a long way from down South to up here, 'specially in th'snow. No use in workin' yerself up."

Angus stopped pacing and faced Einar. "I said shut up. I know he was here, so don't feed me that line of bullshit, old man. He'll come back. He'll come back, maybe with cops, too, but I'll shoot him. I'll shoot him and I'll shoot the goddamn cops. And if I run out of bullets, I'll hack 'em to bits with the axe, you got that, old man? So you just sit there and think about that. You just sit there and *shut the fuck up!*"

Angus's voice boomed through the barn, causing an echo that surely reverberated through the yard outside, too.

Einar figured later on that the echo was exactly what kept Angus from noticing that Jason had just snuck into the barn and was now crouched behind the tractor.

*　　*　　*

"What do we do?" Eleanor asked Ginny as they both sat in the idling truck parked on the side of CR44.

"I don't know."

Silence. Eleanor put the car in Drive and pressed her foot on the brake, unsure of what to do next. "Should we go to Fort Kent, get the police ourselves?" She asked.

"I don't know." Ginny replied.

"We could go back to Einar's house. Maybe we could...I don't know, help somehow. What do you think?"

"I don't know," Ginny replied.

"Well, what do you think if—"

"I don't know!" Ginny screamed, then buried her face in her hands. She pressed her head against the passenger side window and sobbed once, but that was all. When she removed her hands from her face, no tears had fallen and her face looked completely composed.

"I didn't mean to upset you," Eleanor said. "I just hate sitting here, you know?"

"Yes, I do. We should do something," Ginny said. "But I don't know what." Another moment of silence passed, and both women listened intently to the sound of the idling truck engine, as if it might have the answer, something intelligent to say, some great suggestion to save the day. As usual, a V6 drinking unleaded didn't have much of anything at all to lend to the conversation.

"He's a goddamn idiot, my husband is," Ginny said finally, and they both laughed a strained laugh that seemed to accentuate the tension.

"I'll get on board with that," Eleanor said. The truck was still in gear, so Eleanor hit the gas.

"Where are we going?"

"No idea," Eleanor said. "But it beats sitting here, right?"

"I suppose."

She drove north on CR44 for a few minutes in silence, thinking about her dog for no real reason other than the calming image of him, something to think about rather than Angus McCausland. She thought about walking Spurs through the snow, the cool air, maybe on CR44 closer to town, or maybe down by the lake on the hiking trail, the same trail on which she had run into Frank that day they had hiked out together, up to the road and—

"I think I have an idea, or at least part of one," Eleanor said. She pulled over a minute later.

"I'm all ears," Ginny said.

"Do you know the trail that goes along the shore of the lake?"

"Sure."

"It leads right into Einar's back yard, you know."

"Of course I know," Ginny said. "So what?"

"We can walk the trail to get to Einar's. at least that way we won't be noticed. Angus is probably watching the driveway like a hawk, but I'd be willing to bet a damn lot he has no idea the trail's there."

"Okay," Ginny said, trying to process this proposal. "So we take the trail. What the hell do we do once we get there?"

Eleanor thought for a moment, then said, "I have no idea."

Ginny let out an exasperated sigh.

"Look," Eleanor said. "I know it isn't much of a plan, but what the hell can we do? Wait for the police? It will be morning at least before they get out this way, probably even later than that. Who knows what will happen to Jason or Frank or Einar. We have to do something."

Ginny unbuckled her seatbelt. "Where is the trail?"

"Just up there a ways," Eleanor said, pointing out the front windshield.

Ginny sighed. "Okay. How about weapons? You have a gun in here?"

"No."

"You live up here in the damn sticks and you don't have a gun?"

"Don't need one."

"Jesus. How about a knife? Anything at all?"

"Let's check the bed of the truck."

Both women got out and dug through the bed of the truck, brushing away snow and sorting through a mess of rusted tools and scraps of particle board. Ginny pocketed a rusty wrench and Eleanor grabbed onto a screwdriver that was more than likely older than she.

*   *   *

Jason stormed through the front door of the house with his eyes half closed and his heart thumping somewhere in the upper regions of his throat. He ran through the living room and into the kitchen, a rock from the yard raised high in his right hand.

No one was there.

Only a mess.

As he stood in the center of the room, breathing hard in the darkness, the absurdity of what he had just done struck him. *A rock?* He thought. *You're goddamn lucky no one's in here. You'd already be...*

"What? Dead? Come on, asshole." He spoke as though he were speaking casually to some old friend in the room, but the words struck his ears as lonely and confused. Where was his Pop? And what the hell had happened in the kitchen? Jason went to the closet in the hall and swung it open. The shotgun, along with a box of shells, was gone. "Shit," he said, realizing that someone had to be in the house and he was still in a heap of trouble. All of a sudden that rock in his right hand didn't seem silly anymore. All of a sudden it seemed incredibly important. Life or death, maybe.

He was about to leave the kitchen and check the upstairs when he heard a throaty sort of mumble. Jason froze instantly, straining to hear the noise again, wondering if Angus was waiting for him, ready to pounce him at any moment. He could barely see anything in the kitchen, so he flipped on the light above the stove. It revealed the true mess that lay before him, and for the first time, Jason noticed the massive gashes in the door to the refrigerator and another in the door to the basement. He cautiously made his way across the room to the basement door, unaware that Einar could see the kitchen light turn on from the barn but Angus could not because he was busy pacing and spitting and kicking up dust, and Einar hoped like hell that Jason would just turn off the damn light quick, just turn it off and leave, get the police and end this mess, but the light stayed on and so Einar spoke to Angus to try to distract him.

But Jason knew none of this. He crept across the kitchen and, in one sweeping motion, threw the basement door open.

Frank Jordan lay in a heap at the foot of the stairs.

When he looked up at Jason, he mumbled something Jason didn't understand. He started to run down the stairs when Frank shouted, "Stop!"

Jason stopped immediately.

"Go turn off the light," Frank said. It sounded like "Go tumm oth thwight."

"Why?"

"Just do it! Quick!" *Juthdoot, kiick!*

Jason ran to the light switch and turned it off. Everything disappeared into darkness.

"Now come help me," Frank's distorted voice said.

"I can't *see* you now, asshole. How can I help you?"

"Follow my voice," he said. *fo'ow m'voish.* His voice sounded atrocious, as if he had no teeth left at all. Whatever had happened to Frank had happened in grand fashion. He was hurting.

It took him some time, but Jason eventually made it down the steps to the basement. "Where are you?" He said, and Frank reached out and grabbed Jason's arm. "Here," Frank said. "I'm hurt."

Jason worked his hands underneath Frank's armpits and dragged him toward the steps, but then Frank let out a stifled groan. "Won' make it," he said, his voice garbled and broken. "Leave m'here."

"No," Jason said. "We have to get you out of here."

"Leave m'here," Frank said, this time more forcefully. "I thin' thurrin th'barn. Go."

"I can get you up the stairs, Frank. It will hurt, but I can do it."

Jason started to move toward Frank again, but Frank stopped him.

"Then what?" He said, this time crystal clear, and Jason stopped. That was a fine question. He could get Frank upstairs alright, but then what? Jason suddenly wished he had brought Ginny and Eleanor with him. They could take him to the hospital, or at least take care of him for a bit. But they were gone, for all Jason knew, and he was here alone with Frank. He had gotten inside the house just fine, but he just hadn't bothered to consider the all-important question: then what?

"Okay," Jason said, taking a step back toward the stairs. "I'll be back then." He climbed up four steps, then stopped again. "Don't you go running off."

"Fuck you."

Jason couldn't help but laugh quietly. It faded quickly and he ran back up to the kitchen. He peeked out the window on the opposite side of the kitchen from the basement door and looked out at the barn. Sure enough, a slight, faded light threw some of its beams out upon the snow in the yard. They were in the barn, alright. Jason could get there without being seen, but that damn nagging question still hung on: then what?

"Fuck it," he said to himself as he opened the back door and snuck out into the yard.

*　　　*　　　*

Robert and Jason took a trip to New York City the summer of Jason's senior year at the University of Maine. They went for two reasons: one, the New York Rangers were putting on an open tryout, and since Jason had not been drafted, they decided this might be good exposure for him. Two, neither of them had ever been to New York City and it seemed like the kind of place where they could get into a lot of trouble, which of course meant fun.

They were right on both counts.

They arrived on a Thursday and stayed in a cheap motel in the Bronx. The motel was nowhere near Madison Square Garden, but it was the cheapest place they could find and the subway rides, they found, were actually pretty fun. So that first night, they took the subway to Manhattan and partied in clubs they couldn't really afford and in bars in which they probably did not fit. They were both piss drunk by two thirty that morning and neither could remember what subway stop was theirs, so when they got to the Bronx four stops too early, they wandered the streets for almost two hours before they found the motel. As they collapsed into their respective beds, the sun not quite over the horizon but not far off, Jason felt for the first time since he had crushed his brother's leg that things might be okay between them.

They both spent Friday recovering and doing a few touristy things, like walking by Madison Square Garden and gawking at the lights in Times Square. It took up most of the day and that night, they settled into some cushy seats at a sports bar just north of Rockefeller Center and watched the Yankees game on the nineteen televisions that surrounded them. They didn't speak much, but when they did, their exchanges were generally jovial and silly. They went to bed early that night.

Saturday was the day of the first tryout. Robert and Jason were at the Garden two hours earlier than was necessary, so they registered and sat in the stands, staring at the ice as if it were some compelling movie playing out before them. They felt sated just feeling the coolness of the ice. Finally, the staff opened the locker rooms and Jason went to suit up. If you had asked Jason even hours later what that first day had been like, he would have been at a loss for words. He could not remember much of it at all, only skating harder than he ever had before and getting checked into the boards by guys twice his size with a force that seemed to shatter his skull each time. That night in the motel room, though, he could tell Robert nothing of what it felt like to skate on that ice, to look uup at those seats and imagine them filled. It had been beyond surreal.

That notion would not last. The next day was round two of the tryouts, and this day proved to be even more difficult than the day before. Jason found himself exhausted halfway through the day and his legs moved without his consent.. That night, he did not feel like drinking or going out. He just wanted to lie in the bathtub with ice water surrounding his legs, which he did for almost an hour before passing out at eight o'clock.

The next day. Monday. The big day, the third and final day of tryouts. Jason shot. Jason passed. Jason finished his checks and skated hard. And by the end of the day, he felt good, felt as though he had made an impression, felt as though he could play at this level. The New York Rangers felt the same way and drafted him in the fourth round at that summer's NHL draft.

Robert seemed happier than Jason did about it all, but Jason chalked that up to shock. Had that really happened? It had, and he was headed for pro hockey. That 'some day' dream had become definitive, had become an actual date to be processed.

Unfortunately, he would never see that day come.

Shortly after he graduated from UMaine, Jason moved to Hartford. But when he got there, something happened, something he could not explain even years later after he had time to process it all. Jason Coates had a mental breakdown. Robert would tell him later he could not cope with the prospect of success or some other bullshit like that, and Jason could not have explained it any better than that because he did not know why he did not show up to the first, second or third day of training camp for the Hartford Wolf Pack, The Rangers' AHL affiliate. When he showed up on the fourth day, the general manager kindly told Jason to pack his bags and fuck off.

He did, but not before going on a drinking binge the likes of which Hartford, Connecticut had never seen before. He ended up in the drunk tank that night and Robert came down from Portland the next day to bail him out. They drove up to Portland in silence, stayed the night at a mutual friend's apartment, then made their way back up to Northern Maine, back up to their Mom and Pop's place, back up to familiarity and the same ol' same ol'. Jason's parents did not ask what happened and he did not tell. For almost two months, not a word was said in that household about Jason's experience in Hartford, but Jason knew Robert was brooding. Robert was angry. Robert was, most of all, disappointed, and that dug into Jason's mind the most.

One night in early September, Robert came home to an empty house. Willie and Sarah had gone to a neighbor's house for dinner, and all the lights in the house were off…but Robert smelled fire. He bypassed the house altogether and limped into the back yard, where Jason stood with his hands in his pockets in front of a fire in the middle of the yard.

"What are you doing?" Robert asked as he approached.

"Nothing," Jason said, not bothering to raise his eyes from the fire. As Robert came closer, he saw exactly what was going on. Jason had put all his hockey equipment in the fire, even the skates.

"Wow," Robert said. "That sure is dramatic of ya."

Jason did not reply. Instead, he handed the bottle of lighter fluid in his right hand to Robert and walked away. That was all. Robert let the fire burn for another ten minutes, then turned the hose on it to douse it. The next morning, a pile of smoldered hockey equipment lay in the yard like the carcass of a deer fallen victim to a hunting party.

As the case had always been between them, they did not speak of what had happened in Hartford or that night in the back yard. They simply let it pass and analyzed it personally in their own minds, chewed on it and spit it out and thought of it as moments past with no need to revisit them. And they solved nothing. Jason knew from that point on he would always be a disappointment to Robert, the only person who really mattered, because Willie and Sarah, well, were they really even paying attention at all? He

271

thought not, and if they were, they hid it damn well, the way Mainers do, the way they ignore until it goes away, and then what need is there, really, to talk about it ever again? He had disappointed Robert, and he knew it was better to be rid of the entire possibility of success than to try and fail again.

As far as he was concerned at that moment, Jason Coates would never play hockey again.

And Robert said nothing about it.

*   *   *

Jason made his way out the back door and into the yard only to stop suddenly a few feet from the steps.

Someone was down by the lake.

He would not have noticed if whoever was down there hadn't moved just slightly, or if he hadn't coincidentally looked that way at just the right time, or if the moon had been behind a cloud...but he saw movement down there, so he stopped. It was snowing again, only slightly, but Jason looked up and saw the clouds rolling in again and knew this storm hadn't screamed its last. Through the few flakes that fell from the sky and the many swirls of snow that kicked up from the breeze, Jason watched. He could not see whoever was down there clearly, but he could see a vague shape and occasionally heard whispers.

Whispers?

Jason figured if Angus did have Einar's shotgun, he would not bother to whisper, nor would he bother to hide down by the lake. Besides, Frank said they had gone to the barn, and though he never bothered to ask Frank how he knew that (he would find out later that Angus had made the announcement quite clearly, and Einar had made a point to repeat the information on the off chance Frank was listening down in the basement), Jason believed him. So instead of standing like a moron in the middle of the yard and staring at some blob of a shape down by the lake, Jason ran full speed toward that blob.

When he got close enough, he realized the blob wasn't a person but two people. Eleanor and Ginny. He crouched next to them behind a felled log. Before they could say a word, Jason overtook them.

"Frank's inside in the basement. Pop and Angus are in the barn. You two have to go get Frank to a hospital. He's hurt real bad. I'm going to the barn."

"Frank's hurt?" Eleanor said.

"Yes, and you need to—"

"How bad?"

"He's alive, he's talking, sort of, but he needs to get to a hospital. Can you do that?"

"We'll get him out," Ginny said. The confidence in her voice, the sheer lack of fear, made Jason smile. He gave her a peck on the cheek.

"So what are you going to do, Coates?" Eleanor said.

Jason did not reply immediately. He did not have a good answer to that question, but he knew one thing at least: "I'm going to the barn to fetch Pop."

"*Fetch* him?" Ginny said. "He's not a newspaper and you're not a dog, Jason. Angus will kill you."

"I gotta go. You do, too." With that, Jason stood up. Eleanor and Ginny followed suit. Then they all stood there silently, staring up at the yard and the house beyond.

"Should we just go?" Ginny said.

"No."

Another moment of eerie silence passed.

"What are we waiting for?" Eleanor said.

"Can't just go all at once. He'll see us. We should wait." Jason said.

Ginny put her hand on Jason's arm. "For what?"

"I don't know."

They waited some more.

Maybe five minutes.

Then Jason said, "Okay. I'll go first, then you two."

He did not wait for a response. Jason ran up to the side of the barn. When he got close, he made sure to be quieter and snuck his way toward the door. He could hear his Pop saying something to Angus, but he couldn't make out the words. As the storm clouds moved in, the moon dimmed and the dark became darker, and Jason waited. Then it happened.

Angus began screaming. He was incensed, but Jason did not bother to listen to find out why. Instead, he peeked in the doorway, saw Angus's back to him, and slipped in as he heard Angus's voice boom, "You just sit there and *shut the fuck up!*"

As he crouched behind the tractor, Eleanor and Ginny ran across the yard and slipped silently through the back door into the kitchen of the house.

*   *   *

Jason didn't know exactly how much time passed between the moment he crouched behind the tractor and the moment he knew he was probably going to die. Enough time had passed for his legs to stiffen up and become tight. He was shivering now, even though his blood had been boiling when he first got inside the barn. Maybe ten minutes. More likely twenty. Probably forty-five.

But when he heard the front door of the house close and footsteps cross the porch, his shivering and stiffness did not matter. He knew what was going to happen before it happened. Either Ginny or Eleanor, or maybe even Frank, would step on the board on the porch and the gunshot-sound of the tricky slat on that damn porch would erupt.

And so it did.

Angus immediately reacted. He swung around with the shotgun pointed at nothing in particular and said, surprisingly quietly, "What was that?"

Einar did not offer a guess.

Angus turned back around and faced Einar. "You move and I'll kill whoever's out there, then I'll kill you. Got it?"

Einar made no reply.

Angus started to head for the barn door when Jason stood up. "Hey Angus," Jason said, calm as ever, as if he had just passed Angus in the school hallway rather than put himself in danger of being shot to death.

When Angus turned and saw Jason standing there, his disbelief took over, but only for a moment. He aimed the gun at Jason. "Well howdy, Coates. I'm going to kill you now."

Angus held the shotgun tightly as he approached Jason, but he stopped short. Jason had no idea what he was supposed to do in this situation other than to get shot, but strangely, it did not come to that. Not yet, at least.

"You know something, Coates? I think we'll have some fun first. How does that sound? Do you want to have some fun?"

Jason stared blankly at Angus.

"Answer me!" Angus yelled.

"Sure," Jason said. "Let's have some fun, Angus."

"Good. I'm glad you want to have some fun. I have an idea, Coates. How about you stand there as I blow your Pop's face clear off? How does that sound?"

Jason again did not reply. He just stared blankly at Angus again, and again Angus bellowed. "You listening, Coates? *Fucking answer me!*"

"You're here for me, Angus. Don't you think you've already hurt him enough?"

"Enough? Tell me about that, Jason. Tell me about *enough*. Because I know all about it. I know all about *enough* because I spent *enough* time in jail to think about it. I know you put me there, you fuck. I know I'm out and I'm going to kill you, because it's supposed to happen that way. But first I want you to know what it's like to have nothing, to watch your shitty life get shittier. I want you to know, just like I do, Jason, what *enough* really is. Get out from behind there."

Jason did. He stood only a few feet away from Angus, the muzzle of the shotgun still centered on his chest. Jason kept his eyes on Angus's but spoke to Einar. "Hi, Pop," he said.

"Hi, boy," Einar said as he lay in the hay.

Jason made an attempt to put himself between Angus and Einar, but Angus would have none of it. "Get over there," he said, pointing the muzzle of the shotgun toward the far end of the barn. Jason backed up about ten paces and stood in the middle of the barn in the dark. "Now I just want you to watch," Angus said as he pointed the gun down at Einar.

Before Jason could register what was happening, Angus swung the gun around and shoved the butt of it into Einar's gut. All of the air rushed out of him all at once, and the sound it produced reminded Jason of the sound those booth cushions at Pizza Hut make when you sit down—an empty, wheezy sound. Angus heard it, too, and laughed loud.

"You like that? You like it, old man? How about another one?" He sent the butt into Einar's stomach again, but this time there was no air left to rush out.

As this was happening, Jason was slowly moving to his right behind the wooden pillar that held up the center of the barn. But as he did so, Angus turned to him. "You like that, Jason? You—"

That was when Angus realized what Jason was doing. Angus wheeled around, pointed the gun in Jason's direction and fired.

*   *   *

Ginny screamed when she heard the gunshot.

Eleanor had gone ahead, running up the road to get the truck. Ginny stayed behind with Frank where the driveway met CR44. They sat on the side of the road, Frank's wheezing lungs and swollen face a constant source of worry, when they heard the shotgun blast. She couldn't help it; the sound leapt out of her mouth before she could stop it. Frank immediately sent his broken right hand up to her mouth to cover it, and though his hands hurt like hell and were swollen now, he felt Ginny's tears fall onto them.

He wondered fleetingly if Jason was dead now, then figured he probably was.

*   *   *

Jason dropped with a hollow thud. The sound of it made Einar suddenly queasy. Angus had a look on his face that bordered on both fear and satisfaction, but Einar did not look at that face long enough to decide which one it genuinely was. Instead, he stood up. It happened in no smooth flow of a motion, but he got to his feet as Angus slowly approached Jason. Pain soared through Einar's body and he almost fainted from it, but he did not make a sound as he propped his crutches underneath his armpits and made several sweeping steps toward Jason. When Angus heard the crutches digging into the dirt earth of the barn, he turned just in time to see one of those crutches hurling at him. Einar struck Angus in the forehead with the end of the crutch and Angus flew backward to the ground. Einar did not bother to wait and see if Angus was down for the count—he figured there was no way that swing had subdued Angus—but he also did not care. Einar propped the crutch back under his arm and went to Jason.

Blood soaked the back of Jason's shirt and seeped down off his neck. A small hole at the back of his head intermittently spurt blood at an angle toward his left ear. Einar struggled to get to his knees but eventually did. He placed his left hand in the center of Jason's back.

"Boy," Einar said, his face contorted from the pain of his battered body and the sight of his dying son. But that was all he said. Angus had stood up behind him and fired a single buckshot into Einar's back. It bored a hole through him the size of a dinner plate. Einar William Coates fell face first to the ground next to his son, his arm wrapped around Jason's shoulders the way young boys, young best friends, would do as they walked down the road at sunset, hoping to catch dinner instead of a whoopin' from Pop for being late.

And they died there together on the cold, hard dirt of the barn.

*   *   *

Angus stood over the two bodies for almost ten minutes with that same confused look on his face, that same mixture of fear and satisfaction. To anyone who might have seen him there, he probably looked as though he were savoring the turn of events, taking it all in and congratulating himself on a job finally well done. But that was not the discourse taking place in Angus's mind at that moment. He felt no pride at all. In fact, he felt an intense shame, the same kind he had felt so many times growing up when his Pop took the belt, or even worse, the wrench, to him for ruining dinner or forgetting to do a chore or just because Pop was drunk and needed something to wallop. It was the shame of being who he was, the shame of knowing he would never be anything else but what he was in that moment: a damn murderer and a damn fool.

Angus dropped the gun and sat on the ground next to it, watching steam rise up off the backs of the two dead men as the sun began to rise over the Northern Maine horizon that December morning after the first real snowfall of the season.

* * *

Frank's heart stopped on the way to Fort Kent. He sat propped against the passenger side door of Eleanor's truck, Ginny sitting next to him with her feet on either side of the gear shifter. Neither Eleanor nor Ginny had noticed it happen; Frank's heart simply stopped.

Ginny hardly took her eyes off Frank during the ride, but even so, she never noticed a difference in him. He looked as though he were sleeping, or at least trying to, and Ginny said nothing until Frank's heart had been stopped for nearly a minute and a half. Finally, she pressed her hand to his shoulder and said, "Almost there, Frank. How are you doing?"

She expected some sort of muffled reply, like a "Hangin' in there," or maybe something more sarcastic like, "oh, just peachy, sweetheart." But Frank said nothing and did not move a muscle. As the truck bounced along the rutted, snowy road, Frank's body swayed and bounced in unison, and Ginny realized then that something was wrong. "Frank," she said. Eleanor recognized the sudden worry in Ginny's voice and said the same: "Frank?"

Ginny placed her hand in front of Frank's slightly open mouth. "He's not breathing," she said, and Eleanor began to pull over. "No, don't stop," Ginny said. "Keep going. Go faster."

Eleanor did.

"Ginny tried to slump Frank to a slightly reclined position but the cab of the truck was just too small. His knees buckled and he accordioned into the space in front of the seat, and his head lolled to one side. Ginny pressed her ear to Frank's chest and could not hear a heartbeat. She checked for a pulse in his neck and on his wrist and felt nothing. "Shit," she said. "His heart stopped."

"Oh God," Eleanor said, and though her voice actually sounded calm, she began to cry. Ginny blew a breath into Frank's mouth. His lips tasted like dirt and salt, and she did not miss the metallic taste of blood in it, either. She blew again.

"How do you do CPR?" She said to Eleanor.

"I don't know…press his chest, right?"

Ginny did. She pressed ten times before stopping. "I'm not doing anything here."

"Press harder. I heard you have to…"

"Have to what?"

"Break his ribs."

I'd be willing to bet they're already broken, Ginny thought, but she pushed harder nonetheless. After ten more compressions, she felt his ribs give way with a sickening series of pops. She gasped out loud but continued to press.

"I think you need to breathe into him now," Eleanor said, and Ginny did. She blew a solid breath into his mouth and waited.

"I don't know if this is helping," she said.

"Just keep going."

More compressions. More breaths. By the time Eleanor drove the truck into Fort Kent, Ginny could hardly breathe herself anymore. As they pulled into the emergency room hospital, Ginny reached hysterics. She punched Frank's chest with a balled-up fist and screamed.

Then she continued CPR as though she had never stopped at all.

Eleanor parked the truck in front of the ambulance gate and ran inside.

* * *

I killed them.

I killed them.

Angus could not say he regretted killing Jason Coates much, but he hadn't meant to kill the old man. That hadn't been part of his plan. As he stood above the two bodies on the floor of the barn, he could see steam rising off them as the early morning sunshine poked through the windows and onto Angus's face. He had long since dropped the gun; for a while, he sat on the ground next to the bodies, but his legs had fallen asleep, so now he stood. He could not take his eyes off them. When he had killed Thomas Moon Griffith years ago in high school, Jason Coates had sent a punch into Angus's face, knocking him unconscious. Angus had no idea until hours later that he had killed someone. But now, looking at the bodies of the two Coates men, he knew for sure. He intended to kill one of these men. He did not feel the same satisfaction he felt when he had roughed up the Griffith kid; he hadn't meant to kill the damn Hippie, but who really cared if he died? He was just a lazy sack of crap granola cruncher. And he hadn't meant to kill the old man. Why did it feel so bad to know he had?

Angus did not try to feel remorse for killing Jason Coates. He had spent too many years pining to do just that, and now the job was done. But this was a mess. This didn't feel good. This certainly didn't feel any better than the cell in which he had wasted away for years now. The steam. The steam rising off the bodies somehow made it all much worse, somehow took away the satisfaction of knowing he had finally completed the job he dreamed every night about completing. Something about how that steam kept rising, would not stop, not even now, two hours later, the sun up, the light shining into the barn and making all of this real, this scene an actual moment in reality. Angus didn't like it.

He took two steps toward the tractor to his right and vomited onto the frozen ground. Then he picked up the shotgun and waited.

The police finally came early that morning after the sun came up. Angus had been sitting alone with the two dead bodies for almost three hours. Two cars pulled into the snowed-in dirt driveway of the Coates home. They poked around the house first, and Angus watched them through the barn window. They went inside. They went behind the house. They circled in the yard. And then they opened the barn door.

Angus aimed the shotgun at them. The two cops facing him shouted something, but he heard nothing. He simply held the gun in front of him, his finger on the trigger, the knowledge that there was no bullet in the chamber bouncing around his mind vaguely. The cops shouted at him some more. He did not hear them. He cocked the shotgun.

The police fired, each officer sending off four rounds into Angus.

He fell to the frozen ground with a dull thump, and though he would never know it, steam rose off him as he lay there for the next three hours as more police came to see what he had done, to see how he had finished the job.

*   *   *

It felt odd to think it, but Ginny sort of felt like laughing. As the E.R. staff came running out of the hospital, Eleanor not far behind, the scene became a television show, a bad movie in which the same thing that happened in a thousand other bad movies happens again in this one. The medics run out. They shove Frank onto a crash cart and rush him inside where a doctor shouts orders and nurses comply. And that was somewhat how it happened, minus the extremely rushed feel of it all. The doctors seemed much calmer as they wheeled Frank inside, and though they were all shouting, no one said anything like, "stat!" or "cc's!"

Ginny watched it happen and felt like laughing.

Why do we laugh when every indication around us tells us we should cry? Or scream? Or drive a knife through our skin or punch a wall? She remembered being on a flight to Italy once, a few years ago, and though she hated flying, she slept through most of the flight. But about an hour before landing, the plane flew right through the heart of a storm. Rain pounded against the plane and streaked backward off the windows toward the tail. The plane bounced up and down, left and right. It was dark in the cabin and the stillness of the thrumming engines was interrupted by the occasional scream from some woman toward the front of the plane. Otherwise, most people braced themselves, exchanged nervous glances, and hoped for the best. Ginny was terrified. She grabbed onto her seat and braced her left arm against the seat in front of her and shook through every inch of her body.

But then the plane jerked right and the man sitting next to her fell into her shoulder. It felt strange then, too, but she started to laugh, and somehow the laughing helped. She was still terrified and hated every second of that bouncing and hurtling storm, but the laughing helped. It didn't quite calm her or cheer her up, so to speak, it just... helped, as if by committing this strange, antithetical action somehow negated the horrible reality of it.

As the nurses and doctor rushed Frank into the hospital, Ginny laughed to negate the gunshot she had heard just before getting into the truck. She laughed to negate the horrible drive through the snow, the moment she realized Frank wasn't breathing, the crunch of his ribs as she broke them to try and get his heart started again. She laughed to negate it all.

Three hours passed before they heard any word on Frank. During that time, Eleanor spent a significant amount of time on the phone with the Fort Kent police, who finally confirmed they had sent some officers out to the Coates place, but would say nothing more on the matter. Ginny sat in the waiting room and stared at the walls. She tried reading for a little while, but she would get two or three paragraphs into an article before her mind took off and wandered. Eleanor joined her eventually and fell asleep with her head on Ginny's shoulder. Ginny passed the time by stroking Eleanor's hair.

At around ten that morning, a doctor entered the waiting room to talk to Eleanor and Ginny.

"Is there any family we can contact?" He said.

Eleanor immediately burst into tears. "He's dead?"

"No, no," the doctor said. "He's alive, but we need to contact any immediate family if there is any."

"Shit," Eleanor said, suddenly realizing who that meant. "Gerald, we left Gerald at home. I have to go get him."

"What are you talking about, Elly?" Ginny said.

"Frank's father. He's...well, he's not okay on his own. I have to go get him." Eleanor put a hand on the doctor's arm. "Tell me he's okay," she said.

"He's okay," the doctor said. "He'll be here for a long while, but he's going to be fine."

Eleanor smiled and left the hospital in a hurry. Ginny found herself standing in front of the confused doctor, trying to piece this all together just as he was surely attempting to do.

An hour passed before Eleanor returned with Frank's father. "Ginny, this is Gerald. He's—"

"Billings! I need Billings!" Gerald Jordan shouted at the top of his lungs.

"He's sick," Eleanor said.

Ginny had taken a step back. "I see that," she said.

"I would have been back sooner, but he made a mess and I couldn't leave the kitchen the way it was."

"It's okay."

"Any word on Frank?"

"No. Still the same."

Eleanor sat Gerald down in a chair in the waiting room. "Can you watch him while I call the police station again? Just don't let him wander, okay?"

Ginny nodded and watched as Eleanor went to the nurse's station to use the phone. The room had taken on a glossy feel, a sort of ethereal sleepiness that made Ginny finally want to close her eyes, but she did not. She watched Eleanor talk on the phone, trying to read her lips to figure out what was being said, but she could not. Eleanor had been on the phone for almost ten minutes when she turned to Ginny. The look on her face was unmistakable. Eleanor had just heard something awful. She put the phone down on the counter top of the nurse's station and walked over to Ginny. "They want to talk to you," she said.

Ginny walked to the phone with no thoughts at all in her head. She already knew what she was about to hear. Jason was most certainly dead. She knew that the second Eleanor had put the phone down. Still, hearing it stunned her; she dropped the phone after hearing the words: *Your husband is dead.* What had surprised her more, though was hearing Einar, too, was dead. Ginny's mind shut down and she dropped the phone. Her knees buckled and she fell to the floor in a heap, her face blank and her eyes vacant. Eleanor ran to her, but Ginny did not see her. She did not see anything. No laughter could negate this. Jason was gone.

*   *   *

Ginny disappeared for three days.

Bethany was nowhere to be found for three days.

Eleanor sat in the waiting room for three days.

Gerald sat by her side, and in rare moments of lucidity, comforted her.

Frank spent three tense days in and out of consciousness. His heart had re-started the night they brought him to the hospital and had been beating steadily since then, but he had to have surgery to repair a lacerated spleen and a badly shattered leg. His various other injuries began to heal, slowly and painfully, and he was rarely coherent enough to acknowledge Eleanor's constant presence.

He healed, though, and was released from the hospital after two weeks. When Eleanor brought him home, he fell asleep immediately and did not wake for another twenty hours. When he opened his eyes again, Eleanor was sitting in a rocking chair by the side of the bed.

"How long have you been up?" Frank asked through his clenched teeth. His jaw had been wired shut and his eyes were still puffy-swollen almost all the way shut. But he could see Eleanor.

"Three days," she said, and gave a slight chuckle. "I'm tired."

Frank's left arm was in a cast and rested solidly across his chest, but he lifted his right arm and motioned to Eleanor. She stood up, then lay next to Frank, his good arm wrapped around her as tightly as he could muster. She began to cry, and though his swollen eyes wanted to do the same, Frank did his best to look down at Eleanor's head.

"Spurs come back?" Frank asked.

Eleanor sighed. "No. I wish he would…but he was old. If he hasn't come back by now, I don't think he's going to."

They lay in silence for a minute or more, Eleanor's mind flip flopping between worry for Frank and despair for Spurs.

"Tell me again," Frank finally said to Eleanor. Frank had spent much of his waking moments asking Eleanor to recount what had happened that night, how he had survived, how Jason and Einar had not, and what became of Angus. She told him each time, the facts paining her, the vividness of it giving her nightmares on the rare occasion she got to sleep. But she told him anyway.

"You were in the basement after he hit you," She said. "He threw you down the stairs and—"

"No, not that part," Frank said quietly. "Fast forward."

"They went to the barn and—"

"No," Frank said. "Later."

"We took you to the hospital. Your heart stopped in the truck."

"Later."

"Nothing happened after that, Frank. You were mostly unconscious and I waited in the hospital to hear anything they could tell me about you."

"Yes," Frank said, slowly and deliberately. "That part."

"I just waited."

"Yes."

She had dropped off Gerald at the convalescent home yesterday. Part of her had been sad to see him go because he had been her only responsibility, her only distraction from the other task at hand: Eleanor hadn't done much but wait for word on Frank for weeks. And to Frank, that meant more than anything.

"Thanks, Elly," he said.

Eleanor said nothing, only patted Frank's chest with her palm.

"I love you," he said, and Eleanor immediately clenched harder around his chest.

"Love you too."

VII

GOD'S HOUSE, WHILE HE WAS GONE

The Boston that Bethany saw in the two days after leaving Askar was not the same Boston she had seen day to day ever since marrying her husband. In fact, it had been difficult to see the city at all during those years because Askar spent most of his time either traveling to New York City or talking on his cell phone to someone who *was* there. Any remaining free time he had was spent trying to convince Bethany to move to Queens so he could be closer to the stock market.

But since Bethany refused to move any farther away from her family than she already had, she and Askar spent a significant amount of time fighting about where they lived, and therefore not actually *enjoying* where they lived. And so the night she left Askar, she checked into a motel near Fenway Park. When she woke the next morning, she spent several hours walking in a circle around the stadium, admiring it in a way she had never had the opportunity to do before. She didn't even *like* baseball all that much, but seeing the stadium felt good anyway. She wondered why she and Askar had never come to see a game, but she knew the answer to that question as soon as she asked it.

Her immersion in to this new side of Boston did not last long. Eleanor Phillips tracked Bethany down to tell her that both Jason and Einar had been killed, and for three weeks after that, Bethany spent her time in a sort of catatonic autopilot mode. She buried her father, then her brother not long after. And while she was immeasurably sad about what had happened, she also felt somewhat strong—*dignified*, almost—taking care of all the arrangements for two funerals. If there was to be a bright side in such a situation, that was it.

But then she sat in Einar's house, the house in which Bethany herself had spent her youth, and did nothing. She sat by the wood stove, sometimes she cried, most times she did not; sometimes she walked down to the lake, and other times she just sat on the porch in the cold and let the snow dive into her face and chest.

Askar never called her, never saw her. Not once.

And then, after three weeks, she put the house up for sale and left for the last time. She returned to Boston, continued to explore this new city she had not had the privilege of intimately examining in all the years she lived there, continued to gape in awe at Fenway Park or Bunker Hill or Cambridge or the U.S.S. Constitution. She filed for divorce, she ate at diners, she applied for jobs (but did not actually get hired for any), she was granted her divorce, and then she made a decision that surprised even herself.

She moved to New York City.

Queens, to be specific.

And for years after that, since she had no family to return to in Maine and no reason to stay in Boston, she lived in New York and loved it. Part of her felt a little guilty that she had never trusted Askar's assertion that she would love the city, but as time passed, she realized she could not have enjoyed this place, either, had Askar come with her—or more aptly, lead her there.

Askar stayed in Boston, much to Bethany's surprise. That was fine by her. She grew to love baseball and examined Yankee Stadium in much the same manner she had examined Fenway Park, and bought Yankees season tickets that spring. By the beginning of the following baseball season, Bethany had landed a job as an administrative assistant in the Yankees General Manager's office.

And though she missed Askar terribly, she never spoke to him again after they met to finalize the divorce.

Nor did she remarry. She dated, of course, but could not bear the thought of committing her life to another person, especially another person that would not love her back. Or would leave her alone like her brothers did. Or who would be taken the way her father was. The thought of it made her sick, and so she remained married only to her own life and her own surroundings.

And for that, finally, she was thankful, was appreciative of the simplicity of living in a chaotic place that had no interest in dictating who she was or who she would become. As Einar would say, that suited her just fine.

*   *   *

Ginny returned to Maine after three days she had intended to spend in New York City. If answers were what she had sought there, she had certainly found none, but she was not entirely convinced that's why she had gone. On her way down to the city, she stopped in Waterbury, Connecticut—not under her own volition, but because her car had begun to violently shudder while she sped by at eighty miles per hour. She pulled off the highway and sat in the mechanic's waiting room, staring out at the road as cars waited at the stop light.

Two churches sat opposite each other only a block away. She had noticed several, in fact, on her way through town and wondered if the fine citizens of this town honestly believed God resided here. From what Ginny could tell, if this was, indeed, God's home, he'd been on vacation for quite a while and had neglected to hire a housekeeper before he went. Even so, the town boasted several churches and even more cemeteries—Ginny had counted four on her way through town, the first of which bordered Interstate 84 as she pulled off the exit.

The mechanic told her something about a ball joint and recommended she come back in two hours, so Ginny walked down the street toward one of the churches and kept walking right on past it. Eventually she came to the city's center, a large Green with a brass horse at one end and a life-sized Crèche scene at the other. She sat on a bench and watched people shuffle past, some toward the YMCA across the street and others to the bank or to yet another church that bordered the Green. Unlike Maine, the ground in Waterbury, Connecticut boasted no snow yet, but a few flurries dove and sped past Ginny's face occasionally. She watched the buses stop, the buses go, the stoplights change. She heard the traffic noise, the wind around her, the voices, some in English and some in Spanish, some in what may have been Italian. An hour passed, then another. She crossed the street and bought a bagel and a cup of coffee from a dingy little diner, then walked back to the mechanic's garage.

He needed parts. Wouldn't happen until tomorrow.

Ginny was spending the night.

Not far from the Green stood a building that looked uncannily like the Flatirons building in New York City, only with hard edges. Traffic bustled around it at its street level the way ants would divert around a rock, and the donut shop at its base shone a brilliant fluorescent white in the fading light of the early evening. Ginny did not know why this sight so captivated her, but she watched for a good ten minutes or more, trying to get a sense of what cosmic force or unintended irony had thwarted her from reaching her destination and instead had her staring at a pseudo-Flatirons building, a stand-in for the scenes the real celebrity couldn't make. Maybe a stuntman; maybe the building was preparing for the final scene, the great demise that would see the city burst into flames or fall into a deep black hole.

But nothing at all happened, aside from what would pass as normal daily life in this normal, daily city. Ginny walked on toward the hotel the mechanic had recommended, which was three more blocks down the street. She passed storefronts, most of which stood empty and dirty, but some that bustled with some semblance of activity. She had walked past a small college campus that looked brand new, so Ginny suspected this had something to do with the evening activity downtown, but the town, otherwise, looked almost sedated, sleepy and groggy from what must have been several decades of inactivity.

She finally reached the hotel, a tall, dirty-white building that sat adjacent to—not surprisingly—a church. Salvation always came to those starved for it, Ginny thought, but in the strangest forms. This town certainly seemed as though it needed a whole hell of a lot of salvation at one point. All Waterbury eyes seemed to be fixed on God.

After checking in, Ginny took the elevator to the eleventh floor, peeled off her clothes, climbed into bed and fell asleep fast. She did not dream of anything in particular and when she woke up the next morning, the sun shone through the curtains and Ginny felt refreshed… energetic, even. When she called the mechanic, she heard exactly what she'd expected to hear: a few more hours, a few more parts, blah blah blah. She took a shower, dressed and left the hotel in search of nothing in particular.

Through all this, Ginny thought very little, if at all, of Jason Coates. Occasionally she would catch herself lapsing into that world, the one in which her husband had been shot to death along with his father, but she caught herself quickly and distracted her mind with some particularly nice bit of architecture or a curious feature on a passer-by's face. She knew she was not quite ready to deal with Jason right yet, so she avoided the topic. That was why she had left, after all, and that was why she walked around a strange city in a small state on her way to a place she'd never been before.

Willie Coates had once told Ginny something that had at first made her laugh, but now, given what had happened a few nights ago, she took very seriously. Any normal human, Willie had told her, has a natural inclination to *not* like you. Ginny heard this and took it in as the ramblings of an old man, but Willie really wasn't one to ramble—or talk much at all, to be perfectly honest—and so Ginny stored it in the back of her mind to chew on later. At the time, Willie had made an offer to his neighbor down the way to lend the struggling farmer some men from the Coates farm, but the neighbor—hardly a neighbor by proximity, given his farm was almost fifteen miles down the road—had taken the offer as an insult, much to Willie's surprise. His name had been something like Heinz or Hunt, Ginny couldn't remember, but Willie did not lose his cool when Heinz-Hunt barked at him. Instead, he returned to his own home in his pick-up truck and imparted his wisdom upon Ginny, who happened to be the first person he'd seen on his way into the house.

While Willie had officially sold his farm several years prior, several of his former employees remained loyal to him, which seemed an-tithetical to Willie's claim that people's natural propensities leaned toward cynicism, but as she walked around Waterbury, Ginny knew Willie had been right. No one trusted anyone. She hadn't known that about herself until Jason had cheated on her. Couldn't she have just forgiven him? Couldn't she just accept an apology and move on?

No. Of course not. The fact of the matter was, she *wanted* to dislike Jason. *Wanted* to hate him for what he had done. She had that natural inclination toward cynicism and hate built into her makeup. In the grand scheme of self-discovery, this did not strike Ginny as a very original or mind-blowing revelation, only a disconcerting one.

And this, she supposed, was one of the many subtleties of life she'd missed out on while living in Maine. Blame never occurred to her; rather, she felt a certain distance from her own motivations, the kind that makes a person realize it was they all along whom drowned their ambition or at least their motivation to travel down the interstate to see how others lived. In relation to her impetus for leaving Maine a day earlier, this revelation had nothing to do at all with what had burdened her mind. But now that she was here in Waterbury, her priorities seemed to have shifted. She got on a random city bus to see where it would take her, and when she arrived at nowhere in particular, she found herself thinking about one of the Coates men, but not the one she expected to be thinking of.

Robert.

The nowhere in particular in which she ended up after stepping off the city bus appeared to be, for all intents and purposes, suburbia. But she didn't feel exactly right calling it that; no, this place seemed to actually hold a cohesion, a feeling of *neighborhood.* And yes, upon further inspection, it seemed as though people here talked to each other, stopped by a neighbor's place, walked their kids to school, maybe even closed off the streets in summer to have a block party. Would suburbia have done so? Ginny thought not; neighbors would, though. This appeared to be a neighborhood.

Two schools neighbored each other on Congress Avenue, and Ginny walked down this road and back up it just to pass both schools. One was a parochial school called Our Lady of Mount Carmel and boasted clean, beige bricks and a line of windows Ginny could only remember ever having seen in schools, as though the windows themselves had been designed with that specific purpose in mind. The older, darker building next door housed a public school called Tinker Elementary. This building, Ginny thought, more closely resembled the one she had attended as a child and the school yard out front on the corner of Congress Avenue and Highland Avenue could have been an exact replica of the one she had played in as a child, right down to the massive elms in each of the far corners of the yard.

Ginny walked on up the road and eventually took a left turn—a random decision, but she had time, so why not?—on Rosemount Avenue. Tucked away at the end of a short driveway was a park with a swing set and basketball court, and a long metal slide. Ginny wandered into the park and saw that the grassy expanse extended farther down than she had anticipated: the faded markings of a soccer field stretched to the left and a tee ball baseball field sat situated in the far right corner of the park. Ginny admired the empty space for a minute or more without moving.

Then she thought of Robert again.

How strange it was for him to kill himself. Despair, Ginny believed, manifested itself in difficult situations, and Robert's situation certainly was difficult, but hopeless? Probably not. Maybe the booze played a part in it, but Ginny thought something else had elbowed its way into the forefront of Robert's mind, and it only had one part to do with his former fiancé and another part to do with the booze that was choking him. The third part, the biggest part, was Jason. Ginny felt she had a sort of inherent obligation to defend the man she had loved, but now he was gone and so was Robert, which lent a certain uncomfortable objectivity to her thinking. Sitting on the bench in Town Plot Park, Ginny felt as though it might be time to hold the trial in her own head with Robert as the plaintiff and Jason as the defendant.

To say the two had fostered a tenuous relationship over the course of the last ten years would certainly put a politically-correct spin on it, but Ginny also knew how much the brothers loved each other, almost painfully so. In fact, it would take a blind man (or woman) to not see how much Robert admired his younger brother. Watching Jason fuck it up, as it were, must have been heartbreaking.

But enough to promote suicide?

Ginny thought not. As a witness herself, she knew how composed Robert could be ninety five percent of the time, and it seemed the other five percent of the time, the ugly times when the whiskey took over, got spent in the sole and privileged presence of his future wife, Maggie. Could it have been a perfectly timed storm, with Maggie leaving, with Jason the impetus for such an occurrence, and the resurgence of the booze and everything it brought with it? Possibly.

But hope. Hope always plays a part, right?

Two boys crawled through a hole in the chain link fence that butted up against the bushes lining the entire perimeter of the park. They walked side by side, their just-too-large winter coats hanging off them and their backpacks slung securely over both sets of shoulders. Neither saw Ginny sitting there, maybe fifty yards away, suppressing the urge to shiver. They walked all the way from one end of the park to the other, chatting endlessly the entire way, occasionally throwing a fake punch into the air at some invisible super-villain, before disappearing into yet another small opening in the chain link fence and the bushes beyond.

Why had he chosen Jason's apartment? Yes, of course he meant it as a message to his younger brother, but if the act itself seemed so perplexing, didn't that mean by association that the location, too, might seem incongruous? After all, Jason had made attempts to reconcile, or so he had told Ginny. He'd made attempts with her, too, and in those attempts Ginny felt a sincerity uncommon in her husband, most likely prompted by a fear of losing everyone he loved. Hell, he certainly was on his way, wasn't he?

A breeze kicked up and sent Ginny's hair back in a frenzy. She closed her eyes against the wind and thought about Robert sitting on the couch. Whiskey in hand. The television staring at him with a blank screen. The smell of the place, the feel of it as Robert prepared to kill himself. And then the moment, and the blood, and—

Ginny opened her eyes suddenly and drew in a deep and panicked breath. In an attempt to shove that image as far away from her mind as possible, her brain landed instead on another tense topic, finally: Jason.

Okay, she thought. *Let the healing begin. Fine. Let's open the wound. Tear open the ol' heart. What other clichés can we think of, dear?* Almost at once Ginny felt angry and terrifically sad at the same time. "Jason," she said out loud. "Jesus, Jason." She closed her eyes again, expecting some graphic imagining of what that barn must have looked like with Willie and Jason lying next to each other in a mixture of their own blood and the dirt below them. But that wasn't the image that came to her. No, the image that came to her surprised and shook her far more than any graphic image could have. She remembered Jason playing hockey.

He had relegated himself to Men's leagues in and around Portland for years after his days with UMaine and the subsequent Rangers tryouts afterward, and Ginny had made it a point to stay away from those games. It wasn't a matter of whether or not she enjoyed watching Jason play—she did, in fact—but instead had more to do with what her presence did to him. To dissect Jason would be to reveal two distinct vessels, the first being Jason Coates the husband, son and brother, and the other being Jason the fighter, the drunk and the piss-poor communicator. It had been Robert who had quelled that side of Jason and honed only the good vessel, the one that could care about himself and his family and still play good hockey. But at those Men's' league games, with Robert off somewhere else and Ginny standing behind the glass, Jason reverted back to that bad vessel, the one that simply could not control itself.

It occurred to Ginny then, sitting on the bench in the park in the town she had come to only coincidentally, that Robert had, as if by some strange osmosis, taken on the exact traits he had purged Jason of. The image of jumping on a grenade struck her, except different. If the two brothers had been soldiers and Robert the one to jump on that grenade to save his brother, the grenade did not destroy him; instead, it filled Robert up like a balloon, inflated him with it and made him walk on with it all floating around inside him like hot nails and shrapnel.

But eventually, that grenade *did* do its job and kill Robert.

Maybe.

Maybe not.

It was just a theory, after all.

After an hour or so, Ginny stood up and walked across the grass and out of the park with at least some semblance of a theory as to why Robert was dead now, and though it did not feel good to know it, she felt not at peace but at least *settled* with the loss of a man she had sincerely considered a friend in the years she had known Robert Coates.

But Jason.

How could she settle him?

Ginny caught the bus back to the mechanic's garage only to find out that she would be spending another night in Waterbury. Not only did her ailing car need a ball joint assembly, but it also needed a new wheel bearing, and gosh darnit, wouldn't you know that mechanic got so tied up today that he just couldn't get to it?

No matter. Ginny thought spending one more night in town might not be all that bad. Might be good, in fact. It wasn't so much that she *liked* this town, but it did seem to have a calming effect on her. As she wandered around town for the rest of the day, sometimes walking beside the ghost of Jason—debating his life and contemplating his death with him—and sometimes just walking alone, Ginny felt as though the answer had come to her. Not the answer as to why Jason was dead, or why Einar was dead right along with him, but the answer as to how life simply kept on going, despite the overwhelming feeling that life and love had stopped with the death of her husband. The idea of Jason had hurt Ginny long before his death; it was only now, with him gone and this lethargic town plodding along around her, that Ginny understood how the world really worked. Living wasn't so much about moving on as it was about slowing down. Taking a look around. Seeing death for what it was: a temporary bypass to something else. A transition. A breaker in a chapter, a frame of black in a film. A blip until whatever else happens next goes ahead and actually happens.

This town seemed to exude the very core of what it meant to be dead, and yet people walked these streets and cars still honked their horns and kids still crawled through holes in chain-link fences. Somehow, everyone here knew there was something else beyond the current, beyond the now. Beyond the stale stink of rotting buildings and empty storefronts. That wasn't to say it didn't hurt them all—at least Ginny assumed—to see their home wither into something to be mourned, but the grace with which everyone seemed to realize this death was not an end but rather a temporary state of being seemed to make some sort of acute sense that Ginny hoped to hone in on further once she got back to Maine.

And she returned the next day, without having completed her intended trip to New York City.

As far as she could tell, only the slightest hint of hope existed that someday she would have that epiphany that would make sense of Jason's death, but as she drove back up to Maine with a new ball joint and even newer wheel bearing, she thought that might be okay, at least for now. She had left Maine in fear that she would not be able to face whatever came after death, but that was because she did not have any idea what came after death.

Maybe now she got it.

At least enough to get her through that breaker in the chapter, that black frame in the film.

Or maybe she didn't.

But she was willing to go back to Maine and try—not necessarily to move on, but to slow down. That seemed like a feasible option.

*   *   *

Einar William Coates ascended the steps of the front porch. With a hammer and nail in hand, he chose a spot and planted the nail. The wooden placard he hung there felt right. Once it hung solidly there, he ran his fingers over each word: Einar. Then, William. Then, Coates. Here he would raise a family. Here he would live with Sarah, his wife, and forget what he had done in the war. Here he would try to make the lives of his children better than his own.

He turned and looked out at the driveway. Sarah stood at the foot of the steps, smiling up at him, her arms wrapped around herself to keep warm against the early December cold. Einar smiled, too, and went to her, wrapping his own arms around her. When he did, Sarah took a long, deep breath in and smelled Einar, his neck, his chest, the slight scent of his clothes, the odor of wood and dirt and work. The cold scent of December, the one that would stay with her until the day she died, the one and only way she truly knew her husband.

ACKNOWLEDGMENTS

First and foremost, thank you to my mother Susan, father Gus, and step-mother Lorie, brothers Chris and Tim, niece Jada, and the rest of my family for everything and anything I am and ever have been.

Thanks to my very encouraging and very patient wife Rachel, who makes just about everything in life easier and more fun. A big, heartfelt thanks is definitely reserved for Cat Morris, who helped edit this book and gave me the boost I needed to get this manuscript in print.

To Joe and Jen Arthur, thanks so much for your support, ideas, laughs, and couch space that a writer so often needs. And to everyone else who helped me through this process of writing, editing, revising, publishing, and hoping for the best: I am appreciative and quite lucky to have you all in my life.

DAN CAVALLARI is a freelance writer and photographer. He holds an English degree from the University of Maine, and he is a former high school English teacher. His stories and poems have appeared in several magazines and publications both online and in print, and he is the editor of the online literary and photography magazine Waterlogged August Magazine (www.waterloggedaugust.com). He lives in Flagstaff, Arizona with his wife, Rachel, and their dog, Molly, where he is currently working on his next novel, Men Waiting For Sleep.

For more information on DAN CAVALLARI:
danielcavallari.com
d2photos.net

11400534R1020

Made in the USA
Lexington, KY
01 October 2011